DRAGON FIRE

Michelle Janene

DRAGON FIRE

Michelle Janene

STRONG TOWER
PRESS

Strong Tower Sacramento, CA 95829
http://strongtowerpress.com

Cover Art by: Whetstone Designs
Images: Side view oh happy boyfriend and girlfriend touching hands; DepositPhotos; IgorVetushko / Abstract flames; DepositPhotos; majcot / Red and Blue Fire; Unsplash; Patrick Hendry / Set of three vector sacral Celtic symbols. Dragon. Ma; DepositPhotos; balashovmihail38.gmail.com / Misty Fantasy Forest; DepositPhotos; algolonline
Fonts: Title - Aviano Serif; Adobe / Author - Semplicita Pro; Adobe / back cover - SabbathBlack OT and Semplicita Pro; Adobe
Interior Images: flame - free pixabay - fire-car-flame-sports-motor-42600; fairy wings - free pixabay - faery-fairy-female-creature-2789592; Dragon Silhouette: www.123rf.com/photo_28504871_dragon-silhouettes-on-the-white-background

ISBN: 978-1-942320-45-6

To all those who have felt alone.

To those who search for love.

There is One who loves you more deeply and fully

Than you can ever image.

He is the lover of your soul.

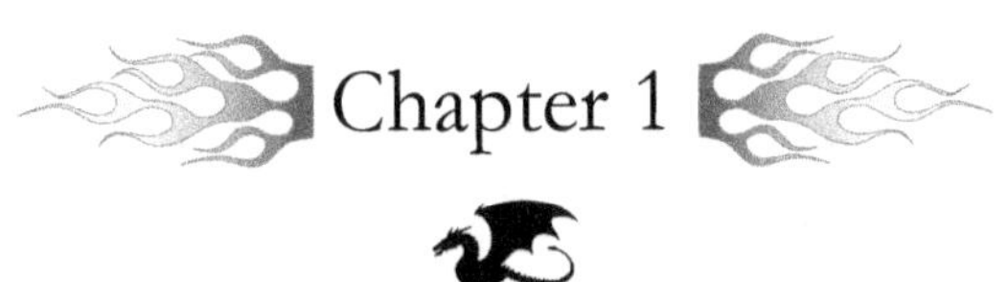

Chapter 1

The low, metallic reverberating of the sacrificial gong drew Jydryn's attention. Smoke from his sigh skimmed up his snout and into his eyes. He stretched his wings and pivoted to change directions away from his hunt. Dinner would have to wait. Unlike his kind who killed only for food or when threatened, humans were cruel, violent creatures. Not just to the other species they shared the kingdom with. They were even more likely to turn against their own, which was why Jydryn had selected the cave where he lived.

The Tetling Ridge was a narrow, rocky outcrop with three human settlements at the west end. He knew Beardrift to the north for its brutal treatment of all its citizens. Greenburn, at the west end of the ridge, sacrificed their own young in the green flames of their hideous altar. The town south of the ridge where he was now summoned was Cragholde. They offered their young maidens to the dragons to appease their hateful gods. All of it disgusted Jydryn, so he lived here to rescue all he could. Today would see another damsel relocated to a new town where she might find a life better than in a place known for sacrificing their own.

Jydryn made a wide pass over the clearing east of the town. The villagers were still retreating toward the walls where they would huddle in their homes as he took the poor woman away. The people of Cragholde were acting quite different today.

In all the past, when these wretched citizens offered him a *gift*, she stood washed and in a white, flowing gown. They would secure the woman to the post on one side of the clearing, and all but one of the townsfolk would leave. The remaining man was a fast runner who would summon Jydryn with the gong and race for the gate.

This was not the case today. Few townsfolk were within the walls when he arrived. The maiden's filthy, ragged dress hung from her. They'd left her unbound in the clearing. She could flee but stood still, arms limp at her sides, staring at nothing across the wide, empty expanse. Why didn't she run?

Jydryn decided he would land rather than snatch her as he flew off. He noted the empty pole and coiled ropes nearby. He made a tighter circle over her head. She was ghastly thin. Her dirty and matted hair left the color indistinguishable. He tossed his head to free the scent of her from his nostrils. As Jydryn landed in front of her, she still didn't move.

There was a fresh cut on her left cheek in the hollow below her sharp, protruding cheekbone. An older, wide scrape crossed from above her right brow to her cheek. Both eyes shone in the afternoon sun. Her sight didn't appear to be affected by the injury.

The air from his wings buffeted her, but she showed no reaction. His back feet and tail found purchase as he tucked his wings. Before his front feet came to rest on the hard packed dirt, the maiden dashed from her spot. To Jydryn's great surprise, she didn't run away from him, but toward him. She darted under him and stood behind his left front leg as it came to rest.

Women fainted when Jydryn reached for them. Many screamed and wept at the sight of him. Never had anyone—except men dressed in armor with long lances—charged *at* him.

He raised his left leg to get a glimpse of her, but she scrambled out of sight behind his right leg. Jydryn lowered his head. His horns scraped the ground as he peered at her. He spotted the flutter of her dress as she trembled in the great shadow of his wide body. As he moved his leg to get a better view, she retreated closer to his hind feet. Her pounding heart echoed in the living cave she hid within.

Clang, clang, clang. His head rose. The villagers who had left the safety of their town again. They banged their farm tools and kitchen pots as they shouted.

"Take her away."

"Be gone, foul creature."

Did they call him foul or her? Why did he sense a dragon-sized sadness in her?

Their behavior compelled Jydryn—more than most—to save her. But he oculdn't take her from this hateful place if he wasn't able to get a hold of her.

As the villagers' angry shouts grew, Jydryn lowered to lie on his belly. With no room to hide, he hoped she'd scurry out from under him, and he could snatch her in his paw.

Again, she surprised him. She fled up his hind leg and onto his back. She took a place below his wings out of reach of his mouth, tail or paws.

Jydryn didn't know of any dragon who allowed riders, so how did she come to settle in the one spot he couldn't dislodge her? With the ferocity of the villagers growing, Jydryn spread his wings and launched into the sky. He figured he'd scoop her from the air when she fell, and they would be on their way.

But she didn't fall. She straddled him as she clung to one of his spine spikes. They flew high out of the reach of the town's venomous words and leveled off in a steady air current. As he made wide circling passes over the Tetling Ridge, Jydryn tried to figure out what to do with this odd woman.

Most often, he flew them hundreds of miles away to areas he hoped would be kinder. He'd place his charges on a road near a large town and release them.

But this woman was in no shape to enter any respectable town. The scent of fresh blood made him turn his gaze back to her. Of all the smooth spines she could have chosen, she'd picked one of his three jagged broken spines to cling to.

He might take her back to his cave home, allow her to clean and treat her injuries, but then she would learn the truth. Jydryn was a shifter. He never allowed anyone he rescued to know of his ability to change forms.

If one he'd rescued didn't leave the road where he left them, he'd land out of sight a distance away, shift to his human skin, and retrieve a stash of hunting clothes and weapons he kept hidden in the thick forest nearby. Then, he'd *happen* upon the woman he'd saved, lead her to the nearby village, and make introductions in the market. He'd slip away and return to his cave to await the call to the next person in need.

But this damsel's choice of what to grasp, complicated matters. Still, he wouldn't shift right before her eyes. Jydryn continued to circle.

Few shifters still survived in the Kingdom of Keyaral. Among the dragons, there were three types. 'The Isolationists' lived most of their lives in their dragon scales far from humans. They were the first to accept sacrifices to repay the humans for their cruelty and make them pause before they thought of attacking again. The largest group, 'The Balanced,' lived in cities much like the humans. They spent equal time in their human and dragon forms, but avoided shifting where humans might see. Jydryn belonged to the smallest group of dragon shifters, 'The Activists.' They spent more time in their human skin, but they weren't afraid to approach the humans as dragons to save lives.

Jydryn glanced back at the woman again. She still clung tight to his spine, deepening her wounds. Another dragon damaged those spines in a fight when Jydryn tried to save a group of humans from him. Jydryn had saved most of them, but he had suffered for days from the injuries he'd sustained.

He turned toward his cave and landed on the wide shelf at the opening. His sleeping chamber lay through a smaller archway in the back, only accessible when he was in his human form.

Jydryn curled into a circle, lowering the spine she held close to the ground so she could slide off with ease.

It took a few moments before she left his back. When she found his chamber, Jydryn took to the air again. He moved three large boulders from the wide path so she could leave after she had cleaned and dressed her wounds. Once he cleared the path for her escape, he resumed his interrupted hunt. She should be gone by the time he returned with his dinner.

Chapter 2

The sun touched the horizon when Jydryn returned to his cave with a large mountain goat in his claws. He sat it at one end of the entrance, where he cleaned his kills and turned to take to the air and return the boulders that kept out the dragon killers. The woman's pungent odor caught him and he sniffed around the small opening. Her scent remained strong. He stilled and found her heart's whispered beat that assured that she still lived. So, she hadn't left. This woman didn't behave in any way he expected.

But with her still here, he had an additional problem. All his clothes were in the same chamber where she was. His only saving grace was that she'd let the fire go out. With the inner chamber dark as midnight, perhaps he could enter and retrieve his pants without her noticing. Dragon vision was far superior to humans.'

Out of sight in the large outer entrance, he shifted. Naked in his human skin, he stepped into the chamber. A chill rose gooseflesh over his body. Dragons didn't like the cold, which is why he fought not to let the fire go out. Two quick strides brought him to his trunk at the end of his massive bed. He pulled on his pants and scanned the dark room.

The woman sat in a back corner, bent knees pulled close to her chest. She crossed her arms on top of them, and her forehead rested on them. Again, the wave of despair he felt at seeing her hiding dejected in the corner made his heart shudder and his stomach twist. Or maybe it was the gnawing ache in his belly from not eating all day.

Jydryn pulled on his tunic and rekindled the fire. She didn't move.

After cutting a large piece of meat from the goat, he brought it back to prepare a stew. He added vegetables he'd purchased at a human market and water from the tumbling stream near the edge of his cave entrance. He lit several candles and scanned every surface. She hadn't touched anything. All the fruit remained on his table. The water for washing was still in the pitcher, and the chairs never sat in. Still, she huddled in the corner.

The stew bubbled and filled the chamber with its savory aroma. Her stomach grumbled. He filled a bowl for her and set it on the table to cool before filling another for himself. "Will you come and join me?"

She flinched at his words but didn't move otherwise.

"Please, you have had a long, tiring day. I know the food will do you good." He waited, but she refused to move.

He stood and took both bowls to the corner where she sat and joined her on the floor. He sat her bowl beside her. "I've used this cave for a while. The dragon comes and goes out front, but he didn't mean to frighten you."

At last, her head rose. Her arms were a bloody mess from where her wounded hands rested on them. Her eyes were hazel, speckled with blue and green. He wondered what she'd look like clean with her hair brushed.

Jydryn smiled to reassure her. "The dragon scared you, didn't he?"
She shook her head.

"No?"

She tossed her head again.

He took a bite and pointed to the bowl beside her. "You're very brave, but you need to keep up your strength. Please eat."

She glanced at the bowl and back at him. A tear left a muddy trail down her cheek.

"Do your hands hurt?" He set his stew aside and reached for her.

"Let me have a look."

She recoiled from him. Horror crossed her gaze; the centers grew wide as the dark centers took over the color.

He left his hand hanging between them, but stilled. "I won't hurt you."

Her head shook back and forth as she pressed herself in to the rocky corner, trying to avoid him.

"Please?"

Her head shook more as her hands disappeared between her and the wall.

Jydryn sighed. He didn't want to frighten her more, so he collected his bowl and moved out of her sight to the entrance. He seldom slept in his dragon skin, but he would tonight to allow her privacy in his chamber. Rubbing a shudder from his arms, he tried to quiet the thought of her sleeping in his bed. He whirled, snatched up the large caldron, and went to the stream. When he returned with it full, he hung it over the fire to warm.

A large tub used for bathing served as the base of his table. He leaned the tabletop against the wall and moved his two chairs. Then, he moved to his trunk and dug to the bottom and found a long tunic and pants that were too small for him. They would be far too large for the woman, but better than anything she wore now. He sat them on a chair with a towel and his hairbrush. If she could get hers clean, his brush might help to get the tangles out. He placed it beside the other items he'd offered. Another glance at her and he wondered if cutting her hair would be easier. But only a shamed woman ever had their head shorn.

He poured the warm water into the tub and balanced a block of soap on the edge. "There. Now, you can clean before you sleep. I promise to remain outside." He grabbed a blanket and small pillow and moved to the entrance.

While he thought he might sleep in his human form in case she sought him, the cool early spring air caused him to shift and sleep in his dragon skin. The warmth from the inner chamber stopped heating his back. She'd let the fire go out again. He never heard her move or the water ripple.

Jydryn sighed, releasing a puff of smoke into the weak light of the waning moon. This was far easier when he left them with others to watch over them. How was he supposed to care for a woman who never attempted to do anything for herself?

Chapter 3

The following evening, when the woman had still failed to move, Jydryn scooped some of the cool water from the tub and added more hot water. Then, he stomped toward where she continued to cower in the corner.

"You've been here for over a day and a half." The deep grumble of his dragon filled his human voice from deep inside him. "In that time, you've refused to eat, bathe, address your wounds, or sleep in the bed. Now, the cuts in your hands are festering." The sour scent of putrid flesh and decay assaulted his nose.

"What does it matter? I should've let the dragon eat me."

A shard tore through his heart at her whimper. "Dragons seldom eat anyone. This one saved you. Are you going to throw away the opportunity for a new start?"

Her face remained buried on her knees.

"If we don't take care of those wounds right now, you could lose one or both of your hands or your life. Now, either you are getting in that tub on your own or I'm putting you in there."

Again, she recoiled from him. When he continued toward her anyway, she staggered to her feet and turned away from him. "Don't touch me." Terror laced her strained voice.

"I will not hurt you. I'm trying to help."

Her head shook. "It doesn't matter. Touching me will hurt you."

Jydryn froze midstride. "What?"

"Anyone who gets near me gets sick. Most die."

His hands balled into fists. "Who told you that?"

"The villagers who sent me to be eaten by the dragon. I should've let him devour me. But I was afraid if my mere presence makes people ill, then eating me might have killed him. He may be a huge, feared creature, but I couldn't do that to him."

Jydryn fought to swallow the lump in his throat several times before he could speak. "Those people sent you to be killed because they blamed you for a sickness ravishing your village, yet you wanted to save your executioner?"

At last, she turned from where she huddled against the corner and raised her tear-filled gaze to his. "He is a beautiful dragon. He didn't deserve to die because of me."

"You can call me Jy. What's your name?"

She shrugged as her breath caught. "I don't know. I've been called all manner of vile things, but my mother abandoned me long before I can remember. She feared I was a curse and wanted nothing to do with me."

Jydryn smiled as he slid forward and closed the gap between them. "Then I will call you Keena. It means brave, for you are by far the bravest person I've ever met. To endure such cruelty and then try to spare the dragon—and me. You have no hate in your heart, Keena."

As the space between them disappeared, she again turned to the corner. "Please."

"I can't let someone so brave and kind die—not for a lie." His hand rested on her shoulder and he felt nothing but bones. He groaned, sure his heart was tearing in two. "Oh, Keena, you are so very thin. No one deserves to be treated this way."

"Children in the village got sick," she protested.

"Which is the nature of illnesses, but as malnourished as you are, if you carried any illness in you—you'd be dead—not fighting to live. I've been around you for two days. I'm not sick. You bled on the dragon and he's not sick. This is not your fault, Keena." He turned her and her gaze searched his. Her hazel eyes focused on him as her brows arched. Soon they fell as her gaze darted away. She seemed to want to believe him, but couldn't. What had happened to this woman?

She kept her exposed skin from touching him as he led her to the tub. "Do you need me to help you?"

Bright pink blossomed on her hollow cheeks as her eyes widened. She shook her head in slow sweeps.

"Can I trust that this time you will clean yourself?"

She offered him a single nod.

"Very well. I have faith in you." He pointed to the chair where he'd left the clothes yesterday. "You can put those on afterward. They will be too large but better than what you're wearing. I'll get you something more appropriate next time I go to the market."

"Please, don't bother—"

"It would be my honor." And he meant it. Something about this shattered woman made him want to wrap his arms around her and hold her until she knit back together. The lone thought made him tremble. No woman had ever affected him this way. "Now, while you bathe, I'll check the mountain trails for some *iddika* root to mash up for the cuts on your hand. If you clean them well, the root should keep the skin from worsening and help it heal."

Her hazel gaze glanced at the things he had provided.

"Do you require anything else?"

She shook her head and didn't speak until he reached the doorway into the larger entrance chamber. "Thank you, Jy," she whispered.

His shortened name on her tongue made his heart flutter. He glanced at her again, where she still stood and stared at the water. She remained motionless, with her back hunched, head down, and hands pressed to her chest. If she could cave in on herself anymore, she'd turn inside out. "It is my pleasure, Keena. Enjoy your bath."

He waited long enough to hear the water ripple and a brief splash over the sides before he climbed the trail, crossed back over the stream, and hiked to the higher pass that held the needed healing root. In the days after the fight with the black dragon, he'd used a lot of it. He hoped he hadn't dug it all up.

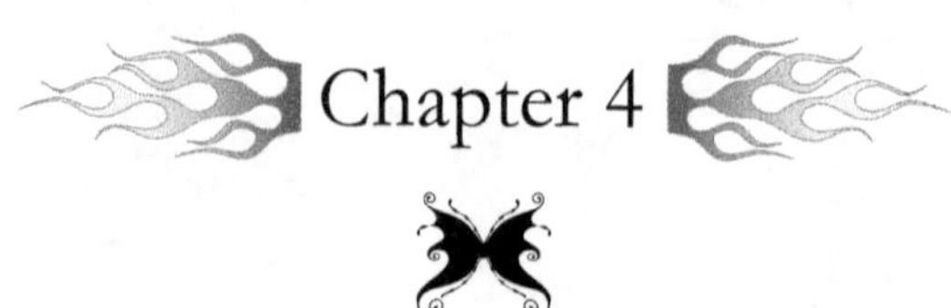

Chapter 4

She slid down and the warm water welcomed her, much like Jy's smile. But it wouldn't last. He'd get sick soon and curse the name he'd just gifted her. Too many people had grown ill in Cragholde and other villages she'd lived in to hold on to the hope that anything would be different now with him.

She jerked her palms from the hot water as tears pricked her eyes. They stung like they were being cut afresh. It took several attempts and biting her lip to submerge her injured hands. Wouldn't it be better to let the rot set in and sap her life? She wanted it all to end, but she feared death—terrified that what waited for her beyond this terrible existence was something far worse. One who had caused so many deaths shouldn't expect a paradise to await them.

The sting of the soap added to her pain but didn't overshadow the excruciating anguish in her soul. No one could heal that.

She worked the lather into her hair. Oh, how her head itched. When was the last time she'd been allowed a proper wash? She scrubbed, worked at the knots, and washed the freed strands again. Section by section, she cleaned her head until the water chilled and her skin puckered, but she still hadn't finished. She stepped out and dried with the towel he'd left her. Never in her life had she felt anything so soft against her skin.

With care, she pulled on his pants and tunic, trying not to get blood on them like she had the towel. The bath had washed away the dried blood and caused her palms to bleed again.

The sleeves and hems extended well past her fingers and toes. Careful not to soil the shirt, she wiggled out of it, wrapped her hands in a bit of cloth she found, and rolled the sleeves before putting it on again. She moved a chair near the fire, rolled the hems of the pant legs and continued to work on her hair near the fire.

With a small knife she found, she cut out the worst knots. She wove those shorter areas with the longer strands nearby into small braids and tied each off with twine. Six small braids later, with most of the rest of her hair free of tangles, she looked up to see Jy standing in the doorway staring at her. He always seemed to smile, but at the moment, his gentle grin gaped open a little. His eyes were the lightest blue she'd ever seen. The man was almost a head taller than her and his tunic stretched over his muscles. He trimmed his beard and moustache short, but his light brown, wavy hair hung past his shoulders.

Still, he continued to stare. Her body warmed as though he'd built another fire in the stone chamber.

She pulled her gaze from him. "Is something the matter?"

"Not at all, Keena. You look … radiant."

The way he said the name he had given her made her insides wobble. The hum of it danced over her skin. She didn't understand him. Calling her brave, caring for her, complimenting her was a stark contrast to how she had lived for almost twenty-two years.

She glanced up as he pulled the other chair to face hers and sat across from her. His sleeves were wet where he'd pushed them up near his elbows. There were scars on his forearms and another one across his nose.

"If you are searching for any sign of illness, I can assure you, I am quite well."

A long breath eased out, and her shoulders relaxed.

"You *were* frightened." He reached for her hands.

She pulled them behind her. "I can do it."

"Keena, I assure you; you will not curse me with some sickness if I touch you."

She couldn't surrender her hands. This was the first person in her entire life who showed her any kindness. Well, not entirely. But she would never forgive herself if something happened to him. "Do you have gloves?"

He stood and returned with a small towel over his palm. "Rest your hand here and let me examine it." She searched his face, doubt making it impossible to move. "God did not give us a spirit of fear, Keena. You are His precious daughter."

She shook her head. "If I am anything to any god, it is as a weapon of his wrath."

His powerful hands gripped her shoulders. "You were fearfully and wonderfully made for the Almighty's great pleasure. There is nothing hateful about you."

Tears blurred her vision. She had never been one for tears. Why did this man's kindness stir them? "You haven't seen what I have done." Her voice choked on her words.

"I *know* you have made no one sick *or* caused anyone's death. And I *will* prove it to you someday." He took a deep breath and his words softened. "But for right now, let me see your hands, please."

With a shudder, she laid her hand in his. He was careful to use the corner of the towel to work the cream into the many cuts there.

"I'm sorry this stings and reeks, but it's the best for quick healing."

"Thank you." The whispered words didn't express the balm his kindness was to her soul. His actions and words were far more powerful than any cream.

When he finished, he cut up one of his shirts. She tried to stop him, but he wrapped each hand in the clean cloth. Once he'd covered both palms, he roasted meat over the flames, tossed out her filthy dress, scooped the dirty water from the tub, and reset the table on top.

As she moved her chair to the table where a plate of sizzling meat and steaming vegetables waited, he glanced at her feet. "Don't you have any shoes?"

"I've never had shoes. It was only so no one had to risk further exposure at the sight of me that they ever gave me a dress to cover myself."

Jy closed his eyes. The muscles in his cheeks flexed and rippled as a small growl escaped his throat. "Father in heaven above, grant me the strength to forgive those who have treated your dear daughter with such cruelty. Help her hands to heal. I thank You for the honor of sa—of having her here in my home where she will be safe. Shower her with Your love. Show her she is precious to You and You have always known her name. Help her see You do not hate her."

Years of unshed tears cascaded down her cheeks and pooled on her plate as she fought not to sniff and disturb his prayer. She had heard many invoke the names of their gods as curses against her and pleas for their protection against her. But never had she heard anyone speak to any god as Jy spoke to the One he called Father. Who was this God? And why did she want to know Him?

"Bless this food that it would nourish and restore Keena. Make a way for her in the days ahead that will lead to great joy. Watch over her and protect her as her loving Father until You call her to Your presence. In the name of the Son, my Savior, Amen."

Her food sat untouched as the tears continued to fall.

"Things are going to be different for you now. This I swear." The last words were ground out as if he spoke an unbreakable vow, and it made her quiver.

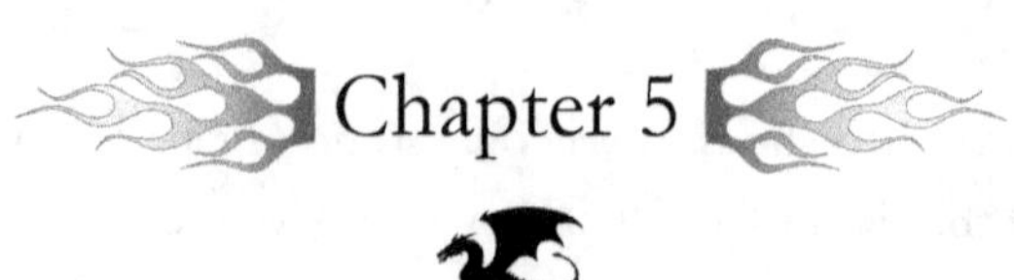

Chapter 5

The beleaguered woman Jydryn had left to bathe and the one he returned to was not the same. Keena was striking—even as gaunt as she was. Her clean hair was russet, though the light playing on it from the candles and fire made him see hints of pink and even blue. Her tanned skin glowed in the flickering flames of his chamber. But most striking was the scent that greeted him now that she was free of all the dirt tainting her body.

Every creature had their own special scent that made it easy to track with a dragon's sense of smell. Most women smelled like some variety of flower mixed with strong spice. Keena's scent brought to mind an open meadow in spring with fresh wild flowers in rich moist loam. She was the best part of the earth, the area where one found the most beauty. No other woman he had ever rescued affected him as she did.

After dinner, he convinced her to take his bed as he moved back to the entrance. He listened for her steady breathing of sleep, shed his clothes, and shifted. Though he craved warmth, like most dragons, there was something about flying just after the sun set. The cool air sliding over his leathery wings, and the quiet of a world where only the night insects made any noise, filled him with a peace that often lasted for days.

Here, he could float on a breeze without the shrieks of women and children at the sight of him. Men didn't turn their bows and ballistas his direction to shoot him from the sky. Here in this quiet solitude, he was free to be all God had created him to be—the body of a mighty dragon and the soul of a son of the Most High.

He sang praises to his God, and he let the peace of communion seep into his spirit. He took seriously his task of rescuing those like Keena. Ones who the Father wanted free of their pain, but this was where he found his greatest joy—on the wing, worshiping God.

Before midnight, he returned to the cave, added wood to the fire as he drank in Keena's earthy scent again, and he curled in his dragon skin at the entrance and slept.

The sun had not cleared the horizon when he landed and shifted outside a town he favored, an hour by the wing to the south. Eagle's Nest housed almost a thousand souls. The people had no grotesque altars to blood-hungry gods, and there was no clearing for the sacrifice of maidens within several leagues. The people greeted him with smiles and waves. Many in the market called him by name as he often came to purchase their wares and produce.

He entered Eagle's Nest as they opened the gates and ambled to the town center. Most of the shops weren't open yet, but the market already had many vendors ready for customers.

"Jy, my friend, you have returned. Weren't you here only three days ago?" The vendor was a lean man that seemed to be all arms and legs. He had a narrow face and a rather long nose that hooked at the end.

"Aye, Tom. Your potatoes and green beans were so good, I ate them all and need more."

"And I am happy to supply them." Tom filled Jy's bags with the produce. "Enjoy, my friend."

Jy dropped a couple coins in Tom's hand. "I will indeed. Can you tell me, do you know of anyone needing a worker?"

"I thought you had land of your own to work. Grapes, wasn't it?"

"Forgive me for not being clear. I've heard of a young woman needing employment on my travels. I thought I'd ask here and pass on the information on my return."

"Hmm." Tom rubbed his pointy chin. "Sarah, the laundress, is always in need of more hands. Bert the baker might need help now that his daughter is married."

"Jenny is wed?"

"She turned seventeen this past winter. It was time."

Jy didn't agree but as long as the girl was happy and the man kind, he had no grounds to object.

Tom named a few others before Jydryn ambled off to see to the other purchases he needed.

After he'd talked with all those who might employ Keena, and with his back loaded down with all he'd purchased, he strolled out the gate toward the hidden clearing he used. He'd never brought a woman he'd rescued here. He wasn't sure why. Perhaps he feared finding them in a place where they were still unhappy after he'd saved them. That he wanted to bring Keena here now so he could catch sight of her from time to time spoke again of her differing from any other he'd saved. But the thought of her someday greeting him with a husband at her side made his nostrils flare and his skin burn. It seemed safer for her and her future husband if he never saw her again. Why did his heart clench at the very thought of losing her?

Chapter 6

Keena—she still struggled with having a proper name—stretched and rolled to her back. Carrying a name was no less strange than being clean, in men's clothes, or lying in an actual bed. Somewhere between the town's folk running her all the way to the clearing at the point of their pitchforks and riding on a dragon, she had fallen into a dream world like nothing she'd ever known. She feared the moment when she would wake to the stench of her own body and the hateful cries of her victims.

She glanced around Jy's chamber, again aware of his smoldering scent lingering in his bed and on his clothes she wore. Where did he sleep now?

She snuggled into the blanket and turned to the fire. Only a few glowing embers remained. With a sigh, she slid out of bed and—being careful of her injured hands—added a log. She turned from the hearth. The sunlight coming from the entrance drew her attention. How long had it been since she'd slid off the dragon's back? Two days? Three? With slow, cautious steps, she inched to the doorway and peeked out but found neither the dragon nor Jy.

Keena's gaze roved over the huge opening. From what she remembered of the dragon it looked tall enough for him to stand in, wide enough to stretch out and not touch his nose or tail tip to the sides, and deep enough to spread his wings. She followed the sound of running water to the opposite side of the opening. As she crossed the large stone surface, she noticed a blanket folded against the back wall with a small pillow on it.

Keena swiped at a tear with the back of her bandaged hand. That anyone would give up the comfort of their bed and lay out in this chilly space on the hard ground for her was inconceivable. There was no cause for him to care so much.

Her feet brushed the grooves cut by the dragon's talons. Where was the dragon, and what relationship did he have with Jy? It seemed unthinkable for a dragon and a man to be friends.

A clear mountain stream cascaded over the far edge of the opening. It welcomed her with a fine mist blown in by a cool breeze. The water landed below the opening and she followed its meandering down the rocky mountain until it vanished from sight around a bend. Moss and clusters of tiny white star-shaped flowers and many-petaled lavender flowers lined the banks of the stream.

From the flowers she turned her attention to the land that stretched out far below the ridge. Bright, muted, and dark green trees filled the land in every direction. Some were tall and pointed, others were broad and spread out. She could see places where the path of a road or river wound through the forests. In other places there were no trees, only wisps of rising smoke—no doubt villages. Was one of those Cragholde? Were the people there safe and recovering now that she was gone?

A powerful wave of wind swept her hair in her face and ruffled her baggy clothes. She brushed her hair aside and blinked away the dust in time to see a long gray-green tail vanish above the opening. The top of the mouth of the cave hung out farther than the shelf where she stood, so she couldn't lean out and look up to see where the dragon had gone.

Jydryn floated around to the entrance of his home and found Keena standing near the spring. One quick pump of his wings and he shot up. Had she seen him? She didn't scream—but then she hadn't shown fear the first time they met.

He landed on a flat area above the cave and took a moment to let his thundering heart calm. Why was he so concerned about what this woman thought? He tossed his massive head, trying to clear it. It wasn't her. He was a shifter and if he had landed and she had seen him transform, his life would be at risk. That had to be the reason. Or maybe it was the fact that he'd never brought anyone he rescued back to his cave before. Yes, that must be it. He wasn't accustomed to having to guard his identity in his own home. Well, he'd solve that soon. Eagle's Nest would make a pleasant home for Keena.

Why did that very idea send his heart pounding again?

Thankful he'd left his clothes in the bag with his purchases, Jydryn shifted, dressed, shouldered his heavy bag, and descended to the cave.

Keena stood in the entrance looking up. "Where's the dragon?"

"He's always close." Jydryn moved to the inner chamber.

Keena followed. "Are you friends?"

"You don't sound like you believe that."

Her brows pinched as her face scrunched.

"Does no one in Cragholde have a dog, cat, or horse that they care for, talk to even?"

She shook her head. "There are dogs out in the streets. They steal food. People yell at them and kick them if they can. A few cats live on the mice in the barns. People use horses for riding, pulling carts, for plowing, but they are also yelled at—whipped too."

Jydryn stopped pulling items from the large heavy cloth bag to stare at her. "I am very glad you no longer live in such an awful place." He smiled. "You'll like your new home. It's nothing like that pit Cragholde."

He drew a cloth bundle from between the sacks of potatoes and beans and offered it to her.

Keena stared at it and glanced up. Tears pooled in her eyes and her voice was a shaky whisper. "I'm not staying here?"

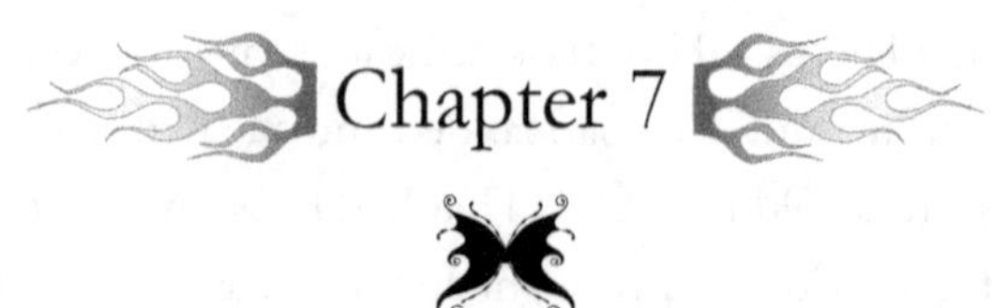

Chapter 7

Jy wanted her to leave. Was it possible for a broken heart to shatter more? His sweet smile hid a fearsome weapon, for his rejection was the deadliest of all. At least the town's people never pretended to be nice to her.

He offered her a dress; the most beautiful she had ever seen. It was dark green with a fitted bodice and trimmed in light green ribbons with tiny bows at the end. It would have been a wonderful gift if not for his intention to be rid of her.

"I live in a dusty cave. It is not a good place for a woman." He held the dress toward her with long, outstretched arms.

She only wanted one thing from him. To stay.

Her arms folded in and she held herself against the freezing air that came from within her empty soul. Her voice was little more than a whisper. "It is the cleanest place I've ever been allowed to stay."

He took a step toward her, and his smile grew.

She staggered back and flinched.

"All the more reason to go to Eagle's Nest. You'll have your pick of jobs. Do you enjoy baking? Or maybe working in the inn or the laundry? If you work in the inn, you'd have a room provided."

She could offer to clean his clothes, be his maid, but if he didn't want her, what was the point? There was an answer to all her pain. A way to put a permanent stop to the hurting.

Why did everything she did surprise him? He'd bought the dress because he thought she'd look stunning in it with her auburn hair. But she seemed hurt by his thoughtful gift and his idea that she needed to be some place where she could live a pleasant life.

A small vibration tickled the soles of his feet. It had no source, and quakes weren't common here. But it matched the way Keena shuddered. "You don't want me here."

"That's not true!"

She recoiled from his outburst.

Jydryn draped the dress over a chair, took a deep breath, and returned to unpacking the food. He'd been stunned at his own reaction and needed to consider a new tactic. "I said nothing of the kind, Keena. It has been a very long time since I lived among others. I enjoy having you here, but it is not what is best *for you*. You need to find a home where you can find—love." Why was that so hard to say? "You deserve that. And a family of your own." Again, the words caught in his throat.

"I'm sorry I have caused you so much trouble."

When he turned from putting several items on the shelves he'd carved into the cave wall, she was gone. "Keena?" She didn't answer, so he went out to the entrance. She stood at the edge. The path was still open for her to walk away, but she didn't intend to leave. As her toes slid over the high perch, he knew she planned something far worse. His dragon pushed against his skin, ready to burst forth and save her—again.

He held control of his other nature and spoke in a calm, firm tone. "The dragon saved you from that horrible place, and this is how you plan to repay that kindness?"

Her arms still gripped her as she continued to inch off the edge. "My own mother never wanted me. The town's people hated me. The dragon didn't want me. And now you. There is no place for me in this world."

"Keena, stop!" His deep voice growled with his dragon's fear.

Dragons had a bit of magic besides their ability to shift. They could, to a small degree, compel someone to do something. Now, he couldn't make her do anything that she would never do—like kill someone or eat something she knew was poisoned. But with a little push of his thoughts to hers, he might prevent her from jumping. "Keena, stop and step away from the edge."

She tossed her head as if a gnat had flown at her face. Again, vibrations tickled through his boot soles as tiny bits of rock trickled down from above.

She didn't move from the ledge. Her being human, his compulsion should have worked.

As his fear provoked his dragon more, he had to try something else. He had to stop her. "The dragon stays here and guards you. And I *never* said I didn't want you. I want more *for* you. Please come away from the edge. Nothing is going to change for a while. Your hands need to heal and you need time to gain some strength from eating proper meals. That is why I traveled to Eagle's Nest. To get you food, a dress, and shoes."

She'd stopped moving forward but hadn't stepped back from the precipice either. "I have cost you so much. It would be—"

"*Thoughtless* to let it go to waste." He inched toward her. "Keena, please. I have seen too much sacrifice. Don't force me to watch yours."

He took hold of her upper arms and pulled her from the ledge until her back rested against his chest. She must feel the drumming of his heart against her gaunt frame. He released her as the urge to wrap his arms around her and hold her overwhelmed him.

He cleared his throat of the foreign need. "Why don't you try on the dress? I'd very much like to see you in it."

Keena turned without looking at him and staggered back into the cave. He removed his shirt, moved to the cascading stream and let the cold water wash away his railing thoughts. What was this woman doing to him?

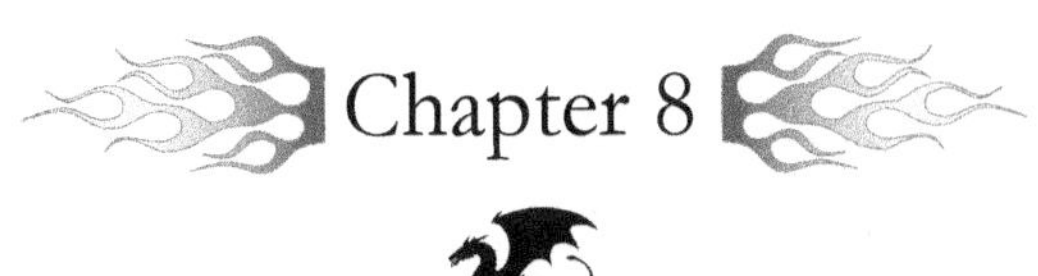

Chapter 8

The atmosphere between them changed after he returned. Keena huddled again on the floor in the corner. She hadn't put on the dress.

"Cragholde always dressed their sacrifices in fancy gowns before they fed them to the dragon," she told him.

He didn't expect her to view his relocation as his personal rejection of her. Would this have happened with any of the other women he'd saved? If he brought them here first, would they have wanted to stay too? Jydryn glanced at Keena. Why was everything about her different?

"Keena, will you walk with me?"

"Why?"

"So I can show you the view from the peak above us."

"And see all I will have to leave when you can't tolerate my presence anymore? No."

All right, he admitted his offer sounded cruel. He cooked the last of the goat. They'd need fresh meat tomorrow—but he didn't dare leave for fear she'd hurt herself. The thought alone near stopped his hammering heart.

He left her in the inner chamber and went out to sit on the edge where she'd stood. The rocks below were jagged and numerous at the bottom of the twenty-foot fall. She'd never survive that—and neither would he. What was she doing to him?

Whatever was at the root of Jydryn's trouble with this woman, he knew it wasn't attraction between them. Dragon shifters mated for life with other dragon shifters. On rare occasions in generations past, they might have found their mate among one of the other shifter clans. But things were different now. Fewer females were being born to any of the shifter clans. As the years passed, there were fewer shifters because of the lack of females.

The humans had no problem growing in number. They seemed to reproduce like fleas and cared little for their young, as the sacrifices proved. But a pairing between a human and a shifter—especially a long-lived dragon—hadn't happened in over a thousand years.

Jydryn sighed and rolled his neck. Attraction couldn't be his problem. He'd known when he chose the life of an Activist over joining the Isolationist or the Balanced, he'd be alone. He would never find love and never sire offspring. It was part of the lifestyle of those who helped the humans. He didn't harbor those desires. He'd chosen this life to help those victimized by the hate of others. Keena was one he was most proud to have saved. She'd suffered so much. To free her to live a fulfilling life seemed like the highest calling he'd ever completed. So why was it turning out so horribly?

He pulled off his shirt and crossed under the cascading stream. The cold water bit, but was refreshing to his knot-clenched muscles. Once on the other side, he climbed to the high plateau he'd wanted to take Keena. From this height, he saw for hundreds of miles—thousands if he used his dragon vision. But, instead of looking down at the land, he turned his gaze skyward to the wispy trails of clouds and beyond. He could almost make out the stars past the light of the late afternoon sun.

Jydryn inhaled the breeze peppered with the first buds of spring. The sun warmed his back and dried his hair. He closed his eyes and raised his hands. "Father, the wonders of Your hands declare Your glory. You are the source of all life, and I praise Your holy name." He left his hands stretched to the heavens as he lost the words he wanted for worship.

As much as he loved his Lord, there was a need on his heart he couldn't contain any longer. "Father, Keena needs You. I can't help her."

Something pushed against him as though he'd received a playful shove. He opened his eyes and looked around. He was alone. There was no scent in the air but his own and the sandstone, the blue mist shrubs—though they would not grow blooms for several months—and hawthorn also grew nearby. Grandmother used the bright red berries for medicine for the heart. The pungent odor of a group of ground squirrels was there too.

Jydryn moved to his knees, raised his arms, and closed his eyes. "Father, comfort her and show her Your mighty love."

Once more, he felt a physical prodding.

He sat back on his heels; resting his hands on his thighs. When he was confused, there was only one option. "What is Your will, Lord?"

You.

God spoke to him in many ways. The words of the hymns he'd learned as a fledgling were the most common. But situations often revealed the will of the Father too. Never had he received an audible word spoken straight to his heart. "Me? I don't understand."

Teach her of Me.

He remembered his lessons well enough to obey that instruction.

Love her as I do.

"What?" The word choked in his throat. No one could love like God. He was perfect and complete, and His love unconditional. And love—no, he wasn't prepared …

But he would not refuse his God. Jydryn stood and hurried back down to teach Keena her first lesson of the Father. Creation was always a good place to start.

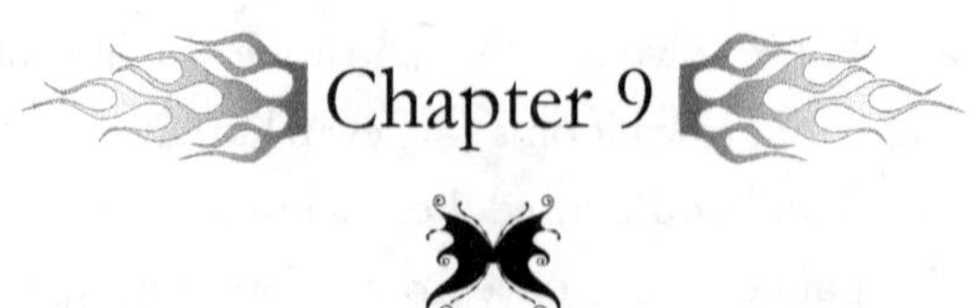

Chapter 9

Jy was an odd man. First, he treated her wounds with kindness and bought her a dress—and shoes. Then he wanted her to leave. Now, he spent part of each day teaching her about his God, and he'd quit talking about her leaving.

The deity Jy spoke of differed from any she'd heard of before. All powerful and in control of all things. Jy said He loved all His creation—including her. She waited to hear what her devotion to this God would cost. There had to be a price to pay. Her being sent to the dragon to make some god happy and stop the illness in Cragholde was proof enough.

Keena swayed on her feet. Perhaps it wasn't Jy but something in her that was the problem. For days, she'd felt off. Her sense of smell dimmed, her hearing dulled, and her sight blurred. Ever since she donned the fancy dress and slid on the leather slippers Jy had brought her, she felt disconnected from the world around her.

Jy finished clearing the table of their evening meal and came to her as she added another log to the fire. "Let me see your hands."

And there it was again. A strange buzzing in her head at random times when he spoke. It was like his words came straight to her mind and forced her to do what he said. The pressure in her skull made her head ache and her eyes water. "They're fine." She studied her hands, picking at the dirt under one nail.

"You haven't let me see them in a week. I must insist that I look at them."

Keena kept her back to him and stared at the dancing flames.

He took hold of her elbow and whirled her around. He snatched up her wrist before she could hide her hand behind her back. Thankfully, the cuff of her dress kept his skin from touching hers. "Keena, you must get over this fear. You've been here for weeks and I'm not sick—not even a sniffle."

"Maybe the dragon protects you somehow." She held her fist closed until he reached for her fingers. Fear for him forced them open so he wouldn't touch her. It might be better if he got sick—a little. She could stay and take care of him, and he'd be too weak to take her to another town.

He undid the knot and unwound the dirty strip of cloth. Closed pink scars added to the lines in her palms.

So that was it. He'd send her away now.

His smiling face rose, but his perpetual grin faded when he glanced at her tear-filled eyes.

"I don't want to go," she mumbled.

He sighed. "Is that what you've been worried about?"

She nodded.

His head snapped up as his whole body jerked. He turned as he released her. "Stay here."

The buzz pierced her head again.

He hurried toward the opening out to the entrance.

She took a step to follow. "What's going—"

"Stay. Here!" His voice growled as the muscles across his shoulders tightened under his shirt. "Don't come out of this chamber." He ordered as he vanished from sight.

Jydryn hopped as he pulled off his boots and crossed to the edge of the entrance. The chants of the vile priests of Greenburn found him through the breeze. What day was it? He glanced at the sky and jerked off his shirt. The first new moon of spring. He should have known there'd be a sacrifice tonight. Keena's presence distracted him.

A rustle behind him stilled his hands as he jerked the leather laces of his pants open. "Keena, stay inside." Why didn't his compulsion work on her?

A glance over his shoulder said she'd not come out. He yanked off his pants and shifted as he leapt into the air.

He tucked his wings and dove for the altar, already glowing with its sickening green flames. The wail of an infant stole his breath. He was too late.

He sped over the altar. Flames licked at the child's legs and set her tiny white dress on fire. He snatched her with a roar of pain. While the skin on the pads of his feet was much thicker than human skin, they were one of his more vulnerable spots. He'd need some of Keena's healing ointment when he got the child to the cave.

In pain, the child shrieked in his paw as he whirled back on the worshippers in a rage. The priests shouted and raised bows to stop him. Jydryn opened his mouth and bathed them in his fire. If they so desired to appease their wicked god by flame, they could sacrifice themselves.

The child grew silent and still. He'd been too late. If the child was dead, Keena would find herself in Eagle's Nest, or some other town, by morning.

# Chapter 10

Keena wasn't at the entrance when he returned. He sat the child on his shirt and shifted. The babe woke with a wail and he hurried to get his pants on before Keena came to investigate. Several blistered fingers made his task difficult.

The child had burns on the back of her legs and one heel. He'd snuffed out the flames on her dress when he'd closed his paw around her. The ragged, blackened edge now didn't even cover her round belly. Her skin there was red with a shallow burn, but nothing more.

Jydryn snatched her up and ran for the inner chamber. "Keena, I need your help."

"What happened?" The tears in her words made him glance up from the screaming child as he laid the babe on her stomach.

"They tried to sacrifice her."

Keena gasped. "Who?"

"The loathsome inhabitants of Greenburn." He remembered the dozen he'd left writhing from his wrath with a shudder. "Come help me."

"I—I can't. She's—a—a baby. My touch …"

Jydryn left the infant on the bed and stomped toward Keena. She backed from his aggressiveness. "She needs your help. Your touch won't hurt her," he said, grabbing both her wrists. "If you don't help, she could die." He pressed his thumbs through the fabric of her sleeves into a curve on each of her wrists.

Keena bit her lip at the pain he caused, but her fists opened with her fingers almost straight.

He pressed her palms to his bare chest. The skin-to-skin contact almost doubled him over as though a young dragon had kicked him in the gut.

"What is that?" Keena's panic added to his own shock as a line of tiny blue tongues of fire appeared to hover on her hands. Each dot of flame formed a row up both arms. The tip of each was—pink.

"Zyrsog!"

"What?" Keena struggled to break free of his grasp. Of course, she wouldn't recognize the curse word in an ancient dragon dialect that few dragons remembered.

He watched the flames find a rhythm that matched his frantic heart. They didn't—couldn't—burn her. It didn't even singe her dress. "Dragon Fire," he whispered. How could that even be?

"Dragon Fire? What is that?"

If he released her, the image of the flames lining her body would disappear and she'd understand that he was—at least in part—responsible for it. He took a deep breath, more to calm himself, and offered her as reassuring a smile as he could manage. He leaned away so her hands no longer touched his chest and let his hands slide up her sleeves as though he wiped the tongues of flame away. Without their skin-to-skin contact, the flames went out. "You are under the dragon's protection."

"Protection?" She rubbed her arms as if continuing to remove the now dormant flames. "Why?"

That was an excellent question, but the wail from the bed pulled his attention back to the more pressing need.

He took Keena by her elbow—assured the fabric of her sleeve would prevent the Dragon Fire from reappearing—and led her back to the bed. "We'll have to discuss it later. Right now, she needs our help." He turned to Keena and pushed her to sit. "Hold her while I collect the medicine I need."

He only made it a step away. He needed the baby held still while he worked to treat her deep burns. Everything in him told him Keena carried no sickness and would cause the babe no harm. But the thought poked at him for a moment. What if …?

"I—I don't know how."

Exasperation flashed through him again, threatening to release his dragon. The inner chamber was much too small for that. How could anyone not know how to hold a child? He whirled to see terror flash in Keena's eyes as a single finger hung quaking over the child's forehead. A wave of cold pity squashed the wrath. Of course, Keena wouldn't know. No one touched her, or allowed her to touch them, so why *would* she know how to hold a child?

Jydryn slipped his hands under the child's armpits with a wince of pain. One of his blisters had opened when he took Keena's wrists. He placed the squalling child against Keena. Stomach to chest. He wrapped the babe's tiny arms around Keena's neck. Who was more uncomfortable? Him, the babe, or Keena? It was hard to tell. To avoid touching Keena and reigniting the flames, he directed her to place one hand at the back of the child's neck and head, and the other under the babe's bare rump. "Firm, but not tight," he whispered.

Keena gave him a wide-eyed nod.

Keena held the babe against her while the poor girl's tears soaked Keena's collar. The horrid burns on the baby's legs made her gag.

Jy returned from the other side of the chamber with his arms full of clay pots and glass jars. He set them on the table beside the bed, pulled the chair she used from the dinner table, and sat beside them.

"Is she going to be all right?" Keena whispered over the child's continued bawling.

"I will do everything I can for her. The burns are deepest on the backs of her legs, but they do not cover a large area. If the Lord grants us His favor, disease will not set in, and she will survive the trauma of dressing these wounds." He dipped a slender metal tube into a dark green glass bottle. He set the container aside and put the tube in the girl's mouth.

"What is that?"

"Something to kill the pain and help her sleep while I treat her." His gaze rose to Keena's. "Two drops would see me sleeping for a day. You should have only one." He brushed the top of the child's head. "If I don't give her enough, she'll suffer as I work to clean her wounds and the pain might kill her. If I give her too much, her heart will stop."

Jy looked at Keena again. "Can you feel her heart beat against you?"

Keena closed her eyes and separated the sensation of her pounding heart from the baby's frantic beating. "Yes."

"Good. I need you to tell me if that changes more than slowing a little."

She nodded and looked down as the child whimpered and hiccuped.

"The medicine is taking effect. She should be asleep in a moment."

The child grew heavy and became deathly quiet. But her heart still beat. Keena fought to breathe.

# Chapter 11

As the child settled in Keena's arms and Jy turned to treat her wounds, Keena's mind tumbled with questions. "How old is she?"

Jy cut away blackened flesh. "Eight months, maybe more."

As blood leaked from the babe's injuries to soak Keena's dress, she had to close her eyes.

"Why did they do this to her?"

"To appease the evil they worship." Jy's words spit his anger.

"Did her parents allow this?" Keena fought not to tighten her hold on the babe. Her own mother had abandoned her, but this was something quite different. To murder one's own blood in such a horrible manner was unthinkable.

Bottles clinked and jars thunked as Jy worked. "The priests have fed the people lies that this is the only way to assure plentiful crops or health for the entire village. Most don't seem to question it or try to stop it from what I've see."

"What sacrifice does your God demand."

"My God is nothing like that!" His nostrils flared and it almost looked like a tendril of smoke slipped into the air. "There is a penalty for all who have gone against His perfect law—but His Son paid that price for us." He took a deep breath and his next words came quieter. "We need only accept the gift of the sacrifice that *He paid* in our stead."

It sounded too easy and unbelievable. Keena decided not to ask him more as he concentrated on the wounds. He muttered angry words at the men who had done this to an innocent child. His intense rage frightened her, and the room seemed hotter than it ever had before—even as the fire grew low. Keena never wanted that anger directed at her.

"Keena?" She opened her eyes. He'd cleaned the wounds and now stared at her. "Is her heartbeat still strong?"

She nodded. "She's asleep, I think."

"I'm going to put the ointment on now. It's her best hope, but you know the pain it caused your shallow cuts."

She nodded again and cradled the child more snuggly against her.

With a tenderness that seemed impossible from such large hands, he smeared the bleeding wounds with the gooey yellow cream. "I owe you a new dress. I'm afraid holding her ruined this one."

"It's all right." She wanted to say that she didn't need another one if he would allow her to stay here with him. The stains would fade. But she feared speaking about her leaving again.

When he finished with the girl, he applied the cream to several fingers on his right hand.

"You're hurt?" Keena thought to reach out for him, but she feared letting go of the child.

"Just a few blisters. I won't even notice them in a couple of days." He stood, put his jars aside, and wiped off his left hand.

When he came back to the bed with a piece of another shirt he'd cut up, his gaze raked over her in an odd way. It was like he was seeing her for the first time. He watched her as he wrapped the cloth around his hand. "I'm going to leave her burns exposed and we need to keep her on her belly as the wounds are worst on the back of her legs. I hope this will speed the healing and be less painful for her." A little of his customary smile returned. "Can you stand and reposition yourself with her on her chest as you recline on the bed?"

Jy placed pillows behind Keena as she reclined back into them. Once she settled, he lowered his ear to the girl's back and listened. "I don't hear any rattle in her chest and her heartbeat is steady." He straightened and placed his hand on the baby's head and closed his eyes. "Father, this dear child of Yours needs You. Great and powerful Healer, come and touch her tiny body. Ease her pain. Give me wisdom to know how to help. Spare this precious one of Yours. I pray in the Savior's name. Amen."

"Amen," Keena whispered.

Jy smiled. He moved to his trunk and cut up another garment. This one was a heavy cloak.

Keena smirked as she wiggled back into the pillows to get comfortable. "You'll not have any clothes left if you keep treating all these injuries and cutting them up to dress them."

He kept working and shrugged one shoulder. "I can replace clothes."

"What happens now?" Keena couldn't silence the tremor in her voice.

"I'd like to get a nappy on her before I leave." Jy held up a square he'd cut from the cloak.

"Leave?" Panic jolted her heart.

Jy's hand rested on her shoulder. "It's all right. I—the dragon and I need to find a doe or ewe from a flock nearby. The babe will need milk when she wakes. I won't be long."

"And then you'll tell me about Dragon Fire?"

Something flashed across his gaze that she didn't understand. "Aye, we'll talk. For now, rest and keep monitoring her heartbeat." He stopped in the doorway before he left. "Do you need anything before I go?"

She started to say no, but her gaze lingered on the pitcher of water he always kept filled from the stream.

He followed her gaze, brought the pitcher, and sat it on the table next to all his medical jars. He filled a glass for her. She drained it and he refilled it, but this time she set it beside the pitcher for later.

"I won't be long, Keena." There was something different in the way he said her name, now. It both warmed her and made her tremble.

 Chapter 12 

Jydryn shifted and launched into the dark night devoid of any moon. It was well after the middle of the night. No flames remained around the altar of Greenburn. He banked away from the town he hated and the death that he had caused there.

He exhaled a long breath and just floated for a moment. If the baby didn't develop a fever, she should survive. Treating her had bought back memories of his grandmother. Their time together tending the sick and injured shifters served him well now. His dragon form wasn't prone to tears, but for her, they shed a few. Grandmother's loss was one reason he left the community and his family and lived alone. But even now, two decades later, the grief still filled him.

He tried to push his thoughts aside and focus on the search for a goat whose kid was old enough not to miss its mother.

The thoughts of his family—those who awaited him in paradise with their Lord, and those he'd left behind to live this solitary life—spun his thoughts to Keena.

Dragon Fire! The tongues of fire had appeared on Keena. It hadn't been a dream. He didn't even think such a thing was possible? *Lord, what are You doing?*

A chuckle tickled over his scales with the breeze. It was not sinister or cruel. It was the sound his shifter father would make when he'd given Jydryn a gift he'd always longed for. Without Jydryn ever speaking his desire, his father had known and presented his son with that very gift. The present always brought both of them great joy.

In the Dragon Fire, his heavenly Father had just revealed this type of gift. Jydryn had found his life mate in Keena. She was the one who would love him and whom he would love all his days. With her being human, he would far outlive her, but he would know love. From before the foundations of the world, God had planned for this woman to share his life and give him children.

Children. Like the tiny girl Keena cradled now. Milk! He was out here to get the wee thing a goat or sheep so she'd have milk. He struggled to focus. Thoughts of his current task intertwined with the horrible memory of burning the priests and the current wild emotions for his life mate.

Life mate!

Him! Keena was his, and he was hers. So much made sense to him now. From his desire to bring her into his home, to his protectiveness and the pain of thinking of her with another, they were evidence of his connection to her. Even Keena's reluctance to leave—though he was sure she understood this destined bond between them even less than he did—proved she experienced the connection as well. It also made complete sense that his attempts to compel her hadn't worked. Mates couldn't force one another to do anything, but he hadn't realized their deeper connection when he'd tried.

Light kissed the eastern sky. Where was he? He'd been floating around aimlessly for hours, trying to wrap his head around the thoughts his heart already knew were true. He loved Keena. Now that the Dragon Fire had been lit between them, if they didn't complete the bonding ritual before God to unite them mind, body, and soul, they would die.

Keena didn't even know he was a shifter. That conversation couldn't wait much longer. But there was a bigger issue. His mate didn't share his faith. God made it clear that His followers couldn't be bound to one who didn't believe.

At last, he passed over a flock of goats on a hill. He selected one doe heavy with milk and turned back toward the Tetling Ridge.

Jydryn couldn't see it on the horizon. He'd flown farther than he'd realized.

The memory of God telling him to love Keena and teach her about Him came back. If God had called them to be life mates, she would one day soon claim God as her own too. He did a few loops and spirals and roared with joy. His playful antics made the goat in his claws squeal in terror.

The sun had cleared the horizon before he landed back at his cave. His heart fluttered, knowing he'd see his mate in a moment.

He secured the goat in a corner with a long lead, pulled on his pants and shirt, and inched to the opening of the inner chamber.

Keena's eyes opened, and her gaze locked on him. Worry furrowed her brows, causing small wrinkles to form.

"Is everything all right?" he whispered as he crept toward her.

"Did you find a goat or sheep? What took so long?"

He crouched by the bed and squeezed her arm with one hand and brushed her hair back from her face with the other. He was careful not to touch skin and thus ignite the Dragon Fire again. It would be hard for him to explain its reappearance. But the urge to hold her had only grown now that he knew who she was. "I'm sorry." He grinned. "I'll milk the goat and prepare a bottle for her. Has she woken at all?"

Keena relaxed back into the pillows. "Twice, but not for long."

"The trauma of her injuries took a lot out of her. It's best she sleeps as much as she can."

Keena nodded.

He milked the flighty goat of enough to fill a small jar and then found a glove he'd never worn and cut off a finger for the nipple. The child drank about half of it before she fell asleep again.

Jydryn moved to the other side of the bed, added wood to the fire, and sat on top of the covers. "Here, let me hold her while you get some sleep. We'll have to keep a constant watch on her for the next couple of days and pray she doesn't develop a fever."

With the child comfortable on Jydryn's chest, Keena got up and used the privy bucket behind the screen he'd set up on the far side of the chamber. When she returned, she stood by the bed. "I can sleep out—"

He pulled back the covers and patted the bed. "Don't be silly. Come, rest. You have done well. I know you must be tired."

She nodded and yawned to prove his point. Instead of lying with her back to him, she curled on her side, facing him. When he was sure she was asleep, he brushed a single finger along the soft skin of her cheek. Tiny tongues of Dragon Fire emerged where he touched her, over her shoulder, down her arm, all the way to her feet. Though most Dragon Fire was a single color, Keena's blue flame also had tops of pink. Regardless of the color, the flames marked her as being his.

Now, the only problem was breaking the news to her.

Chapter 13

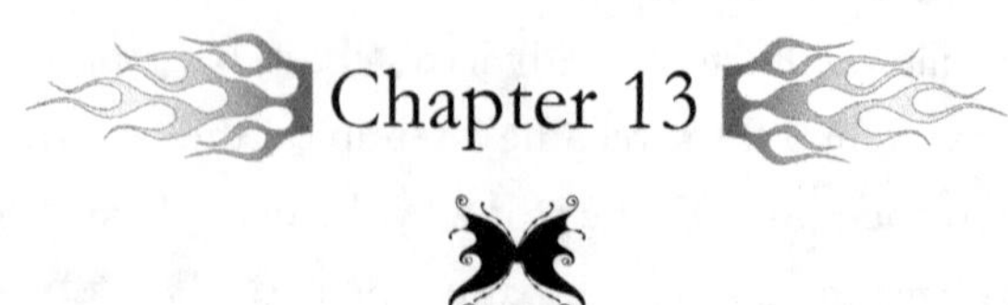

Keena startled awake when the baby cried. As her eyes fluttered open, she thought she saw flames on her again. She blinked and rubbed her eyes as the bed moved.

"It's all right. She needs to be changed and she's hungry." Jy laid the baby on her back on the bed but kept her legs from touching the sheets. "Can you fetch me another piece of the cloak?"

Keena pushed herself up and glanced around the chamber.

"I think it's on my chair," Jy said with a tip of his head.

Keena slipped into the one shoe she could find and stood. Her bare foot rested on the cool stone as a full breath filled her lungs. The scents of ointment, herbs, and smoldering musky man overwhelmed her. Many types of birds chirped outside. Everything in the room was sharp and crisp in her vision. She spotted the cloak.

The hum of the stone welcomed her as she strolled the couple of steps to the fabric and back. She found her other shoe at the foot of the bed.

Keena knelt on the bed and brushed the girl's face as Jy removed the old nappy and put a new one on her.

"Here, sit back against the pillows again. You can hold her while I get a bottle ready." He again laid the child on her stomach against Keena's chest. Her cries echoed off the stone walls around them.

When Jy returned with the bottle of milk, it took a while to get the baby to drink. "You said we were going to talk about the Dragon Fire."

He smirked with a small nod. "Aye, we still need to do that." He caressed the baby's head and spoke to her in soothing tones. "Come now, my sweet. You need this to keep your strength up."

At last, the baby drank, but soon she was asleep again. Jy stood and shook the bottle. "Only half again."

"She's not eating enough."

"No, and that worries me." Jy spun and sat the bottle where he prepared the food. "I'm going to fl—go to the village and get her something else."

Keena sat up, making the child whimper. "You're leaving again?"

"I won't be long."

"You said that last night." Keena glanced up at him. A wild mix of emotions warred inside her. She wanted him to touch her and speak to her like he had the baby. Still, she feared he'd get sick or send her away. She didn't know what to do with this injured infant in her arms, and she didn't want to be alone again. "I don't know what to do for her."

He flashed her a grin. "You'll be fine, and I promise, I won't take as long this time." He was out of the chamber before she could stop him.

It hadn't gone unnoticed by her that he avoided explaining Dragon Fire. What was the man hiding?

Jydryn landed back in the cave entrance. He'd gone to Easthelm, another city with a market he favored. It was smaller than Eagle's Nest, so it didn't have the variety or everything he always wanted, but it was closer.

"Jy!" Keena's cry came before he completed the shift back to his human skin. He jerked on his pants and thrust his arms through his shirtsleeves as he moved toward the inner chamber. One quick pull and his shirt was over his head before he entered. "What's the matter?"

"She so hot."

The baby's thin, light brown hair—so similar in color to his own—was as wet as the front of Keena's dress.

Tears dribbled down Keena's cheeks. "I'm sorry. I never should have touched her. She's sick, and it's all my fault."

"It's not your fault. It's mine." He threw off the tabletop that covered the tub with a crash. "I must have missed something." His anger at being too distracted by finding his life mate to pay proper attention to the child's wounds filled his words.

He scooped up the bucket he used to retrieve water, looked at the tub, and at the baby. He cursed and hurled the bucket against the wall, creating a large hole in it.

Keena tucked the child under her chin in an attempt to shield her from his wrath. "What's the matter?"

"I need to cool her. That would mean a cold bath for most. But her wounds are too deep to be submerged in stream water that is full of impurities and will only add more infection. I could lay her so her legs remain out of the water, but that would put her both face down, and head first under the surface. I don't know how to help her." He shouted his last words and made Keena close her eyes and cringe.

"Could you cool her some other way?" Keena whispered. "Maybe with a damp towel …" Her words faded as he stomped toward her.

He took hold of Keena's shoulders and kissed the top of her head. "Thank you. That's an excellent idea." He snatched up a towel. "I couldn't think over my failure," he called as he raced out of the chamber.

When he returned, he draped the cool dripping towel across the child's back, careful not to cover her wounds. He kicked the wood in the fire apart. "We are going to get cold, but until her fever breaks, I don't want any added heat in here. If fact—" he pulled a pillow from behind Keena and sat it on the bed "—lay her over this. She doesn't need our heat either."

Jydryn propped the baby so she still laid on her stomach, but not flat. He pointed to a shelf carved into the stone wall not far away. "Grab another towel and wet it too. You keep rewetting them, so she always has the coolest one over her. Stay close and make sure she still draws breath."

Keena pinched the shaft of a feather poking out from the pillow between her fingernails. She drew out the downy white puff and laid it near the child's nose and mouth. It fluttered with each breath.

Jydryn relaxed more. He squeezed Keena's arm before she moved to wet the new towel. "That's brilliant. I don't think I could do this without you."

"Are you sure it wasn't my touch?"

Jydryn pointed to a burn on the baby's calf. "Do you see how much deeper the red is here than anywhere else?"

Keena nodded.

He wiped away the yellow cream to reveal what was underneath. "Not all that is cream. Some is puss from the flesh growing sick because I didn't clean it well enough the first time. This is my fault."

"No, it's the fault of those who tried to kill her."

"Aye." He growled the word and had to close his eyes and roll his neck to wash away the image of the tiny babe laying in the flames on the altar and his continuing desire to destroy the entire village.

Chapter 14

Keena kept changing one wet towel for the cooler one as Jy worked to clean the wound. He swore it was his fault and not a sickness Keena could have given the child. He'd praised her twice and even kissed her on the head. The memory still startled her.

Once Jy had reapplied fresh ointment, he retrieved the items he purchased from the entrance. He pulled out a small dressing gown for the baby and two new dresses for Keena. One was blue and the other a butter yellow, and both were much simpler than what she wore now.

She folded them and laid them aside. "I'll wait until after she is better to wear them."

Jydryn nodded without comment as he prepared a gruel with the water hanging over the now dead fire. He separated a couple of spoonfuls into a small clay pot about the size of his fist, added a large spoonful of cool water and a squirt of milk from the goat. He stirred it and grabbed a pouch from what he'd purchased. Then he stopped and stared at the baby.

"What's wrong?"

He sighed. "If you were sick with a fever after an injury, I would know what to do. Use one large pinch and make a strong tea that I'd have you drink."

"But she's so small."

"Exactly." He bowed his head. "Lord, please let me bring no more harm to this precious babe. Control my hands, clear my mind, help me help her."

Jy spoke to his God about everything. He'd talked to God as he'd worked on the baby, muttering his pleas under his breath as one long prayer. Still, the child was sick with fever. Did any of the gods pay attention to their worshippers' needs?

Jy sprinkled a few flecks from the pouch into the gruel and stirred. "Lord, let this work."

He instructed Keena how to hold the baby. With her back against Keena's chest, one arm around her tiny body and the other between her legs so that her wounds wouldn't touch anything, Keena cradled the babe. Then, he dribbled the gruel into her tiny mouth little by little.

The infant was only half awake. Jy huffed a deep sigh. "That is all I can do for now. God has to do the rest."

Keena laid the baby on her stomach again. "Will He?"

"God always answers our prayers."

"You prayed before and she has only gotten sicker."

Jy took the warm towel from her. "Sometimes God says yes to our requests. Other times no, and sometimes wait. But He is always faithful. The delay in the child's healing could be to teach me to continue to trust or to pay better attention next time. Or He might wait until the only way for the little one to recover is by a display of His power."

"If He wants her to survive, why wait?"

"Perhaps He is proving Himself to you." There was a strange grin on Jy's face.

"To me?"

"Aye, Keena. He loves you and wants you to know He'll do anything to make you one of His own."

Keena's stomach knotted. "He'd let an innocent child suffer to capture me?"

"She's too little to remember any of this. It will do her no harm. But God will do anything for one of His own—not to 'capture' you, but to set you free."

"The dragon did that when he carried me from Cragholde."

Jy smiled as he took the warm towel to the cool stream and returned a moment later with it wet again. He draped it over the baby and dropped beside her on the bed.

Keena crossed her arms and sat in the chair beside the bed. "Dragon Fire?"

"Umm." His grin was huge. "The mark of the dragon."

"Why does the dragon want me?"

Jy yawned. "It's not so much the dragon—as he does not pick who gets his flame—but God who chose you long before you were even born."

"Your God picked me for this too?" This God was very pushy, in Keena's opinion.

"Aye, you were always meant to meet the dragon."

Keena wet the next towel. She was tired of cryptic talk about this God of his. "What happens if she gets better?" Keena asked, moving their discussion to a safer topic.

Jy slid his arms under his head as he yawned again. "In the past, I took the babes I rescued to a monk in Ironfair. He'd care for each child until he could find them a loving home. Brother Paul died over the winter. I don't know who else to trust now."

"She can't stay here?" Keena bit her lip and waited for Jy to say he was going to send both of them away. Maybe he would place them in the same village.

Jy pulled his head up and one light brown brow arched high over his faint blue eye. "Wasn't it only yesterday that you were terrified because you didn't know how to hold a child? Now, you want to keep her?"

She shrugged.

He smirked as he fell back with his eyes closed.

Keena rewet one towel and traded it for the warm one. "Have you noticed her wounds?"

"I've inspected them for two days. As they heal, we'll have to work her left leg, so the scar remains flexible enough for her to work that leg with ease."

"I mean the shape."

Jy yawned and rolled toward the baby as he propped himself up on one elbow.

Without touching the sores, Keena pointed out what she saw in the scar that snaked back and forth over the back of both the baby's legs. "It starts on her left heel with a curved line and the wound appears again on her right foot with a flare like a leaf around her ankle." She followed the meandering wound with her finger hovering over it. "This thin line resembles a vine and continues to another teardrop-shaped leaf. This blob looks like a bud. And the wound continues to her left leg again, forming the biggest area—the spot that is over the back of her knee—it blooms like a full rose."

"A beautiful image for such an ugly injury." He dropped to his side and brushed his hand over the baby's cheek. "What do you think, little one? Shall we call you Rose?"

The baby made no sound, but Jy stood and took the towel from Keena. "I'll get this wet. Why don't you lay down for a while?"

"I think you're more tired than I am," she said to his vanishing back. Keena turned to Rose. Something in her wanted to ask Jy's God to save baby Rose, like Jy had. But she couldn't trust something she couldn't see, no matter how much she wanted to believe.

 Chapter 15

Jydryn woke after the sun had set. Keena sat slumped in the chair beside the bed. One of the two towels they were using dangled from her fingers. He pulled it from her weak grasp. "My turn to cool her so you can get some rest."

Keena didn't argue. She lay beside Rose by the time he returned with the towel drenched in cool water. Rose's condition didn't look like it had changed, though her fever might have gone down a little.

Jydryn covered Keena with a warm blanket and Rose with the cool towel and started his watch as he made trip after trip to the stream to re-cool each towel. If the fever didn't break soon, Rose wouldn't survive. He shouldn't have given her a name until he was sure she'd live. What would Keena think of God if Rose died?

"Your reputation is at stake, Father," he whispered. "Reveal Yourself and Your power, so Keena knows You are real and not one of those false gods worshipped by the villagers."

Keena woke to sunlight pouring through the entrance to their chamber. Rose's towel was warm and Jy wasn't sitting in the chair. Keena sat up.

"I'm here," Jy's gentle voice drew her attention to where he worked on the other side of the table. "I'm making her some more medicine."

"She isn't getting any better." Keena rested her hand on Rose's back. She was so very little. The wounds she suffered from could be deadly to a grown person. What chance did Rose have?

"Nor is she any worse," Jy said as he came toward the bed. "Can you hold her again?"

Keena slid her arms under Rose and held her so Jy could dribble a couple more spoonfuls into her mouth.

Rose's hands fisted, and she tried to knock the intrusive spoon away in her half sleep and pain.

Jy smiled. "She has some fight in her. That's good." He put the pot down and held her hands out of the way to try again.

Rose threw her head back against Keena's chest, making Keena cough and huff with the shock. Rose tossed her head side to side and cried louder than she had since she'd first arrived.

Jy chuckled. "You keep fighting, little one. That strength will serve you well. But taking a little medicine will do you even better." Jy got the tip of the spoon in her mouth, but Rose jerked away and spit out the few drops he'd gotten in.

Keena wiped the mess off her arm. "Do you have any honey?"

Jy smiled as he turned to his food supply. "Excellent idea. I suspect she hasn't had anything but her mother's milk yet."

He returned and stirred the ingredients in the small pot again. "Not only will it make this mash taste better, but honey is good for healing in lots of ways." He raised his wide grin to Keena. "Thank you. I think the lack of sleep is muddling my brain."

After a couple of attempts, Rose took the sweetened mixture with more ease. Jy then prepared her a small bottle, helped Keena coax Rose to suckle, and then the baby fell asleep again.

Jy fell asleep on the bed beside them too. Keena watched the rise and fall of his chest as an ache grew in her own.

She'd watched some folks in the villages she'd lived in find love as she grew up hiding in the shadows. Some would marry, while others would live together for a time, have a child, and then the man would leave to father other children with different women. Many of the children abandoned by their fathers joined her on the streets, begging for scraps when their mothers found new men. But there had been a few who had married and raised a family together. She'd always stayed near those homes. The couples were kinder in their rejection of Keena, and some even left her scraps or let her stay in the barn on wintry nights.

Keena swiped at a tear. She wanted a man like Jy to love her like those men had loved their wives and children, like Rose.

Keena looked down at the baby. Sweat covered Rose again. Her breaths seemed labored. Still holding her, Keena carried Rose out to the falling water of the stream as it cascaded over the opening and stood under it.

Keena let the cascading water hit her back, run over her body, and soak Rose while protecting her legs. "Please, Jy's God, if You are real and as powerful and caring as Jy says, please, help Rose. Don't let her die. Please."

Shivering, Keena moved to the center of the entrance of the cave and turned so the sun warmed her back as she rocked Rose and hummed to her. Once she'd dried a little, Keena rewet the towel and wrapped it around Rose. She returned to the cave and sat in the chair. She was unwilling to put Rose down. Unless Jy's God did something, the sweet thing wouldn't have long to live.

Keena jerked upright before she tumbled from the chair with Rose in her arms. How could she have fallen asleep? The chamber was dark. A few candles still had flames that were gutting in the remaining nubs. Keena shivered. She was cold and so was Rose. She turned Rose toward the weak light. Did her lips look blue?

The erratic pounding of Keena's heart added to her trembling body. She reached for Jy. Light flooded the area around the bed as the Dragon Flame sprang up across his shoulders and down her arms.

Keena jumped back with a gasp, extinguishing the needed light. She rested a single finger on the back of his hand with no more pressure than a feather, and the tiny tongues of fire returned. It was him! Not the dragon, like Jy had said. What did it mean?

Rose's head slid across Keena's chest to her arm. The truth of the Dragon Fire would have to wait.

Keena gripped the front of Jy's tunic and jerked. "Jy, wake up. Something's wrong."

 Chapter 16

Jydryn came to life and to his feet with such speed, Keena staggered back. He pulled the cold towel away and pressed his ear to the child's back. He had trouble hearing over his own heart thumping in his ears. "She's still alive. Her fever broke, but now she's too cold."

He leapt over the bed and suffered splinters as he crammed wood in the hearth to rekindled the fire. He'd worry about them later.

Keena inched near as he fed the flames until the fire roared. Keena's teeth chattered as the flames tried to fight back the cold that now blanketed the chamber.

He needed to calm his racing heart and clear his thoughts. "Can you milk the goat?"

Keena nodded.

Stitches popped as he yanked off his shirt and reached for Rose. "Let me hold her." Keena seemed reluctant. She didn't understand that his normal temperature was hotter than most humans because of his dragon nature. He smiled to reassure her. "I've laid covered in bed. You've held her with a wet towel and you still look damp. I can warm her. The fresh goat's milk will work from the inside as the fire and my skin heats her from the outside."

Keena passed Rose to him, being more than careful not to touch him. Were they back to that again? She didn't seem to have any problem touching Rose.

Keena grabbed the bottle and worked off the glove tip as she hurried out of the chamber.

Rose was like a block of ice against his chest. Making sure he remained in control, he brought his dragon closer to the surface to speed her warming, while he took care how close he allowed the flames in the hearth to get to her injuries. If those areas became too hot, it would cause painful stinging.

Keena sat the makeshift bottle on the trunk at the foot of the bed. She tugged several times until the blanket from the bed pulled free.

As Jydryn tried to work the nipple into Rose's mouth, Keena wrapped the blanket to encase him and Rose. The baby's head poked out, but it worked to trap Jydryn's natural heat.

Neither of them spoke. Keena no doubt held her breath as he did.

Rose stirred against him. Her tiny hands opened and closed on his chest. Then, she stilled again.

"Please, Lord," he whispered.

"Please," Keena echoed.

Rose turned her head so her other cheek pressed against his skin. It was cooler than the side that had been there, but far warmer than when he'd first taken her. Her head turned again and her fists rubbed against her eyes.

Jydryn wiggled the nipple near her lips as they opened in a small whimper. Rose jerked away and rubbed her face against his chest. Her arms and legs kicked and she let out a loud cry.

He took the opportunity to get the nipple in her open mouth. When Rose bit down to take another gulp of air to prepare for a second hearty cry, milk must have squirted in her mouth. In only moments, she was sucking hard. Her left arm worked between their bodies so she could hang on to the bottle with both hands herself.

Jydryn handed the empty container to Keena who raced to refill it. He moved to a chair as he drew the blanket around him to drape over the front of them. He placed Rose against his shoulder and patted her back.

Rose cried as he burped her before Keena returned. Then, the little one grasped the bottle and drained it again.

Keena filled it a third time. Rose held it and looked up at him—watching, smiling. She looked at Keena, the bottle in her mouth forgotten.

This tiny babe wound her way deep into his heart. He couldn't help chuckling at her. "Are you going to finish this one too, Rose, or are you going to smile at Keena?" Rose kept the nipple in her mouth, but her lips were curled in a lopsided grin so she couldn't suck.

Keena knelt and brushed the child's silky hair. "Is she going to be all right now?"

"Aye. God has saved her." Jydryn released the full breath he'd held trapped in his lungs since he'd startled awake. "Lord God Almighty, we thank You for Rose's life. For Your kindness and faithfulness to her and to us who have come to love her so. May she grow to praise Your name too."

"Mmm," Keena nodded. "Thank You," she whispered.

"Do you want to hold her again?"

Keena shook her head and stood. She rounded the bed and added a log to the fire before she moved about the chamber and a lit candle.

"There are more on the shelf," he pointed.

With the room bathed in light and warming, Keena yawned and glanced down at her filthy dress. He followed her gaze when it landed on the bucket they used to bring in water from the stream. It lay broken on the floor from his earlier outburst.

He stood and offered Rose to her. "I can fill the large pot over the fire if you'll hold her. I'm sure a warm bath would feel good."

Keena stared at him with her arms limp at her sides. Was more than exhaustion weighing on her? She retreated from him, leaving Rose in his arms, which told him there was something more at the root of her troubles.

She walked past him, giving him a wide berth, stretched out the drier of the two towels on the bed, and lay down with her back to him as she faced the fire.

Jydryn draped the blanket over her and pulled his last dry towel from the shelf to cover Rose where she still lay in his arms. Her tiny eyes drooped. She startled and sucked on the nipple a few times, grinned at him, and the entire process would start all over until she was asleep.

Jydryn laid Rose on her stomach over a pillow beside Keena. He drew the edge of the blanket over her before he moved out into the entrance, stripped, and shifted. He took to the sky in the predawn light, praising God and praying over whatever troubled Keena.

God had been faithful all his life. Jydryn never questioned the truth of God's provision in all ways. Somehow, now, with these two destined to be his family, Jydryn struggled to release the care of them back to his heavenly Father. His mind kept wandering from his prayers to all he needed to do to keep them safe on his own. He'd repent and trust again, only to fall into worry in the next moment.

Jydryn landed back at the cave, shifted, dressed, strolled to the edge of the entrance, and let his gaze wash over the land. To make Keena, and Rose, family, he needed to tell Keena who he was. His stomach tightened so much he had to brace himself on his knees. If the mere thought of confiding in the one who would be his, made him nauseous, how was he ever going to tell her? His fist pressed against his middle as an uncommon fear overwhelmed him.

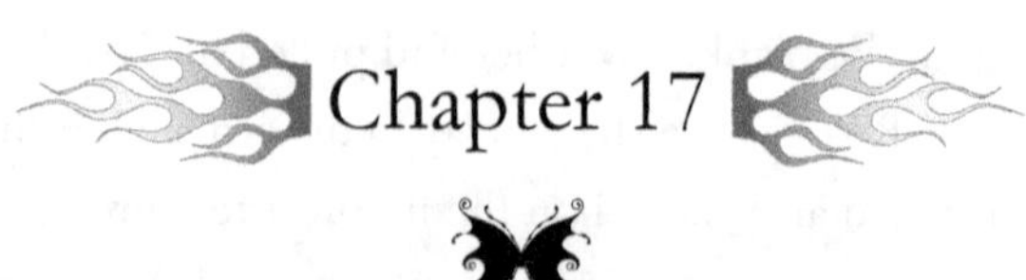

Chapter 17

Keena chopped vegetables as Jy left Rose on the bed and came toward her. Over the last ten days Rose showed steady improvement, and Keena and Jy had found a rhythm, but things had changed between them. While Jy taught her how to prepare editable food, she kept him at a distance.

Jy never spoke about the Dragon Fire. If Keena tried to question it, or ask for any information about him, he talked around the question. She didn't trust him. He was lying to her about something.

His shoulders slumped. His skin had a gray pallor, and the area below his eyes lay shadowed and dark. He didn't look like he'd slept in the near month she'd been with him. Jy released a heavy sigh. "I'm going into the village market again. Do you need anything?"

She scanned their food supply. "Potatoes, more gruel for Rose—"

He reached his hand toward hers as she cut a carrot to add to the stew. She jerked out of his reach. His eyes closed for a moment, the last hint of his smile vanished, and his head hung. When his gaze came up again, he stared for a time before he spoke. "I know what food items we need. What can I do for you? What can I get you, Keena?"

She banged the knife down. "Where do you sleep?" The question burst from her lips before she could stop it.

His head tipped as his brows scrunched together. "At the entrance."

"I've seen the dragon there, but not you."

He turned from her to collect the bag he used to carry back the items he purchased. "The dragon makes sure I stay warm and protected while exposed to the night air."

"Where does your money come from? You don't have a job."

"My grandfather left me a fair amount of coin when he passed." He stopped at the end of the table and watched as she finished cutting an onion and reached for the last of the potatoes. "May I ask you a question?"

She shrugged.

"Have I upset you?"

Keena shook her head. "You've been kinder than anyone I've ever met." She brushed the chopped vegetables into a bowl and carried them to the pot warming over the fire. "I used the last of the stag. Maybe you could bring something back or send the dragon to get us meat. Does he go with you?"

"He is never far."

Rose giggled. She knelt on her hands and knees on the bed and rocked her weight back and forth, but didn't move across the bed.

"She'll be crawling soon," Jy said.

Keena returned to the table and cleaned her mess. "Perhaps it is time you take me to Eagle's Nest."

"What?" Jy staggered and gripped the back of a chair.

She narrowed her gaze and pointed the tip of her knife at him. "You said you wanted to leave me there. Rose could stay with me."

The last of Jy's color drained, and he looked about to collapse. "You want to leave?"

She stopped to stare at him and rubbed the chill from her arms before she braced her hands on the table. It needed to be said—even if it would cut her heart out. The heart he had almost brought back to life. "Though you have been kind, of a fashion, I don't want to stay where someone lies to me."

"Lies? Keena, I have *never* lied to you."

She reached out and covered his hand with her own. Weak Dragon Fire flickered over their bodies.

Jydryn had never felt so horrible in his life. If he didn't know Keena was his true mate, he might agree with her fellow villagers and think she caused those around her to become ill. But his distress was not her fault. He bore the only blame. He'd refused to pursue her. At first, they'd focused on getting Rose well. Then Keena had withdrawn from him. She'd grown quiet and distant. Terror prevented him from telling her of his true nature.

Now she wanted to leave. He'd die without her—she would too, now that the Dragon Fire had been lit between them. He couldn't breathe. His chest ached and his heart struggled to beat.

Her accusation that he lied stunned him. He startled when her small, warm hand covered his. The tongues of Dragon Fire were smaller and weaker than they had been the first time.

"It's you. The dragon isn't doing this. You are. You lied."

Jydryn covered her hand with his other, trapping it between his. He needed her touch to ease his discomfort. "I swear to you, I have never lied." He sighed. "I have not told you everything, but I never lied," he whimpered.

"Keeping things from me is just as bad."

The spirit of his dragon reached out, strengthening the connection between them. Each breath came easier. Each beat of his heart grew stronger and the flames larger. "Will you come with me? I will reveal everything to you."

She tried again to pull her hand free, but it was a half-hearted attempt. Perhaps she found his touch as comforting as he did hers. The tongues of fire lining her slight frame grew in size and brightened. "Where do you want to take me?" Her voice held a tremor.

"Just to the cave entrance. I need to show you something."

She glanced at Rose, who was still trying to discover the secret to crawling.

"She'll be fine here. It will only take a moment."

Keena's gaze darted from looking at him, to their hands, to Rose, and back again. He'd betrayed her trust.

"Please. I need to show you something and then I will answer every question—tell you anything you want to know."

At last, she gave him a single, small nod.

Jydryn pulled off his boots as Keena went to the bed and moved the pillows to the edge to wall the rocking infant in the center.

He stepped out into the entrance and pulled his shirt off as Keena joined him. "Stay there at the opening to the inner chamber." He put his hands on the laces of his pants and froze as a full shudder of terror raced the length of his body. "For modesty—propriety—you will want to turn away. I ask that you don't. You need to see this."

"What are you thinking of doing?" Fear laced her words and soured the air.

"I will not, could never, hurt you. I won't even touch you."

Her arms hugged her tight as she nodded, and he turned so she had a view of his side and back as he pulled the leather cord free and let his pants drop.

Chapter 18

Keena had never seen a fully naked man. She tried to fix her gaze on his broad shoulders as heat flooded her face. A huge, jagged scar marred the cords of muscles in his lower back, which allowed the edges of her vision to take in his chiseled, round bum. Her gaze shot up to his long wavy hair as she rocked her weight between her feet and tried to swallow.

The air filled with a cracking sound. His skin turned green as his limbs extended and changed shape. His body enlarged to fill the entrance, more than doubling in size. Wings sprang from his back, their leathery skin covering her in shadow. His face elongated and filled with rows of sharp teeth as long as her forearm. Keena's heart stuttered as her mind tried to comprehend what she was seeing. His hand and feet formed paws larger than the goat bleating at the opposite end of the opening. Claws sprang from each toe and scraped across the stone. The dragon stood before her. The broken spine she'd clung to emerged where Jy's scar had been.

Images returned of the dragon sweeping down on her, his claws sparkling in the dying sun as she waited at the edge of Cragholde. She wanted to turn and run to Rose. Hide in the corner. But her feet wouldn't move and her hands hung numb at her sides.

The dragon turned his head. One stunning bright blue eye divided by a slit watched her. His wings and limbs tightened against his body, and the enormous creature trembled.

Keena's chest ached from the air trapped inside.

Again, the sound of crunching, like a giant walking over dry branches, filled her ears. He shrunk in size, and his flesh returned. Jy knelt on one knee in front of her. At last, her muscles responded, and she turned from him.

Jydryn remained on his knee after Keena left. This was his soul mate, the one God destined for him to meet so they could share a life and family. His body convulsed as the bond that had just begun to sparked between them threatened to go out. He had to fix this.

He staggered to his feet and forced his limbs back into his clothes before he entered the inner chamber with her.

Keena sat in a chair on the far side of the bed, clinging to Rose as she rocked back and forth. "What … what are you?" She choked out a whisper.

Jydryn moved to the other chair opposite her, keeping the bed between them so he didn't frighten her further. "My full name is Jydryn, the Champion of Life. I am a shifter of the dragon clan."

"Shifter?" The word stuttered from her lips.

He offered her a single nod. "Aye. Some of the peoples God created can change from a human form to an animal."

Keena continued to rock. She seemed to be unaware of Rose squirming to be free from her tight hold. "Animal? You mean dragons?"

"Some are dragons, but there are other clans. I've met those of the lion, tiger, bear, and wolf clans. There are more, but we are few compared to the humans and the fae."

Keena shook her head and almost came out of her chair. Her voice rose. "Fae are real too?"

"Aye. They live in a hidden realm called Shimmerbourne."

Keena stopped rocking. Rose stilled on her lap. The baby giggled and reached for him. Keena's head tipped and her gaze narrowed. "What does the Dragon Fire really mean?"

"I didn't lie. You are under the dragon's protection."

"Your protection."

He nodded.

Her gaze bore into his.

He swallowed the lump lodged in his throat. "I will die to protect you." He took a deep breath as Rose's plea became more vocal. "The Dragon Fire marks destined mates."

Her nose crinkled, and her lips pursed at the word. "Mates?"

"Before God formed the earth, He planned for you and I to find one another and create a family."

"I have no choice?"

The pain tearing through his chest was beyond what the old dragon had once done to his back. "I would never force you. If you want me to take you to Eagle's Nest, or someplace else, and leave you there, I will. I can do nothing to hurt you." He raised his gaze from the whimpering baby writhing on her lap to look into his mate's fearful gaze. "I love you, Keena. I always will."

She gasped. Rose slipped from her hands and landed on the bed.

Rose gripped the bed coverings, kicked, wiggled, and inched toward him.

Keena didn't stop her. "Love?" The word was a breath.

"With every fiber of my two bodies, all of my heart, my every thought. I only love my God more. Nothing else matters to me but God and you …" Rose came within his reach and he scooped the giggling child up. "… and Rose. I can't live without you."

Keena stood and turned to gaze at the flames. She added another log. Embers burst off in every direction. "Then why didn't you tell me when the Dragon Fire first appeared?"

"I should have. There were a few reasons, I guess. First, I was as stunned as you—"

She turned and looked at him with an arched brow and a smirk.

"Fair enough. I at least knew what it was and what it meant. But it has been a millennium since a dragon and a human were destined to be mates. Shifters keep to their own and avoid humans most of the time. Once people learn what we are, they want to kill us. There is also the fact I never expected to find a mate as fewer female dragon shifters are born every year, and I left my community to live where I could save humans. Seeing the Dragon Fire on you was a shock I struggled to recover from."

"It appears on you too."

Rose caught a handful of his beard and pulled, making his next words pitch higher. "On me?"

Keena's lips turned in a small amused grin at his discomfort. He deserved that. "Yes, on you." She turned to face him. Her features tensed as she alternated between biting her lip and pursing them. Her brows furrowed at first before they relaxed and her head tipped. She took one deep breath and released it with a huff before she moved toward him.

Keena pulled Rose's hand from his beard. Then she faced her palm toward him.

Jydryn raised his and pressed it against hers. The pink-tipped blue flames came to life along her arms.

"See?" She pointed with her other hand to high on his shoulders, where a dozen tongues of flame danced. His were a wild mix of color: green, pink, orange, and yellow.

Rose reached for the dancing lights and Keena broke their connection. "Will they hurt her?"

"No. Dragon Fire only marks paired mates until the ceremony binds them together."

Keena sat on the trunk at the end of the bed. "You said there were other reasons you didn't tell me the truth about the fire."

"I had just returned with Rose. Her injuries had to be treated."

Keena stared at her hands where her fingers fidgeted. "She's been well for over a week. Was there any other reason?"

"I was afraid," he said with a defeated sigh.

"Afraid?"

"Next to God, you are my world now. I need you and love you as much as my own breath. But I didn't know how you'd react to learning who I am. I've hidden from humans for so long—I didn't know what to expect." He offered her a wry smile. "I'm still not sure. What are you thinking?"

Chapter 19

What *was* she thinking? Jy—or Jydryn—asked an excellent question. Why did it also bother her that he hadn't even shared his real name with her? It was like during their time together so far, nothing had been the complete truth. How could they move past that?

Keena stood again and moved back to stare at the leaping flames of the fire. "A little like those flames, I suppose." She considered them for a silent moment. "One flame leaps up like the brightening of understanding a world where men become dragons. Another turns once living wood to ash as I consider I'm fated to be with someone—whether I choose to or not. Others warm me with your profession of lifelong love. Little ones spring up with the hope of a family and belonging. And still others get snuffed out as the wood shifts, like my fear and doubt, at something so unfathomable and all the truths that were hidden from me."

His chair creaked.

He stood behind her. "All relationships have their challenges, whether they be parents, children, friends, or lovers. Anything worth pursuing has to be fought for, worked out, and misunderstandings overcome."

"I never knew my parents or had any friends. And, well, the other —" heat filled her cheeks again—"always seemed like an impossible dream." Thoughts and emotions whirled in her like a great storm that ripped up trees and tossed them miles away. She wasn't sure she wanted the answer to the next question. "What happens now?"

"Don't leave." His hand rested on her back with his plea.

Even through the heavy linen weave of her dress, his warmth and strength eased the storm within her. Part of her wanted to turn and throw her arms around his neck. Another part wanted to snatch Rose and run from the cave. She pressed her fingers to her temple and rubbed circles.

"Please, give me a chance to prove my love to you. Let me make right what I have broken between us. Ple—" He growled. "Zyrsog."

He thrust Rose into her arms as he turned toward the entrance. "Stay here."

Keena raced after him. "What did you say? What's going on?"

He gripped her shoulders. The color of his skin shifted as he pushed her back into the inner chamber. "Stay inside. Knights are climbing the mountain to kill the dragon."

Keena pushed back, clinging to his shirtsleeve with her free hand to keep him close. "How do you know that?"

"Keena please. I have to lead them away from you. And Rose." He mentioned the babe in her arms almost as an afterthought. "I have to keep you safe."

Panic in his voice sped her already pounding heart. She was going to be sick. She spoke each word slow and distinct. "Why do you believe they are coming to kill you?"

"Dragons have hearing far more sensitive than humans. Their crunching steps approach with the sound of the rocks they dislodge tumbling farther down the mountain. Their mail and weapons clank."

"But you know they come for *you*—the dragon?"

"That is the only reason armed men climb to a high cave. That, and they said, 'We go silent from here. We can talk again when the dragon is dead.'"

Keena tightened her grip on his arm. Every other thought fled her aching head except the image of the dragon pierced with spears, fallen in a crumpled heap on the mountainside as his blood soaked the jagged rocks. "Don't go." The words choked her.

Jydryn took a slow, deep breath. "When I first brought you here, before I understood you were my mate, I removed the boulders that blocked the trail to the cave mouth. I wanted you to have the option to leave if you wished. There is nothing to stop the knights from reaching this cave and finding you and Rose. You have to be safe."

So did he. Everything in her said she couldn't lose him.

Her gaze shifted to the three giant boulders at the side of the cave. "Can you move the smallest one to cover the opening to the inner chamber?"

His brow rose.

"Hide the opening but allow a person to still slip inside behind it?"

"Aye. Then will you hide?"

She shook her head. "No. You will."

"Keena." His tone deepened as he growled.

"You want me to trust you. Prove that I can by doing what I ask. They aren't coming to kill a skinny woman and a baby. They want you. Man or dragon, *you* will be a threat."

His voice was quiet. "You know what some men do with unprotected women?"

"I'm not unprotected." She released him and took a step back. "Will you trust me?"

"Always." He stripped again, shifted, moved the stone, and shifted back. "Why don't we all hide?" His arm encircled her to guide her inside.

She put her hand on his bare chest, sparking the Fire between them as she pushed him away. "Go," she whispered. "Even I can hear them now." She glanced at the hidden opening. "Put out all the lights. Hurry."

When Jydryn was out of sight, she noted their footprints all over the entrance; her small woman's prints, large male boots, bare feet—and dragon. Keena crouched and pressed her fingers against the dusty stone. It welcomed her as much as Jydryn's touch. The prints faded, leaving a smooth, untouched surface. She'd always been able to hide her trail in dirt roads, gravel lanes, and dusty barns. It had left her undetected hundreds of times.

Keena walked to the path and glimpsed the gleam of sunlight off helmets not far below. Wandering in hurried steps all over the entrance, she made new prints everywhere but near the now dark, hidden opening. She freed the end of the goat's lead from a rock and walked her around too.

As the sound of the approaching men grew, Keena returned the goat and crouched in a dark corner near it. The stench of the animal's waste burned her nose and made her eyes water. That could help her.

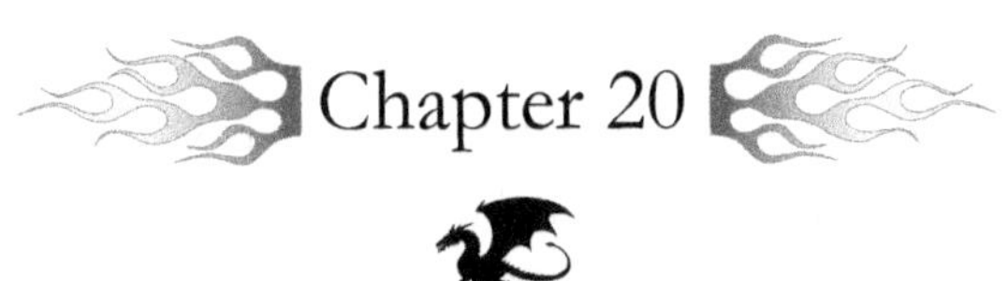

Chapter 20

Jydryn pressed his forehead to the stone hiding the opening to the inner chamber as he leaned against it and fought to keep his dragon contained. Keena and Rose were on the other side while men with murder in their hearts approached. She'd forced him in here with her challenge to prove that he could be trusted. This wasn't how it was supposed to be. He did the protecting. He was the dragon. She was a small, fragile human with a baby.

"There's nothing here, sir."

The goat bleated.

Rose whimpered.

"Who's there?" a deeper voice demanded. "Light the torches."

"It's a goat, sir," a third voice said, "and a woman."

"Woman?" the leader's deep voice said. "My lady, what are you doing here?"

"Please, don't hurt us." Keena's moaning voice covered some of Rose's growing cry. "Please." Their sobs provoked Jydryn's dragon all the more. His fingertips bled as he gripped the rock and fought shifting.

"We are honorable knights of the Keyaral Kingdom. We would never hurt a lady and her child."

"I'm only a simple peasant, sir."

"It doesn't matter," one of the other knights said. "We protect all people in the kingdom."

"Aye, we only came to kill the dragon."

Keena's scoffed chuckle came before her words. "Do you see a dragon? Who said you'd find a dragon here?"

"One of the villages at the foot of the ridge hired us. A dragon killed some of their citizens a fortnight ago, and they believed he came here," the leader said.

Jydryn cringed. Now she knew he was a killer. She already struggled with him being a shifter. What would this do to the fragile trust between them?

"If there was a dragon anywhere on this ridge, don't you think it would have eaten my daughter and me, and the goat, by now?"

Light rippled around the slim opening to the chamber where Jydryn had hid. Someone seemed to search the cave entrance as they carried a torch. "Captain, I don't see any proof of a dragon ever being in this cave. There are no bones from his kills, no waste, and the only prints are the woman's and the goat's."

Jydryn's head rose. How was that possible?

Rose's cries grew. It was time for her next bottle—which was in the chamber with Jydryn.

"Maybe there is another cave somewhere else on the ridge," the captain said.

"The people of Greenburn said—"

Keena screamed, and Jydryn's fingertips tore more as he gripped the rock to hold himself in place. "Don't kill my baby!"

The captain huffed. "Woman, what is the matter with you?"

Keena's heartfelt cries only grew. "Please, I beg you, good sirs, don't kill my baby."

"I already told you, we don't kill women and children."

"Greenburn does. They laid my baby on their altar of green fire to sacrifice her. I hid nearby, weeping in horror at the sight. But there was a disturbance, and I pulled her from the flames and came here to hide."

"Sir, do you think Greenburn is a village that still kills their own children?"

"It can't be," the other soldier said. "Our order of knights stopped the practice everywhere in Keyaral."

"You missed one." Keena's words filled with her tears. "See for yourself."

She must have shown the men Rose's scars.

"Fie. I'd have burned that village too, if I were a dragon," one of the knights said.

"Indeed. Well, I'll not hunt a dragon under those circumstances. Greenburn can burn to the ground if this is what they do," the captain said and the two men agreed.

"Can we take you somewhere safe, miss?" one of them asked.

"No. No, I can't go back down there. They'll find her and kill her. I can't."

"We can take you to a town where you will be safe, I swear it," the captain coaxed.

"Just swear that you won't tell anyone that she lived. Please don't tell Greenburn where we are."

"I assure you; we'll not be returning that way. Now, why don't you come with us?" The captain seemed like a good man.

"No. I sent word to a distant relation before I climbed the mountain. They'll fetch me soon." Keena's tears added to Rose's pitiful wails.

"As you wish. Come men. We have a long journey home." The stomping steps of the men receded into the distance.

Jydryn waited for Keena to come to him. When she didn't, he inched out of the gap to go to her. Rose's cries had stopped. She even giggled from time to time.

Before he rounded the stone, he heard footsteps again—a single set. "Miss, I noticed you didn't have a blanket."

"Oh, I couldn't take yours, good Knight," Keena said.

The warrior's mail rustled, and his kind voice calmed Jydryn's dragon nature. "Please, if you won't come with us, I'd feel better knowing you had a way to keep you and the baby warm."

"Thank you." Jydryn heard the smile in Keena's voice.

"Aye, miss." His steps hurried away.

Soon, the soft swish of fabric approached, and Rose's whimpers grew.

 Chapter 21

The knights sent to kill the dragon had left at last, and Keena's heart slowed from its frantic pounding. The narrow passage between the boulder Jydryn had moved and the entrance was dark. It would have been impossible to find if she didn't know it was there. She slid sideways and her back brushed against the boulder as she used her hand to guide her along the wall in front so she didn't hurt Rose, who cried on her hip.

A large, rough hand captured hers and the black chamber lit with the Dragon Fire that covered them.

Rose giggled and batted at the flames on Keena's shoulder.

A slim grin raised one side of Jydryn's lips.

Keena smiled too. Rose couldn't capture them with her clumsy toddler skill, and they flickered away at any attempt.

"Don't do that ever again." Jydryn's ragged words came with his uneven breathing.

She tightened the grip on his hand and noted the moisture. "I'm confused by all the information you shared—shifters, fae, fated mates, your feelings … But when you told me they came to kill the dragon—kill you—I couldn't breathe. I couldn't shake the image of the dragon dead on the rocks and it terrified me."

Jydryn smiled. He pulled her forward until their foreheads touched. "That is the pull of a fated mate. The care of the other will always override every other thought of self-protection."

Peace and contentment flooded her spirit, as warmth filled and relaxed her body that was still tight from her panic. She drew in the first full breath. Her hand released his and slid across his hard muscled stomach and over his hot skin until her arm encircled him.

Jydryn pulled her close, and she melted against him. "Why are you wet?"

She chuckled. "Rose was hungry, but I couldn't retrieve the bottle, so I tried squirting some from the goat into her mouth."

Jydryn's firm frame rumbled with quiet laughter as one hand brushed up and down her back. "Let me get a bottle filled before she tires of chasing the flames."

She didn't want him to let her go. The thought about mates and being destined for someone still confounded her. One thing was certain; she'd never felt more at home, right, whole, or safer than she did in his arms.

As he drew from her, their Fire vanished, plunging them into darkness. Rose cried, and Jydryn snatched Keena hand again. "Let's get a few candles lit before I leave." His words filled with his smile.

It only took a moment to light a candle, and Keena used it to light the others while Jydryn filled the bottle for Rose. He'd bought her a much larger bottle the last time he'd gone to the market. He handed it to Keena as she sat on the bed, back against the stone wall at the head and legs stretched out down the length. Rose yanked the bottle into her mouth, as Jydryn knelt to rekindle the fire in the hearth.

He stood and watched them for a moment once he finished. Rose stopped drinking and grinned at him with the tip still in her mouth.

"I'm going to go find us a new place."

Keena fought the strangled breath and stumbling beat of her heart. "Please, don't."

He turned to look at the stone hiding the chamber entrance. "Greenburn will send others when these men don't return with confirmation of the dragon's death." He released a long breath and his shoulders sagged forward. "They want justice for their dead citizens."

Keena glanced down at the sweet babe in her arms and brushed her curls. Memories of Rose's cries and the horrible burns soured her stomach. Her words were bitter. "As they received the punishment for their own cruel evil, there is no more justice to be gained."

He inched toward the bed, his voice almost a moan. "Keena, you don't understand. I kill—"

Her gaze rose to hold his unwavering. "The dragon defended Rose from the threat against her life. That was right and just. Even the stories of your God spoke of innocent blood crying out to Him. He can't be angry with you for righting a wrong and stopping it from happening again in the future."

He straightened and paced at the end of the bed. His long hair brushed his shoulders as he shook his head. "Perhaps if I had done it to save Rose, but I already held her safe in my claws when I turned and raked them with my flame. In that moment, pure rage poured out on them. It had nothing to do with Rose."

"No, it had everything to do with her, and all the others who would come after her." She swung her feet off the bed. "Jydryn, didn't you teach me the stories of how God's chosen people came to the kingdom He was giving them but there were people already living there? Those people also sacrificed their children to other gods and your God hated it so much that He had His people kill everyone. Not just the priests demanding the offering, but every man, woman, and child—sometimes even the animals. If He asked that of them, wouldn't He praise what you did?"

Jydryn stilled. "I don't think praise is the right word, for the Father wants none to perish. It is why He sent the Son to pay for our sins."

"Then, your sin—if that is indeed what it was—is paid for. Either way, I don't think He is mad at you." She rested back again.

Jydryn turned to her with a small smile. "My God does not get mad at His people like the other say the false gods do. He loves His children. He offers comfort when we come to Him."

"Then do that."

He walked toward her and brushed her cheek with his large hand. The instant sensation of peace and comfort overwhelmed her. She closed her eyes and leaned into his touch. "I have been seeking Him, but I hadn't heard His answer until you spoke it."

She startled and looked up. "You think your God talked through me?"

"I know it. His peace returned with your words."

Keena didn't feel as if any god had taken over her body to use it to speak with Jydryn but the man seemed assured and happier. "Well, since you don't believe your God is mad at you, will you stay, Jydryn?"

He brushed his hand over her head and down her cheek like he did with Rose. The action sent a hum over her skin. "Will you say it again?"

She scrunched her brows and tipped her head. "What you think God told you?"

"No." He chuckled and brought his face closer to hers. His thumb slid across her lower lip and made her tremble in the oddest way. His voice was low and husky when he spoke again. "My full name. Will you say it again?"

"Jydryn." His name whispered from her lips like a spell. One that healed her brokenness.

His hand cradled her cheek as he pressed his forehead to hers again and closed his eyes. "I did not know it was possible to love another person so much." He lifted his head and pressed is lips to her brow.

Heat filled her body, and she gasped.

He stared at her.

She closed her eyes as she tried to find words to explain. "There are so many sensations and emotions I don't understand."

Again, he gave a quick chuckle. "The bond strengthens between us. I feel it too. It's a bit overwhelming."

She arched a brow as she considered him again with a smirk. "A bit?"

He released her and turned back toward the cave entrance. "All the more reason I'm driven to find us another place."

"Jydryn, please." He stopped and glanced over his shoulder. "Not this moment. What if the knights are still on the mountainside? They could see you, or someone from Greenburn, or some other dragon hunter." She choked on a lump in her throat as she put the bottle aside and moved Rose to her shoulder. Rose wiggled and fussed when Keena squeezed the child. "I'm scared," she whispered.

"I know. I am too." He looked to the stone blocking the entrance again. "For now, I'll only move the boulders back to the path so no one else can find their way to the entrance. I won't leave until long after dark."

"After you hide the path, will you come back here?"

His smile grew. "Of course."

 Chapter 22

Jydryn stretched his wings and banked back over their cave toward the east. There was an icy mountain lake not far away, and he needed a cool dip.

After he had returned the boulders to the path, he had come back into the smaller chamber as Keena had asked. Even as confused and unsure as she was, she wanted him near. At least she wasn't talking about leaving.

But she had beckoned him closer until he sat beside her on the bed. When Rose fell asleep in her arms, Keena had leaned against him. She had no idea the desire she sparked in him. While she fought to accept the knowledge of them being mates only hours after hearing the information, Jydryn had known since the day Rose joined them. His desire to bond with her ran deep.

When Keena fell asleep, he'd tried to leave, but she'd grasped for him each time he moved. It was the middle of the night before he extracted himself from her hold.

The light of the moon glinted off the unmoving surface of the lake as Jydryn drove. The icy depth welcomed him and quenched much of his desire. He knew now that he'd found his mate. The longing would never go out again, but at least it was manageable.

Jydryn slogged from the water as it streamed off his scales and soaked the shore. Able to think once again, he returned his focus to finding some place safe for his family to live.

He launched into the air. The cities at the western foot of the ridge were out of the question. He would never allow Keena to re-enter Cragholde, or Rose Greenburn, and Beardrift was the worst of the three. Ironfair and Easthelm were better, but still too close to where they were now.

He made a long loop over the ridge as he considered his options. Eagle's Nest to the south had to be one of the nicest towns. The people were kind there. They even had a small chapel known for its instruction of the one true God.

Jydryn had never lived among humans. He'd visited many towns to purchase what he needed, but he'd never stayed the night. It would be best for Keena, and even Rose, to live among others. Keena needed friends and Rose needed other children to play with as she grew—beside the siblings Keena would no doubt birth.

He, on the other hand, would have to find a job. As Keena had pointed out, it was odd for a man not to work to earn a living. Yes, his grandfather had left him his horde, and he'd added to it over the years. People offered the dragon more than just their women.

There was the issue of his dragon, of course. If he lived among the humans, enjoying his dragon scales would be rare. He loved to fly. Loved this side of his nature. His absence would leave those he watched over and rescued at the foot of the ridge with no one to intercede for them. Children would die. He held out some hope the knights would spread the word about Greenburn and stop their sacrificing ways for good. But there was no guarantee they would before the next sacrifice.

Jydryn turned and headed north. He'd never ventured far in this direction because of the undesirable cold. But spring was in full bloom and many said the summers were pleasant. Perhaps he could find a workable cave near a friendly village. There he could have a house for Keena and Rose, and escape to the cave to free his dragon from time to time.

The sun warmed his scales as he swept east to west and back again, working his way farther north. The villages became less frequent and only low, cave-less hills broke up the pine and fir forests.

He turned back south, still searching. The Tetling Ridge peeked up on the edge of the horizon when the *twang* of an enormous weapon releasing its projectile grabbed his attention. Two more followed. Something shot into the air past his left wing, but it wasn't an arrow or ballista bolt. As the other two rose above him on the right side, they burst open, each releasing a heavy wire mesh weighted at the edges.

Before he could avoid them, the traps covered him. The weight and awkwardness snagged at his wings and prevented him from drawing them up to push himself away from the ground. The sting of magic seeped under his scales, paralyzing him.

Jydryn plummeted to the earth. He smashed through trees and landed with a crash, breaking a wing and a rear leg. He roared in pain. Several men in heavy armor, hidden behind tall shields, approached him. Unable to fuel his fire with the air knocked out of him and possible broken ribs, they advanced unharmed.

The men's shields parted to reveal a child's cart holding bellows three-times the size of any he'd ever seen. It puffed out a cloud of blue dust. His vision narrowed and darkened as the men retreated toward the trees. His world spun and tilted as the darkness grew.

# Chapter 23

Keena jerked awake. Her back and chest ached and her leg throbbed. Rose babbled beside her as she put her toes in her mouth. The fire was out. Where was Jydryn?

Keena lit candles, prepared a bottle for Rose, and rekindled the fire. There was no sign of Jydryn anywhere. He'd wanted to find them a new place to live. Somewhere safe from the dragon hunters. He said he wouldn't go until after dark.

Keena stood at the edge of the entrance. The sun neared midday. He should have been back by now.

She rubbed at the back of her neck and turned her head. She clawed at her collar, yanking it away from her neck as she fought for breath. The peace she'd experienced since Jydryn had confessed everything was nowhere to be found now. Her breaths came shallow and quick.

Rose whimpered and Keena turned to the inner chamber as she rubbed her wrists. Pain cut into them. She held them up to the light but saw nothing wrong.

She changed Rose's nappy and tried to distract herself by playing with the baby. Rose shook the rattle Jydryn had bought for her and whacked Keena in the head with it. Dizziness tickled her thoughts.

What was wrong with her?

She took the rattle from Rose, which made her fuss. "Here, play with this while we wait for Jydryn to return." She handed Rose a bit of sheepskin fashioned into an animal shape.

Rose gripped it in her stubby fingers and shoved it into her mouth. She drooled and chewed on everything. Jydryn said her teeth were growing. He'd brought her a mala fruit. The dark purple, tube-shaped fruit was about the size of a carrot, but not as long. The skin on the outside was soft but difficult to break, so it was a good thing for a baby to chew on to help with the pain of the emerging teeth.

Keena handed Rose the mala and then walked back to the entrance with the baby on her hip. The rays of the sun struck her face, and she shielded her eyes. "The sun will be down soon. I hope Jydryn found someplace to stay hidden all day." She bounced Rose. "He'll return once it grows dark."

Rose giggled and cooed as drool ran over the mala root and soaked the front of her dress.

Keena wished she was as content, but the aches and pains riddling her body told her something was wrong.

Keena didn't sleep well. Her tossing and turning woke Rose several times. The night had passed without Jydryn returning. She paced and nipped at her fingertips. It was a bad habit that left her fingers torn and bloody.

Though Rose had been awake much of the night too, she didn't want to nap. Even a bottle didn't interest her. She pushed the gruel away and fisted her little hands over her mouth.

Keena left Rose alone on the bed. Her fear was affecting the child. For a second day, the sun shone from overhead with no sign of Jydryn. She needed to find him. But how would it be possible? He could fly. In this much time, he could have covered the entire length and breathe of the kingdom. She didn't even know where to begin.

What would Jydryn do if she or Rose were missing? She shook her head, annoyed with herself. He'd fly over the entire land and find them. That wasn't an option for her.

Keena threw back her head, ready to scream—or cry. But she had never done either—not until she'd met Jydryn, anyway. To show such deep emotions when being tormented by another gave them power and made them increase their harassment and prolong the abuse. Better to stay quiet and act as though nothing hurt.

But losing Jydryn was a pain she had never imagined.

She turned from the view across the ridge toward the inner chamber.

"Ask and it shall be given. Seek and you will find." The words echoed around her.

Keena whirled, looking for Jydryn. No one was there. She remembered him saying those words in one of his many lessons about his God. But this voice hadn't been Jydryn's.

She stared at the billowing clouds again. "All right, Jydryn's God, I seek Your help to find him. How can You help me?"

Tongues of Dragon Fire formed on her left arm. They slid toward her hand, congealed in her palm, and vanished. A moment later, a single stream of the Dragon Fire flowed out of the tip of her first finger. It hung in the air about the length of her finger and then turned right for the same distance.

Keena stared at the cord of Fire that started out blue but ended up green, pink, yellow or orange by the end. "Jydryn is that way?"

To test her theory, she turned. No matter which way she faced, the fire always pointed to the right of the cave entrance.

She closed her fist, and the flame went out. Racing into the inner chamber, she started grabbing things she thought she'd need for a journey. At first, she stuffed them in the bag Jydryn used to bring back his purchases from the market, but she ran out of room. She dumped the contents on the table and started again. She chose with more care, folded when needed, or wrapped things to take up as little room as possible.

The bag had a long handle; she realized now so the dragon could carry it in a claw with ease. But with it on her shoulder, following the Dragon Fire seeping from her fingertip, and leading the goat, she couldn't also carry Rose. She'd have no free hands.

Keena looked around for something that might help and spotted the blanket the knight had given her. It was much narrower and thinner than the one she'd packed from the bed. She'd seen women carry their babies strapped to them with a long strip of cloth.

She folded the blanket in half down its length and tried to wind it around her body. It took several attempts before she figured the best way to secure Rose in a proper sling.

Rose woke as Keena worked her inside the cloth against her chest. She cried at being so confined. "Sorry, Rose. I know you don't like it, but we have to find Jydryn, and this is the only way I can carry you."

The baby continued to fuss as Keena slid the bag on her shoulder. She glanced around for anything else she should take. Nothing seemed important. Jydryn could fly back and retrieve it if he wanted anything here.

She moved toward the goat and took it's lead. The animal didn't want to come, but Keena tugged against her stubbornness. The animal bleated and dug in her hooves. "Goat, you *are* coming with us."

Keena stopped and stared at the blocked path. It was going to be hard to get around the boulders.

She froze. This was an absurd idea. She didn't know where she was going. Rose continued to fuss and fight the swaddling sling. The goat continued to pull against her. She was one small, weak woman. What could she do?

None of it mattered. Nothing mattered without Jydryn. She had to find him. "Jydryn's God, I'm going to do something I vowed never to do. I'm going to trust a god. If You see me safe to Jydryn's side, and I find him alive, then we'll talk again." She took a deep breath and let it ease out. "Maybe at the end of this, You will be my God too."

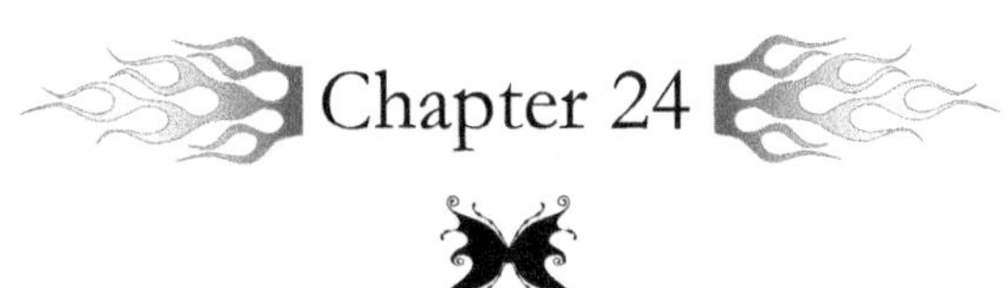# Chapter 24

Keena startled from sleep as Rose fussed. Light flooded the eastern horizon with bright orange and pink, but the sun hadn't appeared yet. She sat up and rubbed her back with a moan.

Rose fisted her hands above her head. Then, she swung down and hit her sides as her legs kicked out. Her cries grew.

"I agree, Rose. How is it I grew accustomed to sleeping in Jydryn's cushioned bed so fast?" She turned to milk the goat and her heart jolted. The doe wasn't where Keena had secured her last night when darkness made descent down the ridge too dangerous. She spotted the animal not far away, stretching to the limits of her lead to nip at a lone clump of grass.

She fetched her and brought her back closer to Rose. Keena alternated between milking the goat and rubbing Rose's stomach.

Rose's cries grew more insistent until the crisp air filled with them.

How close were they to Greenburn? It was one of the three villages she'd spotted at the bottom of the ridge yesterday. Cragholde was another. The third was a town she'd always avoided. Her heart rate increased until it pounded.

"Shh, Rose, before someone finds us." Keena changed her nappy and finished milking the goat. She took a long drink of the warm, thick liquid before refilling the bottle.

"Come, my precious girl. Let's get you back in the sling." Keena tucked her in with the bottle and reaffirmed her direction with the

Dragon Fire. The rocky path looked treacherous, and she glanced toward the heavens. "Remember our deal, Jydryn's God. I can't follow You if I'm dead."

Her feet never slipped once.

Sweat soaked her dress and grew uncomfortable as it clung to her. The sun shone down from right over her head as Keena stepped off the ridge onto the flat plain. "We'll be under the shade of those trees in no time, my sweet."

She stretched out her left hand, and the Fire pointed to a narrow path almost invisible in the thickening forest. Why did her stomach knot and her hand tremble? Under the canopy of thick shade, she sat on a rock and fought to collect herself.

Since meeting Jydryn, her thoughts and emotions were as wild as boars. They raged inside her, tearing away all the ways she'd learned to cope with the cruel world.

After a quick glance at the limp child against her chest, Keena moved again, though she didn't make it far. She jerked her skirt free from where it had snagged on a branch. Pain stung her hand as she tripped over roots. She couldn't see around Rose, but found her balance with the help of a rough tree.

A buzz filled Keena's palm, soothing her scratched skin as she tried to slow her erratic breathing. The mere thought of her dragon shifter renewed the ache in her heart and made tears blur her vision. Would the fire lead her to him? Why hadn't he returned? She panted for breath, but the questions hammering her thoughts wouldn't quiet. "The only way to find the answers is to keep going, right, Rose?"

Within an hour, the gurgle of a cool stream greeted her. Keena raced to it. The bank was low and the water easy to reach. The goat walked right in. Keena filled the bottle and drank the contents dry twice before dumping three more over her and Rose.

The baby sputtered and blinked her eyes the first time. Rose smiled the second time. The third time, she giggled and reached out her hands to capture the stream.

Keena added more water and secured the tip before handing it to Rose. When she took her first drink, Rose stopped and pushed it out of her mouth, letting the water escape. She pushed the bottle beyond the confines of the sling and let go.

"You're going to want that later." Keena retrieved it from the ground before she re-filled her waterskin and checked for direction. "What will happen to us if I can't find him, Rose? I struggle to care for myself." She fought for a full breath as her heart threatened to beat from her chest. Never had she experienced such emotions before.

"Get yourself under control, woman. You have the means to care for Rose today. With God's favor, we'll find Jydryn tomorrow and he will know what to do next," she mumbled to herself.

Rose put her thumb in her mouth in response.

Perhaps Jydryn had changed his mind and didn't want to be found—especially by her.

Keena stopped again and leaned against a tree. A subtle calm filled her. Find him—then worry if necessary.

She pushed from the trees and started walking again. With the creek close enough to hear, she picked her way through the woods. "You would think there would be a wider path or a road that would allow us to move faster. I have this terrible feeling Jydryn needs us to hurry."

Rose didn't make a sound.

Keena lurched forward and fell to her hands and knees in the growing dimness. Rose didn't seem to notice the jostling in her tight swaddling. "It's too early to stop." She sat back on her heels and swiped at an errant tear with the back of her hand. "I need him." She shook her head as the tears fell too fast to rid herself of them. "I want him in my life. Please."

The long shadows made trudging through the thick forest dangerous. Next time she fell, she might not catch herself and injure Rose.

She pulled the baby from the sling and laid her on the large blanket.

Rose kicked her legs and threw up her arms, joyous in her freedom. She flipped to her stomach and continued her ecstatic movements as she rocked on her belly.

Keena milked the goat, now tethered to a nearby sapling. At last, Keena sat and drew a corked jar from the bag. The little bit of cold stew she'd placed inside didn't fill her aching stomach. She laid down beside Rose, who wasn't interested in sleeping yet, but Keena couldn't escape it. She yawned. "Where do you think he is, little one? Do you think he is all right?" Her eyes hooded as the baby giggled.

Two sets of footsteps crunched through the woods toward Jydryn. He'd smelled them coming before he heard them. For two days, he'd laid staked to the ground with heavy chains connected to bands around his neck and both front legs. They'd also wrapped his tail in a chain and anchored so he couldn't swing it.

They'd infused the chains and bands with magic that prevented him from breaking them or shifting to get free. He couldn't have shifted until his injuries healed, anyway. All the broken bones would have left him defenseless and maybe even dead in his human form.

"Now, son, I don't want you to be frightened. It can't hurt you. We have it secured." A man and a half-grown boy stepped out of the tree line on his right.

"Fie, it's a dragon!" The boy was plump, with short arms and legs. He wore torn and stained rough clothes like his father. The grease filling his dark hair made it appear even darker. Deep brown eyes stared at

Jydryn from a round and reddened face.

"It is." The father stood with his hands on his hips and chest puffed out. His black unkept beard hung to his collarbone, and his hair brushed the top of his shoulders.

The boys words were breathy. "How did you catch it?"

The father's hands moved to draw images in the air. "Well, the man who hired us has metal nets we shot out of a special ballista."

Glancing up at his father, the boy asked, "Why doesn't it break free or try to burn us up?"

"They say they filled the bands holding it with magic," the father said with a flourish.

The boy chuckled. "Really, Dad?"

The man shrugged. "It hasn't gotten away or burned anyone."

Their gaze turned back to Jydryn. "What do you do with a dragon?"

"Many things. People sell the organs to healers for medicine, claws and teeth to dragon hunters to claim rewards for killing a dragon. The leather of the wings is strong and flexible. Some favor the spikes to make weapons, and many can sell the scales as souvenirs."

"Is that why you caught it?" The boy's gaze held Jydryn's.

Dad's head shook. "No, the man who hired us needs to catch a live dragon for someone in the neighboring kingdom of Farfell."

The boy's eyes widened. "Why would anyone want a live dragon?"

"For power, son." The father placed his hand on his boy's shoulder. "He plans to starve the dragon and only feed it his enemies. Dragons refuse human flesh, you see."

The boy moved a little closer and stared into Jydryn's eye. "Dad, does it look sad to you?"

The man chuckled. "Now, Oscar, don't go soft on me, lad. It is a dumb creature. It has no more feeling than the rabbits you trap or the cows we raise."

The boy pointed. "But, Dad, it looks like it's crying."

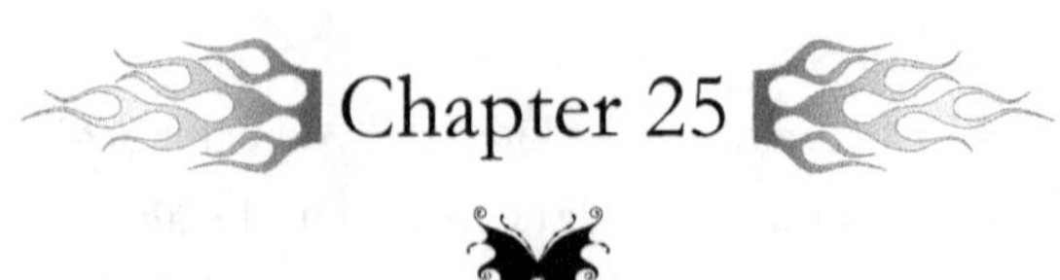

Chapter 25

Keena braced herself against a tree as tears overwhelmed her.
When the anguish in her spirit grew too heavy, she slid to her knees and
sobbed. Something was terribly wrong. But whether it was wrong with
her, or with Jydryn, or it sprouted from being alone and caring for Rose,
Keena couldn't decide. Maybe it was all of it.

She pushed to her feet and stepped from the trees onto a hard
packed road that stretched out across her path. She looked to the left and
right but saw no one. On the other side was a wide, well-used trail
bending toward the left, and a narrow, almost non-existent, path leading
to the right.

She scraped her sleeve across her face to dry it and raised her left
hand. The Dragon Fire pointed to the smallest trail. "Of course, *that* is
the way I have to go."

Between her rolling emotions, a cranky baby, and an ornery goat,
Keena didn't have the strength to fight through the woods anymore. She
remained on the road and headed right, facing the sun as it neared
midday.

The Dragon Fire vanished.

Her hands fisted at her sides. "I have to do it Your way or You won't
help?"

There was no answer, and the flaming pointer didn't return.

"Agh!" she screamed, which set Rose to crying.

Keena turned back to the two paths on the far side of the road and the Dragon Fire returned. But when she stepped onto the wider path, it went out. "Now, You are just being mean!" She stomped her foot. The emptiness carving a hole in her heart compelled her to take the harder path.

She marched to the other trail and started working her way through the dense undergrowth.

Keena hadn't gone far when hooves thundered down the road she could no longer see. She crouched behind a large bush, wrapped her arms around Rose, and allowed the goat the freedom of the full lead to munch on whatever she wanted.

Male laughter added to the sound of the horses coming through the forest. As they passed, the cries of a woman snaked through the trees too.

Keena shuddered at the cruel laughter fading into the distance.

It took her a while before she stopped shaking enough to continue. Had she stayed on the wide easy road like she'd wanted … "Thank You. I'll listen better the next time."

Keena dropped to her back without eating. Every part of her ached, from her blistered feet and cramped legs to her sunburned scalp to where her hair had snarled again and again in branches and pulled out.

Rose flipped to her belly and started scooting off the blanket.

Keena removed the sling and tied one end around her wrist and the other around Rose's waist. When Keena fell asleep, the tether would assured Rose wouldn't travel far.

"Ouch," Keena growled as her left arm stretched above her head and continued to pull. "What?" she muttered. She pried one eye open first and then the other. The Dragon Fire glowed fat and bright and had pulled her halfway off the blanket.

Her heart thundered as she forced her stiff body to comply. Keena had the sling wound around her again and Rose tucked inside in moments. She folded the blanket and stuffed it in the bag. The goat wouldn't get up. She pulled on it and the Dragon Fire pulled on her.

The animal was Rose's only source of food. She couldn't leave it. But Keena had no other choice.

Though her hands trembled, she filled Rose's bottle and the empty stew pot with milk. Rose had gone back to sleep, so Keena tucked both containers in the bag and removed the lead from the goat. "Don't get eaten."

She picked up her hem and lumbered forward as fast as she could. The flame pouring out of her finger lit her path and urged her on. "Please, he has to be all right. I have to make it in time."

According to the conversation between the guards Jydryn had overheard, the man who wanted to make him into a weapon of terror would arrive today. Not that he would ever live long enough to be forced to eat anyone. Jydryn had no fight left in him. The separation from Keena had already sealed his doom. He'd awakened the bonding connection with his mate, but without its completion, he would die. Keena would too. And without them, Rose would soon starve to death.

How had he gone from being on the precipice of having everything he'd never allowed himself to dream of to the death of all he loved? *It's not fair, Lord.*

Jydryn closed his eyes and released a long breath. The sun baked his scales, but it didn't matter. Nothing mattered now.

The breeze tickled his nose with wild flowers and rich earth. Keena's scent. He sighed with gratitude that his last thoughts would be of her. A soiled nappy and sour milk greeted him next. Then, he smelled blood.

The wildflowers and milk seemed to circle him. He filled his mind with images of Keena lying beside Rose as the two laughed. For a few days before his capture, he'd known the love of a family. He wanted more.

Snap!

"Who are—?"

Thump!

Crash!

The aroma of blood filled his nostrils again. Stronger this time.

Jydryn opened his eyes halfway and watched a figure in a dirty dress stumble out of the woods toward him. Sunlight caught in her messy hair, revealing the red with splashes of green and pink.

A crossed band of cloth surrounded her chest and a baby's head poked out of the top under the woman's chin.

A vision of his mate and the baby they loved as their own would carry him to his Lord.

Keena.

"Oh, Jydryn. What have they done to you?" Her hands brushed his snout and his senses flared to life like the Dragon Fire covering her and his scales.

No, you have to leave.

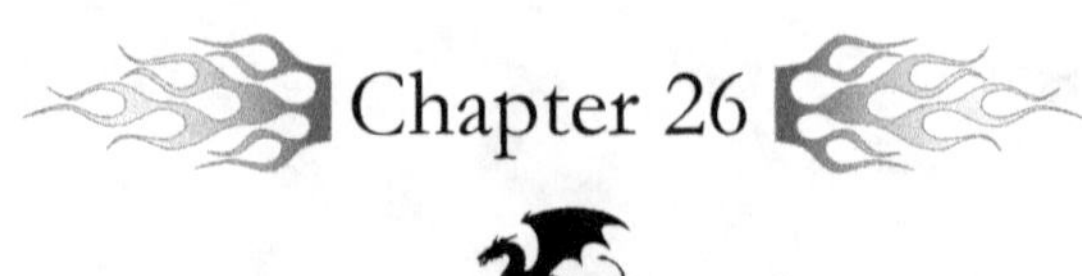

Chapter 26

Jydryn jerked his head up as far as the chain would allow. *No, you can't be here. Run!*

Keena staggered backward and gripped her head as her eyes squeezed closed.

Had she heard him? She shouldn't be able to perceive his thoughts at all—not until the binding was complete. How had she found him?

"Yes, I heard you. Stop yelling." She reached out her left hand and a ribbon of Dragon Fire leapt from the tip of her first finger, wound through the air, and touched the end of his nose.

She moved to his side. "Why can't you break free?"

Magic, he tried to make his thoughts whisper.

She moved to the lock that secured the band around his neck The chains ran to the post on either side of him.

No, Keena. Run! The guards …

"Not without you. I knocked out the too that I found."

That must have been the blood he'd smelled.

Keena pulled Rose from the wrap around her chest and placed the child on the ground in front of him. "Watch her." She pulled something shiny from his bag. She flung the strap toward his back and it caught on one of his spines.

Keena, stop.

She marched to the end of his snout, dug the fingertips of her left hand into his tender nostril, and waved a knife with her right. "I haven't walked for four days through dense forest with a fussy baby and a maddening goat, for you to tell me to go away." Her anger fled as she wiped her many tears away. "Please, don't make me leave without you."

I am held by magic chains, and men come to claim me today. I couldn't bear it if you died.

Her fists perched on her hips. "But I'm supposed to let you die?" She kicked him in the chin and stomped back to the lock and knelt. "If you can't, I can't. One way or the other we are *all* going together. Either away from here or to the afterlife." Metal grated against metal. "I can't open it."

It's no use, my love. Please go.

She rose and stomped her foot. "You may not call me your love and send me away at the same time. God got me here. He'll help me get you free too." She muttered her next words. "We have a deal, and He hasn't finished His end yet."

She pulled a wide metal bead from one of her small braids. "I need you to warm this." She put it on a stick near his mouth.

I can't breathe fire in these chains.

"Good. I don't want it melted, only soft. Can you generate some heat?"

Aye. He pinched it between his teeth and closed his lips. As he worked to heat the metal, she found a smooth rock that fit in her hand.

The bead just flattened.

"Good," She reached for the stick and pulled the softened metal from his mouth. She dropped it on a boulder sticking out of the ground and pounded it with the rock in her hand.

Rose gurgled, and he turned to see her reaching for him. Did she recognize him as the man she knew?

When Keena shaped the bead to a long point, she returned to the lock. Using it in conjunction with the knife, she wiggled them until the lock popped open. She tossed it aside as she pulled the band open and freed his neck.

Jydryn stretched and tossed his head.

"Stop wiggling around." Keena had moved to his left leg to work on the next lock.

How do you know how to do that?

"I have lived on the streets all my life. I've needed to get food and find a warm place to sleep that weren't always open to me." She freed his leg and ran to his other side.

As she tossed the band around his right leg aside, Jydryn caught the voices of men approaching. They came with the scent of horses and the rumble of a wagon.

It's too late. They're here. Go now.

"Stop yelling at me. There is only one chain left." She ran the length of his tail. "What's that word you're always saying? Zygross something?" She huffed. "There's no lock."

Then it's time for you to take Rose and go.

"You are maddening." She scanned the chain as she followed the length of his tail again.

And you are stubborn.

"Found it," she muttered as she slid the knife in a link. She raced back toward him while she unwound the cloth crisscrossing her body. "But you love me anyway."

He did. Oh, how he loved that she fought for him. Keena believed God had brought her here. She trusted in His divine leading and protection far more than Jydryn did at the moment.

As she looked around, she submerged the cloth in his water trough. "Can you pull up one stake?"

Aye. Keena, the men are close. Please.

"So help me, if you don't stop pushing me away I'm going to kick you again. Now, get me a stake, and grab Rose."

He tried not to smile, despite his fear, as he gripped the tall stake in his teeth and jerked it from the ground. It was about as long as Keena was tall.

Free of most of his bindings, he sat on his hunches as he watch her wind the wet cloth through a link of chain as thick as her wrist. What did she think she could do? Next, she wrapped the wet cloth around the stake and secured it. Then, she twisted the stake, making the fabric tighten. She continued to twist, even bracing her foot against his tail to force it around. The wet fabric and long lever of the stake created a force that allowed a small woman to bend the heavy metal of the chain.

But it took too long. The voices were so close now. Closer than his escape.

"Sir, the wagon can't proceed through these trees."

"Well, we can't bring that immense beast to it. Start cutting them down."

Leather creaked, and several men grumbled.

Jydryn wrapped his paw around Rose.

Keena grunted and pulled the fabric aside to look at the link. She had bent it open enough to unhook it from the next. She freed the fabric, unhooked the chain, and tossed it over his tail.

They are only feet inside the trees, Keena. Take Rose and hide.

"Lift your tail," she whispered.

Axes struck wood, and branches shuddered.

He wanted to refuse her, but he didn't dare slow her progress. It took her a moment, but she found the loose end of chain, pulled it free under him, and tossed it over the top of his tail. Loop by loop, she pulled it out from under him and tossed the growing length over as she unwound the binding. She worked down the length of his tail until she couldn't lift the heavy chain over him.

Voices again drew his attention from her progress. "You men finish up here. I want to show Duke Pritchard his prize."

A tree crashed to the ground, and Keena gasped.

Ten loops still wound around his tail and their magic hampered his escape.

Another tree fell.

Keena leapt over his tail and dragged the chain off him. She leapt back and pulled it free from under him. Back and forth she worked at a frantic pace. Covered in sweat and panting for each breath, she never slowed.

Horses approached.

Hurry.

"Where's the guard?"

"He's over here, sir. Someone has struck him in the head."

"My dragon." The voice sent a chill down Jydryn's spine. Hooves pounded toward him.

With only three loops remaining, Jydryn tried to shake free.

Two men burst from the trees. "He's escaping!"

"Men, to the weapons!" the other yelled and two more trees fell.

Jydryn reared back and coughed out bursts of weak fire.

The horses cried and threw their riders.

"Give me Rose and get us out of here." Keena climbed his rear leg and held up her hands.

He couldn't reach his paw to his back, so Jydryn took the tiny baby in his mouth and craned his neck over Keena. Rose dropped into Keena's hands as he spread his wings. He prayed he'd healed enough to get into the air.

Chapter 27

Soldiers burst from the woods with their bows raised and their swords drawn.

Duke Pritchard and the man he hired staggered to their feet as their horses disappeared into the forest. "Get the iron nets in the air!"

"Don't let him escape or it will be your necks."

Jydryn flapped his aching wings and rose off the ground. He only made it a few feet before he came to the end of the chain. One last loop had caught on two small spikes at the end of his tail.

Keena followed his gaze down his long body and rose to stand.

Be still and hang on.

Jydryn spit fire at his attackers and knocked a couple off their feet with a hard stroke of his wings. Then, he lowered enough to create slack in his tether. He whipped his tail. The spike linked to the chain loosened from the ground.

"Hurry, before he escapes," the duke shouted

An iron projectile launched into the air. Knowing what it was now, he snatched it in his teeth before it could open and form the large net. He rained the shattered and melted pieces down on the knights in front of him as the stake jerked from the ground.

He whipped his tail around in front of him and caught the duke and his man square in the chest, sending them flying into the trees behind them.

Free from his hold to the ground, Jydryn pumped his wings and rose. A few more shakes and the chain fell away at last. Free of the suppressing magic, he bellowed out a blast of fire.

Another net launched at him and he tipped to catch it in his claws. Terror sliced through him as he searched the sky for Keena and Rose. When he didn't see them hurtling to the earth, he glanced at his back and found them safe inside a bubble of Dragon Fire that secured them to his scales.

"Get us out of here, please," Keena called to him.

With a twist to avoid another net, he climbed out of reach of their weapons, pumped his wings, and sped away. He glanced back at his family again. Through the blue tint of the flames, he saw Keena laying on her side next to Rose. Her hand rested on the baby, keeping her from rolling over.

Rose's legs and arms moved in excited fits.

Is she all right?

Keena chuckled. "I think she enjoys flying as much as I do."

How can you tell? He tipped to the right and then the left. Rose's movements only sped up. He dipped and twisted and she squealed in delight.

"That would be a yes, Daddy. Your girls like to fly."

His girls. Daddy. The wind snatched tears from his eyes. He was free. He had his family. They were safe.

Jydryn spread his wings in a strong current and floated for a moment. *Thank You, Father. I doubted and accused You of failing. It was me who failed again. She trusted You. She believed where I couldn't.*

"I guess that is why we need each other."

He hadn't expected her to hear his prayer.

He glanced back at her. She also shouldn't have been able to control the Dragon Fire.

Keena opened her eyes the moment her dragon stilled as he landed.

Rose quieted and kicked out with a cry.

I think she's mad we stopped flying.

Keena yawned. "Either that, or she's hungry. I set the goat free early this morning. I gave Rose the last of the milk a couple hours before I found you." She scooped the baby into her arms, looped the bag over her shoulder, and climbed to the ground. She threw out the blanket and tossed the bag in front of him. "You'll find a shirt, pants, and your boots inside."

She turned her back to allow him to shift and dress as she knelt to change Rose. She couldn't finish before a firm hand grabbed her elbow.

Jydryn pulled her to her feet and spun her around. His large hands captured her face as his lips covered hers. Warm and hungry, his kiss deepened.

She closed her eyes and gave herself to the wonder of his affection.

His tongue probed and parted her lips and his hot cinder scent invaded her mouth.

She reached out to hold him, and he withdrew with a gasp. His entire middle was dark, with a hideous bruise above his pants. "Jydryn." Her voice and heart broke at the sight.

His hand slid under her hair, and he pressed his forehead to hers. "I'm all right. The worst of the injuries have already healed. I'm thankful the magic didn't suppress that too." He lifted his head and kissed her forehead. "Thank you and never do that again." He offered her a smirk.

She swung at his bruised body, but stopped before she made contact. "Don't get caught ever again, and I won't have to."

His lips found hers again in another deep kiss. When the kiss broke at last, he asked, "Do you know how much I love you?"

"I think I'm starting to understand."

Jydryn's gaze slid over her shoulder. "I told you it wouldn't be long before she was crawling."

Rose shimmied off the blanket and reached for a bright yellow flower.

He ran to her, scooped her up, and tossed her in the air above his head.

Rose squealed and kicked him as she landed against his chest. He whistled and winced in pain.

Keena reached for Rose. "Here, let me hold her."

"I'll see what I can find for us to eat." He kissed Rose's cheek and then Keena's as he turned toward the woods.

Keena moved back to the blanket, finished securing the nappy, and sat with Rose in her lap. She found the mala root in the bag and offered it to Rose to keep her busy.

Keena glanced at Jydryn's retreating back. It was as black as his front, and there was a slight limp to his gait. Her gaze moved around the small clearing where he'd landed. Nothing but thick forest surrounded them.

A glint caught her eye in the opposite direction from where Jydryn had gone. She gazed at it. Something was there, just inside the shadow of the trees. Her skin tickled. Not to disturb the contented baby, she left Rose and stood. As she ambled toward the spot, a tiny cabin came into view. One moment it had seemed mere vapor; the next, it stood solid with light reflected off the window no bigger than her hand.

She knocked, but no one answered. Keena pushed open the door to a room with a dusty bed, and table, one chair covered in cobwebs, and an empty fireplace. "Jydryn," she called over her shoulder, "there's a tiny house here."

"What?"

Was there panic in his voice?

"It's empty. Doesn't look like anyone has used it in years." She stepped all the way inside.

"Keena stop! Get out of there!"

The door slammed closed behind her. The walls blurred. Motion lurched her forward and jerked to a stop, causing her to stumble forward.

"Secure her."

Her vision still blurred and her stomach ready to heave. She could only feel her hands being grabbed and a stinging rope wrapped around them.

"Let go of me."

"Welcome home, princess."

Chapter 28

Jydryn turned at Keena's call, but he was too far away to stop her. He shouted as he raced across the field. He scooped Rose and his shirt up in one smooth motion, but he watched as Keena stepped inside the fae trap. The door closed, and the house vanished before he arrived.

He screamed his rage, and Rose cried. Jydryn cradled her against his chest as she kicked his bruises. "I'm sorry, Rose. Don't worry, I'll get her back. I'll bring Keena back for both of us."

He had to.

Jydryn paced as he bounced Rose, trying to calm her. She was hungry. How was he supposed to find her an alternate source of milk, watch her, and find a way into Shimmerbourne all at the same time? He wanted to roar again. The meddlesome, loathsome fae. If he never saw another fae again, it would be too soon.

He reached for some ripe gooseberries, put one in his mouth, and mashed it before he offered it to Rose. She spit it out and screamed even more. He kept trying, knowing the juicy fruit would do her some good even if it didn't fill her up.

As he searched the edge of the clearing, he bumped into Shimmerbourne's barrier. He could feel the magic and see a dim wall of light. That shouldn't have been possible. The warding that kept the fae kingdom hidden was oddly weak.

Keena was right to have searched for him, stayed, and fought to free him. Now, he needed to do the same. Problem was, he couldn't wield the Dragon Fire like she had. She shouldn't have been able to, either. Dragon

Fire only appeared at the touch of a fated mate. It appeared on its own until the joining rites were complete, then each partner could bring it forth to show they were bound after that. But no one had ever used it to track a lost partner or to create a shield like she had to keep her and Rose on his back.

He shook with rage at losing his mate after just being reunited. The anger brought his dragon to the surface. Rose squirmed in his arms. If he didn't get control, he'd burn her again.

The fae had hidden Shimmerbourne out of sync with this reality. There was no way in except by capture, escort of a fae—which never happened—or a fairy ring, and they were more rare than female dragon shifters.

He moved to the place where the trap had been.

Rose's pitiful wails grew desperate. He needed to find her milk before he chased after Keena. With a loud shriek, the frustrated child hurled herself so her back arched over Jydryn' arms. Her fisted hands reached over her head and disappeared through a magical barrier.

"Oh, you brilliant girl—just like your mommy." He pulled her close and kissed her head. Rose was an innocent who carried no malice. Like all children, they could often see the fae and some even found their way into Shimmerbourne by accident.

Jydryn pulled on his shirt and groaned with each movement.

Dressed to hide his injuries and weakened condition, he took Rose's wrist and pushed her hand through the hidden gate. It vanished again as muted light danced around where her skin touched the opening. He pushed his own hand through. There was resistance, but now that he had found the access to get to his mate, he wouldn't let a little fae magic stop him.

He pushed until Rose's right leg and arm, and her face slipped through. Then he pivoted to ensure that his entire body, except his arm around Rose, was inside the fae kingdom before he pulled her the rest of the way across the barrier. It wasn't beyond the irritating fae to yank her from his arms and leave him on the outside.

Jydryn stood in the same dense forest he had just left. He closed his eyes and drew in a deep breath. His tongue slid over his lips to taste his mate's sweetness again. Though Keena wasn't visible, her scent was easy to find.

He glanced at Rose, who had quieted to sniffles as they crossed the magic threshold. "She's here, Rose. Mommy is here." He walked as fast as he could with an aching body and a hungry baby in his hands.

Keena's vision cleared. Three men and two women surrounded her. But they weren't human. They each had a different shade of hair, from green, blue, orange, pink, to purple. They were her height or a little shorter, lean, and attractive. Their skin glowed. Each of them wore clothes made from leaves or flowers. The females had tight bodices covering their chests and short, skirts of bright colors. The males only wore pants made from the same flora.

Keena tried to shake free. "Let go of me."

"The queen has summoned you," the female with pink hair said with a bright smile.

"Jydryn will hunt you down for this." Keena knew his temper would provoke him to protect her with force.

"Your weak man can't cross the Shimmerbourne barrier." The tallest one with green hair was the one who'd ordered her to be bound.

Drawing on the strength of her bond with her dragon, she stared the glaring green-hair fae down. "He's not weak, and he will come for me."

The leader gripped her arm above the elbow and squeezed until she closed her eyes. "That is enough. Now come on."

The male with purple hair took her other arm and they marched down a trail following the pink-haired girl.

"She *is* the queen's *daughter*, Nightshade. Her Majesty will not be happy if she arrives battered," the male with orange hair behind them said.

"She is a halfling, Echo. I'll treat her as such." Nightshade tightened his grip.

"You have the wrong person," Keena muttered.

The pink-haired fae turned around and seemed to float backward. "Oh no, you are the princess. We made sure."

"Magpie, shut up." Nightshade motioned for her to turn around.

The fae pushed out her lower lip and stuck her tongue out at Nightshade before she whirled.

They plodded along until Keena's feet ached before they stepped from the dark trees into an open area covered in yellowed grass. A low horn blew and echoed around them.

Nightshade and the other fae never slowed as they marched her toward an odd structure that seemed to be made of nature. They climbed four steps formed from cracked roots. Other fae opened two large doors of vines with withered leaves and inside they crossed through a group of fae men wearing thigh-length tunics over pants in a rainbow of bright colors. The women wore long, flowing gowns adorned with sprigs, flowers, or small plants.

The floor of the room was a carpet of a thick gray groundcover. Trees with only brown leaved lined the entire room like columns. Brown vines with sickly leaves covered in dark spots wove between the trees to form walls. A dry, woody vine stretched overhead to create a roof—not that it would keep the rain or sunlight out.

They stopped at the far end of the long room in front of a raised platform and waited. The green-haired fae gripped Keena as the sounds behind them told her the room filled. After several minutes, an elegant woman with light blue hair topped with a crown came from the back of the dais and sat on a large throne made from a stump and woven vines. "What is the meaning of this commotion in my hall, Nightshade?"

With a disrespectful nod of his head and a raised chin, Nightshade acknowledged the woman. "We have captured the halfling as you demanded."

"Why would you bring that creature into my court? Get rid of it."

Keena knew this wasn't her mother. She wasn't fae—not even a little bit. But the words still stung.

# Chapter 29

Jydryn did his best not to jostle Rose as he raced through the dense forest. He had to get to Keena, but his mind whirled as it searched for some reasonable explanation of why the fae wanted her. They had no use for humans. Oh, there were old myths about fae kings kidnapping beautiful maidens, but last he heard, a queen ruled the fae.

Jydryn stopped and leaned his back against a tree. He wiped sweat from his brow and closed his eyes against the blurring forest. The queen would know of his displeasure if they met.

As he gulped air, Jydryn took in his surroundings. The ground was dry, the leaves on the trees were brown, and the bark gray. No flowers were in bloom.

Rose whimpered and rubbed her fists over her face. Now she was hungry *and* tired. "We need to find your mommy. Then it will all be better, my sweet girl." He kissed her head and started again.

He raced through the bleak woods, weaving between the sickly trees for a while before he took another break. He laid Rose down in the path and watched from behind a tree. Without a sound, a blue-haired young male fae crept out of the shadows and bent over her.

Rose cried, and the youth staggered back.

Jydryn seized him by the throat, pinned him to a tree, and covered his eyes. With the fae only able to whisper a few words at a time in Jydryn's tight grasp, the creature couldn't summon any spells. Covering his eyes prevented him from summoning the natural surroundings to defend himself. "Tell me what you have done with the woman you stole."

"I didn't … steal anyone," the fae croaked on his strained words as he clawed at Jydryn's hands.

"The fae took an auburn-haired woman from a meadow in the northern territory of Keyaral. Where was she taken?"

His pale face reddened. "To … the fae … court."

Jydryn stared. "Why?"

"Queen … ordered … it." The fan's hands dropped limp at his side.

"Why?" Jydryn's volume grew as he pulled each bit of information out of the troublesome fae. Not that he believed anything he was told.

"I don't … know."

Still laying on the ground, Rose kicked and cried.

"You are going to take me to her." Jydryn tightened his grip to let the vile creature know it was his only option if he wanted to live.

"Sure," the fae youth smirked.

Jydryn let his dragon growl and blow hot air against the boy. "You will swear a binding royal oath to take me without delay to the woman you took with no harm coming to me or the child."

The smug smile faded. There was one thing to keep at the forefront when dealing with a fae. If you managed to get them to swear a royal oath—with the right words—it was binding and no fae could brake it.

Jydryn squeezed the youth as Rose's cry grew to a pitiful wail. "Swear."

"I swear … to take you … and the child … unharmed to the woman … I took." The smirk returned with the last few words.

Jydryn shook him and slammed him against the tree he pinned the fae to. If Jydryn hadn't needed the fae, he might have smacked his head hard enough to render him unconscious. "First, that was *not* a royal oath, you manipulative fae. And second, let me be absolutely clear, I don't want to end up with any woman the fae kidnapped in the last few days. I want the auburn-haired woman, known to me as Keena, who the fae stole from the meadow in the northern territory of the Keyaral Kingdom through a cabin trap, about an hour and a half ago. We are to arrive as quickly as possible *today*, unharmed and unmolested by any magic or warding. And we are to remain unharmed until all three of us leave Shimmerbourne."

Jydryn must have closed all the holes the slimy little fae might have slipped out of, because he snarled before he spoke the full oath. "I swear … on the royal blood … of my queen that—"

"Name your queen."

The fae wheezed out a shallow breath and began again. "I swear … on the royal blood … of Queen Nashala Ever Blossom … to take you … and the child …" The fae repeated what Jydryn had said word for word.

"Seal it." His dragon's snarl leaked through Jydryn's human lips as he squeezed again.

The fae bared his teeth, but shuddered. "I, Flamo … seal this unbreakable … oath … in my blood … and bind myself … to this man … until the oath … is complete."

Jydryn drew forth one claw for a moment and pricked Flamo's neck. He twisted his hand on the fae's neck and let the large drop of blood fall to the ground from his fingertip. He only removed his hand from the fae's eyes in time for him to watch the droplet hit, but not stop it. A burst of magical energy leapt from the ground and washed over the three individuals.

Rose quieted again with the wave. Jydryn picked her up and kissed the top of her head. "Let's go get Mommy."

The fae coughed as he rubbed his neck. "She has a child?"

Jydryn glared. "Is that a problem?"

The youth shrugged and stepped away. "The queen won't be happy."

"It is no concern of mine what makes your irritating queen happy.

Let's go." Jydryn hurried the fae along. Bound by his oath, Flamo couldn't desert him, but the sooner Jydryn and Rose were with Keena, the better.

After a short time of dashing through the dying woods, Flamo led Jydryn to the dilapidated fae court. They pushed their way inside. As they worked through the grumbling crowd, Jydryn spotted Keena at last. She stood between two male fae. The light through the rotting ceiling shone on her rich red hair streaked with—faint *green* and *pink*.

Chapter 30

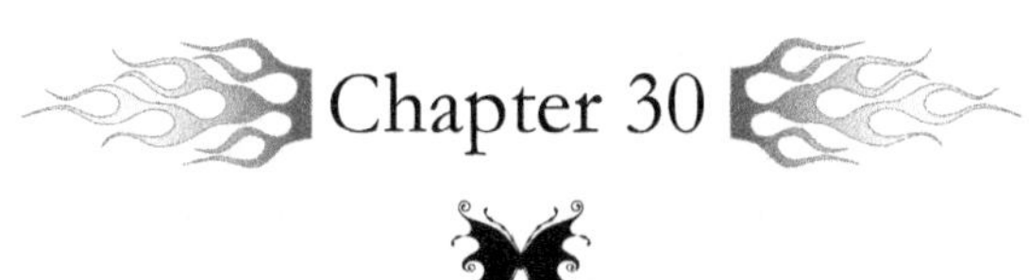

Keena fidgeted as the queen glared at her. Even after her time with Jydryn and Rose, the hateful words of 'get rid of the creature' stung.

A petite fae with sea-foam-green hair knelt next to the queen and talked to her in soothing tones. "Majesty, she is your daughter."

A rumble of voices and shuffling built behind Keena. A sizable crowd of beautiful fae now filled the room.

"Oh, you silly girl, Lilly. Is this one of your jokes? I don't have any children. I'm much too young."

"Majesty, I am Petal. You gave birth to a daughter in the human kingdom," the fae said.

She gasped and glanced around. "Human kingdom. Father forbids …" The queen grinned and leaned into Petal with a giggle. "I know ways to sneak out of Shimmer-*boring*, Lilly."

"It's Petal, majesty. Your father banished Lilly. But you know many ways out of the kingdom. You used them and found a handsome human."

"Oh, he is a right beautiful man isn't he, Lilly? And we have such a pretty child. You can tell she's fae because she's so beautiful. I wish you could meet her, Petal."

"She is here now, Majesty."

The queen gripped the younger fae's arm. "No, Lilly. You can't bring Lay here. Father will kill her."

Petal or Lilly, or whoever the little fae was, patted the queen's hands.

"King Nix is dead. You rule as queen now, and you have brought your daughter home."

At last, the queen's stare turned to Keena. "That is not Lay. My daughter is only a wee sprite."

"That is your daughter, Majesty. It has been many years."

The queen tipped her head, and her brows pinched. "Lay? Is that you?"

How did one prove she was not—or was—a long-lost child?

The crowd grumbled behind her.

Keena, can you still hear my thoughts?

Keena smiled and released a long breath. Jydryn would know what to do.

Flamo stopped in the middle of the crowd. Jydryn could see Keena, but he couldn't reach her because of the many fae blocking his way. *Keena, can you still hear my thoughts?*

Her shoulders relaxed, and she turned her head.

Don't turn around, but if you can hear me, give a gentle toss of your head.

Keena shook her head, and her long hair swished across her back.

Jydryn looked to Flamo. "Your oath is not complete, fae, until I stand beside her and we have the opportunity to leave."

Flamo glared, but pushed the rest of the way through the crowd. As Jydryn stepped between Keena and the fae on her left, he spoke to her again. *Don't touch me and don't tell them who I am.*

"Nightshade, what is all that commotion?" the queen asked. She didn't sound right. More like a lost child than a powerful ruler.

Keena turned to the green-haired fae on her right. "I told you he'd come for me."

The fae's lip curled at Keena before he answered the queen. "Just another intruder, Majesty. I'll remove him at once."

"Queen Nashala, why have you brought this woman here?" Jydryn called as he shook free of a guard trying to grab him.

Rose whimpered, leaned out of his arms, and reached for Keena.

The crowd behind them rumbled.

"How dare you speak to our queen!" Nightshade stepped around Keena to come at him.

Keena showed Jydryn her hands bound with vines covered in black splotches.

The queen leaned forward. "Is that my daughter? Lay, oh Lay, is that you?"

Jydryn elbowed Nightshade in the gut and looked at Keena. "Daughter?"

Keena shook her head. "They're mistaken. The queen seems quite confused."

"That explains so much," Jydryn whispered as he struggled to keep Rose in his arms and keep out of the grasp of the guard. "Put your hands out to me and pull them apart."

"It burns."

"It will only be a moment," he promised. Here, in the walls of the fae court, he struggled to bring even one claw to the surface. Just this morning, fae magic had him trapped in his dragon form. Now it trapped him in his human one. Keena was the key to getting them out of this place—just like she had been this morning.

He slid his claw between her hands and cut away the magic vine. He passed Rose to her arms as he fought off another grab by Nightshade.

"Why is she holding my baby?" the queen whimpered.

"A baby. She has a child," the crowd muttered.

"Majesty, your daughter is the older one," the little fae beside the queen said.

As shyly as you can, take off your shoes.

Keena gazed at him out of the corner of her eye. "You can't believe this," she whispered.

He nodded as he turned and shoved Nightshade and a couple of other fae guards away.

"Nightshade, whatever you are doing down there, stop it. I want to meet these people." The queen smiled at Jydryn like she'd had too much twilight ale. "I like humans, you know." She clapped her hands. "They are ever so entertaining and lovely."

Jydryn took his place at Keena's side once more. "Your Majesty, if this is your rightful daughter, call her by the name you gave her at birth."

The fragile fae court swayed with the collective gasp of those gathered.

The queen slid to the edge of her throne in full control of her faculties. "Who are you to demand such a thing?"

"I am Jydryn, the Champion of Life; son of Govam, the Protective; nephew of the Dragon King."

The crowd whispered with muttered words. "A shifter."

Chapter 31

Keena struggled to focus.

Jydryn had found her—but he was acting strange, almost as odd as the fairy queen. He didn't shift into his dragon and carry her away. He handed her Rose and told her to take off her shoes. Then, he demanded the queen say the name she'd given her baby.

With her shoes off, a deep breath filled her lungs, and every fear vanished.

Rose wrapped her little arms around Keena's neck and laid her head on her shoulder as the crowd buzzed.

The dry, gray growth under her feet softened and warmed. Keena glanced down and noticed a growing ring reaching out from her hem. The groundcover now had healthy, flat, succulent, blue-green leaves. White flowers budded and bloomed too.

Jydryn introduced himself.

"You're the nephew of the dragon king?" she whispered.

He smiled ridiculously big at her. "You're the daughter of the fae queen," he whispered back.

The trunks of the trees nearest her on either side mended and darkened to a deep brown. New, bright green leaves unfolded from the branches. The vines between them lost their spots and bloomed with large yellow and pink blossoms sprinkled with white spots in the center.

She leaned closer to Jydryn to whisper in his ear. "What's going on?"

Jydryn winked at Keena and turned back to Queen Nashala, who looked nothing like her. "There is power in a name given to all fae, but especially to a fae of royal blood. As princess of Shimmerbourne, and her future queen, her people should know and revere the princess' name."

The queen shook her head. "No, I don't have a daughter. I am princess." She seemed so confused.

Petal patted her hand again. "Yes, majesty. You had a child with a human. You call her Lay."

"Lay. My sweet girl." The queen's ramblings grew too quiet for any to hear, except maybe Jydryn.

Jydryn chuckled. "How very perfect."

He turned to face Keena with his enormous grin and hummed. "She gave you a name that in fae means 'of earth,'" he pointed to her, "'and sky,'" he pointed to himself.

He took a step back and his next words were loud enough for everyone to hear. "Court of the fae people, your long-lost princess has returned to you this day. Take a knee and greet Princess Arlayna, Bright Star!"

A wave of energy burst out of Keena in a visible ripple of light. It washed over everyone around her and up the walls, speeding the regeneration of healthy leaves and bright flowers that had started when she removed her shoes. The roof filled in with fat, green vines and long stems of heart-shaped flowers dangled from them. Each burst with light like a chandelier.

Gasps filled the room around her.

"She *is* the princess."

Jydryn stepped close again and took her hand. Dragon Fire covered both of them with huge flickering tongues of flame.

"Our princess is mated with the shifter."

"The prophecy!"

"No. Can she be the one?"

Nightshade knocked them apart with a punch to Jydryn's tender back and stepped behind Keena. He grabbed both of Keena's upper arms and pulled back until she feared she'd drop Rose. "We have found our lost princess. Secure her. Take the child and the beast away."

Vines shot out of the ground and wrapped around Nightshade.

A branch swung down and batted away another fae who approached with outstretched arms to seize Rose.

A storm of flower petals swirled around another guard as he reached for Jydryn.

Keena fought for breath. "What's going on?"

Jydryn encircled her with a powerful arm and turned her to the side of the room as vines, branches, and flowers opened a path for them while blocking anyone who might stop them. "What you did this morning, in releasing me from the chains, has happened to you. Announcing your name here set your magic free."

Keena jerked to a stop in front of the wall now standing open for them. The meadow—now vibrant green and full of flowers—awaited them on the other side. "Magic!"

Jydryn sighed as he kissed her cheek. "Aye, Princess Arlayna. Powerful fae magic."

"I'm not doing any of this."

"Not consciously, but others threaten those you love and your magic is protecting us."

Keena—Arlayna—Lay, she wasn't sure who she was. She turned and looked at the woman who now stood in front of her throne. "My mother …"

"Aye. But there is something wrong with her." Jydryn tugged Keena through the wall and it closed behind them. "We need to figure out what is going on before your people tear us apart."

Her legs ached as she tried to keep up with his long strides. They raced across the open field into the trees. Rose cried and Keena stumbled on her hem. Jydryn was quick to catch them as they hurried into the cover of the trees.

"Don't let her escape." The shouted cry of those following them sent a shudder through Keena. Their thundering footfalls matched the pounding of her heart.

"Stop him from taking her back to his world." They were getting closer.

The trees closed the paths behind them as she staggered forward.

A pink-haired fae with deep scars across her face and only one eye appeared before them. "Princess, I'm here to help."

Jydryn's hand covered Keena's eyes, and the breath of his words tickled her ear as he wrapped her in his mighty arm. "Peace, my love."

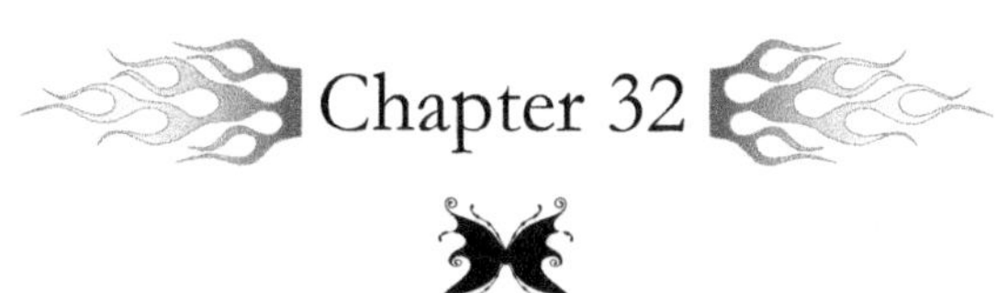

Chapter 32

Keena's heart thundered in her ears as Jydryn kept her in the dark with his warm hand. She gasped for breath and leaned her weight into his sturdy form.

"You're in no danger," Jydryn whispered. "Rose and I are safe."

"Why are you telling me that?" She pulled at his hand that still covered her eyes. "Why won't you let me see?"

"Fae bring their magic to life in two ways; through spoken incantations—which you don't know yet—and by seeing nature around you and bending it to your will. If you can't see the trees and vines, you can't use them to hurt this fae."

"You trust her?"

"I do."

Her head dropped to his shoulder. A long nap—for about a week—sounded divine. "Why?"

"Are you calm?"

Her heart rate had slowed and her breaths were more even. "I think so."

Jydryn eased his hand away. No trees moved more than what the breeze caused. Nothing flowered, and the vines remained inert on the ground.

The deep scars on the fae's face were as bad as those on Jydryn's back. "What makes you trust her?"

Wrapped in his embrace, he stroked up and down the length of

Keena's arm. "There are a couple of reasons. First, fae—by their nature —are not known to be helpers. It is not something they will even lie about. She has offered her aid. She called you princess, so she believes you are who the queen suggested you are. But most telling to me is the fact fae are vain creatures." He glanced at the one-eyed female, who tipped her head and shrugged in agreement. "They do nothing that could cause an injury to themselves that would leave a scar—that is why their magic controls nature. It goes into battle for them. If, by some freak accident, they suffer an injury, they will use a glamour, an illusion spell, to hide the blemish from the world. That this fae has suffered such a grievous injury on her face and she does not—or more likely—cannot hide it, says a great deal about her."

Tired enough she couldn't lift her head from Jydryn's shoulder, Keena asked, "What happened to the others?"

Rose fussed again.

The fae offered a bottle. "I have hidden us from those following you. It won't keep them out forever, but it should buy us some time to talk."

Keena didn't take the bottle. "Aren't there tales about eating what fae offer while in their kingdom and never being able to leave?"

The fae smiled. "That is not true, and I will do nothing to hurt my princess or her family. I swear on the blood of Queen Nashala Ever Blossom, the contents and the bottle are safe and will only nourish the poor babe." She pricked her finger with a thorn and let a drop of blood fall on the ground. A wave of magic rippled away.

Jydryn looked at Keena. "It is a royal fae oath. Said and sealed in this manner, she can't ever break it." He took the bottle and offered it to Rose.

At first, Rose continued to fuss, not understanding the bottle would make her feel better.

"Why don't we sit?" the fae waved her hand and a long bench with a high back formed from a fallen log behind Keena and Jydryn.

He pulled Keena down with him and, once Rose reclined in her arms, she sucked hard from the bottle.

The fae sat cross-legged on a stump in front of them. Her bare knees poked out between the petals of her multi-colored skirt. She tucked her pink hair behind her pointed ears, fidgeted with her fingers, stared, and then she released a deep sigh. "First, Princess, I need you to know how very sorry I am. I hope you can one day forgive me."

"Perhaps you should start at the beginning," Jydryn said as he snuggled Keena close.

"Your grandfather, King Nix Dark Oak, chose a wife from among the many beautiful fae females of court. His deep love caused him to bind them as a mated pair."

Keena kept her head on Jydryn's shoulder, but twisted to look up at him.

"Unlike shifters, who have destined mates appointed by God," Jydryn winked, "the fae can choose to create that permanent bond or not."

The fae nodded. "Your mother was his firstborn, their only child. High Lady Phoebe White Stag died before she could have any more children. There were rumors humans had something to do with Phoebe's death, but to this day, no one knows the truth of what happened to her. Nashala was only five when her mother died. It broke the king and made him a bitter male. He'd wanted a son to take the throne after him, but all he had was Nashala." The fae scowled and grumbled. "His every word cut her down, and he tried to keep her locked in the palace."

"And how do you come by all this knowledge?" Jydryn's voice reverberated with his anger.

"I am Lilly. Nashala was my best friend as a child. We did everything together, including getting into trouble with the king. When King Nix punished me and sent me away from court, it left Nashala all alone. She learned to conceal the evidence of her magic and to slip from Shimmerbourne into the human kingdom.”

“That is how she met my father,” Keena said. Even saying the words sounded odd.

Lilly smiled. “Nashala does love humans. They were kind to her in ways she had never experienced in her own home. She met Lord Rycharde of Wealdstone in a village east of the Tetling Ridge. She returned many times to see him. He is a tall, broad man, much like your Jydryn. Your father even has a similar strong jawline. He has warm-colored skin, kind eyes, and a very long nose.” Lilly giggled.

Keena squirmed as Jydryn tightened his hold on her. The heat from his body grew uncomfortable. “What happened to him?”

Lilly closed her eyes and bit at her lip as she picked at the edge of a purple petal on her skirt. “They fell in love. They married in secret in a human chapel, and Nashala sealed them with a mated bonding. Her father had forbidden her to create a mate’s bond—even with a fae—but she feared what he would do to Rycharde if she didn’t seal him to herself. She was right.”

The fae unfolded her slender legs and slipped off the stump. She paced for several moments before she continued the tale. “When King Nix realized Nashala had left Shimmerbourne and not returned, he sent others to find her and bring her back. He brought me before him and told me of my duty to safeguard our kingdom by bringing the princess home. I refused at first, knowing how unhappy she had been, but the kingdom couldn’t survive without her.”

“Unlike the human kingdom, ”Jydryn explained, “the fae succession must proceed from parent to offspring. It is almost unheard of that a fae ruler dies without a living heir. In those times, it has plunged Shimmerbourne into decades of destruction, disease, and chaos. They avoid such a situation at all costs. Which would explain why they would seek you when their queen’s mind suffers.”

"He's correct," Lilly said. "It was only the king's promise that I could return to the court and care for my friend if I brought her back that made me join those searching for her. But your mother's magic at hiding was like no other's."

"No doubt honed under years of evading her father," Jydryn snorted.

Lilly nodded. "It was almost three years before we found her."

"And by then, I had been born."

"Nashala came back willingly. She hoped to change her father's mind or, at the very least, appease him until he died and she took the throne. But her father flew into a rage when he learned she'd mated to a human. He stripped the memory of you and your father from her mind."

Keena's eyes filled with tears. "That's why she is so confused now?"

"And why Shimmerbourne looked to be dying until Arlayna's magic was freed," Jydryn said.

"It is. My daughter, Petal, serves her now. We have been trying to help her remember, but until she reunites with your father, I don't think she is going to get any better."

Keena sat up, disturbing Rose from her sleep. "My father's still alive?"

Chapter 33

Every muscle in Jydryn's body clenched in tight knots. Had he not been in the magic kingdom of Shimmerbourne, his dragon would be raging and setting the place on fire.

He closed his eyes and pinched the bridge of his nose. His mate—the woman he loved more with each breath—was a despised fae. The way her grandfather had treated her mother was proof enough that Jydryn's feelings about this species were justified.

But his Keena was Princess Arlayna Bright Star, heir to the fae throne. And at the moment, her mother was in no condition to rule.

Keena pulled from him. The heat of his dragon nature soaked her dress. She rested her hand on his knee. "I thought mates were for life. Why would King Nix erase Nashala's memory of him?"

He covered her hand with his, bringing their fire to life. "He made her forget, but couldn't break their bond. She isn't able to connect with any other male. There is no chance of love or the ability to produce children without him. The desire for her love would still be there—but she wouldn't know who her heart yearned for. That unfulfilled longing would tear her mind apart."

"Didn't the king understand what he was doing to her?" The lament of Keena's heart spilled into her words.

Lilly sighed. "Only when it was too late. But even on his deathbed, he wouldn't relent and reverse the spell."

Keena pursed her lips. "You said the only way to help Queen Nashala is to reunite her with Rycharde."

Lilly released a deep sigh and nodded. "Now, that is our only choice."

"Now?" Keena looked between Lilly and Jydryn as the fae and the shifter exchanged glances.

"They will need to produce another heir," Lilly mumbled.

"Why?" Keena turned to Jydryn. "What are the two of you not saying?"

Jydryn leaned forward and braced his forearms on his thighs. "The fae are not welcoming to other species, as your grandfather proved. Your mate is a shifter. To rule Shimmerbourne, you'll need to live here, but they won't accept me. And I can't take my dragon form while in this magic-filled land."

"And the other reason?"

Jydryn smirked. His mate was too good at realizing when he was keeping something from her.

Lilly spoke first. "Long ago, we all lived as one people—fae, humans, and shifters."

He didn't care for the way she said shifter, but it was no worse than how he said fae. "We each had our rulers, but one emperor united us all. There was a blood connection in this high ruler to all the species of the kingdom."

Lilly stared at Keena. "Prophets have long foretold we will one day find one to unite us again."

Keena glanced between them again. "And you think this emperor is me?"

"Empress, yes," Lilly said with awe.

Keena shook her head, but Jydryn captured her hand and squeezed it which ignited the Dragon Fire again. "You are the offspring of a fae and a human, and your mate is a shifter."

"Then one of our children will be bound by blood to all three peoples, but not me." Keena's voice quaked.

Lilly smiled. "The mated bond is the same as a blood bond in this case."

"You are delusional if you two think I will ever be queen of the fae, let alone empress of all the land."

Jydryn squeezed her hand again. "That is a discussion for another time. Right now, we have other concerns." He turned his hard stare back to Lilly. "For Shimmerbourne to be whole, we need to know everything they did to her father and where to find him."

The fae slumped down on the stump again. "You must know, princess, I regret every part I played in what happened to you and your father."

Keena shook.

Jydryn swallowed a growl. "Tell her everything. It is the only way to be free of your guilt."

"It was not enough to have Nashala back in Shimmerbourne. King Nix demanded we deal with Lord Rycharde and you."

"Deal with us?"

Lilly nodded. "The only thing that saves us now is during his life, King Nix never left the fae realm, and you and your father are either royal blood, or bound to one of royal blood."

Keena turned to him; her brows pinched together.

Jydryn explained. "Because of the right of succession among the fae, no one can kill one of royal blood—except another royal. Since Nix never left Shimmerbourne, and you and your father never entered, you were spared and therefore the kingdom."

"But even this connection didn't afford you complete protection." A tear slid from Lilly's one remaining eye. "When the guards found you and your father, Nightshade blew forgetting dust in your father's face and erased his life. Your father can't remember you, or his love, or even who he is. Nightshade compelled him to wander the earth with no memory."

"That's terrible," Keena moved to stand.

"You were too young to have much of a memory to erase. But that didn't stop Nightshade. He put a ward around you to suppress your magic and repel anyone from caring for you."

Keena leapt to her feet. "I was two years old. What harm would I have been to anyone here? To have deprived me of any kindness and now expect me to stay here and help your people …" She plopped down next to Jydryn again; tears streaked her face. "It is a wonder I made it to my third birthday."

Lilly hugged herself tight, but it didn't stop her shaking. "I had returned to court with your mother, but when I learned what Nightshade had done, I searched for you. I wasn't powerful enough to remove the warding, but I stayed with you and did what I could."

Keena shook her head. "I've never seen you before."

Light shimmered around Lilly. Her thin, smooth legs and flower dress faded into the body of a plumb, large bosomed woman in a dirty dress. The illusion stopped before it reached her damaged face.

Keena gasped and sat straight. "Ol' Laura."

The glamor vanished, and the fae sat before them again. "I stayed with you for the first few years. Kept you hidden and fed. But I had to return to Shimmerbourne from time to time to keep King Nix from knowing what I was doing."

"He did find out though," Jydryn said with a growl as he indicated her face.

"You were almost seven when I left the last time. Nightshade captured me as soon as I crossed the border and took me to the king. Nix tortured me for months. But not even when he did this to me, " she pointed to her scarred face, "would I tell him where you were."

Keena sniffled. "How did you escape?"

"Echo, Nightshade's lieutenant, knew what I had been doing. He condemned the king's actions—saw them as a threat to our way of life. He aided me when he could without revealing himself. We both believed we'd benefit if he stayed close to Nightshade and the king. He rescued me from the dungeon and nursed me back to health. He is Petal's father, though he cannot claim her before his people."

"Why come for your princess now?" Jydryn asked.

"Without my glamor, I couldn't leave Shimmerbourne. When I healed enough for Echo to leave my side, he came to find you, but you weren't in Ravengap any longer."

Keena shuddered as her eyes squeezed closed. "The people there were so mean, and I struggled to get anything to eat. I looked for you and ended up in Mudwood. There were lots of kids on the streets. I learned to survive by watching them."

"How did you find her *now*?" Jydryn asked again.

Lilly scowled. "With the princess' magic suppressed, we lost her." Her features softened. "A few times a year, Echo leaves Shimmerbourne to search. Several weeks ago, he sensed her magic. We don't know why."

"Dragon Fire," Jydryn said with a groan. The thing that had marked her as his had also helped make her easy to find by the fae.

Keena glanced from Jydryn to Lilly again. "What do we do now?"

Lilly leapt from her stump and turned to scan the surrounding area. "They have almost found us. We need to hurry."

Chapter 34

Jydryn stood and pulled Keena up with him as Rose slept against her. Keena's eyes closed and her head tipped back. It was all too much. She needed sleep.

Lilly stood between them and took each of their hands. The world around them blurred and Keena swayed.

Trees came back into focus—but they were not where they had been before. These trees here were thinner, the leaves a lighter shade of green, and longer. "What just happened?"

"Fae quick leap," Jydryn said before they did it again.

"It is the way they brought you to the fae court." Lilly tightened her grip as they jumped again.

When they stopped next, Keena jerked her hand free and braced herself against a tree. She closed her eyes. She leaned her spinning head against the rough bark and pressed her hand to her churning stomach. Bile touched the back of her throat.

Lilly crossed her arms. "Forgive me Princess. Though you are unaccustomed to traveling in this manner, we'll need to make several more jumps to hide where on our border I'm leaving you. The more we can confuse your pursuers, the better chance you'll have."

Jydryn came to her side and supported her, so she didn't drop Rose. "She's exhausted, fae. She was up well before the light to save my scaled hide. We escaped the magic chains holding me only moments before you captured her. She's met her mother, had her magic released, and now this."

Keena's head dropped to his muscular chest as she clung to a fist-full of his shirt. "I'm too tired to escape them. But I can't lose you and Rose."

He kissed her forehead, bathing them both in Dragon Fire.

Lilly's brow rose as she stared at Jydryn. "You two need to do something about that. It's like a beacon." She took their hands again, and they leapt three more times. This time it happened so fast, Keena couldn't catch a breath in between.

Lilly scanned the small clearing around them. "We have only a few more moments before they locate us again."

"What are we supposed to do now?" Keena couldn't think of any way they'd ever escape the magical creatures who chased them.

Lilly looked at Jydryn. "As soon as you're through the barrier, take them away from Shimmerbourne lands."

He nodded.

Lilly dipped in a curtsy. "Princess, find your father."

"How am I supposed to find a man who has no magic, who I don't remember, and who is under a spell that compels him to roam around?"

They leapt again. Keena's head throbbed. She looked down at Rose, who hadn't stirred during all their magical travels, and then tried to hand Lilly the bottle.

"Keep it," Lilly said. "There is a spell on it so it refills anytime the wee one is hungry."

"Well, that would have been handy earlier today," Keena mumbled.

"It will save me from needing to find a new goat to drag along with us." Jydryn smiled before they leapt again.

"I told you what your father looks like, but I assure you, you'll know him. There has been a familiar face throughout your life. Someone who has showed up no matter where you went." They leapt again. "A man who stared at you a little too long, but it didn't frighten you. He will be drawn to you because he needs you, but he doesn't remember why,

Princess."

"And what—" another leap. Keena swayed and gasped for breath. "What am I supposed to do when I find him? I don't know how to use magic."

"The key is you, Princess. Just being with you will start to open his mind. Take him home to Wealdstone Castle. There is a man there I met once named Herbert. I put a ward of protection on him and the castle. He witnessed your parents' marriage, knows of your birth, and awaits his master's return."

They leapt again.

Keena leaned forward as more bile washed over her tongue. It was a moment before she could speak. "How is this Herbert to believe me?"

Lilly stepped in front of them. "Tell him, 'Roses are the first to bloom each spring.'"

"They aren't," Jydryn said.

"True." Lilly nodded. "But it will unlock his memory of me and he will remember all he needs to do."

The fae turned and pointed to a spot between the divided trunk of a single, slender oak tree. Light shimmered inside the opening, and a wide field shrouded in fog glistened in the light. "Exit through there. Inform me as soon as you have your father home and I'll bring Nashala to you."

Jydryn wrapped his arm around Keena and led her toward the opening.

Keena glanced over his shoulder at Lilly. "How am I supposed to get a message to you?"

"Tell the trees." Lilly laughed as her image popped and she vanished.

Jydryn drew Keena close, wrapping his arms around both her and Rose. "We have to go together. I can't pass through without you."

She nodded, and they stepped from the forest to the meadow bathed in the fading light of the day.

Jydryn's human form vanished, and his dragon took a protective stance over them. *Quick, climb on my back.*

Keena took a deep breath and clambered up. She dropped between his wings and covered her and Rose with her Dragon Fire. "I don't have any clothes for you. Are we going back to the cave?"

I know a place.

Chapter 35

Jydryn landed less than an hour after they fled Shimmerbourne near Arrowfall. He shook. *Keena, wake up, my love.*

She slid off his back and staggered a few steps in the tall grass. "Where are we?"

He shifted. "Close to a town called Arrowfall." He talked as he headed for the trees to her right. "Over the years I've brought a few of the women I saved here and released them on the road near a small field closer to town. If they didn't leave, I came here, shifted, changed into clothes I have hidden, and then I'd lead them to town as a helpful farmer."

When he returned from the tree line, Keena lay curled on her side with Rose tucked close to her body. Both slept. A thick bed of grass spread out under them and flowers continued to spring up all around.

Jydryn pulled on his shirt and dropped to his back behind them. The grass grew and formed a tight weave over them until it blocked out the last of the light but still allowed air in.

Keena's magic was incredibly powerful if she could conjure up such concealment in her sleep. He hoped those chasing them wouldn't sense her power in it. But that was a concern for another time. He let his eyes close as sleep claimed him too.

Keena's hand clamped over his mouth, waking Jydryn with a start. She'd rolled over to lie facing him. Her eyes were closed and her breathing deep. She wasn't awake, not fully anyway.

Whispered voices approached, and he tried to remove her hand to put out the Dragon Fire.

An angry voice challenged. "Are you sure you sensed her magic here?"

The next voice was softer and contained an uncertain quake. "I thought I did, Nightshade, but they aren't here now. Perhaps they only stopped here for a few moments?" The last was more a question than a statement.

A third voice joined the others. This one sounded bored. "They need to sleep at some point."

A foot landed on the top of the woven dome covering them. The grass dipped under the weight but didn't get close to Jydryn or Keena. He held his breath.

"It's impossible to believe that half-breed can control her magic already," Nightshade's voice snarled, "but how can she keep slipping away?"

"I don't know, sir. Could the shifter be helping her?"

The sound of a punch filled the still air. "That mongrel has no magic." The weight lifted off the grass enclosure. "Come on," Nightshade ordered. "We have to find her and bring her back."

Their movement paused, and the air burned in Jydryn's chest.

Nightshades voice was farther away now. "But this time we do it right. We kill the mate and the whelp. Like her mother, she's bound so she'll never have another male. The bloodline will end with her."

The third, most reasonable voice spoke again. "But what about Shimmerbourne?"

Nightshade's response was quick. "It will rise again from a stronger, purer bloodline."

"Yours?" both the other two said.

The sweet tenor of Nightshade's voice made Jydryn shudder. "When

I take the throne, I will give glorious reward to those who assist me now."

A smaller, quieter voice, perhaps a female, spoke for the first time. "What of the prophecy?"

Slap. "Never mention that again," Nightshade roared. "Arlayna Bright Star is not the one."

Footsteps rushed off. The fae couldn't jump from location to location outside their realm, but their speed on foot was beyond any humans and many clans of shifters.

Keena's hand relaxed over his mouth, but she still didn't stir. Her magic was indeed powerful.

Something hit Keena's thigh and brought her to the surface of consciousness again. Warmth surrounded her. The gentle sucking of Rose as she enjoyed her bottle tickled her ears. She must be in Jydryn's cave—safe with those she loved. Had it all been a nightmare? *Fae … my mother? …Wait, a chase?*

Another hit against her thigh made her pry one eye open.

Rose lay beside her, drinking and kicking her legs.

Keena's stomach growled. When had she last eaten?

"I'd be happy to get us something to eat if you can set us free." Jydryn's voice rumbled from behind her.

Keena flipped to her back and stared at the woven grass encasing them. "I didn't—"

"Not consciously, but you did."

"Why?"

"To keep us safe. It worked."

She turned her head to look at him. "Why? What happened?"

Jydryn sighed.

Her heart stuttered. Would he lie to her this time, or keep things from her as he had before? "Please. Don't hide the truth. I feel like lies have infused my entire life."

He rolled to his side to face her and interlaced their fingers. Each tongue of fire covering them was now about the size of his hand. "Nightshade and a couple of other fae found us this morning."

"Morning?"

He smirked. "You've slept almost an entire day."

"I'm still tired," she said with a yawn as she bathed in the love she saw in his eyes.

"You're also starving. I don't think you've eaten since yesterday morning." His stomach grumbled too.

She frowned. "But it's been even longer for you."

"Just release us and I'll go catch the first large animal I find."

She stared up at the grass, trying to think of a way to make it open. Lilly said she could send a message by talking to the trees. Would it work? She paused. "How do you know Nightshade found us if the grass trapped us in here?"

"I heard them talking, and a male with him called him by name."

"Why didn't I hear them?"

He smiled, making her heart flutter. "You did, but like a sleepwalker who can fetch food or dress and not realize it, you acted in your sleep. You slapped your hand over my mouth and woke me up."

Her brows crinkled as she stared at him. She'd been tired, but never walked in her sleep before. "Why didn't they see the grass mound, or the Dragon Fire, or sense my magic?"

Jydryn shrugged and rubbed her arm. "I don't know a lot about fae magic other than it is most often used to manipulate others."

She stared up at the unmoving grass dome again. "You don't like the fae."

"Not in the least."

That hit her like a punch. "Oh."

He turned her face toward him again as he caressed her cheek. "You're different, my love."

"I'm fae—half, at least."

His tender smile and gentle touch washed away her fear. "But they didn't raise you in their ways. Your magic has done nothing but protect, and it is powerful."

She searched his face for a long time but only saw love looking back. "What did the fae say?"

His smile vanished. "I would rather not say."

She pursed her lips. "Then I think I need to know."

He rolled onto his back with a deep sigh. His eyes remained closed for a moment and Keena's returning fear tried to wash away her hunger. "Nightshade wants to capture you and bring you back to Shimmerbourne to restore some order and health to the land."

"We already knew *that*." She couldn't keep the frustration out of her tone.

Jydryn turned his head and looked at her. "He doesn't want to make the same mistakes of King Nix. He plans to kill Rose and me, so the royal bloodline ends with you."

"What?" Keena sat up and the grass dome parted, freeing them.

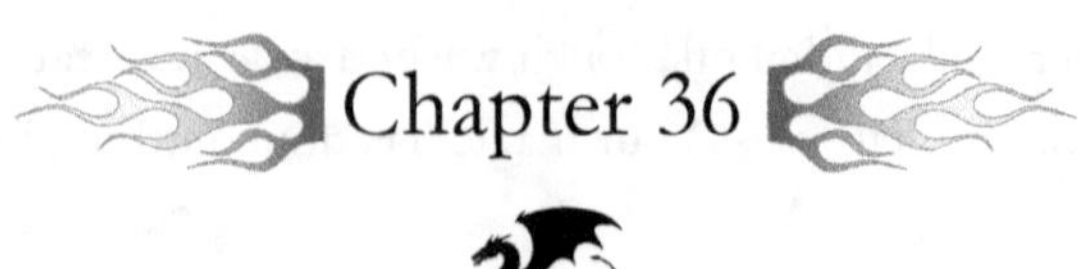

Chapter 36

Jydryn stood with Keena as the rest of the grass enclosure melted away. Nature continued to act without her conscious thought which added to her confusion. As the grass cocoon fell away, he wrapped his arms around her. His need for her was growing intolerable. As soon as they had some food in them, they needed to think about the bonding ritual. "It's all right, love. You kept us safe."

She trembled in his grasp. "Lilly and Petal have to know. They can't trust him."

"I don't think they do."

Keena wiggled free and paced. "But you said without a royal heir on the throne, it would throw the fae kingdom into chaos. What does he hope to gain?"

He wanted her back in his arms, but her need to understand was too powerful. "He wants to be the new king."

Keena staggered a step. He captured her again and pulled her back against his chest in a tight embrace. "They are gone for now. We have other matters to address."

She glanced over her shoulder, her muscles relaxing as her weight leaned more against him. "Like eating."

He almost couldn't speak for the need clawing at him. What he managed to say came out as a strangled rasp. "And our bonding."

He loosened his hold, and she spun to look at him. "What's the matter?"

"The need to complete the bonding rites grows past my limits to deny them."

"Then don't." She cradled his face between her hand, brushed against him as she rose on her toes, and pressed her delicate lips to his. She tightened her hold as the kiss deepened. Her body hummed in his touch.

He pushed her away with a gasp and braced himself on his knees. He sucked in air like a drowning man surfacing moments before it was too late. "We need to complete the rites," he stammered. As he straightened, he caught sight of Rose over Keena shoulder. "And it would be better if the little escape artist was asleep during the ritual. Once we start, we aren't going to be able to stop," he chuckled as he hurried past her to scoop up Rose who had crawled several feet away.

She fussed at him for a moment, but he tossed her in the air and she squealed with delight.

Keena reached for Rose when he returned. "Why don't we eat first? I think my headache will go away when my stomach is full."

He cradled one of her cheeks as he kissed the other. "Aye, my love." He paused for a moment before he prepared to shift. "Can I ask what you prefer to be called—"

"Keena." Her response was quick and forceful. She took a breath. "I prefer Keena. I don't remember ever being Lay or Arlayna. You—my mate and soon-to-be husband—gave me that name for a special reason. That is the one I want to be known by. The other is from a different life I never lived and has ties I'm not sure I want to be bound by."

"Keena it is." He smiled as he pulled off his shirt.

Oh, that man did things to her that made her head spin. Keena watched him shift and smiled at his mighty dragon form. Rose laughed in her arms. "Sorry, little one. We aren't going flying with him this time."

Rose reached for Jydryn as he lifted into the air.

I won't be long.

"I'll try to get a fire started." Keena glanced up at the trees on the edge of the clearing. "I need to get a message to Lilly—but no one else can know."

The trees waved in a unique manner that looked more like a nod.

"All right, trees, tell her of Nightshade's plan to kill my family and take the throne."

One tree bent into the next, which bent into the next. The motion continued out of sight.

Keena turned back to Rose, who was still reaching up to the empty sky. "I wonder how I'll know if she got the message?"

She released a long breath as Rose wiggled in her grasp. Keena set her down in the grass. "Now, how do I keep you from crawling off?"

A hundred small vines crawled into the air and surrounded Rose. Their fat leaves and tiny flowers burst out. They filled the space between them and made a living corral around the child.

"Those flowers won't hurt her if she puts one in her mouth, right?" She wasn't sure who she spoke to, but the area of the vines within Rose's reach changed. They lost their leaves and flowers and grew thick and woody. The foliage that remained was out of reach. Good thing Rose hadn't learned to pull herself up yet.

"Thank you," Keena murmured.

Leaves whirled around her. They carried the whispered response from Lilly. "We will be on our guard and prepare for his downfall."

She stood for a moment and let the sun warm her. She had never known such peace. But it wasn't safety or even being connected to the earth that filled her.

She glanced at the sky; its deep blue-purple leaned toward black. The evening sky from the east to west spoke of her life. From the darkness of being stolen and abandoned, a spell cast to keep anyone from loving her, to learning to survive on the streets … From the unexpected meeting with Jydryn, taking care of Rose who filled her with light and hope, to the brightness of knowing that she was born of love and cherished … It all flooded into her and filled her with joy. Yet it was the One behind all of it—the One who was the source of the light that filled her life with the pinks and oranges of a glorious future Who was behind all of it.

Keena lowered to her knees. Her life had been miserable, but if her father had raised her, as her mother had hoped, Cragholde wouldn't have sacrificed her to a dragon who ended up being her mate. Had she not learned to steal for her food, she wouldn't have been able to free Jydryn from his chains. Had a spell not deprived her of love, she would not know the depth of its sweetness now.

Tears slid down her cheeks and dripped into the grass. A wildflower grew from each drop. He had gifted her this too. This God of Jydryn's— this God she now chose as her own. "Thank you!" The next words would not form on her tongue as she staggered under the weight of all He had done for her. It was some time before she could whisper. "I am Yours. I will go where You lead."

The peace she had marveled at only moments before increased tenfold and pushed her down to sit on her heels. She reached her hands to the heavens, but she could do no more than revel in the power of this true God's presence. "Thank you," she whispered.

Chapter 37

Jydryn landed and dressed. Rose was in a vine enclosure. She flipped from her hands and knees to sit on her rump and reached for him as he came near. A ring of stones with bare dirt in the center waited nearby.

Keena stepped out of the tree line with her arms full of wood as he sat Rose on his hip. "I'm afraid I didn't find anything other than rabbits. We must be too close to the village."

His mate was radiant—more so than normal. Her smile spread wider than he'd ever seen. She dropped the wood beside the ring.

"Are you all right?" Jydryn couldn't take his eyes off her.

"Of course." She kissed his cheek. "I have you and Rose." She kissed the child's head. "And my parents loved me and wanted me. I have crazy fae magic and all of it was part of His loving plan."

Jydryn's heart did a tiny leap and continued to vibrate. "What's happened?"

"I told Him I was His," she said with a shrug. "Which way is the village?"

He pointed to the east in the direction she faced. She walked away. Jydryn watched her for a moment before he snatched up Rose's enspelled bottle and hurried to catch up. "Just to be clear—you've chosen to be known as a child of the Father? You believe in the one true God?"

"Yes." The word floated out of her on an awe-filled breath.

Jydryn moved Rose to his other hip and took Keena's hand. He raised it to his lips and kissed it. "I'm so happy for you."

"I'm giddy to the point of bursting." She released his hand and twirled for a moment. Leaves left the trees and petals fluttered from flowers and danced with her.

Jydryn had never seen anything so beautiful in his entire life.

The sound of a cart rumbling nearby brought him up short. Keena twirled past him, turned, continued walking backward, and waved him to follow.

He raced to her side and pulled her to a stop. "Where are you going?"

"*We* are going into town. We'll find food and a place for us to stay."

He remained rooted to the ground. "That's not a good idea."

"Why not?" Her brows crinkled. "Don't you have any coin?"

"Human villages aren't always safe for our kind. I stop to purchase things, but I've never stayed."

Her enchanting grin made a smile play on his lips. "As long as you don't shift, how are they ever going to know?"

Jydryn turned his gaze back in the direction they had come. A trail of bright flowers showed her every step.

"Oh, I need to find a way to turn that off." She sighed. "You've been in this village, right? Do they have dirt streets or are they covered in stone?"

One brow rose. "Arrowfall is quite large. They have stone streets."

She turned again and walked toward the village. "Well, that should help until we can get me some shoes."

He came to her side, took her hand, and tried to slow her. "Keena, I don't think this is a good idea."

One hand perched on her hip. "Will you protect me and Rose?"

"Of course!"

"And I will protect you." She gave him a quick kiss. "Are the fae that are hunting us likely to enter a human town?"

"Never!"

She pulled him as she continued forward. "So, as long as you have some coin, we can get something to eat, sleep without fear of being killed, and buy some needed shoes and new cloth for a sling and nappies when the market opens tomorrow."

It all made perfect sense. So, why did the hairs on his arm stand on end as the gate of Arrowfall came into view? It was one thing to come alone into a human town. If danger arose, he couldn't get out of, he could always shift and get away. But now he had his love, who was a powerful fae princess and a baby to think about. The dangers were greater for human women and children—Keena being a fae only added to his concern.

She tugged on him again, and he followed at last. *Lord, protect us.*

Arrowfall was nothing like Cragholde. The streets were wide and covered in flat stones. Keena's breaths came harder and her headache increased. Her vision and hearing dimmed as she lost connection with the earth.

She swayed and Jydryn tightened his hold on her arm above her elbow. "I understand separation from the earth can be difficult," he whispered.

"The separation is what I felt much of my life with my magic suppressed, but now I know the difference, so I experience it more as a loss." She turned to him and smiled. "It is only for tonight. Let's get something to eat. We're both hungry. I'll be fine until we can go to the market tomorrow, and then we'll be on our way. Unlike when they cursed me, it won't be forever."

He lifted her hand to kiss it, but stopped before his lips touched her bare skin. He winked.

She looped her arm in his, and they strolled toward the center of town. They followed the noise and smells to a lively inn. She glanced up at the carved wooden placard over the door. A green frog leaned to one side.

"It's called the Tipsy Toad." Jydryn smirked.

"Then, I guess we should be careful what we drink in here." Keena stepped through the door he held open. About two dozen square tables filled the long room. Each had two to four chairs around it. A bright fire burned in a hearth, almost as tall as she was, at the far end of the room.

Jydryn handed Rose to her as he pressed his trembling hand to her back and led her to the counter on the rear wall. She tried to glance at him, but he wouldn't look at her. He removed his hand as they came to the end of the long counter.

"How can I help ya?" a burly man with thick arms and a dirty black apron asked. His mustache moved with each word, though his lips hid under its thick growth. He wiped a silver tankard, filled it with a foaming golden liquid, and thumped it down on the counter, which slopped some contents. A woman in a dress that revealed the bulging mounds of her breasts came to take the drink. Stains covered the faded apron around her waist. She stared at Keena and Rose for a long moment before she turned. Her long black braid swung across her back as her wide hips swayed.

"I'd like a meal for my wife and me and a room for my family for the night."

The owner nodded. "Two dinners are five coppers. Room's half a silver. A bath or fresh sheets is more."

Jydryn laid a full silver on the counter, but kept it under his finger. "Two of your best meals and clean sheets in a room near the rear exit."

The man glanced at the coin, at Jydryn, and then at Keena and Rose. "Agreed." He took the coin the second Jydryn released it, slid it into a pouch at his waist, and pointed to a table opposite the window, closer to the fire. "Please sit."

Jydryn led Keena to a chair where her back was to the hearth. He took the other one and moved it, so he sat beside her with his back to the wall opposite the door.

"I'm sorry."

He stopped scanning the room to look at her.

She moved Rose to sit on her lap and squeezed his arm. "I didn't realize how hard this would be for you."

"I've visited many villages." He'd left out the word human, but his raised eyebrow told her the full story. "I've never done more than pop in to make some purchases and left again. Then it was just me. Now I have you and Rose to protect." He offered a forced smile. "I'll be fine." He squeezed her wrist. "Are you okay?"

She winced. "It's the wood floor. It hurts."

He leaned close. "Is it cutting your feet?"

She shook her head. "It's dead." She blinked away tears, unable to say more.

He seemed to understand as he nodded and patted her arm.

The same black-haired woman came toward their table with two steaming bowls on a tray. She only looked at Rose as she sat them down with a thump. She lifted Rose's hand with her finger, trying to get the baby to grasp it. "'Ello, my sweet. Can I getcha anythin'?"

Rose jerked away with a squeak.

"Our child is fine, miss. That will be all." Jydryn's words were terse.

Keena wasn't sure the woman heard the growled threat rumbling in Jydryn's words, but it made her hair stand on end.

Chapter 38

The dark-haired barmaid left their table at last, and Jydryn turned his attention to his meat pie. But it smelled off. He rubbed his nose. Something was wrong. *Don't eat it*, he warned Keena as he took Rose into his arms.

She glanced at him with her brows pinched. She left the spoon on the table and returned her hand to her lap.

A man at a table farther in the room stood and staggered toward the door. As he passed, Jydryn stretched out his leg and bumped the man's heel as Jydryn focused his attention on Rose. He babbled to the child as the man stumbled.

The man's flailing arms pinwheeled to stop his fall. The back of one hand struck the side of Jydryn's face.

Jydryn tucked Rose under his chin and covered her with his hands.

Losing his balance, the drunk fell back onto their table. The table pitched under his weight and sent their pies flipping through the air. Their food landed with a crash near the bar as the man groaned and rubbed his head.

"Hank, ya drunk fool." The owner stormed out from around the bar with his fists clenched.

Jydryn passed Rose back to Keena as he stood, arresting the owner's advance. "It was an accident. I think our feet might have tangled when my daughter distracted me." He pulled another silver out of a hidden pouch under his belt. "Will this cover the replacement of the table and our meals?"

The owner crossed his arms and glared while the drunk struggled to his feet. "That's mighty kind of ya, stranger, to pay for your meal twice."

"Names Jy." He extended his other hand toward the owner. "I've traded in Arrowfall on numerous occasions. Seems best to always leave on good terms and assure another welcome next time. And it was in part my fault. I'm happy to pay for another meal and the trouble."

After another long moment, the owner accepted the coin and grasped Jydryn's forearm in a fearsome grip, "Baglen," the man said with a nod.

"I don't want to bother your maid, Baglen," Jydryn said as he watched the woman's frantic attempts to keep the inn's hounds away from the spilled food. "I'll follow you back to the bar and grab our replacements."

"'Fraid we're out of meat pies."

Jydryn shrugged. "We're too hungry to be picky."

Baglen kicked Hank in the romp as they all moved toward the door. Hank left as Baglen and Jydryn went into the kitchen.

Jydryn returned to their table a few minutes later with two new plates heaped with food. Keena had righted the table. He kept his eye on the barmaid.

"What was that about?" Keena whispered when he sat again.

"Thought I sensed something wrong with the pies." He tipped his head over his shoulder. "See the way she won't let the dogs lick up any of our meal?"

"You think someone poisoned it?"

"Smelled like it."

She stared at the slices of mutton and boar surrounded by a large potato and sliced carrots and peas.

He cut a slice of the meat and put it in his mouth. "This is fine. Baglen took a bite from the reaming hunk of boar after he cut our portions."

She considered him with one high arched brow. After he took a few more bites, she gave in and ate too. Rose snatched a carrot off Keena's plate and stuffed it into her mouth. Keena tried to fish it out.

He chuckled. "Let her chew on it. They're soft."

She glanced at the maid, who glared at her now. "Maybe you were right; we shouldn't have come."

He'd been thinking the same, but he wanted to reassure her, so he smiled. "You're not alive unless someone is trying to kill you."

"Are you serious?"

He had to laugh. Even he didn't believe that.

Keena's stomach churned with her need for food and her fear of being poisoned. At some point, her hunger overrode her anxiety. Their second dish tasted good, and she finished the entire meal.

She'd monitored the maid, who seemed to look at Rose anytime she could. At the moment, the woman stood behind her, taking the order of a man with fat legs, scarred arms, and a broad nose that hung over his unkept, dark beard.

"Keep yar hands to yarself, Cai. I ain't on the menu."

Cai's low voice rumbled in Keena's chest. "Don't be like that, lass."

"Stop!" the woman slammed into the back of Keena's chair, pushing her and Rose into the table and shoving the table into Jydryn.

He leapt out of the way and jerked the table aside to free her and Rose.

Keena stood and turned as she bounced a whimpering Rose.

Jydryn stomped toward the man.

"This ain't none of yer concern, mister," Cai stood, and while he was twice Jydryn's size, the man only came to the shifter's shoulder.

"When your bad manners cause injury to my family, it becomes my concern. Now, you can get your food and drink and eat in peace, or you can leave with your lechery to an establishment more suited for those pursuits."

"And what ifin I don't? Whatcha gonna do about it?"

"Cai!" Baglen called from behind the bar. "Behave or get out." The owner slapped the head of a large club in his palm twice.

Cai glanced at the woman, but Keena could only see her back. Cai lunged at Jydryn, wrapped his arms around the shifter's waist, and drove him to the floor.

Keena sat Rose in her chair and picked up a serving tray from a nearby table. She brought it high above her and crashed it into the back of Cai's round head.

The man groaned, and Jydryn shoved the dazed man off him.

Keena turned to grab Rose before she fell. But she wasn't in the chair any longer. In fact, she was nowhere around the table.

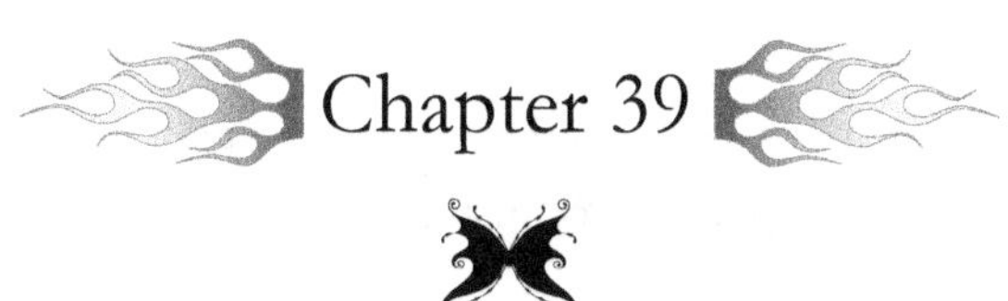

Chapter 39

Keena fought to draw breath into her lungs. Her heart lay still in her chest as she scanned the room for Rose.

Baglen stormed toward Cai and Jydryn, but over the owner's shoulder, Keena spotted the maid with the black braid hurrying toward the kitchen. A tiny foot poked out above her hip.

Rose shrieked.

"Stop!"

The woman jerked to a stop and struggled to move forward again.

Keena remembered Lilly and Jydryn talking about the ability to compel people to do what you wanted them to. If this was a magic she possessed, she needed it to work now. She raced across the room and stood in the woman's path before the maid could free herself.

Rose cried in her tight hold.

"Give me my daughter."

"I was just getting her some place safe," the woman said, but there was hatred in her eyes.

Rose tried to push away from the woman. When that didn't work, she cried louder and reached one hand for Keena.

With her arms outstretched to accept Rose, Keena focused every thought on making the woman do as she wanted. "Give her to me! Now!"

The barmaid thrust Rose toward Keena with a snarl.

Keena cradled Rose in her arms and moved back toward Jydryn.

He spun Keena, wrapped his arm around her waist, and led her toward the door. "We'll find lodging elsewhere for the night."

"There is no need—" Baglen called, but they were out the door before he could finish.

Jydryn found an inn closer to the market and paid for a room on the second floor near a rear exit. Once inside, he braced a chair under the handle.

Keena plopped on the edge of the bed and rocked Rose, who was still sniffling. "What is going on?"

"I'm not sure. I've never stayed in an inn before." He went to the window, looked out, and made sure he locked it before he closed the curtain. He grabbed the one lit candle and used it to bring four others to life.

A small warmer sat in the corner. Jydryn knelt in front of it and grabbed the coal bucket. Chunks of coal tumbled into the metal pan before he lit it too. At last he stilled and he sat beside her rubbing her back. After a few minutes, her tremors stopped.

"Is she asleep?"

Keena peeked at Rose and nodded.

"Why don't you lay her on the bed?" He helped her stand and drew back the sheet and blanket. After she covered Rose, he turned Keena and drew her into his arms.

"Cragholde was a filthy place, and people there didn't like me, but no one tried to poison me. And no one started fights in the taverns. I sneaked food from several. People behaved, or they weren't allowed back." She pulled from him and looked up into his pale blue eyes. "Could the fae have put a spell on these people to kill us on their behalf?"

"No, I don't think Nightshade thought of it—though he might in the future. There are towns who try to take advantage of strangers, assuming they will be easy marks." He drew her close again.

In Jydryn's embrace, her mind calmed, her heart rate slowed, and she drew in a deep breath. As long as they were together, he would keep her safe. Keena pressed her hand to his chest. "You said Rose should be asleep for us to …"

He chuckled. "Here?"

"You were the one who wanted to complete the binding as soon as possible." She felt the need now too. She needed the assurance they would always remain connected, no matter the dangers they faced.

He let her go and pushed his hands through his hair, smoothing it after his scuffle with Cai. "I've wanted to complete the rites with you since I first saw the Dragon Fire."

She perched her hands on her hips and one brow rose.

His smirk made her knees wobble. "Okay, so I didn't fully think about the rites until after we finished with Rose that night." He raked his hair again. "Rose was so hurt from the flames; her injuries became my only focus. But as soon as the treatments stopped, and there was nothing more to do for Rose, all I could think about was the Dragon Fire and my found mate."

Keena steered him back to the present. "What is involved in these rites?"

Jydryn pulled an extra blanket from a trunk in the corner. He left it folded and dropped it on the floor in the only open area of the room. He took her hand, adding their Dragon Fire to the light around them, and lowered to his knees on top of it.

She followed and knelt in front of him so that only a few hand spans separated them.

"The bonding ritual knits together two separate individuals so they are of one mind, and one soul, and…" He paused and considered her. His next words were husky. "… and one body."

She swallowed, nodded, and at last found her voice. "Are shifter and fae rites the same?"

He dropped back on his heels and his hands fell limp on his thighs. "I do not know. I assumed a mate bonding would be the same for everyone."

"A human marriage is different, I assume—as Rycharde and Nashala thought it important to do both."

"That's a good point." His shoulders slumped as he released a long, noisy breath. "Do you want to wait until we learn what their bonding consists of?"

She smiled, inched closer until their knees touched, gripped both his hands in hers. "I don't want to—I can't wait another moment."

His smile returned, and he rose on his knees again. He pulled his hands from hers and cradled her face as he brought her head forward until their foreheads touched. "You are my mate. The one I have waited to find since my first breath. The one who will share my thoughts, see my every secret, and know me in depth. Only our Creator will know me better."

He kissed the spot where their heads had touched. *Say those same words to me.*

He replaced his forehead against hers as she repeated his speech.

A hum filled her thoughts, followed by a growing pressure.

Don't fight me. Let me in and share your memories with me.

She released a long breath and closed her eyes. She let the hum grow and welcomed its already familiar presence.

You are my love. The one I will cherish until…

He jerked away from her, planted one foot on the floor, and braced his hands on his upturned knee.

Keena's head throbbed. Tears filled her eyes, but more from a profound loss than pain.

He leapt to his feet and snuffed out three candles. *Grab Rose and go to the window.*

Chapter 40

To not bind with your mate was bad and yet … to start it but not be able to finish it was worse. So much worse.

Jydryn had just opened his mind to Keena and her to him. He'd caught glimpses of her life on the streets as a child. Then his dragon had interrupted. Sounds from outside their room drowned out her precious memories.

A woman's voice leaked through the door. "Ya've got ta do it right this time, Cai. Kill him first while I grab the baby."

Cai's low voice stuttered. "Are ya sure this is where they got to?"

"They were easy to follow. Now get to it."

"They'll know it were us after what happened in the Toad." Cai mumbled.

"They'll be dead."

Cai tried again. "Baglen'll figure it out."

"As soon as I have that baby, we'll leave this town." There was a pause and only the creaking of the floorboards interrupted the silence. "If ya love me, ya'll get her for me."

Jydryn motioned Keena, who held Rose, toward the window he eased open. He pointed to a tree he'd noticed earlier growing over the city wall that ran along the back of the inn. *Can you get to the edge of the roof and have the tree help you down?* His thoughts passed even easier now— though the bonding was nowhere near complete.

She stared at him as the handle of their door rattled. *Even if I could, I can't hold Rose and skirt across the roof to reach it.* Her thoughts were loud and clear in his head.

The handle rattled more forcibly. "If ya're goin' ta make that much noise, ya might as well break it down," the barmaid hissed.

Jydryn whirled toward the bed and jerked the sheet free. He covered Rose where she lay asleep against Keena's chest and wrapped a new sling around her.

A loud bang rattled the door and shook the walls.

"Go!" Jydryn told her as he turned at the next thud against the door and the room filled with the cracking of wood.

Keena stepped out of the window onto the sloped roof and yelped as wood splintered behind her. She didn't dare look back. "Tree, can you help us get down?" she begged. This far above the earth, she wasn't sure the sprawling oak would respond.

The branch hanging over the wall lifted toward her and wrapped around her and Rose. Her feet dangled in the air as the tree lifted them off the roof.

Jydryn?

The flexible branch bent and twisted until it slipped through the narrow gap between the wall and the inn.

Her feet brushed the ground.

"Oh, praise be. There you are, child," a raspy ancient voice called out of the darkness.

The tree released them, as Keena stared through the inky black to find the person she almost imagined she'd heard.

"Where is he?" the voice asked.

Jydryn dropped beside her, and Keena covered her mouth to quiet her yelp.

"Good, good. Come," the voice called, followed by a shuffling sound.

Can you see anyone? Keena asked.

"It's an old woman," Jydryn whispered as his arm encircled her and led her through the dark. They wound between builds Keena suspected were homes but appeared little more than black blocks.

"Come, children." A door pushed open in one of the dark shapes in front of them, revealing the dim glow of a low fire.

Jydryn stopped Keena in the doorway of a tiny structure. It only had space for one narrow bed against the wall and a table with one chair. "What do you want with us?"

"The Father sent me to fetch you." The woman stepped out of the shadow into the light that flickered from the small stove in the corner. Her thin, white hair framed a wrinkled face. She stood hunched over. Each of her quaking hands gripped a short stick that kept her from toppling.

"The Father?" Jydryn still hadn't moved from the doorway.

"May the Lord bless thee and keep thee …" The old woman dropped to the chair with a huff.

"The Lord make His face to shine upon thee …" Jydryn continued the passage of the ancient blessing he had taught Keena before Rose arrived.

"And be gracious unto you?" Keena added with less confidence that she remembered all the right words.

"Yes, child." The old woman smiled. "The Lord lift His countenance upon thee …"

"And give thee peace." Jydryn eased them into the room and closed the door.

"Now, dear, you and the babe take the bed. Use the old towel to change her." The woman's gnarled finger pointed to the narrow, raised pallet against the wall and to the towel folded at the foot. "But you, child," she pointed at Jydryn, "must lie there." The direction of her knobby finger shifted and pointed to a tattered blanket on the floor near the stove. "You two have not wed, so it is the only proper thing to do." She crossed her arms on the table and lowered her head to lay it on top.

Keena looked at Jydryn, who just shrugged. "We can't take your bed, ma'am. I've slept on the floor and in the dirt and don't mind."

"But I do, child. You are as tired as the babe. There is a long journey ahead of you. Best get sleep whilst you can."

"I don't feel right about displacing you. I don't even know your name." Keena again looked at Jydryn.

"I'm Annabelle. Now, sleep. The sun will be up soon and you have to find your father, child."

"How…?"

Annabelle sighed a long breath, and Keena almost feared it had been her last until a rattled snore escaped.

How did she know all that? That we would be out there, not being married, and that I'm looking for my father?

Jydryn shrugged again and moved to the blanket. *God speaks in intelligible words to some.*

She looked at the bed and slipped the sling off her shoulders to free Rose. She changed her nappy, then laid the child next to the wall while Keena lay on her side on the edge to protect Rose from a fall. *Do you trust her?*

There is a familiar peace here. I think we'll be safer here than at the inn.

Annabelle released a stuttered snore. "Children, it's time to sleep now."

There's no way she can hear us, right?

No.

Chapter 41

A knock jerked Jydryn out of sleep.

"Sister Annabelle? It's Brother Isaac. I came as you requested."

The door pushed open as Jydryn scrambled to his feet. He squinted against the morning light spilling in as the robed holy man entered.

"Who are you?" Brother Isaac asked.

Keena sat up and pulled Rose into her arms.

"Who are all of you?"

"Stop fussing, brother," Annabelle said. Her voice was even weaker today. She didn't lift her head. "He sent them. You are to marry them before they continue their journey."

"All right." Isaac moved into the room, lit two fat candles, and came to Annabelle's side. "But first I'm going to get you back in bed." He raised a chin toward Jydryn who leapt forward to help ease the old woman onto the pallet Keena and Rose left.

Jydryn moved to Keena's side as she straightened from changing Rose again. He pulled the bottle from his shirt and Rose took it with a smile.

Brother Isaac stepped beside them. He was about as tall as Jydryn. He'd shaved the center of his scalp while a ring of his light brown hair hung about the length of a finger.

Jydryn rubbed his nose at the smell of incense emanating from Isaac's robe. "You marry any couple she tells you to?"

"Sister Annabelle is a faithful follower of the Lord. In all the years I've known her, she has never said anything apart from His ordained will.

Most in my parish believe her to be a prophetess."

"Prophetess?" Keena whispered.

Jydryn glanced at here with a nod."One whom God speaks to with messages for His people."

"So yes," The priest nodded as his gaze held Jydryn's in a serious—while not unwelcoming—stare. "If she says I should speak the rites of holy union over you, I'm happy to do it." His gaze lingered on Rose for a moment. "It seems you need to formalize your partnership as you already have a child together."

Keena's cheeks pinked. "She is not our blood, sir. Her people placed her on a fiery altar as a sacrifice and Jy—" That was the name Jydryn had given her in the beginning and the tavern owner yesterday. "Jy saved her." Keena raised the child's long dress, exposing Rose's scars to the man.

Isaac gasped and placed one hand on Rose's head and the other on Jydryn's shoulder. He tipped his head back and lifted his face toward the ceiling. "Holy Father, we thank You for sparing this precious life. May she grow to know and serve You. And I thank You for this man, Jy, who was Your hands in rescuing this life. Will You bestow on him mighty blessings for doing this great deed? Walk beside him and guide him in Your will in the days and years to come. We give You the glory for the days ahead in these lives. In the name of the Christ, amen."

"Amen," Jydryn and Keena said as one.

"Well, let us make this family official. Why don't you place the babe next to Sister Annabelle, child, and we can begin?"

When Keena returned to Jydryn's side, the monk instructed them to kneel.

Keena slipped to her knees beside Jydryn. *Is this all right with you?*

Jydryn offered her a small shrug as his attention focused on Brother

Isaac. *Your parents did both—a marriage and the rituals of bonding.*

"Now, Jy, are you a follower of the Most High?" Brother Isaac's hands unclasped and one pointed toward Jydryn.

"Aye. From my youth, I have chosen God's will and His lordship over my life. I still continue to study the ancient text of His Word."

"Very good. It is a pleasure to meet you, brother." The man turned his large-eyed gaze to Keena. "And what of you, child? What is your name?"

She paused for a moment.

"Tell him all, child." Annabelle's croaked whisper sounded pained.

"Jy gave me the name Keena when he rescued me from a similar fate as Rose's a few months ago. My parents gave me the name Arlayna."

Isaac smiled and rocked back on his heels. "Both are powerful names. So, tell me, Arlayna-Keena, are you also a follower of the Most High?"

"Jydryn has been teaching me. And I have seen God working in our lives. Yesterday afternoon, I told Him I would follow Him."

Isaac stood rigid as his eyes widened. He glanced from her to Jydryn and back. "Yesterday?"

She looked at Jydryn, who grinned. "Yes."

Isaac flapped his arms. "Yesterday? Has anyone heard your confession? Have you completed the sacraments?"

Keena turned to Jydryn again with a raised brow.

Jydryn's hand rested on her back and he answered. "As her belief in God, and her willingness to follow His will, was only expressed less than a day ago, Keena has yet to be baptized or take the holy bread."

Isaac left them kneeling on the floor and took a pitcher from the corner. "Do you confess your sins?"

"Sins?" Keena remembered the word from one of Jydryn's lessons.

Isaac nodded as he approached her with the pitcher. "Those actions against God's law?" Isaac bowed his head over the pitcher and mumbled words she couldn't understand.

"I have stolen many times. Almost always it was food so I wouldn't starve. On a few occasions, I stole items I sold so I could buy food. I only ever wanted to eat."

Isaac raised the pitcher over her head. "Yes, and while I understand the need, you understand the sin, correct?"

Keena shrugged. "It was as wrong as leaving a child on the street to starve."

The man pinched his lips together. He sighed. "Do you renounce your thieving ways?"

"I do not need to steal now. Jy makes sure we are both well cared for."

The pitcher hovered above her. "Have you chosen the Christ and accepted His payment for your sins?"

"Yes." Keena watched the pitcher as it tipped preparing to release its contents on her.

Isaac paused. When one decides to follow God, they are baptized to show their old life is dead and they have new life in His Son. As we have no pond nearby, I will wash you in water as a symbol of this choice and bless you, all right?"

It is a rite, like the bonding ceremony.

"Yes."

Brother Isaac straightened again and drew in a deep breath. "Do you turn your back on your former life and choose to walk in God's will going forward?"

"Yes," Keena said.

"Brother Isaac, the time is short. The marriage," Annabelle gasped.

"It's not even a proper baptism of submersion. I hate to rush it." Water poured on her head, ran into her eyes, and over her ears. It tickled as it slid under her collar. "I baptize you in the name of the Father, and the Son, and the Holy Spirit. You are buried with Him and risen again a new creation." His thumb traced a long line down her forehead that he crossed with another brush of his thumb. "The Lord—"

"Marriage," Annabelle sputtered.

"Very well." Isaac set the empty pitcher on the table as Keena wiped water from her eyes. "Will you, Jy, take this woman, forsaking all others, to care for, love, honor and protect her, in health or ill, in poverty or wealth, until death does part you?"

Jydryn looked at her. "I will."

"And will you, Arlayna-Keena, take this man, forsaking all others, to care for, love, and honor, and obey him, in health or ill, in poverty or wealth, until death does part you?"

"I will."

"Then, in the eyes of the God we serve, I pronounce you husband and wife. Go forth and multiply." Isaac nodded and turned to Annabelle as if seeking her approval.

"Come," the old woman whispered. "He has a message for both of you."

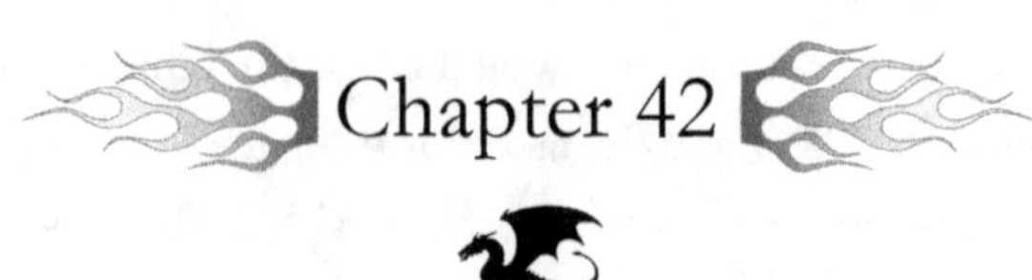

Chapter 42

Jydryn rose to his feet and extended his hand to his bride. According to human law, they were joined. But by shifter tradition, their bonding was incomplete.

Keena rocked back on her heels and extended her hand up. At the last moment, she gripped his wrist, covered by his sleeve. Smart woman. He'd forgotten. Another reason to complete the binding. When they completed the rites, their Dragon Fire would only appear if they wished it. Until then, it would mark them as belonging to each other for all to see.

"Come, Jydryn." Gasps of breath broke up Annabelle's creaky words.

Keena glanced at him. He'd caught it too. The old woman had called him by his full name.

He knelt beside the bed and looked into her clouded eyes.

"You are to train … the little one … in the ways of the Lord. He had you spare her … for a special calling. One day …He will speak to her … as He has spoken to me." A smile parted her pale, cracked lips. "He promised me … I would not see His face … until I saw the one to follow me. Guard her well, dragon. Safeguard them both … for as God is your anchor and source … they will learn from you by your example."

Annabelle's gaze shifted to Keena as Jydryn reeled from Annabelle's revelation. It humbled him to be called to train Rose in the ways of the Lord.

Keena moved closer to Annabelle to hear better as Jydryn staggered a step away. Her gazed locked on Keena.

"And you, dear … He has a message for you as well." She spoke her next words in a strong, commanding voice, nothing like the old woman's. "Be strong and of a good courage, fear not, nor be afraid of them: for the LORD thy God, he that doth go with thee; he will not fail thee, nor forsake thee."

Keena gasped as her hand rested on her throat.

Annabelle relaxed, and her breaths grew shallow. "You are to remember this … in the hard days to come. Difficult times … do not necessarily mean … you are out of His will. He loves you so, child. All three of you. But He especially … wants you to believe, Keena. He loves you now; always has … and always will. He never left you … nor will He abandon you … in the future. What He calls you to … will be hard … but trust in Him … and you will not fail."

Annabelle's eyes opened wide and glowed. "Oh, so much love." Tears slid from her eyes back into her hair. "Love that has no limits," she whispered. The light dimmed, but not her smile. Breath staggered out of her until her chest stilled.

"Lord, accept Your faithful servant into Your loving embrace," Brother Isaac said behind Keena.

She startled at his voice.

Isaac pulled open the door. "I must prepare her body for burial and inform the flock of her passing. The Lord has His own purposes for you three. I bid you safe journey and I hope to see you again one day. Godspeed."

Jydryn scooped up Rose, tucked the bottle back inside his shirt, and wrapped his arm around Keena's waist. He turned her toward the door.

Her feet moved, but it wasn't until he stopped that she noted where they were—on the edge of the market. Keena noted the blur of movement her mind couldn't comprehend.

"We should …" Jydryn's words trailed off.

She struggled to focus. "Has anything like that ever happened before?"

He shook his head. "I've known God was with me my entire life. At times, I've felt Him quite near. But *nothing* like that."

Keena slid her arm in his and rested her weight against him. She allowed her head to fall to his shoulder. "We need to remember it always—especially in the hard times to come, like Annabelle said."

He kissed the top of her head. "We will remind each other of His promises whenever either of us forgets."

Rose reached for her. Keena straightened, took her, and held her at arm's length. "One who will hear God's voice. You are extraordinarily special, my sweet girl."

With excitement, Rose's arms and legs bumped against Keena.

"She looks like she's dancing," Jydryn said with a chuckle.

"I feel like joining her." Keena tucked Rose back into the sling Jydryn had fashioned for her from the bedsheet.

Jydryn sighed as his hand rested on Keena's back. "Lord, we thank You and praise Your name. Guide our steps in this coming journey and prepare the way for us."

"Fill us with Your strength and wisdom," Keena added.

"Amen." He glanced at them with a full smile. "Come on. Let's get the items we need for our journey and be on our way."

They stepped out of the shadow of an alley and joined the busy market. Moving from booth to booth, they found everything they needed, including shoes for Keena.

Jydryn pointed. "There is a tanner on the far side of the square I wish to speak to."

"There is an apple vendor and a baker here," Keena pointed in the direction they'd been heading.

Jydryn hesitated for a moment. He looked from the tanner to the apple vendor and back. At last, he drew three silver coins from his belt and dropped them into Keena's waiting palm. "This should be *more* than enough. I won't be far, but keep your eyes open."

Keena nodded and turned to select five large yellow orbs from the pile on the apple vendor's table.

"Here ya are, ma'am." The older woman passed her a bag with the apples.

"Thank you." Keena handed her a coin and waited for the change. She glanced back in the direction where Jydryn had gone and found him speaking to a beautiful young woman. She was shapely, with hair so fair it looked to be a source of light in the midday sun. They stood close, with their heads bent in conversation.

Seeing Jydryn—her husband—being so familiar with another woman should have sparked something in her, but they had started their bonding already. Keena could sense his feelings for this other woman as though they were her own. Jydryn did not love the stranger, and wasn't drawn to her. But they had met before.

A foggy image filtered through Keena's thoughts. The blond woman stood tied to a stake. Long dragon fingers reached out, encircled her, and pulled her into the sky.

Keena smiled and turned to see what the baker might have to offer.

A wide shadow darkened her path, and fear crawled up her spine.

Chapter 43

Jydryn!

Keena's cry flooded his thoughts, and he whirled from the tanner he had just started speaking to.

Her arms hugged tight around Rose as she leapt out of the way. Jydryn's feet pounded over the cobblestones between them. He fought to keep his dragon contained as Keena stumbled backward. A flash of light bounced off metal. A dagger thrust at his mate!

People bumped into him as they fled from a wild man attacking a strange woman and her child. No one stood in her defense.

"Guard!" Jydryn bellowed as a tall man knocked him off balance and stopped his charge. He let three more people rush past him as he placed his finger between his lips and released a sharp whistle.

Women yelped, and children covered their ears.

With his way at last clear, he came up behind the large, short man. "Cai!"

Be careful, Keena warned. *I think he poisoned the blade.*

Jydryn pulled up short as she dodged another awkward lunge. In truth, Cai swayed on his feet far more than Keena did. He made wild thrusts and slashes. *How—?*

She pointed to a bleeding chicken in a small cage on one of the vendor's tables. It was convulsing in the throes of death.

Jydryn freed the blanket draped over the bag on his hip and wrapped it around his forearm. He kicked Cai in the back of the knee. The large man spun as he stumbled. Only one knee hit the ground before he stood and charged at Jydryn.

"I jusss wantsss the babe." Cai lumbered forward. His eyes were red and his speech slurred.

"What is the cause of this disturbance?" Four city guards in black leather armor stomped toward them.

"Be careful," Keena said as she clutched Rose and worked her way behind a table covered in baskets.

"Who are you telling to be careful, woman?" The lead guard had a deep, puckered scar under his left eye.

"You," Jydryn answered as he blocked another blow with his covered arm. "This lunatic has a poisoned blade."

"Cai, what are ya doin'?" A blond guard stepped between the leader and Cai.

"Ssshe wantsss the kid. Sssays ssshe'll kill me in my ssleep ifin I don't get her."

The leader crossed his arms, took a wide stance, and huffed, "Who said this? And what kid are you talking about?"

Cai staggered. The tip of his deadly blade swung from pointing at Jydryn to Rose.

The blonde spoke to the lead guard but monitored Cai with a hand on the hilt of the sword at his hip. "This man keeps company with the barmaid of the Tipsy Toad."

"Willuma wantsss herssself a kid." Cai's hand lowered as his wobbling grew. "Af'er two yearsss, ssshe won't let me bed her no more till ssshe hasss one." The dagger slid from his grasp, and Cai dropped to his knees. "Just the kid …" His words turned into incoherent mumblings as he dropped back to sit on his heels.

"Secure him," the leader ordered.

It took all three guards to pin the man to the ground and get irons around his wrists and ankles.

The leader turned his gaze to Jydryn as he coaxed Keena out from behind the booth. "She is your child, correct?"

"Of course she is, Captain Vince," Brother Isaac strolled up from behind the captain. His hands rested inside his sleeves and his hood was up. "Sister Annabelle's departing request was for me to bless this family."

Captain Vince swiveled to look at the monk. "Departing?"

"Aye. She drew her last breath and met with her Lord only an hour ago."

As the captain's gaze returned in his direction, Jydryn wrapped a protective arm around Keena. "We only stopped for a meal and a place to rest last night. We have a couple more things to purchase, then we plan to leave your fine city, captain."

Captain Vince sighed, and his arms dropped. "Sorry for the trouble, folks. We'll deal with Cai and his woman, Willuma." He gave a curt nod and spun on his heel. "Take the drunk to the dungeon and find his woman."

The guards hauled Cai to his feet and dragged him away.

"Are you all right?" Brother Isaac whispered as he neared them.

Jydryn looked to Keena. She nodded. "He was so drunk, he could have killed us both instead of just me."

Jydryn turned his attention to Rose. Her eyes were red and swollen, her cheeks wet, and her breathing stuttered. Her little hand wiggled out of the sling and reached for him as her fingers opened and closed.

As he reached for Rose, Keena slid the wrap off her shoulders, freeing the baby. Rose wrapped her arms around his neck and buried her damp face against his skin. He rubbed her back as he soothed her with soft words. "You're all right, my precious girl."

"Indeed," Brother Isaac said. His robe twirled as he turned away. "The Lord has plans for you. No misguided drunk will stand in His way."

As the monk left, the vendors and shoppers returned. Keena's hand shook as she paid for three loaves of bread and put them in the bag Jydryn carried. She folded the blanket but left it over her arms as though it were a shield.

"He's right, you know." Jydryn led her back toward the tanner. "If God is for us, who can be against us?"

"It seems like everyone," she muttered.

"Be strong and courageous," he said with a smile.

She drew in a deep breath, squared her shoulders, and released it with a nod.

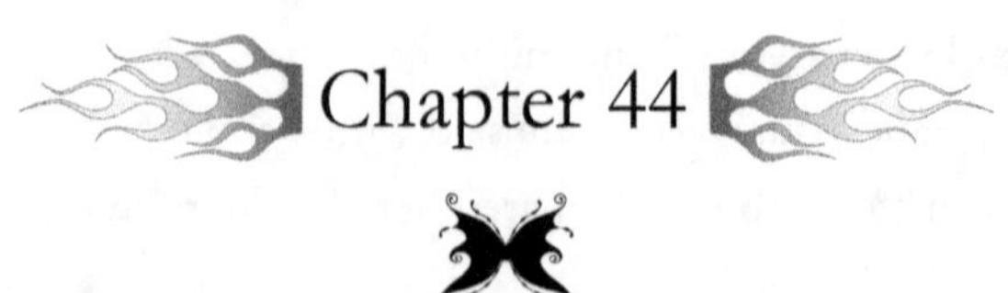

Chapter 44

"What are we doing?" Keena gritted her teeth as she hitched the smaller bag of their purchases up onto her shoulder before it slid off again.

"Looking for your father," Jydryn said with a smirk. He had a pack on his back made with two wide leather straps attached to a long pouch that carried Rose.

Rose faced him, swinging her legs at his sides and pulling on his hair when it blew in her face.

"Jydryn, we are in the middle of nowhere. We will find my father in a town. Cragholde, to be exact. And out here in the open, aren't the fae more likely to find us?"

He grumbled. "I've told you already, you are never to return there." He ignored her fear about the fae.

She scanned their surroundings and set her unease aside as she countered his order. "But I know I have seen him there. We're nowhere near Cragholde or any of the towns I've lived in where I've seen him."

His steps slowed, and he turned his head to look at her. "You know who we're looking for?"

"When Lilly said it would be someone I'd seen often and who stared at me, I knew."

"Merchants always travel a circuit of towns. Share with me what he looks like—"

Keena's skin tickled and goosebumps covered it as if an icy breeze buffeted her. She stopped. "Give me Rose."

"What?" Jydryn walked three more steps before he turned back to her.

She searched their surroundings. The trees to the left of the road bent in an unnatural manner. The grass in the meadow on the right side flattened. She fought to catch her breath. "Give me Rose and shift now."

Nightshade and six other fae charged out of the forest on the far side of the meadow and sped toward them with remarkable speed.

She stepped out of her shoes.

Four more fae approached them from behind.

Tree branches swung down, taking fae off their feet. Vines wrapped around them and jerked them into the air. The fae recovered, freed themselves, and resumed their approach.

Rocks and jagged branches hurtled at her. Keena raised her arm as a useless shield. When nothing hit her, she peeked over her arm. The natural weapons had impaled a wall of leaves in front of her. She dared a glance at her family.

Jydryn stood two steps behind her and to her left. A wild vine sprang up to cover him and Rose, but leaves tore off and the vine ripped away as fast as it grew. Keena couldn't tell if she had created a protective vine to shield them, and the fae were tearing it down, or if the fae were attacking them and Keena's magic was shredding it.

Jydryn looked as unsure as she was, but he swiveled to keep his gaze on those approaching from either side.

She turned her attention back to Nightshade as Rose giggled. Nature flew in chaotic waves around them. The earth heaved and holes opened below a few of the attackers. Branches, vines, leaves, and flower petals hurtled through the air.

Keena quaked. There were too many. With Rose strapped to his back, Jydryn couldn't shift without fear of her tumbling to the ground. Keena's breaths came in harsh gasps as she tried to think of a way to secure Nightshade.

The green-haired fae swore and shouted as he fought against the attacks that kept him several feet away. Leaves covered his mouth, preventing him from speaking any spells.

Still, each fae inched closer. In only a few moments, they would reach her family. She couldn't stop them.

Keena dropped to her knees, weakened by the effort of the magic flowing from her and the fear consuming her. As she dropped, air caught under her skirt. She landed with her bare shins touching the hard-packed dirt of the road, which strengthened the power she drew from the earth. The attacking fae lost a little ground. Still, it wasn't enough.

"God, I can't save us," she groaned in a gasped whisper.

"Do not fear them." The voice who had spoken through Annabelle filled her and she drew in a deep breath from its power. "I am with you."

She glanced back toward Jydryn and Rose. The fae with the orange hair, who had helped bring her to the queen but warned Nightshade not to hurt her, stood behind Jydryn. His gaze met hers and he nodded. What did that mean?

Jydryn, can you move?

I think so. Even his thought sounded strained.

Get behind me. Keena's hands rested palms up on her thighs as she watched the chaos around her with less fear.

Jydryn shuffled closer as the attack of the fae in front of them increased. It was almost impossible to see with all the debris flying in the air.

Get close enough to touch me, and brace yourself.

Jydryn's legs rested against her back, and he leaned forward over her while the vine still grew and tore around him.

Keena slammed her hands together with a crack. A wave of magic burst from the sound and the fae hurtled through the air, away from her. The surrounding air cleared as the debris went with them. Branches snapped off the nearest trees; a couple lost their tops as they bent back from the explosive energy.

Before Nightshade landed, Keena reached out her hand. A vine shot up from the ground and spiraled from his feet upward around his entire body. The vine stem wrapped around his neck as leaves covered his mouth and eyes. "Swear, with a royal oath, you will never attack and kill my fam—"

Nightshade squirmed and disappeared in a puff of black smoke. The six fae who had followed him across the now grassless field watched the empty vine drop and return to the earth. They stared, turned, and fled back into the trees.

Keena dropped forward on her hands as weakness battered her entire body.

The orange-haired fae and the other three with him stood. They brushed themselves off and came to drop to one knee before her. "Princess."

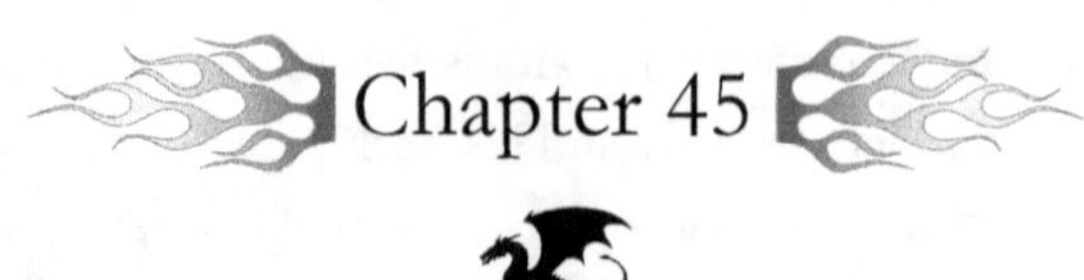

Chapter 45

Jydryn released a long breath. Rose still had a large leaf in her hand. It was the only evidence of the plant that had swirled around them. She waved it in the air in her clumsy toddler way. *Thank You, Lord. She did not know the danger she was in.*

He could sense the cost Keena had paid in the battle. Still kneeling on the ground, she lumbered back to sit on her heels, but she leaned against his legs for support.

Four remaining fae knelt before her. He recognized the orange-haired one from Keena's memories Jydryn had seen when they started their bonding.

"I, Echo of the queen's guard, swear a royal oath. I will never by will, action, thought, or spell do anything to harm Queen Nashala, Princess Arlayna, her dragon mate, or any of her children by blood or choice, alive or yet to come. And I will do all in my power to protect them." So, this was the mate Lilly mentioned; Petal's father. The one who had searched for Keena. Echo proved his loyalty to Keena's family yet again.

The other three fae, Dusk, Badger, and the female warrior, Amethyst, repeated the royal oath. When all had said the words, they pulled daggers from their belts, sliced a finger, and let a small stream of blood hit the ground. The wave of the oath magic washed over all of them and Rose giggled.

Echo stood, and Jydryn pulled Keena to her feet as the others rose. Dusk, Badger, and Amethyst spread out and faced the trees. The grass returned, they anchored listing trees back into the ground, flowers sprouted up, and holes filled in.

As they erased any evidence of the battle, Echo stepped closer to Keena. As she leaned much of her weight against Jydryn, he could feel her tense, even after the fae had sworn to do her no harm.

Echo's gaze rose and met his. "May I have permission to connect with your mate?"

Jydryn nodded.

Keena must have looked confused, because Echo smirked. "It is unwise to come between a dragon and his mate if one wants to keep breathing for long."

Keena found her balance and enough strength to stand on her own. Jydryn took a step from her to allow them to speak.

Echo focused on Keena and bowed his head in greeting. He raised his hands toward her. "Princess, I want to share with you the lessons all fae children learn to control their magic."

"Fae children can use magic?" Keena's head tipped.

Echo lowered his hands and smiled. "We are always aware of our connection to the earth. Nature speaks to us. But it is not until we reach the awakening, what the humans call puberty, that we can learn to command nature to do our bidding."

"How was that snake, Nightshade, able to vanish without the use of his eyes or voice?" Jydryn broke in.

Echo took a step back and brushed his hair over his shoulder with a grunt. "Long ago, the fae divided into two kingdoms. The light fae worked *with* nature and did little harm to it or others. The dark fae, ruled by the king's sister, sapped all energy *from* nature, killing it to strengthen their magic. They did great harm. A battle between the light and dark took place in the time of your three-times-great-grandfather, Princess. The light fae were victorious. The king imprisoned his sister in a doorless chamber in a tower of cut stone perched high in the air. It had no window or any entry point. The only magic allowed her was the ability to create food. Years later, she died there."

Echo glanced at the work of the other fae for a moment. "The king sent light fae soldiers out to destroy all writings containing information about dark magic. They killed those who refused to stop using it. But they spared those who agreed to renounce their dark ways. The king removed all memories of the time of dark fae." He turned to Keena. "Unlike what Nightshade did to your father in erasing all of his former life, King Zephyr only removed those memories containing the dark magic and their time with the dark fae."

"You think Nightshade has somehow uncovered how to wield the dark magic again?" Jydryn said.

"We do."

"How will I be able to fight dark magic when I don't know how to control the light magic?" Keena's voice cracked.

Echo met her gaze. "Your magic is powerful, Princess, almost as powerful as your mother's—which has come as a great shock to Nightshade. You may have inherited all of her power, or what you received is enhanced by your connection to your dragon."

Keena shook her head. "But I have no idea how I am doing anything."

Echo smiled. "In truth, I don't know how much you are doing with conscious thought." He raised his hands to the surrounding foliage. "When you renewed the life of Shimmerbourne, nature was grateful. It watches over you and fights to protect you, even against those who try to use it to harm you. But what I wish to share with you will help."

Echo glanced at Jydryn with a raised brow.

Jydryn nodded his consent yet again. This man meant his mate no harm. He was trying to help. But he could also feel the strain in Keena after all that had happened in the last few days. "Be quick."

Echo focused on Keena again. "Much like a mated bonding which connects two minds, I'm going to share this knowledge with you mind-to-mind."

"Is a fae bonding ceremony and a shifter one the same?" Keena said through a yawn she couldn't suppress.

Echo paused for a moment as his head tipped. "I'm not sure." He shrugged. "I'll share our rites with you as well, then you can compare the two yourself."

Jydryn noted Keena's hooded eyes as she gave Echo a small lift of her chin.

Echo raised his hands so his palms faced Keena. She brought up her arms as well and placed her palms against his. "I'm going to share it all with you, but it will open in your mind a little at a time as you need it so as not to overwhelm you."

Keena nodded again.

Echo whispered a fae spell and Keena's eyes opened wide. They stared at one another in prolonged silence.

Jydryn could sense the pressure and buzz in Keena's thoughts.

At last, the fae released a long breath and broke their connection.

Keena swayed and Jydryn stepped forward to wrap his arm around her waist. She leaned against him, devoid of strength.

"Dragon, you need to take her far from here. I recommend a human settlement. Nightshade abhors to enter one."

Keena tipped her head up to look at Jydryn. Her concern about remaining out in the open flashed from her thoughts to his, but she was too tired to say or even think, 'I told you so'.

Echo glanced at the others who were finishing their repairs. "We will return to Nightshade and tell him we stayed to continue to fight, but you broke free and shifted. We followed as best we could, but it appears you headed toward Crystalbrooke."

"Hmm?" Keena was too tired for words, but even Jydryn hadn't heard the name before.

Amethyst returned to stand behind Echo. "It is a small hamlet far to the south, in what remains of the emperor's capital city. A group of sequestered fae, humans, and even shifters live there hoping to learn the signs that will foretell the emperor's—"

"Empress'," Dusk interrupted with a wink at her and joined them.

Amethyst narrowed a harsh glare on the blue-haired fae. "They search for signs of the return of the supreme ruler, or how *to* recognize him, or her, once they claim the imperial throne."

"Regardless," Echo said with a wave of his hand to the others, "Nightshade would believe you might take her to such a remote place for both safety and to confirm she is the empress we have long waited for."

"Thank you." Jydryn almost resented thanking any fae, but they had helped to save Keena and Rose, as well as a shifter like him.

The four fae bowed. "It is an honor to serve our princess and her family." They turned as a military unit and vanished into the darkness of the tree cover.

Once again alone on the road, it looked as though nothing had disturbed the natural order of things.

Keena stumbled to the closest tree. "I'm sorry," she mumbled.

The trees looked to bow to her like the fae had. She turned back to him with a sigh.

Jydryn slid Rose off his back. "Can you hold her?"

Keena gave a weak nod, as he pulled the supply bag off and sat it at her feet. He stuffed in her shoes, his boots and clothes, and shifted.

Rose squealed, and Keena winced at the sound.

Can you climb or do you need help?

She drew in a deep breath, looped the heavy bag on her shoulder, and lifted her hem. It took a long time as she slipped more than once, but at last she dropped between his wings, and then he leapt into the air. He glanced behind him and smiled. Once again, his beloved had sealed them to his back with a bubble of Dragon Fire.

Jydryn climbed to an air current and headed toward home.

Chapter 46

Jydryn woke in his cave. A chill covered his skin. The fire was out. The only actual light in the room came from the sun leaking through the opening to the entrance. Keena and Rose weren't in the chamber with him. A glance at the entrance proved they weren't there either. The pack he'd purchased to carry Rose was gone and the smaller bag with several supplies was also missing.

Keena?

Jydryn.

Where are you?

She didn't speak into his thoughts, but an image filled his mind of a well-worn, rutted road leading to a city gate in the distance. Cragholde, by the look of it. How had she gotten down the ridge so fast?

Keena!

Jydryn!

Oh, that woman was going to send him to glory far too soon. There was nowhere for his dragon on the narrow road between her and the town. He jerked on his boots, shimmied around the rocks blocking the path, and careened down the hillside.

Jydryn thanked the Lord for his dragon reflexes, even while in his human skin. Otherwise, he would have broken his neck in his wild race down the ridge. As the city gate came into view, he had to force himself to slow. A wild man charging the city's fortifications would raise alarms.

After Keena had showed him the picture of her whereabouts, she'd refused to communicate with him other than to provide him a general sense of her well-being.

His hands fisted and opened in a frantic rhythm at his sides as the echo of his pounding steps matched his thumping heart.

When he neared enough to see past the gate into the town, he spotted a familiar light blue dress with something dark covering the back. Rose's waving arms proved he had his family in sight. They weren't more than a dragon's length inside the walls. Keena crept down the center of the lane. Rose could have crawled faster. It was obvious she waited for him to catch up—but she'd entered the town so he wouldn't stop her.

Jydryn nodded at the guards at the gate. They were pale and gaunt. The color of their surcoats over their mail was unrecognizable. The stench of the bleak city assaulted his nose.

Keena sensed Jydryn's approach. His frantic attempts to speak to her mind and get her to stop or wait had left a dull ache in her skull. But she believed in her heart that she had to be inside Cragholde to find her father. She just couldn't figure out how to convince him.

As she progressed along the street, Keena recognized almost every face. Other than to acknowledge her presence, with curt nods or wide-eyed glances, no one seemed to recognize her as the most recent woman they'd run out of town to give to the dragon.

Rose babbled on her back. Keena found the pack more comfortable for both of them than the tight sling.

Jydryn came alongside her, snatched her elbow, and pulled her to a halt. "What do you think you're doing?" He released his words with a dragon hiss.

Instead of answering him, she jerked him behind her as the contents of a privy bucket poured out on the stone near where he'd stood.

The retched odor she accepted as part of this village made him wrinkle his nose and gag. "We're leaving."

Keena released a little of her power and rooted herself to the ground as though she were a tree. Even his dragon strength couldn't make her budge until she wished it. When he released her with a huff, she offered him a serene smile and turned back to continue down the street.

He moved to her other side. Rose reached for him. *I wanted to complete the bonding rites. You were so tired I thought it best to let you sleep, only to wake and find you gone.*

This is where I need to be. She stopped for a moment. "You're right. We should have finished, but like when you were captured, I felt compelled to leave. I'm sorry." She continued down the lane again. *There is a place.*

He held her elbow again and tried to stop her. *Someone is going to recognize you.*

No one has yet. She glanced at him. *I kept to the shadows here. My hair was filthy—remember? Now, I am clean, several pounds heavier from the meals you have provided. I carry a ten-month-old child on my back when I showed no signs of being with child when you came for me two months ago."* Her hand brushed up his arm. *"And I have a handsome husband at my side. No one will ever think of me as the waif they ran from this city into your arms.*

Jydryn stopped as Keena strolled forward. Human waste caked the bottom few inches of every building. Everyone who passed him looked as ill as the guards at the gate. Some had open sores. Their garments were gray, tattered rags. While the path down the middle was dark, the stained outer edges of the street were slimy with excrement—whether human or animal was impossible to tell.

He followed Keena and watched a woman washing her clothes inside of the well's bucket. When she'd worked the lye concoction, stinging his nose, to a lather, she lowered the entire bucket. No wonder they all looked so unhealthy if they drank from their wash water.

Another bell jingled, and he hastened away from the revolting dumping of another bucket of waste. A few moments later, they passed another well where a woman washed dishes as the first woman had. He pulled Keena to a stop as the market square opened between several buildings ahead of them. "Keena, I know what is making all these people sick."

She eyed him with a raised brow. A calmness came from her, as if the filth and evil around them weren't touching her. When had she become so confident and strong?

Rose jostled and fussed as she reached for him again with a squeak.

He pulled her out of the carrier and rested Rose against his chest. She wrapped her arms around his neck.

Keena smiled. "What were you saying about these people being ill?"

Jydryn tossed his head. He'd forgotten what he'd been about to say. He wrapped his arm around Keena's waist and turned her in a full circle, pointing out the disgusting habits of the citizens of Cragholde.

"This is why they are ill? So it wasn't me," she said with a long sigh.

He shook his head. "Never. They have done this to themselves. Now, can we leave before their dangerous habits infect us as well?"

Keena turned toward the market, but in a few more steps, her shoulders slumped. The vendors had already left for the day. She sighed, turned to her left, and slipped between two buildings. While the ground floors were small enough to create dark alleys between the shops, the homes occupying the floor above were larger until they almost touched the homes on either side.

He had no choice but to follow his wife through the twisting alleys as they crossed street after street. She paused in one larger lane and pointed to a building a few steps away. On the placard was a carving of a blue dragon crawling up it.

"This tavern is called The Sapphire Dragon." She winked at him. "Though most here just call it The Dragon. They serve a decent stew in a round of hollowed-out hard bread. If the customer doesn't eat all the bread and it isn't whole enough to reuse, they throw it out. It was one of the primary ways I stayed alive." A sweet hum came from deep within her. "It appears a dragon has always looked out for me."

She crossed the street and headed down another alley. At last, they came to a tiny listing shack next to the city wall. Unlike most of the places they had passed, it was only one story and had nothing to lean against for support.

As Keena reached for the latch, a small, dark figure darted out of the shadows and reached for the bag on her shoulder.

# Chapter 47

Jydryn watched his love, unable to assist in the narrow space.

Before the thief could connect with its prize, Keena snatched the grabbing child and pulled him in front of her.

A knit cap covered his head down to his brows. His ragged breeches came to his knees, revealing an ankle boot on one foot and a house slipper on the other—both too big for the child who couldn't have been over ten years of age.

Keena captured the lad's other hand in hers. "There will be none of that. Tell me what you *need*. And be honest."

Jydryn marveled at her kind but firm tone.

The boy squirmed and tried to pull away but gave up with a whimper when Keena's grasp held him firm. "I be 'ungry, miss."

Keena straightened with a sigh. "Then I have food for you."

The child's dark eyes looked up and widened. "Ya're just gonna give it to me?"

Keena shook her head, and the kid groaned. "No, I'm going to pay you."

"Huh?"

Keena smiled, let the child go, and reached into her bag.

The boy took two steps back. When the child didn't leave, Jydryn raised his brow. Keena's actions still surprised him.

Keena drew out a large, yellow apple and a hunk of herb bread she'd torn from the round she purchased in Arrowfall. "Now." She held them close to her chest as she looked at the boy, who wiped a dirty hand across his mouth. "You are welcome to these if you will watch over this place and warn us if anyone comes skulking about."

The boy eyed the dilapidated structure with his nose crinkled in disgust. "Ya wanna stay in theres? But the spirits claim it, miss. Ya won't be safe."

Keena beamed. "See, you are already doing a fine job."

The lad looked at her with his face scrunched. He tipped his head and watched her.

Jydryn glanced at the abode and almost agreed.

"Now, as this is a right proper job, we'll provide you with food every morning and evening you're here."

The lad's jaw dropped.

"Do we have a deal?"

With his mouth still open, he nodded his head so hard his cap slid over his eyes. He brushed it away, no doubt fearing he'd find them gone when he looked again.

Keena moved the apple and bread to one hand and reached the other in greeting to the child. "My name is—"

"Eena," Jydryn said. "I'm Dryn, and our daughter is Blossom."

Keena glanced over her shoulder with a raised brow before returning her attention to the child.

The lad wiped his hand on his shirt so stiff with dirt it no doubt added to what was already on his hand. He shook on the agreement, but Keena didn't let go.

"Pey," the waif whispered at last.

"It is a right fine pleasure to meet you, Pey." Keena released the child's hand and held out the apple and bread. Pey snatched it and darted away.

"We'll never see him again," Jydryn grumbled.

Keena pushed open the door with a creak and smirked at him. "*She'll* be back as soon as she's done eating somewhere in secret so no one will steal it from her.”

"Her?”

They stepped inside the single room structure. Two steps inside, Jydryn's left knee bumped the frame of a narrow bed covered by moldy hay sticking out of the many holes in what was once a mattress. A rickety table touched his right hip. An old, round stove sat on the other side of the table. Its door hung off, and the pipe used to carry the smoke outside lay on the floor. He left the door open behind them as their only source of light in the windowless space.

Keena settled into the familiar surroundings. No one looked to have used her hideaway since she left. It wasn't much, but after their experience in the Tipsy Toad, she couldn't bring herself to stay in an inn again.

"I remember the child from my time here,” she said as she pulled up her hem and squatted. The tips of her fingers touched the dirt-covered floor. The filth lay so deep she could no longer see her fingernails. "Her mother was sick and Peyton tried to do the wash brought to them to keep coin coming into the house.” Her magic caused the dust and debris to scurry to the corner by the door in a neat pile, revealing uncut stones.

"She's so young.”

"If she's on the streets trying to steal food, I imagine her mother has died.” Keena stood and turned her attention to the three spiders sitting in webs where the slate roof and the wall met. A spell allowing her to speak to creatures slid across her thoughts. While she heard it in the fae tongue, it came out of her mouth in her language when she whispered it. "Creatures who crawl and creep, hear me now, and listen deep.” Their webs vibrated.

The two fat black ones sat in round, well-formed webs, while the hairy brown one had made a web with no discernable shape. "I ask you three, and any other critters lurking with thee, to please leave and find a new place to weave." None of them moved. She slipped out of the odd rhyming and spoke as herself. "The choice is yours, of course, but if you don't leave on your own, he will smash you." She tipped her head toward Jydryn.

The three spiders scurried through a narrow gap under the roof.

Keena shuddered. She glanced back at the pile of dirt and skirted around Jydryn, who seemed to be an immovable statue in the middle of the room. "Why don't you see if you can connect the stove pipe and then light a fire? It will be our only light until we get some candles."

"Are you serious about us staying in this place?"

"It served me well before." A breeze moaned through the gaps in between the boards forming the walls.

Rose's eyes widened and her tiny hands gripped Jydryn's shirt.

Keena patted Rose, but smirked at Jydryn. "My *spirits*. Those sounds kept most away and me safe." Keena stepped outside and looked around. Peyton returned as Keena stood from scooping a bit of water from a puddle near the door. "Hello."

The girl stood at the back of the leaning cottage and peered at her.

"Is there anyone you know who would like some food for bringing me clean straw and fabric I can fashion a new bed out of? They can't steel it," Keena was quick to add.

Peyton nodded and dashed away.

Jydryn had moved closer to the stove, but with Rose on his hip, there wasn't much he could do.

"You can put her in the pack until we get the bed remade." Keena turned so he could slip Rose into the carrier on her back.

"Keena, I don't think—"

"Ya weren't lying, runt." A lanky boy with hair hanging in his eyes and more holes than fabric in his shirt and pants stood in their doorway. He was a couple of years older than Peyton, but Keena didn't recognize him. "The runt said ya offered food for hay?"

Keena smiled from where she crouched, making mud from the dirt pile and water. "I did." She glanced at Jydryn. *Can you pull another apple from the bag?*

He retrieved it and held it up for the lad to see.

"You get this apple now, and more if you can find—without stealing it—clean straw and fabric so I can remake the bed."

"Don't know why anyone'd want to stay in this spooky ol' place." He shrugged. "I wouldn't want the spirits to steal my soul."

"The Almighty already has our souls, so there is nothing to steal," Jydryn said. He let the apple go. As it fell, he straightened his arm, so it hit his bicep, and popped it in the air toward the kid.

The boy snatched it out of the air with blackened hands and chomped into it. "I'll be back," he mumbled with his mouth full as he ambled off.

As Peyton slunk back to the shadows, Keena raised a handful of mud in her palm. Using another spell, she sent the mud to the crack the spiders had left through and filled it in. "There," she said with satisfaction.

She wiped her hands clean on the remnants of the heavy canvas holding the old straw bed together and turned to Jydryn. Keena gave him a quick kiss as she reached for Rose. "Why don't you take Pey to The Dragon and purchase four stew bowls?"

He raised a brow.

"Two for us and two for the kids." When he didn't move, she cradled his cheek, hoping Peyton was far enough from the door so she wouldn't notice the Dragon Fire. "They need to be cared for by someone, and I'm hungry. Please?"

He took her hand and kissed her palm. "You have a good heart, my love."

# Chapter 48

Jydryn stepped out of the shack Keena wanted to use as a home and called to the girl. "Come with me, Miss Pey, I'm going to need some extra hands."

The girl gasped.

"Don't worry, my friend," Keena murmured. "Dryn would never hurt you and if anyone else tries, he'll pop them in the nose."

Pey slid out of the shadows and looked wide-eyed at them both.

"Rose is littler than you, but she loves him. You'll be safe if you stay close." Keena gave Pey a pat on the shoulder and pushed her after Jydryn as he worked his way down the alley.

The inside of The Sapphire Dragon was cleaner than Jydryn thought possible in this town. Tables and the stone floor were free of food or debris.

"Get out!"

Jydryn stared at the man behind the bar. Ink drawings mired his hairy arms. His pot-marked face held small eyes which looked past him to Pey.

The girl quaked and backed toward the door.

"Stay where you are, Pey." Jydryn said with a firm but quiet voice. He turned his attention to the man and met him with a glare.

"*That* is not welcome in my establishment." The man pointed to Pey with a fat finger.

"Pey is with me. As I have coin to spend, we can either purchase from you or one of your competitors. Your choice." He held up a silver coin pinched between two fingers.

"Well, it ain't eating in here," the owner grumbled.

"We prefer to eat in peace without anyone looking down their smug noses at us anyway," Jydryn barked at the owner.

Another man entered. His black face and arms marked him as a coal miner. He gave Pey a wide berth and snarled at the girl. But he stared at her a little too long and licked his lips. "Henry, whatcha doin' letting the thievin' riff-raff in yar place?" He raised his hand to strike her.

Jydryn slid between the two, tucked the trembling child behind him, seized the miner's flying wrist, and wrenched it until he yelped. He stifled his dragon's growl, but heat flooded his skin. "Look at the big man picking on a defenseless child." His voice vibrated with wrath. "Pey is with me. If you have a problem with that, I'd be happy to teach you what it feels like to be beaten up by someone bigger and stronger."

The miner stared. "I have no quarrel with ya, mister."

"If you have a quarrel with a starving child, then you have one with me. And, my wife promised Pey if anyone gave him any problems, I'd punch them in the nose. Yours looks like a perfect fit for my fist." Jydryn raised his other fist close to the miner's face.

"Listen, stranger," Henry, the owner, broke in. "if yar buying food, get it done and leave peaceful like with the runt." He turned to the other man still held in Jydryn's grasp. "Darrell, go sit down so I can get these two out of here."

Jydryn leaned in and allowed his dragon's snarl and hot breath to wash over Darrell. "You say anything cruel, or strike Pey, or any of the children starving on the streets of your city, and I will find you and reward you in kind—tenfold." He shoved Darrell away.

Darrell rubbed his wrist as he hurried to a table. He sat but watched them both.

Jydryn took a deep breath and released it as his dragon slid away from the surface. He stroked Pey's head and bent to look her in the eyes. "You all right?" he whispered with a smile.

She bobbed her head but gawked at him.

"Come on. Eena and your friend are waiting for their dinner." He kept his hand on her shoulder as he stepped closer to the bar where Henry waited. The owner's gaze focused on Jydryn's other hand holding the coin.

"We'll take four stews served in bowls made of bread—fresh ones, no reused bread another customer didn't eat."

The owner scanned the room to see who might have heard the pronouncement. Apparently, that wasn't common knowledge. Henry nodded with a hard glare.

"And I'll take a full jug of any ale you've not added water to."

"You got more than just one silver, mister?"

Jydryn closed his fist around the coin and turned Pey with him toward the door. "Come. The owner of The Dragon is not only a thoughtless cur; he's a cheat as well."

"Now, you listen here," Henry bellowed as he slammed his fist down on the bar, rattling the metal tankards at the other end.

Pey jumped, but Jydryn kept his hand on her shoulder. He turned again, keeping her safe behind him. "Any man who has traveled as many towns in Keyaral as I have, knows he can get a few meals and a jug of ale for less than half a silver. And you want two. Sounds like you are taking advantage of strangers *and* small children."

Henry waved a barmaid forward. Gray hair slipped from her cap. She carried four steaming bread bowls on a large, round tray. Henry plopped a jug on the bar.

Jydryn handed Pey two bowls, stacked the other two. He flipped the owner half the silver coin he'd heated and bent in half in his palm as they talked. Then, he looped his finger in the jug and turned to leave.

"This ain't what we agreed ya'd pay me," Henry snarled.

"And if you hadn't insulted Pey, or tried to get more out of me than was fair, you might have received more. Something to keep in mind for the next stranger who wanders in here."

Jydryn held the door open for Pey. The older woman put her hand on Henry's arm as if to hold him back. When it looked like he wouldn't follow, Jydryn joined Pey in the street.

"Follow me," he whispered. "Stay close, and try not to drop either of those."

The girl nodded and fell into step right beside him.

They crossed the street to the side where the shack was, but they moved away from it.

Pey raced beside him. "It's the other way—"

"I know," Jydryn whispered back. "But I don't think the two men from the Dragon are going to be content with letting us go." He wound between the houses and shops until he spotted a rotting market booth tucked behind a home.

With his elbow, he motioned for Pey to go behind it. "Sit here and stay quiet." He arranged all four bowls on her lap so they wouldn't spill and sat the jug beside her. He brushed her cheek. "No matter what you hear, stay here and keep quiet until I come for you. I promise I won't let anything happen to you."

She nodded, and Jydryn slid out of the hiding spot. The footfalls and voices of those tracking him were clear with his dragon hearing.

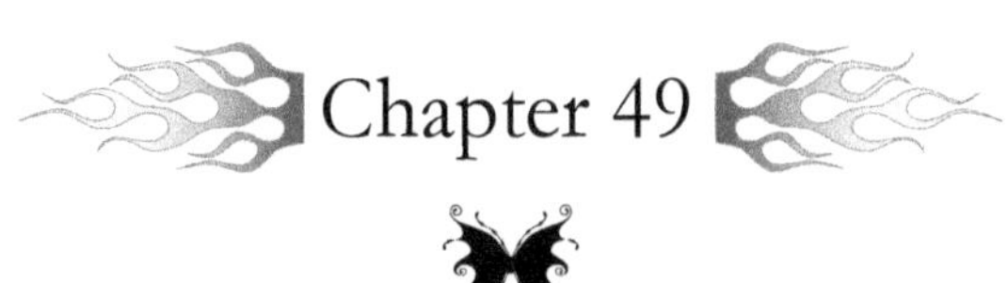

Chapter 49

Keena moved to set the bag of supplies on the table, and it wobbled. She stepped out of one shoe and called a stone up under the shortest leg until the table sat still.

Footsteps approached with a rhythmic clunking until the boy Pey had brought appeared in the doorway, pulling a small cart with broken and missing wheels. A pile of straw sat stacked high in it. The lad carried almost as much on his back, wrapped in a large piece of fabric.

Keena smiled. "Where did you get all of this? And so fast?"

"Peoples toss out stuff." He tipped his chin toward the straw. "Da Hissing Whip be a tavern on the other side of da market. Them swept it out. I gotcha the cleanest bits. The cloth were over a vendor's booth but the corners tored so it blowed away."

"You have done an excellent job, my friend."

The boy stared at her.

"Do you have a name?"

He shrugged. "Urchin, I guess."

Keena moved to stand in front of him and considered the lad for a long moment. "You look like a Jack to me."

He shrugged again. His gaze slid to the bag on the table.

"Well, Jack, you can try to steal my supplies if you like. You'll only get clothes that won't fit you, nappies, one more apple, and a little bread. But if you are patient, Dryn and Pey are collecting our dinner from The Dragon. They should return any moment."

"Yar strange, miss." Jack grunted as he dropped the straw from his back. He inched out of the room and leaned against the wall opposite the door.

Keena sat Rose down on the floor. It was clean as it was going to get, and it wouldn't help to put the infant on a blanket, because Rose would only crawl off it.

She collected the vendor tarp with its straw and dragged it into the room. "Jack, would you mind pulling the old mattress out?"

"Can I have the apple?"

Keena smiled. "Thank you for asking. Of course." She sat her bundle on the sagging slats of the bedframe as Jack tugged the leaking, bug-infested mattress out.

Rose reached for strands of the decaying reeds floating down toward her.

A spell came to mind and Keena called up a small breeze to blow out all the nasty bits behind the lad—who didn't notice.

After tossing Jack the apple when he returned, Keena pulled out a needle and spool of thread from the bottom of the bag and turned back to the mattress. She'd planned to come here before she'd left Jydryn's cave. Though she'd hoped no one had claimed the cottage yet, she knew they'd need a new bed, so she had collected the sewing items from a small dusty box on Jydryn's shelf.

Folding the vendor's tarp one way would create too small of a mattress, so she pushed the straw around until she could fold the fabric the other way. She made sure the bird droppings were on the inside and sewed the fabric closed around the straw. Quick stitches across the top secured one end before she moved to the side.

"Be careful, my sweet," she said to Rose, who had moved to the unlit stove and tried to pull herself up.

Keena smiled at Jack as she pulled an armful of straw from the cart. She took two steps toward the mattress and froze. Thoughts of Jydryn flooded her mind, and her heart rate surged.

She sat on the bedframe with her back to Jack. As she continued to stitch, she sent out her magic to help her husband.

Jydryn tracked Henry and Darrell's voices back three alleys from where he'd left Pey.

"I'll make that stranger pay me what he promised, and I'll take every coin from him for the trouble."

"The filthy runt is mine. I didn't recognize her at first, but she's Mary's kid and would make a sweet treat."

Jydryn fought to keep his dragon controlled. If he shifted now, he'd ruin several homes and hurt innocent people. He closed his eyes and waited for them to get within reach.

As they rounded the corner next to him, Jydryn kicked the side of the first knee he saw. Darrell crashed to the ground with a scream that sounded more like it came out of Pey's mouth than a grown man's.

When the miner fell, he tripped Henry. Jydryn stepped on Darrell's back as he slammed the tavern owner face-first into the wall of a shop. Bits of wood and waddle rained down on them from the overhanging living quarters. Jydryn blinked away the painful debris and punched Henry twice in the back above his hip. The man moaned but shoved against the wall to get himself free.

Fire speared Jydryn's calf.

While still on the ground, Darrell thrust a dagger through Jydryn's tall boot into his leg. Jydryn kicked the man in the shoulder, rolling him out of reach, but the action increased his pain and allowed Henry to break free.

Jydryn landed with a grunt against a wall; the dagger still dangling from his calf.

Henry brought his fist up and caught Jydryn in the chin. Even in his human skin, dragon bones were strong, and the man snatched back his hand with a yelp. It didn't deter the man for long. Henry came at him again with both fists.

"Get him, Henry. Pummel him," Darrell cheered.

After taking two blows to his stomach, Jydryn ducked under Henry's flying left and delivered two rapid punches to Henry's gut.

The tavern owner staggered backward, stepped on Darrell's already damaged leg, and the miner shrieked.

"What's going on out here?" A man stepped out from the nearest door with a candle.

"Lloyd, help me with this brute," Henry said as he pushed off Lloyd's wall and lunged for Jydryn again.

Without question, Lloyd—who weighed about as much as the tavern owner and stood a head taller—leapt into the fight. The candle dropped to the ground and sputtered out. In the failing light, and the shadows of the wide homes overhead, Jydryn had an advantage over the men with their weaker human vision.

Fog slid down the alley toward the men as they exchanged blows. A puff of air escaped Jydryn when Lloyd landed a punch to his ribs from the right, at the same time Henry landed one from the left.

Jydryn ignored the air pummeled from his body, shoved his shoulder into Lloyd's stomach. The blow propelled Lloyd back into the wall. Jydryn straightened and slammed his forearm into Henry's throat. The two men moaned as the fog grew between them and Jydryn. He braced himself on his knees and sucked in cool air.

When water vapors brushed Jydryn's cheek, Keena's love washed over him. His mate fought for him. The fog thickened and obscured Jydryn from the men's sight, but it didn't hamper his dragon's senses.

"Where'd he go?" Henry's voice rasped.

"Where'd this fog come from? Ain't never seen nothin' like it in Cragholde," Lloyd said.

"I'm gettin' out of here. I'll find the girl when the stranger leaves town," Darrell said.

Through the misty barrier, Jydryn landed a knee to Darrell's head as he crawled along the ground. Then, Jydryn reached into the fog and knocked Henry's and Lloyd's heads together. He stepped out of the way as the two men fell.

Jydryn braced a hand against a wall and drew in a deep breath of cool, moist air. *Thank you, my love.*

As the fog melted away and revealed the three unconscious men, a vine tugged at his boot. "Give me a minute," he told the plant. It released him, but waved in the breeze of the retreating fog.

He winced as he pulled the blade free, tugged his boot off, and lifted his pant leg. The vine returned. It wound around his leg, cleaning the blood. One fat leaf pushed the narrow leaves of a yarrow plant into the deep cut, and Jydryn hissed. After wrapping the wound in a wide leaf of the vine, the rest of the plant returned to the earth. The wrapping leaf had small needles on the backside that pricked his skin but deadened the pain. Healing would be quick in his dragon scales, but this would work well enough while he remained trapped in the village.

Jydryn needed to convince Keena they couldn't stay in this town. First, he had to collect Pey.

Keena looked up from her work as Jydryn and Peyton returned. Both children took their stew-filled bread bowls and disappeared.

Jydryn huffed as he held out one of the reaming bowls for her. "You insist on staying here?"

"Just until we find my father."

He leaned against the wall, as they had no place to sit, and ate without talking to her.

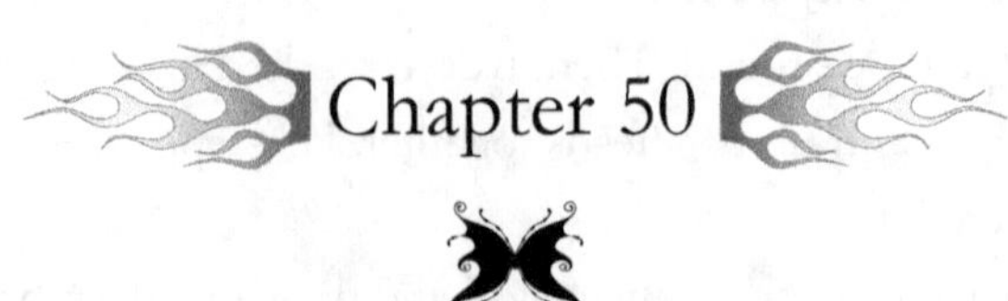

Chapter 50

Knock, knock, knock. "Miss?"

Jydryn jerked awake. Keena grabbed for him and missed as he rolled off the bed and landed on the stone floor with a grunt. His displaced weight almost made Keena tumble off her side, but she gripped the mattress to help save herself. Rose, who'd been sleeping between them, rubbed her nose with her fist but didn't wake.

Knock, knock. "Miss? Sir?"

The sound came a little louder as Jydryn climbed to his feet. He brushed his hair out of his face as he tried to pull the door open.

Keena yawned and released the spell she'd placed on it which had locked them inside. She wobbled to the stove and dropped in another piece of wood Jack had found.

She turned at the sound of shivering and chattering teeth. Pey stood outside, soaked as rain dripped from her chin. "Do …" Her shivering made it hard to talk. "… blanket?"

Jydryn placed his hand on her shoulder. "Get in here, girl, before you catch your death."

The girl hesitated and glanced over her shoulder.

"Tell whoever is with you to come in too, Peyton," Keena said as she waved the girl over to the fire.

A boy, maybe only five, darted to Peyton's side and clung to her.

Jydryn drew them into the tiny room. "Anyone else?" He scanned the alley outside before he closed the door.

Keena pulled one of Jydryn's shirts from the bag and tossed it to him. "We need to get them out of these wet things and warmed."

She drew out a thin shift adorned with ruffles and lace she'd planned to wear the night they completed the bonding ceremony and knelt before the shivering girl.

"How … do ya know … my name?" Peyton was so cold she struggled to move, but raised her arms at last and let Keena pull the soaked shirt off. After draping Peyton in the shift, Keena pulled off her mismatched shoes and pants.

A vision filled her, and Keena's hands stilled. She stood in the town square and climbed the raised platform the village elder used to give announcements. When she turned, she found the market square filled with Cragholde's citizens looking at her and waiting to hear what she had to say.

Keena shook off the image and focused again on the girl. "I knew your mother. She let me help her with the laundry for a little bread when she first got sick." Keena brushed the girl's cheeks and pushed her wet hair away from her face.

Peyton's mouth hung open, and even her shivers quieted. "They fed ya to the dragon," she whispered at last.

"Dragons don't eat people." She tapped Peyton's nose. "He saved me." Keena stole a glance at her husband, who winked at her.

He stood and brought the boy to the fire.

The lad tripped over the hem of Jydryn's shirt and fell into Peyton's embrace.

"And who is this?" Keena said as she caressed his cheek.

"My brother, Callum."

She didn't remember Mary having two children, but he was young, and she had helped the sick woman some time ago. "It is very nice to meet you, Callum." Keena let her hand trail down his arm. "I hope Peyton shared her stew with you."

He nodded, still leaning against his sister.

"I think we have a little bread if you are still hungry."

She got another nod and stood to retrieve it from the bag.

Jydryn's hand squeezed her forearm and, after she'd handed the children the last of the loaf, she turned toward him. "You and the children take the bed."

"But—"

He placed a finger near her lips. Casting a glance at the two children. "I wasn't totally comfortable balancing on the edge. It's too small for just you and me, not to mention Rose. But if you curl at one end and have the children sleep cross-ways, you can all enjoy it."

She blew a kiss at his finger. *I'll make you something comfortable and warm to sleep on.*

Can you hide our flame? He leaned forward for a quick kiss.

"Yuck!" Peyton scrunched her face.

Keena slid her arm around Jydryn and rested her head against his chest. "One day, you will find a man who will prove to you a kiss is sweet and one of the best things ever."

Peyton shook her head hard, splashing her brother with her wet hair.

Keena and Jydryn laughed.

"All right, everyone in bed. The sun will be up soon," Jydryn said.

Keena pulled Rose toward her near the foot of the bed and let Peyton and Callum have the head away from the door. Though she'd warded it against anyone breaking in, she wanted to keep herself between the children and any potential threat.

"Why'd ya come back ta Cragged Hole?" Peyton whispered as she wrapped her arm around her brother and snuggled under the blanket.

Keena laughed at the slur against the town's name. "I am looking for a traveling merchant I saw here many times. It's very important I find him."

Jydryn sat on the floor beside the bed, placing himself between the door and bed. "It is a secret she's back. Can we trust you not to tell anyone about her?"

Peyton nodded.

As the children dropped off to sleep, Keena spoke a sleeping spell over them to keep them from waking and reached her hand over the edge of the bed. Jydryn wove their fingers together, igniting their fire as she called on vines and grass to make him a comfortable bed.

Jydryn kissed the back of her hand. *I will replace your special sleeping gown.*

She hummed as her eyes drifted closed.

Jydryn squeezed her hand. *I guess we'll take them with us when we leave?*

Thank you. Even her thoughts were quiet as she edged toward sleep.

I know your heart, my love.

And I yours.

His thumb rubbed the back of her hand. *Now, can we leave as soon as we check the market in the morning?*

Again, the vision of her on the dais in the square filled her mind. *We'll see how God directs.*

As sleep pulled on her, the words of the fae bonding ceremony floated into her mind. She whispered them. "My thoughts grow with yours as a vine around a tree. We find strength in one another as we become one living being." Their minds touched again, and she experienced his life as a young fledgling.

Jydryn tightened his grip on her hand.

Chapter 51

Jydryn spent much of the rest of the night experiencing Keena's memories. He relished the way she'd spoken the fae words of the rites to finish the first part of their bonding.

In the morning, as he walked through the city, he recognized places from her time living here, and the faces of those she'd met. Most had been horrible and cruel to her, and while he knew it was because of a fae spell cast on her as a child, he struggled to forgive them.

Keena didn't. She smiled at the villagers with no evidence of malice.

How do you not hate them?

She turned and stared at him. *For being under a spell?* She shook her head and turned back to those going toward the market with them. *I hold more against those who laid Rose on an altar.* She turned and brushed Rose's cheek as she rode in the pack on his back. *But even then, I do not hate. For, without Rose, you may have sent me to Eagle's Nest and we might not have ever discovered the Dragon Fire. And we wouldn't have Rose now. She is so dear to me. I can't imagine our lives without her. To know God will speak to her one day … no, I can't even hate Greenburn.*

By her way of seeing the world, if it hadn't been for this village running her out of town to be sacrificed to a dragon, they would never have met. He looked at the people again. They were not hateful. They were terrified. In their fear, they had tried to do anything to aid their survival. They were to be pitied, not hated.

It was so hard not to grab his wife's hand. They needed to complete the bonding ritual.

She smiled and looped her arm in his to avoid skin-to-skin contact. Peyton and Callum followed close behind.

Keena picked up her pace, slipped her arm from his, and sped into the market square. She made a slow turn and looked at each vendor. Her shoulders sagged and her lids filled with tears as she stepped back beside him again.

Through their bond, he'd seen images of the man they looked for. He had a fuzzy graying beard and hair. Deep wrinkles covered his dark tan leathery skin, but his eyes were Keena's eyes, hazel and bright. When he'd looked at her, his mouth had worked but no sound came out. Like her father's memory, the fae had even stolen the man's words.

Jydryn scanned those in the square too, hoping she'd missed him, but knowing he wouldn't find her father. "Maybe tomorrow," he offered. He didn't want to stay here, but he couldn't take her away until they found the man they sought. Once done, and Queen Nashala re-established their bond, the queen would be strong enough to fight Nightshade and any fae who had gone dark with him.

Keena drew in a deep breath and pushed a smile to her lips. "Jydryn, can we impose on your coin pouch again?" Her glance fell on the children.

He followed her gaze and finished her thought. "Clothes, food—"

"Chairs or stools," she added, taking his arm again. "You are a good man, my dear husband."

"You need not flatter me. I had already agreed."

"'Tis not empty words when spoken in love."

"Eww," Peyton said behind them.

He turned and watched the girl roll her eyes. *She is going to be so surprised one day.*

They both chuckled.

They ate meat pies as they moved from vendor to vendor, filling the bag slung across Keena's body. Peyton carried a stool and so did Keena. She'd spotted Jack and sent him to the shack with two chairs. She paid the boy with a meat pie and two apples, and he now followed in their shadow too.

We can't take in every homeless child.

"Hmm?" Keena turned from looking at the platform in the center of the square with a raised brow. He'd caught her at least five times distracted and staring at it.

Jydryn searched the memories they'd shared but couldn't bring up a single one that included the raised space. "Children?"

She turned and glanced at them. "Yes? What about them?"

"They are not stray animals you can collect." He smiled.

The crease between her brows grew until they almost touch, and she nodded.

"My love, where are you?"

She turned and looked at the platform again. "I'm not sure."

"There is still wood and candles to purchase."

"A blanket."

He stopped midstride and glanced at her.

"Maybe two. The children had ours last night. Rose and I could use one, and you too."

"And blankets," Jydryn agreed with a small sigh. If they kept spending at this rate, he'd need to fly to his grandfather's horde and refill his pouch in another day.

He turned back to take Keena's arm, but she wasn't beside him. Callum sat on the stool she'd been carrying, and Peyton on the other. He followed their gaze to find Keena climbing the platform steps.

Her head bowed for a moment, then she pushed back her shoulders, and raised her chin.

What are you doing?

"Woman, get down from there," the baker shouted.

Her voice rang out, filling the entire square, yet she didn't shout. "Do you want to be well?"

Laughter greeted her.

She leaned forward and looked several people in the eye as she turned to gaze at those gathering around the dais. "Do you want to be well?" Her voice rang with excitement and he rubbed at the sensation skipping up his arms. Was she using magic on them?

As she straightened, her gaze locked with his. He took in everything about her: the serenity of her smile, the regal stance of her body, the authority in her voice. He saw an empress standing before them. Only her crown was missing. Until that moment, he'd not put much credence in the fae's assertions. But he saw the truth as he saw the sunlight shining down on her in a ring of light.

Jydryn lifted Callum from the stool, dropped onto it, and put the boy on his knee.

"Listen, woman, we've had too many people come with their quackery to pay you any mind," an old man said with a flip of his hand as he turned back to his shopping.

"But what if this was the time you learn a way to restore your health? What if you never had to bury a child before their fifth birthday because of this persistent illness?" The crowd had been about to dismiss her like the old man but now stepped closer as if they fed on her every word. "What if you never sent another maiden to the dragon?" Her gaze rose to his and the smile shining from her sparkled before it swept over the crowd again. "What if you were no longer covered in sores?"

"And how do ya think yar gonna do that?" the tanner asked, standing in the back of the crowd, stance wide and arms crossed.

She laced her fingers together in front of her and turned in a slow circle until she looked at Jydryn again. "I have no idea. But my husband knows how to help you."

What?

 Chapter 52

Keena stood on the raised platform in the middle of Cragholde with the townsfolk's full attention on her. Her inside fluttered until she thought she'd burst with excitement as she waved her husband to join her.

What are you doing?

Following God. She smiled and waved him up again.

I don't know how to help these people.

You told me as we walked through the town yesterday all the things they were doing wrong. Tell them. She waved once more.

He lumbered to his feet and returned Callum to the stool.

"This is my husband, Dryn. He knows what will help."

Jydryn stepped beside her. She pulled Rose from the pack on his back before she joined Peyton and Callum in the crowd.

"We've had enough of a spectacle for one day. Everyone, go back to your business." Alfred, the town's elder, tried to shoo everyone away before Jydryn could even say a word.

"What if he has the answer?" A woman Keena didn't know clutched a child in her arms.

"You can't listen to this man," an angry voice shouted. "He attacked Darrell, Lloyd, and I last night. Broke Darrell's leg."

Keena handed Rose to Peyton and sat Callum back on the stool as she stood and wiggled through the crowd to see who had accused Jydryn.

"Why'd he do that?" a woman called.

"Refused to pay for food he took," the man shouted.

Keena spotted the man. It was Henry, the owner of the Sapphire Dragon. She narrowed her gaze on him. "Tongue be bound, so only truth is found," she whispered.

"He attacked the three of you in your tavern?" Alfred asked.

"No. Darrell and I sneaked through the streets to attack him." Henry clamped his hand over his mouth.

"But he stole the food and left without paying?" another man asked.

Words blurted from Henry again. "He gave me half a silver for four stew bowls and a jug of ale." This time, he put both hands over his mouth.

The crowd rumbled as Keena glanced at Jydryn with a smirk and returned to the children.

"Half a silver?" a man near the front asked.

"You robbed the man." A woman huffed as she crossed her arms.

"Then, chased him down to get more." The man near Keena grumbled as he balled his fists.

Alfred took control again. "This stranger had every right to beat you senseless, Henry. You best get back to your tavern and hope there is someone in Cragholde that doesn't know what a low-down cur you are. Otherwise, you'll be out of business."

The crowd shuffled as Henry ran from the square.

Alfred directed his next words to the grumbling crowd, now with one hand on his hip, and used the other to point at Jydryn. "And how much are you willing to pay this stranger for *this* cure?"

"Not a single coin," her husband said.

"What?" Several people spoke at once.

She sensed the idea blooming in Jydryn's mind. They shared a smile again.

"I want nothing—well, except maybe a jug of ale each day until the wells are cleaned."

"Cleaned?" Again, several had spoken.

Jydryn drew in a deep breath. "My family and I will leave soon. There is no benefit to us in you changing the way you live in this village. But if you want things to be different, I'm happy to give you some suggestions."

Alfred climbed the steps to stand beside Jydryn. "What makes you qualified to tell us anything?"

"He's a healer," Keena shouted from the stool she shared with Callum. "Trained beside his grandmother, who was renowned in her corner of the kingdom for the power of her medicines and the strength of her cures."

"We have healers. They've never been able to prevent the sickness or the deaths," a man's voice rang through the crowd.

Keena spoke again. She could compel them to listen, but it didn't seem right. She smirked, remembering what Peyton had called the town. It was a filthy, craggy hole of a place to live. "Cragged Hole is your town. If you like living like this ..."

"Cragholde," Alfred corrected her as he sneered at Jydryn. "What would you propose?" Alfred sneered.

Jydryn spent the next hour explaining how they had to stop dumping their privy buckets into the street. They could no longer wash directly in the well buckets. Drainage needed to be built to take the refuge away from the city and the wells and streets cleaned.

"Is that all?" a woman somewhere behind Keena said when he finished. Many chuckled.

Alfred turned back to Jydryn. "You were telling us what to do to clean up our town?"

Jydryn shrugged. "I am not telling you what to do. It's none of my business. But what if you tried it for ... six months? Until the harvest festival? Then, if you find you are no better, sores have not healed, babies are still dying, then all it has cost you is a little time and hard work to dig the canals." He walked down the stairs. "We have other purchases to make. You discuss it amongst yourselves." Jydryn came and stood in front of her. "Is this how you hope to keep me in this town?"

She stood, and Rose flung herself into his arms. "No. If you wish to leave, I will go."

"Then, why …?"

"It was a … vision." She shrugged. "I felt like God told me to help these people. It was the only way I saw to do that."

If only I could kiss you.

She closed her eyes and whispered a spell. "Still and quiet, breathe but make not a riot. Eyes wide open, but remain frozen."

The crowd around them stilled in place as though she had turned them to stone.

Rose and Jydryn were the only ones not affected. The infant giggled and Jydryn reached out a hand and brushed Keena's cheek, igniting the Dragon Fire.

She wrapped her arm around his neck and drank in his smoldering scent as their lips pressed together.

His forehead rested against Keena's. He released a long breath. "I know we are mates, destined for one another since before the foundation of the world, but it continues to astound me how my love can grow for you every day."

She kissed him again. "I never dreamed of love, but between God, you, and Rose, I am filled with it until I think I'll burst." She kissed him again, sighed, and drew from his hold extinguishing the flames. With a breath, the spell released the others, and they resumed their activity as though nothing had happened.

Jydryn had just led her to a woman who sold blankets when Alfred came alongside them.

"Tell us where we begin."

Chapter 53

Jydryn straightened and arched his aching back. This would be so much easier in his dragon form.

Keena grinned at him, and Rose babbled on her back. "You look thirsty." Keena held up a bucket of fresh water.

He drew the ladle out and dumped water from it over his head once before he dipped the large spoon in again for a drink. Rose laughed and kicked on her back, making Keena grunt.

Keena's gaze shifted to the well next to them. "Are you sure Peyton will be all right?"

"I secured the ropes myself, and she insisted she could do it." He followed his mate to the stone shaft and looked at the girl dangling half way down. "How are you, Peyton?"

She glanced up with some of the pitch concoction he'd instructed the town to make marring her cheek. Her smile was bright, even in the dim light of the inside of the well. "Half way done. 'Tis easier the more I go up."

"Dryn," Alfred strode toward them with quick strides. He clapped Jydryn on the shoulder. "Only a fortnight, and already we have seen improvements in almost everyone's health. I thought nothing would ever produce a change in this city."

Jydryn inclined his head. "Once Peyton, Jack, and Luis finish coating the wells, we can light the fire."

Alfred rubbed his chin. "And you believe the flames will clean all the shafts and waterways so we can release the stream?"

Jydryn nodded and explained the process again. "The flame should kill off the disease from the stone without damaging the mortar between them."

Alfred turned to the street. "Once we blocked the stream, the cleaning of the wells has been a fair-sight easier than restoring the street." They'd removed all the stones and taken them out of the city. Then, they also carted away a few feet of the dirt beneath before new soil and gravel were put in its place. At Jydryn's suggestion, the brick makers employed many of the older boys living on the streets. New bricks were being laid to form a clean path through the center of the city. They would replace the other lanes in the months to come.

"It took a long time to foul this town. It will take more to restore it," Jydryn patted the elder's shoulder.

Alfred nodded. "We still have a few who try to keep to the old ways. But once you and the men get our sewage drain installed, I won't allow them any excuse for improper waste disposal."

Jydryn glanced at one of the narrow ditches he'd helped dig. It almost reached the gate. The only thing remaining was to find a location for the waste to go. The town had discussed the option of creating a depression in the ground, but he'd advised against an open pit of waste. People or animals might fall in it, and it had the potential to still spread disease.

Keena touched Jydryn's elbow.

"Well, I'll let you get back to it. I'm on the next water run." Alfred smiled at Jydryn again as he strolled away. "I hope this is our last trip."

Jydryn turned his attention to Keena as she pulled on him. He leaned his shovel against the well, glanced inside, and brushed his hand across Peyton's head. "Almost done."

At another tug, he turned to face a man who appeared to be about Keena's age. His gaze was hard and narrow. His clean-shaven jaw set and his lips held in a straight line.

"Dryn, I wanted you to meet Roger." She flashed him a mischievous smile. He sensed the excitement running through her. "Roger was just telling me the saddest story. He was in love with a woman from here. But a couple of years ago, the town sent her to the dragon—is that not the most terrible thing you have ever heard?" She'd moved to stand at Rodger's side so he wouldn't notice the radiant grin on her face.

"Dreadful," Jydryn managed to say with a straight face.

Keena's gaze looked off in the distance. "Do you remember the woman you met? The pretty one with golden hair you spoke to in one town to the east? What was her name again?"

Jydryn crossed one arm and propped the other on it as he tapped his chin. It was time to trim his beard again. The errant thought wandered through his head as he played Keena's game. "A pretty blond? I can't think of any more lovely than you, my bride."

She rolled her eyes. "She told you an odd tale about a dragon, did she not?"

Rodger stood straight, his arms stiff at his sides. His eyes opened wide as he leaned in toward Jydryn.

He hummed as he pretended to think. "Hmmm, Olive? No, that's not right."

"Olivia?" Rodger bounced on the balls of his feet.

Jydryn tipped his head, still looking off at nothing. "Aye, that might have been it." He shifted his gaze to Roger's again. "Strange woman. She insisted a dragon had carried her to a field outside the city and just left her there. Now, if a dragon had taken her, why didn't he eat her?"

"Where?" Roger struggled to stand still and catch his breath. "Where did you find her?"

"Was it Beardrift?" Keena had never been there, and they'd never discussed the town. She must have pulled it from his memory like she had Olivia.

Jydryn shook his head. "No, it had to be Arrowfall where we met the couple who obsessed about having a babe."

"Arrowfall? You're sure?" Roger glanced between them.

Jydryn waited a prolonged moment before he put Roger out of his misery. "Aye, Arrowfall for sure. Yes, we met the pretty blond named Olivia there who talked about a dragon."

Roger thrust out his hand, clasped Jydryn's forearm, and shook it in frantic, pumping strokes. "Thank you. Thank you so much. I have to see a man about a horse." He ran down the street and shouted over his shoulder. "The gods bless you, sir."

Keena smirked at Jydryn as she turned and strolled away. "Was there any need to play with him so?"

He grinned as he fell into step beside her, down the unfinished lane and out the gate. "Did you witness me talking to her or just the memory?"

"I watched you talking together before Cai attacked. But I also viewed the memory of you saving her. Then, as Roger was grumbling and cursing the dragon and the city for losing his love, I remembered her telling you she was still unwed and how she missed a man from her former home."

"I'm glad for them both."

Outside the town gates, they turned to the south off the main road and walked toward a wide, rocky depression surrounded by a forest on all sides except the road. Closer to the road, there was a hill of rocks.

"There is a sizable cavern under here." She continued to the far side, near the tall pine trees.

Looking back, he could only glimpse the tops of the walls above the rocky outcropping between him and the city. Jydryn turned back to a hole only big enough to peer through. He leaned down and used his dragon vision to explore inside. "You're right. There is no water in it and there seems to be no outlet. This would house their sewage for several decades."

As he rose to his feet beside Keena, fae burst from the surrounding forest. Nightshade led two dozen this time. Echo and the three who had sworn an oath to Keena were again among them.

Chapter 54

Jydryn stepped between his family and the approaching dark fae band as spheres of magic flew at them. Keena covered them with a shield, but the ground vanished beneath her and she lost her hold on her magic. As she shrieked, Jydryn shifted, and cradled her in his open paw so as not to crush Rose, who still sat strapped to Keena's back.

Magic hit him from every side. Most of the blasts burned, but there were some hits, he assumed from Echo and their allies, that soothed. He didn't notice any difference in what the blackened-red spheres of light looked like that might account for the different effect on his scales.

Jydryn spewed fire, but the fae created their own shields against it.

Is there a way you can get me to your back? Keena asked.

Jydryn raised her to his neck. She climbed from there as he rose in the air and tried to get out of the reach of the fae magic.

Keena positioned herself between his horns on the crown of his head and countered Nightshade's magic with her own. Their blasts, his deep red and hers stunning blue, met between them and the dark fae. Blinding yellow light shone from the point where light and dark magic collided and sparked in wild ribbons in every direction.

Some of those with Nightshade stopped their attack and stared.

Nightshade shielded himself and stopped his attack against Keena as Jydryn carried them higher. From this height, they watched Nightshade lead his squad back to the road where he turned his assault against the city of Cragholde.

"No!" Keena raced down his foreleg, placed the pack holding a crying Rose into his paw, and leapt into the air. Trees reached up and grabbed her which slowed her descent until she landed between the fae and the city. She stood behind a shield of her magic that took the brunt of the attack meant for the defenseless village.

Jydryn watched her shield cave inward at the center, forming a bowl until the enemy's magic pooled within it, inches from Keena's outstretched palms. She braced against the force hitting her as she slid back along the road toward the gate.

Nightshade advanced, increasing the magic flowing from his hands to a wide stream.

Jydryn covered the fae within reach in fire, impaled others on his tail spikes, and cut one in half when he bit into him.

Nightshade was only a wagon's length from his mate.

Keena's voice filled his thoughts. *Sweep Echo, Amethyst, Badger, and Dusk out of the way, and climb so you are above me.*

Jydryn didn't waste time questioning her. He whirled in what he hoped would appear as a haphazard turn that batted the four fae away with his wing as he took up position over her head and faced Nightshade with her. Several other fae moved away from their leader as though they believed Jydryn intended to breathe fire at them.

Nightshade advanced despite the ruckus.

Keena stopped sliding backward. Her head shot up. The bowl of dark fae magic gathered within her shield hurtled away as the shield flipped from concave to convex. The magic hit Nightshade and those close behind him, decimating their protective shields and hurling them through the air. Bodies landed hard, two dragon-lengths from her, smoking, and blackened.

Fae who had escaped the blast, glanced from their fallen leader to Keena and back again before they fled into the woods.

The dark fae leader rose and vanished in a puff of smoke before Jydryn could cut him down.

He landed beside Keena, and she took Rose from him.

Echo and their other allies started toward them, but Keena shook her head and they turned to the woods with the others.

"Wrong put right; remove all evidence from sight. Memory too, please undo," Keena muttered through her gasped breaths.

Her powerful magic caused Jydryn to shift against his will. He stood clothed beside her. His breath caught, pain like he hadn't experienced since his first shift radiated through him, and his heart struggled to find an even rhythm.

"I'm sorry," she fell into his arms, crying. "I didn't know it would affect you too."

He stroked her back. "I'm all right. It was just unexpected."

She raised her tear-streaked face. "How are we ever going to stop him?"

Jydryn pulled her close again and held her. "God will show us the way." He hoped he sounded more confident than he felt, but if so much dark magic hadn't taken the evil fae leader out—what would?

They turned back toward the city but didn't make it far before they saw a group of men walking toward them.

"Hello, sir." The man in the lead waved. "Have you found a place for us to send the filth from our town?"

"Indeed, we have." Jydryn gave Keena one last look as she turned toward the gate.

She yawned. *I'm going to take Rose to the cottage. Both of us could use a rest.*

He nodded and turned his attention back to the men as he explained about the cavern below the meadow and how to get the waste into it.

Jydryn fought to keep his mind on the task at hand and the men before him, as his thoughts tumbled with his desire to be with his family.

Chapter 55

Keena stretched and blinked sleepiness away. She pushed herself from the bed and looked around. Everyone was gone. A plate of pork and fruit sat on the table. The pork was cold. Her heart skipped a beat. How late was it?

It nears midday, my love.

Why'd you let me sleep so late?

You were exhausted. The stream is running again, and the channel to the cavern you found is well underway. I thought it best to let you recuperate.

She smiled as she slid into her chair to enjoy the meal. The love passing between their bond served best to restore her. Never had she imagined finding such a deep love.

Now, dressed in a dark green gown, she strolled toward the market square and went through her morning and evening routine of searching the vendors for Lord Rycharde. She couldn't recall how often she'd seen the man who stared at her and tried to talk but never had. It could be months before he visited the city again. How long did she endanger her family and the citizens of Cragholde now that the fae knew where she was? Where else should she look for him?

"Mornin', Eena." George, the baker, greeted her. "I have fresh herb bread." The short man passed the long loaf to her.

She'd stopped trying to pay him a week ago. He always refused. His daughter now worked beside him without fear of being sent to the dragon. "Thank you."

Keena nibbled on it as she walked around the square. Everyone greeted her. Many offered their wares. She declined, as always.

Near the lane that led out of the back of the city to the area where they sent the maidens sat an unfamiliar wagon. The sides were gray and porous with age and the bed tipped to one side. An odd selection of pots sat inside. Some were new, but most had dents and scratches.

Her heart sped up, and her breath caught. The vendor faced away from her. His long unkept hair was more gray than deep brown—almost black.

Keena froze, locked by fear and excitement. Could it be him?

She sensed Jydryn coming toward her. She'd be able to face the truth either way with him beside her.

The peddler straightened a bit. One shoulder hunched lower than the other, and he had the unsteady gait of an old man.

He pivoted to the side, but his hair hid his face. Bending again, he picked up a large stone and placed it behind a wheel. He turned the other way, and she glimpsed a long, dark-tanned nose.

She fought for breath as he placed another stone in front of the wheel.

He straightened once more, but his head remained bowed and his curly hair obscured her view. His shuffled steps brought him toward her.

Jydryn drew near. His energy hummed over her gooseflesh-covered skin and made her shiver.

The man stepped closer, and his head rose. His eyes scanned up her skirt, over her waist, climbed to her shoulders, and at last locked with her gaze. Hazel eyes. Her eyes.

His mouth opened, creating a gap between his mustache and beard. It closed and opened again. Tears filled his eyes, but no words came out.

Keena slid forward on quaking legs as Jydryn's hand pressed to the small of her back. She drew in the strength he offered. "Lord Rycharde of Wealdstone."

He shook his head and turned his gaze to Jydryn as he drew in a deep breath, as though released from an unseen force. His voice croaked. "Nary a lord 'ere. Just ol' Ry."

She reached out and pulled his hands into hers. "Restore what was lost at enormous cost. Return to you what was stolen. Let your mind open. Every memory returned to you; the past I undo."

Rycharde inhaled a lungful of air through his open mouth. He blinked as he held her gaze. His hands gripped hers. As his shoulders squared, his age appeared to revert a least a decade. "Well, you are a beautiful lass. You remind me of someone who was once dear to me." Now, he spoke with strength and polish.

"I am your daughter, my lord."

He shook his head, making his hair toss about his shoulders. "Nay, my Layna is a wee thing." His gaze shifted toward Rose. "Only a little older than your daughter."

"Lord Rycharde, I am Arlayna, your daughter. A spell was—"

"Stolen!" His shout made her step back and let him go. His gaze dimmed and his mouth worked, but no more words came out.

She stepped beside him, leaned against the wagon, and took one hand again.

Like before, he drew in a deep breath and looked at her. His eyes narrowed and his head leaned forward to examine her. "They stole my daughter."

"I know."

"Ripped from my arms."

"I know."

Tears tumbled down his cheeks and drenched his beard. "I couldn't save you. Oh, my sweet, I would have done anything to keep you with me. But I failed you."

Keena couldn't contain her own tears. "No, you loved me. It wasn't your fault."

"King Nix took you away!"

"The king is long dead. Queen Nashala rules now."

He rocked back on his heels, but his hand remained in hers. His lips turned in a goofy grin, and his eyes hooded as they stared off at nothing. "Oh, my sweet Nash. My love. My mate. Mother of my daughter. Oh, Nash."

"She wants to be with you again." Keena wasn't sure Queen Nashala wanted it as much as she needed it, but it was something they both required to be whole.

"No!" He tried to jerk from her grasp. "'Tis too dangerous. Nix will kill you. We can't—"

Keena placed her fingers over his lips to quiet him.

He kissed them. "Layna, oh my precious girl. I've found you."

She slid her hand up his cheek and back into his snarled hair. She drew his head down and rested it against her forehead, like Jydryn often did. Like with Echo, she filled his mind with events in the fae court and images of the feeble-minded queen. In return, her parents' love flooded her spirit.

Through a blur of tears, she looked at his watery eyes. "We have to get you to Wealdstone. Lilly and Echo will bring Queen Nashala to us there."

"Once she re-establishes our bond—"

Keena nodded. "You will both be better."

He brushed her cheek and kissed it. "My sweet Layna."

# Chapter 56

Jydryn walked beside the lumbering wagon. They'd left most of Rycharde's pots behind in Cragholde, to allow room for Rose, Peyton, and Callum to ride in the bed. Keena sat beside her father as he drove the old horse. She needed to maintain contact with him in order to keep his mind functioning.

They'd left before nightfall the same evening she'd found him. Now, almost a week later, they were still over a day from Wealdstone. The territory Rycharde controlled in the name of his king sat on the east end of the Tetling Ridge. From what the lord said in his more lucid moments, he had a castle, which sat on a large hill next to a town three times the size of Cragholde.

Jydryn tipped his head back and forth until his neck cracked. He didn't favor traveling out in the open with dark fae hunting them. But they didn't have any other options. He couldn't carry all of them, and dragons were less tolerated on this side of the kingdom.

His hands fisted and relaxed as he ignored Rose's whimpers to be carried. He needed to be free to shift at the first sight of trouble. The next two days couldn't come fast enough. He closed his eyes for a couple of steps as he tried to relax.

"Whoa!"

Jydryn's eyes flew open at Keena's command to the horse.

Keena leapt down from her father's side as the unwelcome sensation of insects crawling under her skin hit her. She'd come to recognize it as an advance warning of Nightshade's impending attack.

She reached for Peyton, sat her on the ground, and handed her Rose before she pulled Callum out too. "Get under the wagon and stay out of sight."

Jydryn was out of his boots and tossed his shirt in the wagon as a black blur whirled out of the forest. It was still about the width of a dragon from the road as she turned and prepared to fight.

She'd taken too long with the children and didn't have time to create a shield.

Dark magic slammed into her, pinning her against the side of the wagon. Pain laced through her until she screamed.

Jydryn shifted and leapt into the air.

Nightshade materialized from the black smudge with his hands around her neck. "You think hiding them under a wagon will keep them safe?"

The earth rumbled and fell away beneath the wagon. Peyton screamed.

Jydryn roared, but his voice in her head exuded calm. *Vines have pulled the children into the underbrush out of sight. They're safe.*

"How many of these worthless creatures do I have to kill to stop you?" Nightshade pulled one hand from her throat and pointed it at Echo. Magic struck their fae ally in the chest, slammed him to the ground, and left him coated in blood.

"You are doing … my job … for me," Keena choked as she clawed at his fingers.

"I know he sides with you. I know everything."

While Jydryn went after the other fae with fire, claw, and teeth, Keena drew his fire into her own body.

After a moment, Nightshade released her with a yelp. Smoke billowed off his skin.

Keena gave him no quarter as she thrust out her hands and bound him in vines that covered his entire head.

In a puff, he was free and stood to her right. But she predicted his movements and turned to meet him before he solidified. She had him again.

As he vanished within her magic once more, the air filled with his cackling laughter. "This is why you will never defeat me."

Dusk rushed toward her, but Keena turned to face a pink-haired fae who'd fought with Nightshade before. A blade in the enemy fae's hand pierced through Keena. Her scream filled the clearing and dropped every fae still standing.

Matching pools of blood grew on Keena's side and the attacking fae's side as he lay writhing on the ground. Since when did fae use metal weapons?

Nightshade materialized to stand between her, and Jydryn as he flew toward her. His dragon maw opened wide, but the dark fae filled it with blasts of magic.

Her vision blurred and her strength failed and clung to the wagon. She sensed the burning in Jydryn's mouth from Nightshade's attack. Her mate coughed and choked as he fought to stay in the air and not crush her under his falling body.

Keena drew the dagger from her side with gritted teeth. "Royal blood now coats this blade." She rose, staggered forward, and slashed at Nightshade as Jydryn landed hard behind her.

The murderous fae leaned back to keep from being touched by her wild swing.

"It will kill any fae with just a touch."

Nightshade tried to grab her arm, but magic burst from her and smashed him into a nearby boulder. He rose on wobbling legs as he used one hand to brace himself. His lip curled in a snarl as he sent two quick blasts from his free hand at Amethyst and Badger.

Keena deflected the blackened spheres that no longer held any red. Nightshade laughed again. "You can't win. My numbers grow."

"As does my power." Keena stood tall, as blood seeped from her side.

Jydryn shook free of the last of the blast Nightshade had hit him with and took to the air again. He dove straight for Nightshade, his teeth bared.

Keena joined her mates' attack causing the boulder he'd fallen against to explode, showering Nightshade and his men with its sharp shards.

Amethyst, Badger, and Dusk added their blue spheres to the fight.

But the tide turned in her favor, the sneaky cur and fae who supported him all vanished.

Keena dropped to her knees with a gasp. Once the dark fae were gone, Badger raced to her side and Jydryn started to shift. "No," she gasped.

He settled into his scales and walked toward her.

"Use your fire to seal the wounds." Her breaths were shallow and labored.

The great dragon's head shook as his nose hovered over her. *I'll not burn you.*

She caressed his snout. Oh, he was beautiful in either form. *Then, heat the dagger and let Badger do it. You know it is the proper way to stop the bleeding.*

Jydryn growled, picked up the short sword of a fallen fae in his claws, turned his head, and blew flame on it until it was white hot.

Badger took it and pressed it to her wounds front and back.

The screams torn from his mate, shred Jydryn's heart. The fae who had stabbed her echoed with his own shrieks. He'd attacked a royal fae.

He suffered in the identical manner as she did, but his magic offered him no healing. A just punishment for attacking his princess.

Jydryn shifted at last and Dusk tossed him his pants as they passed one another. Jydryn dropped beside Keena and he pulled her into his lap. Her eyes fluttered, and he caressed her cheek.

The children? Rycharde?

Jydryn glanced up. He had no idea.

Chapter 57

Though she tried, Keena couldn't draw in a full breath through the searing pain in her side.

During their latest battle, Nightshade had said she could never win. He didn't speak his last words. They'd come as a whisper on the breeze. "You can't win, because you won't kill."

It was true. She'd prefer to take him alive and lock him in a tower like her great-great-grandfather had done.

"Where are the children and Rycharde?" she asked again.

"They are here, princess," Dusk said as he led them from the bushes on the other side of the road. "Everyone is unharmed—except you …"

"And Echo." She tried to look past Jydryn to the fallen fae. She bit her lip against the pain and returned to her mate's lap.

He kissed her forehead. "If we had completed our bonding, my dragon could help heal you."

She inched her hands upward. Halfway up, she stopped breathing and held her breath against the pain. She pulled his face closer and pressed his lips to hers. As their kiss deepened, some of his healing strength seeped into her. When he pulled from her, she could breathe a little easier as he helped her sit up.

Amethyst leaned over Echo; her magic swirled around his chest.

Keena rested her weight against Jydryn as they watched Badger add his healing magic. When the two fae sat back on their heels with a long sigh, Keena was afraid to ask.

"How is he?" Jydryn spoke the words for her.

"Weak, but still alive," Amethyst whispered. She turned to them. "If you can get him to Wealdstone, his mate can help him heal the rest of the way."

Keena glanced at the old wagon.

"We still have over a day of travel," Jydryn said with a low groan, or it might have been a growl.

Dusk put a whimpering Rose in the wagon. Her little hands opened and closed as she reached toward Keena and Jydryn. The blue-haired fae lifted Callum in as Peyton climbed up herself. "We can help." Dusk nodded.

Badger carried Echo to a transformed wagon with tall, solid sides and fat wheels covered in layers of leaves. Amethyst followed him, leading three powerful horses. The one already pulling the wagon shimmered and grew until he matched their size. Jydryn scooped Keena into his arms as the fae secured the horses into harnesses.

Keena reached for Rycharde, who stood a few feet from the wagon. He staggered forward and took her hand. "Oh, my poor Layna. I failed you again."

"No. I am glad you are unharmed. Queen Nashala needs you to restore order to Shimmerbourne." She offered him a small smile.

Badger gave the old lord a boost up into the wagon bed and Jydryn sat Keena on the end. Badger put his hand on Jydryn's shoulder. "If you can drive this thing, you can arrive in Wealdstone before the moon rises."

Jydryn opened his mouth, but Dusk interrupted. "We've strengthened the horses. They will get us there without tiring or injury."

Amethyst joined them at the rear of the wagon. "Dusk will ride in the bed and watch over the wounded. If Lord Rycharde holds Princess Arlayna's hand to keep him focused and alert, he can make sure the children stay safe while you push the horses to speed."

"Where are you going?" Keena looked between Badger and

Amethyst.

"We will return to Shimmerbourne and alert our allies that Nightshade has discovered our efforts against him. Then, we will gather as many as we can trust and bring Queen Nashala to you," Badger said with a snapped nod.

"Maybe it would be better if we brought Lord Rycharde to her." Keena nibbled on the corner of her lip.

"No, you are almost there. Wealdstone has powerful wards around it. We can get to the court and back before you could reach Shimmerbourne. We'll see you there." The fae woman touched Badger's arm.

Keena slid back into the wagon bed with Dusk's help. "If there is anything written about how King Zephyr secured and held his sister, or their tactics in fighting the dark fae, can you bring it too?"

"Of course, princess." They both inclined their heads before they turned and sped into the forest.

Dusk helped her lie down as Jydryn climbed onto the seat and gathered the reins.

Jydryn glanced back at them. "Ready?"

"Whether we are or not, we need to get moving." Keena nodded.

The reins flapped, and her mate clicked his tongue. The wagon jerked forward and soon their speed increased until they were hurtling down the road.

Keena lay on her left side, keeping her wounds away from anything that could bump into them. Her feet were near where Jydryn sat and her head near the back of the wagon. She rested it on Lord Rycharde's thigh as his legs stretched out across the end. Rose squirmed toward her and dropped in front of Keena.

Echo lay opposite her with his head at the other end and Dusk sat close to watch over him.

Peyton and Callum sat at the front, near Echo's head. Peyton's eyes were enormous and her brother clung to her. "Ya're a … a … *fairy.*" She whispered the last word.

"Echo and Dusk are fae. I'm half fae and half human," Keena said.

Peyton leaned forward, glanced at Jydryn above her, and turned back to Keena again. "And he's a dragon."

"Does that frighten you?"

The girl sat back and snuggled with her brother. Her face scrunched up, but she shook her head.

Keena managed a small smile as her eyes slid closed. Even being jostled around couldn't keep sleep from claiming her.

Keena woke as the wagon slowed. The sky sparkled with a thousand stars as she glanced at those beside her. Only Dusk was still awake.

"How is he?" she whispered as she sat up and watched Echo to see he still breathed.

Dusk offered her a tired smile. "Stronger, like you. If Lilly arrives in the next couple of days, he will make a full recovery."

She stood and used Dusk's shoulder for support as she picked her way between all the sleeping children. She only released him when she held Jydryn's hand. The Dragon Fire illuminated their surroundings. Jydryn smiled as Keena climbed over the seat he occupied and settled beside him. With a contented sigh, she slid her hand in the crook of his arm and lay her head on his shoulder. It plunged them into darkness only lit by the sliver of the rising moon.

"You should rest," he whispered as he kissed her head.

They wound around a city with its gates closed for the night. "We're almost there." She pointed to the eight-tower silhouetted structure rising out of the hill ahead of them. "We should be safe there until Queen Nashala arrives."

Until your mother arrives.

She groaned, glanced back at the sleeping lord, and returned her head to Jydryn's strong shoulder. *I don't know why I can't think of them as my parents. I understand they never abandoned me, and our separation hurt them as much as me. I don't know why they don't feel like family.*

Taking the reins into one hand, he cradled her cheek, sheltering it from the chilly wind and lighting their Fire again. *Give it time. They are still strangers to you, but you know the truth now.*

He released her as the torchlight on the battlements grew and, soon, the raised drawbridge came into view.

"Lord Rycharde!"

Keena lifted her head as Jydryn pulled the reins at Dusk's shout.

The fae lay on his belly with both hands gripping Rycharde's shirt as the old lord tried to get out of the wagon.

Keena jumped down and whimpered at the ache still in her side. She used the edge of the wagon to steady herself as she worked her way to the back. Once his hand was in hers, he stopped struggling and stared at her.

Rycharde and Dusk helped her climb into the wagon bed, and they joined her before Jydryn started them forward.

"Who goes there?" a gruff voice shouted down from the walls.

"We must speak to Herbert," Jydryn yelled back.

"The thane has retired for the night. Come back tomorrow."

"Please, sir," Keena said as she gripped Rycharde's hand. "The matter is most urgent and concerns your lord."

"Our lord is none of *your concern.*"

Keena closed her eyes and drew in a deep breath. "Herbert!" The breeze and her magic carried the shout over the wall and into every room.

"Stop screeching, woman, and be gone."

"What is all this ruckus? How is a man to get any sleep?" An unknown voice called down to them; one full of authority.

"Herbert?" Jydryn said.

"Who is asking?"

"Roses are the first to bloom each spring." Keena spoke the words, and a ripple of magic washed over the wagon and up the walls.

"Open the gate!" Herbert ordered.

"Sir?"

"Open the gate right now. They have Lord Rycharde. Let them in. They are not safe out there."

Chapter 58

Jydryn squinted at the blazing torches in the bailey as they entered Wealdstone castle. Several guards lined either side of the wagon, and two took hold of the lead horses' halters. As they passed under the inner gate into the smaller ward, servants in their nightclothes with shawls or blankets around them poured out of the castle.

"Lord Rycharde, it is good to have you home again." A man with gray hair strolled to the back of the wagon and bowed. Jydryn tried not to laugh at the man in his long nightshirt and heavy boots.

"Herbert. It is good to see you. We need to prepare the men. Nashala is on her way."

The thane took a step back and stared at his lord. "You sound … well."

Jydryn helped Keena slide from the back of the wagon until she stood on the ground while she still held her father's hand.

Herbert's gaze shifted to her. He blinked, and a smile grew to fill his face. He bowed deep at the waist. "Lady Arlayna. Welcome home." He straightened. "You look like your mother, my lady. It is good to see you. We feared we might never find you."

"Thank you." She followed the thane's gaze to her hand entwined with Rycharde's. "My touch seems to help his mind clear."

"Yes, of course. But we can help him from here."

Several servants stepped forward and bowed.

Rycharde patted her hand and smiled. "We all need rest. They will look after me until your mother arrives."

Keena let Rycharde's hand slide from hers, leaned her weight against Jydryn, and turned her attention back to Herbert. "We have wounded, sir. And children."

The thane snapped to attention and waved more servants forward. "Are they human or fae?"

Jydryn glanced back at Dusk and Echo, who concealed their true nature with a glamor to make them appear human.

"It matters because we have a wing of ground floor chambers appointed with no cut stones or rooms on the upper floors of the castle and towers with wood floors and finished stones," the thane said.

"We are fae, sir," Dusk said as he released the illusion covering them.

"Very good." Herbert nodded to three men who stepped forward. A litter stretched between two of them. Dusk and the third man moved Echo onto it. They walked toward the open doors of the imposing stone structure.

"Come, children." An older maid with a messy, graying braid stepped forward.

Keena's warmth slipped from Jydryn's side as she drew Rose into her arms. "It's all right, Peyton. You'll be safe with these women." She coaxed the girl and her brother to the end of the wagon.

Keena kissed Rose's head as the little girl rubbed at her eyes with her fists. "Peyton and her brother Callum are our wards," she told the women helping them from the wagon. She passed Rose to the oldest maid and Keena let her hand rest on Rose's head. "Rose is our daughter."

"Yes, my lady." The older woman's tone was more curt than Jydryn cared for. "We will have them cleaned and put them to bed in the chamber beside your own."

Jydryn and Keena turned back toward Herbert as the thane waved the last two servants forward. A young maid and a tall, lean, dark-skinned man bowed. "These two will see you to where you can bathe before they show you to your chamber, Lady Arlayna and …"

"This is my husband, Dyrn." Keena leaned against him again.

Herbert smiled. "And Lord Dryn, are you fae as well?"

"No," Jydryn said.

The thane's smile never faded as his attention returned to Keena. "It is an honor to have all of you at Wealdstone. Please, make yourself at home. We have long awaited your return." He waved for them to follow the two servants, and he fell in line behind them as they entered.

While Jydryn, Keena, and the servants continued straight through the castle, Herbert climbed the stairs that ran parallel to them.

The structure seemed even bigger on the inside. There were elements that reminded him of his uncle's castle. They walked for several minutes as he savored his love at his side.

The male servant turned to face them, opened a door, and waved him inside. "My lord."

Jydryn glanced at Keena.

"Our lady will only be a few steps away, my lord." The female servant stood at another open door on the opposite side of the wide hallway.

"I'll be all right," Keena assured him as she drew her weight and warmth from his side and stepped toward the maid.

I love you.

She turned a radiant smile to him before she entered her chamber.

And I you.

Jydryn drew in a deep breath as he stepped into a small chamber dominated by a metal tub. A narrow table with a basket of soaps, towels, and grooming tools sat against one wall. A hearth with a bubbling, black caldron hung over the blazing flames opposite the door. The heat welcomed him and his muscles relaxed.

Running footsteps drew his attention back to the open door. The servant took a stack of garments from someone with a nod and the individual darted past the door and a knock sounded on a door not far away.

The servant offered him the clothes. "Do you require assistance, my lord?"

"No, I'll be fine." Though part of the shifter nobility, as an Activist dragon, Jydryn had been bathing and dressing himself for years.

"Very good, my lord. I will wait outside the door and take you to your chamber when you are done."

Jydryn nodded and turned to the tub. Weariness tugged at every part of his body, but it would be better to get the journey and his weeks of labor off his skin before he joined Keena in their chamber.

The tub sat half full of tepid water. Jydryn placed the new clothes on the table and went to the cauldron. He used the large ladle to scoop boiling water into a bucket. He added it to the tub until it steamed before he stripped and settled in.

His head lolled back and his eyes closed. This must be a taste of the paradise that awaited him. The last of his tension melted away as he slid down until the water touched his chin. His dragon added a contented rumble.

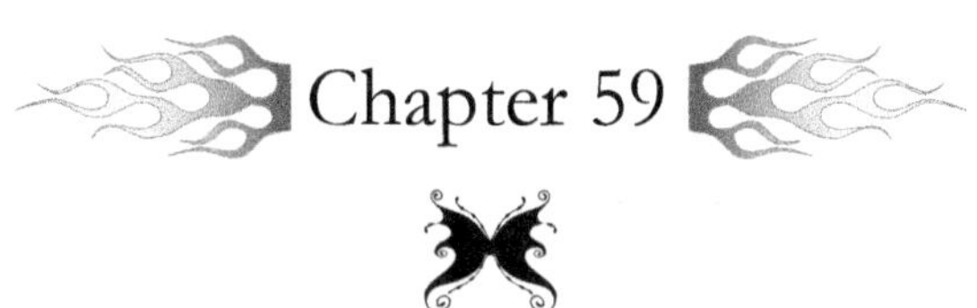

Chapter 59

Keena stepped out from the small chamber where the children slept, into the one she was to share with Jydryn. The hearth's bright blaze illuminated the beautiful tapestries covering two of the walls to keep the night chill far away.

An immense bed that could almost sleep Jydryn's dragon form, filled the space opposite the hearth between two high, long, narrow windows. A desk and chair sat in the back corner opposite her. A small round table and two chairs occupied the front corner near the other door. It opened as Jydryn entered from the hall to join her.

He wore a long nightshirt similar to hers and his feet were bare too. A stack of clothes draped over his arms. He sighed as he looked at her and closed the door. "I apologize for being late. I confess I fell asleep in the hot water."

Keena giggled. "Me too. I only arrived a moment ago after I checked on the children." She used her thumb to point over her shoulder at the door behind her.

He tossed the clothes and boots on the trunk at the foot of the bed and came to her on long strides. His hand brushed her side. "How are you?"

"Well." She slid her arms over his shoulders, threaded her fingers through his wet hair, and pulled him down. Their kiss grew hungry and their tongues danced together.

He pulled from her with a deep sigh and rested his forehead against hers. "It is late and you need your rest."

She tipped his chin up. "I'm tired of waiting." She captured his lips again and pressed her body against his. Need clawed at her as if a dragon tried to escape from within her.

Jydryn pulled from her again, cradled her face, and kissed her forehead. "As you wish, my love."

He pulled a pillow from the bed and sat it in front of the fire. He lowered to his knees on one end and drew her down on the other. Cradling her face again with their foreheads touching, his low, husky voice made her insides wobble. "Our minds are one. Our thoughts shared. Secrets revealed. Hopes known. We are of one mind." One hand slid down to cover her heart as he raised her chin. "We bind our spirits together now."

She placed her hand over his heart. The hard thump caressed her palm.

His eyes danced in the firelight. "As our souls entwine, so do our dreams for our future, our goals, and the notions of what our life together will be. Today, we are of one purpose. One life from two. We will strive together as I seek only what is best for you—"

"—and I seek only what is best for you. Your needs go before my own. Your happiness is my first priority." Keena finished the dragon rite and continued with the fae words. "Unseen, I feel your spirit as we labor for the common good of our family and those who share our life. I hear your heart beating. Mine beats with yours as one." The rhythm of their hearts synchronized in perfect cadence. She smiled. "I breathe when you breathe. Breath to breath, heartbeat to heartbeat."

The dark center of Jydryn's eyes engulfed the ice blue irises as his hand skimmed up from her heart to push the shoulder of her garment off her skin. He warmed the area with kisses from the lobe of her ear as he nipped down her neck and across her shoulder until he pulled a moan from her throat as her head tipped back.

"And they two shall be one flesh. Therefore they are no more two, but one flesh. What God has joined together, let not man tear asunder," he whispered.

There might have been words from the fae rites she was supposed to say, but all thoughts vanished under Jydryn's heated kisses.

Keena's eyes squinted open against the sunlight that streamed through the high windows to flood the room. The remnants of the fire didn't even glow. She snuggled closer to her husband and his natural warmth.

Her hand lay on his chest, and she twirled the sparse curled hairs growing there. It was a shame the Dragon Fire had gone out with their completed bonding.

Her head bounced as he chuckled. "The flame is still there." To prove his point, his multicolored tongues of fire popped up all over his skin. "Now, we can call it forth as we wish. Though you have already shown your power over the flame."

She rolled so she lay more on his chest and looked at him.

"What are you staring at, my mate?"

"There is no city to save. Lord Rycharde is home. Queen Nashala on her way. We are inside warded walls." She dug her toes into the mattress to push herself closer to his lips. "The children have someone to look after them." Her head lowered to brush her lips against his in a quick kiss.

He smirked as his gaze consumed her. "It sounds as though we have nothing more to do."

After another kiss, she laid her head on his shoulder and snuggled into his embrace. "Can we just stay here all day?"

"I would like nothing more—"

"My lady?" Several quick knocks came with the voice. "My lady, are you awake?"

She stifled a groan as she sat up. "What is the matter, Herbert?"

Jydryn pulled on a new pair of dark pants and stood.

Keena sifted through the wardrobe, trying to decide what to throw on for the moment.

"The king approaches the castle, my lady," Herbert called through the door.

Keena drew an orange kirtle with long, dangling sleeves trimmed in red ribbons over her head before Jydryn pulled open the door. "Why does the king's arrival have you so concerned, sir?" Keena pulled a brush through her snarled hair as she watched him wring his hands.

"He is coming with all due haste, my lady. And he has his army with him."

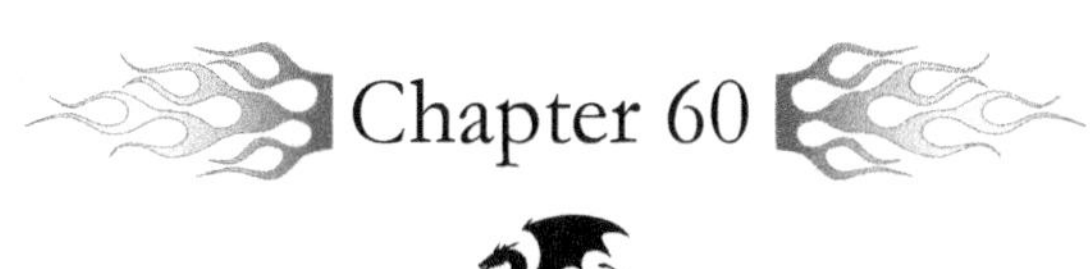

Chapter 60

"His army?" Jydryn fought to constrain his voice as he stood at the open door speaking with Herbert. Jydryn turned to Keena. "Your father is related to the king, is he not? What cause would the king have to come armed to these gates?"

"He is your father's distant cousin, my lady." Herbert wrung his hands as he remained outside the room at the threshold. His weight shifted between his feet so fast he appeared to be dancing. "The man who was king when your parents wed often requested Lord Rycharde at court and sent messengers here to see him. He died last year. His son, King Gallagher, rules now. He came here once, just after he was crowned to take your father to task for not attending his coronation, my lady."

Jydryn tried not to be offended, as the thane did not address him.

"Rycharde has returned home before?" Keena braided her hair in one fat braid and pinned it up in a knot at the base of her head. Jydryn preferred it down.

"At least twice a year he has appeared at the gates. We cleaned him and tended to him, but no matter how we guarded him, or the doors and gates we locked, he always slipped away again. His mind remained fogged, but he knew he'd lost something of great value and he had to search for it—even if he didn't know what it was."

Jydryn needed to get the man back on point. "So, why is King Gallagher charging here *now* with his army?"

"The king is changing many things. He has taken the holdings of other lords faithful to his father and given them to his unworthy companions. It would seem Lord Rycharde's holdings are next."

"He aims to lay siege to the castle until we surrender it to him?" Keena glanced between Herbert and Jydryn.

Jydryn could smell her fear and sense it through their connection.

"I have the kitchens preparing a feast—"

"No!"

Herbert turned with Jydryn to stare at her.

Keena drew in a deep breath with her eyes closed. When she looked up again, she filled her voice with confidence. "Set up a table and two chairs …" She pointed to the one in their room as an example. "… outside the gate. Lord Rycharde, Dryn, and I will meet the king there. You are to keep the drawbridge closed until we indicate otherwise."

"My lady?"

"Keena?" Jydryn spoke at the same time as the thane.

"Have the table set with only the minimum honor demands to greet an important visitor. A cup of friendship or bread—or whatever is required."

"But, my lady—"

"There is no time to argue. Dress Lord Rycharde in his finest and we will meet you in the bailey in a quarter hour." Keena turned back to the wardrobe as Herbert turned and looked at Jydryn.

Jydryn closed the door. "Are you sure about this?"

She pulled him back to the pillow they'd left on the floor last night and lowered to her knees. When he joined her, she took his other hand and bowed her head. "Pray over us," she pleaded.

He wasn't sure what he was seeking the Lord for, but any assistance the Father could provide would be welcome. "Our great God in Heaven, we come to You now in another time of distress. You have been faithful to us in all our trials. Your hand protects us. You guide us. And we come to You again as an army bears down on this castle where we take refuge —"

Keena interrupted. "But You have said not to fear them, for You are with us."

Jydryn smiled at the confidence in his mate's voice. His mate knew to put her trust in God. "We are in Your hands, Father. And if You are for us, who can be against us? You have already written the outcome of this day in Your book. We rest in Your care and love for us. Go before us and put the words we are to say into our mouths. And those not to be spoken, keep far from us. We go trusting in You. In the name of the Son, amen."

"Amen." Keena rocked back on her heels, stood, and whirled to the wardrobe once more. She drew out a bright yellow overdress and added it to her garments. The layers of red-trimmed orange and yellow made her look like a walking sunrise.

Jydryn pulled on his boots and grabbed a short tunic and brocade doublet as he raced out the door after her.

He finished buttoning the outer garment as they came to the gate where Herbert held Lord Rycharde's elbow to keep him from wandering across the lowered drawbridge. The lord's hair was trimmed, so it only touched his ears. His beard now hugged his jaw, much like Jydryn's. Clean and in a doublet even finer than Jydryn wore, the man now looked like a nobleman and cousin of the king.

Herbert looked out at the open field that surrounded the road to the castle. "My lady, are you sure this is the course of action you wish to take?"

"Will the wards the fae put around this fortification allow the king to enter with his army?"

Herbert's already pinched features tightened. He shook his head, causing disorder to his well-groomed hair. "No, my lady."

"Then, yes, I am sure." She took her father by the hand. As always, his eyes seemed to focus, and he looked at her. "Come, my lord. Your cousin wishes a word," she said as they crossed the bridge.

The creak and moan of the drawbridge rising behind them filled the air. Jydryn knew he could always shift to protect them, and he trusted his mate and her fae power, but he agreed with Herbert. Standing here unprotected seemed unwise.

Rycharde grumbled. "What does that whiny weakling want now?"

"Your lands and your title, sir." Jydryn kept his hand on Keena's back as they approached the small table placed in the dirt.

"He wouldn't dare." Rycharde's voice pitched higher than it should for a man with authority of his own.

Keena snatched back his hand and held it firm. Jydryn followed her gaze to the horizon. There, on the road they had travelled only hours ago, a row of horses march toward them. An endless number followed. The mail on their riders glistened in the late morning sun.

Keena helped her father sit. Jydryn noted she rested her hand on her father's shoulder, so her little finger pressed against the bare skin of his neck.

Rycharde sat tall as the army bore down on them.

A dark brown steed broke from the others and thundered toward the table. It reined in at the last moment, kicking up a cloud of dust.

Rycharde waved it from his face and looked up at the helmed man. "Greeting's, cousin. Please, come sit, and let us discuss why you have come."

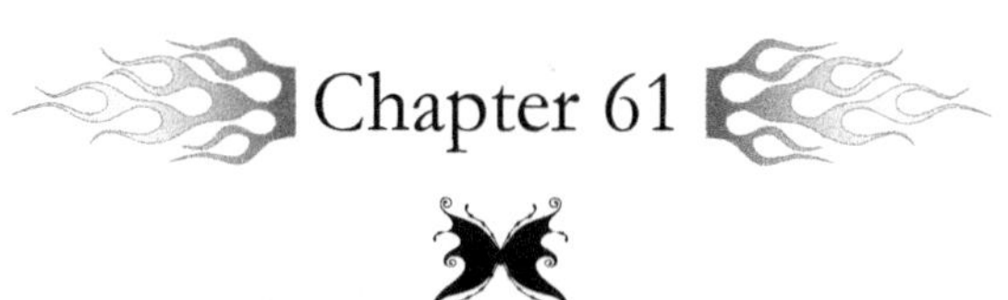

Chapter 61

Keena waited with Rycharde who sat on her right. Jydryn stood on her left with his comforting hand on her back.

The man hiding in the helmet sat still as his horse huffed.

"Your Majesty, do you intend to sit there in such a threatening manner or come and share a cup of friendship and discuss matters like men? We are the nobility of the Keyaral Kingdom. I would hope we can talk things through in a dignified fashion." Lord Rycharde was in full possession of his mind this morning, but his familiar way of addressing the king of all the human realm rattled Keena's nerves.

He tries to prove he is no threat and willing to talk, Jydryn's thoughts whispered in her mind.

At last, the king drew off his helmet and set it in his lap. Keena blinked several times and had to suck her lip into her mouth to keep from sneering. The king had a rather long face with a protruding jaw that hung low. His eyes were small which made them hard to see as he narrowed his gaze on Rycharde. Pale skin, thin, curly, yellow hair, and a small puckered mouth gave the man, who didn't look older than she, a rather hideous appearance. How could they be related?

"You dishonor me, Rycharde." His voice seemed to emanate from the back of his throat out through his nose, pitching the tone far too high for a man.

"How so, Your Majesty?" Rycharde seemed unbothered by the accusation. "I greet you unarmed in the face of your superior forces with a cup of friendship."

King Gallagher nodded, and a squire rushed forward to place a step beside his horse. The king handed the youth his helmet, stepped down, and strode to them on short legs. He was only about as tall as Keena. "You will relinquish your lands, Rycharde."

"There is to be no discussion then?" Rycharde sat taller and placed both clenched fists on the table on either side of the elegant silver goblet. His volume grew so the soldiers settling into their formation behind the king and awaiting their liege's order could hear. "Do the other *rightful* lords of Keyaral approve of your actions? As my men and I hold the territory from here to the eastern border—in your name—we are the first defense against attacks. Even in my frequent absences no one has breached our border in five decades. Can you say the same for the rest of your borders?"

Keena fought to stay connected to Rycharde as he pushed to his feet. His hands still fisted on the table as he leaned over it. She eased forward and pressed one finger to the pulse on his wrist before he could mumble something incoherent.

Rycharde's voice vibrated with anger. "Have I failed to pay the taxes owed by this territory?" He paused, but the king gave no reply. "Have my men failed to come to your father's call or not fought with bold honor in the king's army?" Again, the king gave no reply. Rycharde straightened; his palm covered the back of her hand. "Then by what cause do you come here with your army to strip me of my title?"

"I am the king." Gallagher sneered and sounded like a petulant child. "I hold the power to give and take away my favor. As you have produced no heir, and refuse to attend matters at court, I've chosen one more attentive to my needs. These lands are mine."

"I have an heir."

Gallagher's gaze shifted to Jydryn and swept over him. "Picking some muscular man off the streets does not make him your rightful heir,

Rycharde."

"This is my daughter—"

"Keena, Your Majesty." She curtsied. "And this is my husband, Dryn."

Jydryn bowed deep at the waist. "Your Majesty."

The king erupted in a grating chuckle. "Bedding some trollop does not give you the right to claim her as your child."

Rycharde leaned on his knuckles on top of the table. His joints popped and echoed through the wood while his voice slid forth low and harsh. "You may think anything of me you like, Gallagher, but you will not dishonor my daughter with your slanderous words. I am long wed to her mother. All the castle can attest to our ceremony before the castle priest, Father Aiden. He recorded it in the records of births, marriages, and deaths of the city. You can speak with any you like and see for yourself. And most of my current maids were present for her birth."

Gallagher snorted but with less zeal. "Father left no record you sought permission to wed."

"I'm sure your good father did not write down all his dealings. Nevertheless, it was a love match and no concern of my king's. But her family was against our union, so we spoke our vows in haste. Once her kin learned of it, they stole my family away. I have searched for them ever since. I sought their welfare over your petty need to keep me under your thumb at court."

Keena drew in a deep breath. *Signal them to lower the drawbridge.*

Jydryn swiveled behind her and the chains rattled as the bridge dropped.

"You are vulnerable out here alone—with your family." Gallagher leaned forward and bared his large square teeth. "This castle is mine!"

"King Gallagher!" Keena waited until his gaze slid to her as she placed Rycharde's hand in Jydryn's behind her back. Each word snapped with compulsion. "Get on your horse."

The king jerked straight, his stare blank as he turned.

Take Lord Rycharde inside and raise the bridge again.

Keena widened her stance and dug her toes into the dirt, anchoring herself to the earth and the power flowing from it. It was not magic or some mystical power coming from her, but the touch of her Almighty Creator. He held all power, and He now gifted her access to it to defend her family.

As Gallagher obeyed her command and climbed back into his saddle, Keena bowed her head. "I am Yours, my God. Use me as an instrument in Your gracious hands."

Chapter 62

Jydryn leaped on the end of the drawbridge before it rested on the ground and hauled Keena's father up beside him. They raced down the long boards toward the closed portcullis. "Raise the bridge again."

"What?" Herbert choked.

"But Layna …" Lord Rycharde said as he tried to pull from Jydryn's grasp and turn back to his daughter.

"She is as powerful as her mother, my lord. You should be more worried about your king."

"Raise it!" Herbert ordered. His men seemed unclear what the thane wanted raised so, as the drawbridge closed behind them, the portcullis also rose, allowing them entrance.

Jydryn ducked under it with the lord and handed him off to the same dark-skinned servant who had shown him to the bath last night. As Jydryn scanned the mounted knights before him, ready to ride to defend their castle, he found most of them to be men of warm brown to dark ebony skin; from the captain to the young pages. All were dark but a few. Most wore their long black hair woven into hundreds of slender braids.

He glanced again at Rycharde. Years in the sun had not caused his deep skin tone. He was a man of color.

"We're ready to fight," Herbert said in his rigid form.

"Good. Post your bowmen on the wall, but have them keep their weapons out of sight." Jydryn turned to the nearest access to the battlements and unbuttoned the doublet.

"How can I help?" Dusk fell into step beside him.

Jydryn tossed his outer garment aside as he pointed to two squires. "I need that beam and that stump." He pointed to the items as he climbed the stairs. "Bring them up here."

"Aye, my lord," the boys said as one and moved to complete the task.

Jydryn turned back to the fae at his side. "Find anywhere you can see her and still access your magic to assist her if she needs it."

"It will be done."

They parted ways at the top of the battlements; Dusk moved to the left to stand over the center of the gate behind Keena while Jydryn turned toward the right. He instructed the boys to put the stump down near the corner of the wall and brace the long thick floor beam on it so it went from the battlement up to a crenel on the wall like a ramp. He removed his shirt and boots and waited.

Moving to the midpoint between the makeshift ramp and Dusk, Jydryn looked past his mate to the ranks of mounted knights with their shields on their arms and swords drawn.

Keena's commanding voice filled the field. "I am Keena a' Arlayna. Daughter of Lord Rycharde of Wealdstone—the eleventh earl from his family to labor as a faithful servant of the kings of Keyaral, cousin to King Gallagher—and … Queen Nashala of Shimmerbourne!"

The king's soldiers lowered their weapons as they looked at one another.

My dragon and I are ready to join you in battle, my love.

"My husband is Jydryn, the Champion of Life—"

Jydryn turned and raced for the ramp.

"—son of Govam the Protective—"

He charged up the coarse wood and off the end.

"—nephew of the king of the dragons!"

He shifted as he leapt into the air and roared as he sailed over the soldiers. Many dropped their weapons. Horses bolted. The trained lines of seasoned warriors dissolved into chaos.

The drawbridge lowered behind her as Jydryn banked to hover over her and face their enemy. Voices of those in the castle and those reforming their lines melded together.

"Yes, see your empress!" Dusk shouted as he stepped beside Keena.

"I have no quarrel with you. But we will defend ourselves," Keena said. "I don't believe the claims the fae assert about me. 'Tis a concern for another day. This day, I seek the safety of those in our care and the restoration of Shimmerbourne. I have a battle against a dark faction of fae I must fight." Keena drew in a deep breath. "I bid you, King Gallagher, and all those with you, to leave in peace."

"Never!" Gallagher roared as he hefted his sword in the air—few of his men answered his battle cry.

"Then I offer your men a choice. Face me now …" Huge oak trees burst from the ground, six on either side of Keena to frame the outside edge of the moat. Their trunks were as thick as Jydryn in his dragon form and so tall he had to climb higher in the sky to get out of their way. Their branches only grew on the side of Gallagher and his soldiers. They reached out over their heads and covered them in deep shadows.

The lines of the soldiers were again in disarray.

"… fae magic …" Keena continued.

Beside her, Dusk held a sparkling blue ball of magic suspended between his hands.

"… dragon fire …"

Jydryn swooped low past the trees and released a long blast of flame over their heads. Many men fell to the ground and screamed.

"… *and* swords and bows…"

Rycharde's army of one-hundred men spread out behind her, filled the bridge, and lined the front of the battlements. They beat their swords against their shield in unison through a short-syncopated rhythm before they released a battle cry.

"Face us now as you fight *against* us … or leave this field to fight *with* me on another day," Keena concluded.

"You do not command my men," Gallagher shouted.

"I have not commanded them!" The earth shook, and the trees swayed at her shouted words. The next statement came quieter yet filled with no less strength. "You will know when I command them."

She addressed the king's soldiers as they looked at one another. "Stay and fight. Or leave. The choice is yours. But should you choose to leave, tell your name to the trees. It will pay the debt of your life if you come when the breeze whispers your name and you fight at my side."

The soldiers shifted as they watched one another.

"Captains, cut down any who would abandon their king," Gallagher ordered.

Jydryn looped over the disorganized clump of three hundred soldiers. Three stood out with colorful plumes on their helmets, marking them as captains. Two of them turned and followed their men, leaving the field in neat ranks. The third stayed behind the king but did nothing to prevent the others from leaving.

The king and a few dozen men remained.

"It is time to leave in peace, Your Majesty," Keena said.

"This is not over, woman."

"Of that, I have no doubt, Majesty."

Keena turned. Dusk followed at her side. Rycharde's men jostled to turn their mounts on the drawbridge and re-enter the castle's fortifications. Jydryn sailed over them and scanned for a safe place to land within the walls.

The quiet swoosh of arrows taking flight caused Jydryn to whirl in a tight circle. Two bolts sailed at Keena. Before he could call warning, they hit a protective shield she had at her back, which remained invisible except where the arrows struck and shattered.

Gallagher held another arrow, nocked and readied.

Keena stopped and swiveled until she looked at the king again. "And now your few remaining men know you are a man without honor. To fire at your enemy's back when they have offered you peace is the ultimate in ignoble behavior."

The remaining men, and even his squire, turned their backs on the shamed king and left. With a scream, Gallagher loosed a final arrow.

Keena raised her hand, and the projectile stopped in midflight. It dangled in the air, spun, hurtled back at the king, brushed past him, causing him to squeal, and sunk deep into the ground at his horse's flank. "That is your last warning, King Gallagher. Go home."

He kicked his horse to speed and fled back down the road.

Jydryn tucked his wings as he lowered between several buildings in the bailey. He watched as the others entered.

"Princess." Dusk tossed Keena a pair of men's pants as she came toward Jydryn.

He shifted and dressed behind her skirts. He wrapped her in his arms as she leaned her weight back into him and her head dropped to his shoulder.

In front of them, every knight took a knee as they thrust their swords into the air. "We swear our swords to Lord Rycharde, and his daughter, Empress Keena a' Arlayna."

"And it begins," Jydryn whispered in her ear.

Keena sighed.

A child's shriek filled the reverent air of the ward.

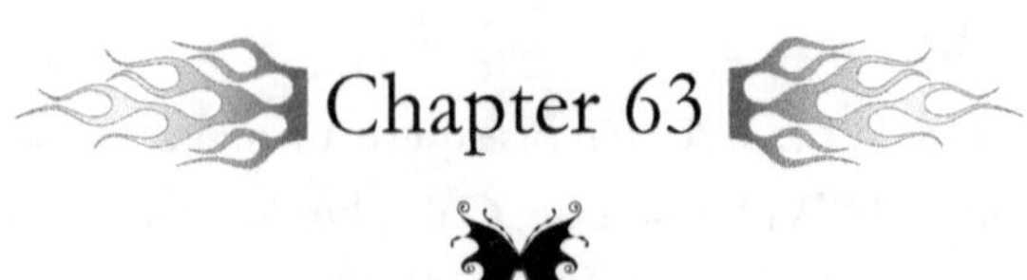

Chapter 63

Every muscle in Keena's tired body tightened at Rose's sharp wail. Soldiers moved out of the way. Horses tossed their heads and shied. Rose released another ear-piercing shriek.

Pushing the last two soldiers apart, Peyton emerged, caught sight of Keena and Jydryn, and hurtled toward them. Callum ran a step behind her. They crashed into Keena's legs with such force she grunted. They clung to her skirts and filled the fabric with muttering and tears.

Dolcie, Lord Rycharde's housekeeper who oversaw all the maids in the castle, stepped through the opening Peyton and Callum had created. Her hair, white from her advanced years, hung in disarray around her face and down her back. She pursed her lips as she struggled to keep a hold of Rose.

The distraught infant pushed against Dolcie's shoulder until her arms and legs were straight against the housekeeper's grip.

"What is going on?" Keena shouted to be heard over Rose's wailing.

Rose stopped pushing against Dolcie, twisted in her grasp, and tried to throw herself at Keena.

Dolcie snatched a better hold of the squirming child before she fell.

Peyton and Callum lifted their heads, and both spoke at the same time as Rose shrieked again.

"Silence!"

Even Keena jumped at Jydryn's harsh bark.

The soldiers cleared their throats or looked away as smiles played on their lips. They occupied themselves with stabling their mounts and left Jydryn, Keena, Dolcie, and the children.

Keena pulled from Jydryn's hold with a deep sigh as the children whimpered. "Peyton, you first. What in all Shimmerbourne is going on?"

"Everyone is mean here." Her words stuttered through her tears.

Keena propped her fists on her hips. The children had been asleep most of their time in the castle. "Mean? I don't understand."

"They makes us stay in ours room," Callum said.

"They wouldn't let us see you." Peyton tipped her head back and lifted her hands. At ten, she was a little too big to be carried around, but Jydryn lifted her to his chest and her arms and legs wrapped around him.

"As we were facing an army of angry soldiers, I am glad they kept you safe inside. There are going to be times when we can't be together. It is something you must all understand," Keena said with a huff.

Keena couldn't walk with Callum still clinging to her legs, but Dolcie came close enough for Keena to take Rose. The toddler buried her wet face against Keena's neck.

Peyton turned her head on Jydryn's shoulders to look at Keena. "They make us eat yucky things too."

"Little balls o' lettuce," Callum explained.

"We brought in a wet nurse for Lady Rose, but she refused to suckle." Dolcie worked to rewind her braid. Her dark eyes met Keena's with a hard stare.

"Now, don't go scolding my daughter so, Dolcie. She has done her best to mother these children while dealing with an absent-minded old man and fighting the fae at every turn." Rycharde seemed very clear-minded at the moment, though Keena wasn't touching him.

Dusk stepped beside the lord with a tight smile. "Your mother must be getting closer," he said with a tip of his head to Rycharde.

"Is your mother coming to visit, young lady?" Rycharde's mind slipped again. It seemed such a fragile thing. He shook his head. "Yes,

Nash is coming. She will be here soon." His words spoke like he understood, but his voice was soft and whispery, as if he didn't.

They didn't speak as they ambled through the inner gate and into the castle. Keena led, with Jydryn, Dusk, and Rycharde behind her, and Dolcie at the tail of their little procession.

"Which way to the hall, my lord?" Keena asked.

He looked at her and blinked. "Are we going to a feast?" He glanced at his attire of dark pants tucked into tall, polished boots, a deep green shirt and gray doublet with gold stitching. "I am dressed for it."

"We are going to share a meal together," Keena coaxed.

"Oh, that is a fine idea. I am quite hungry." Rycharde turned to the right and led them a short distance before he turned to the left. They walked along another hall lined with paintings before he opened a door. He waved them in ahead of him.

Floor-to-ceiling paned windows lined the right wall and looked out on a small garden full of young buds. Weeping trees shaded benches positioned along a winding path. Inside, in front of the windows, sat a long table surrounded by a dozen chairs.

Four maids entered from the far end of the table. One lit all the candles. Two other maids opened cabinets against the wall opposite the windows and drew out plates and cups. The final maid went to a drawer and gathered forks and spoons.

Keena stopped the maids with the dishes before they placed them on the table. "It would be best if the two older children had tin plates and cups."

"Yes, my lady."

Rycharde wandered around the room and looked out a glass door centered in the windows. "What an enchanting garden. Do you suppose the owner would permit me a stroll?"

"It is your garden, my lord," Jydryn said as he pulled out a chair and helped Peyton sit. Callum climbed into the one beside her and sat on his knees. Keena took the one to his right at the corner and Jydryn sat beside Peyton, sandwiching the children between them.

Herbert poked his head in the door they'd entered and huffed a deep sighed. "Oh good, here you are, my lord."

"Herbert, my friend, are these gardens not exquisite?"

"Aye, my lord." Now free of his mail, Herbert straightened his shirt as he strode to his lord's side. "Your mother did a fine job in creating it, and Queen Nashala infused it with a bit of her earth magic to keep it growing and blooming all year around. Keeps Edwin quite busy tending it."

"Fae magic, you say?" Rycharde giggled and rubbed his hands together. "How exciting."

"Your wife is very special."

"Wife, oh you jest, Herbert. What sport is this?"

Herbert drew the lord's attention to the table. "You are long wed, my lord. Here sits your daughter, her husband, and their children."

"The dragon." Rycharde gripped the back of the chair at the end of the table beside Keena and looked at Jydryn with a wide grin. "Oh sir, you are a sight to behold."

Jydryn inclined his head.

"Won't you sit and eat with us?" Keena said as a new string of servants entered the room with trays and bowls of steaming food.

"Excellent idea, my dear. I am hungry." Rycharde took his seat, and Herbert sat beside him, opposite Keena. Jydryn waved Dusk to the seat across from him.

Dolcie stood at the opposite end of the table from Rycharde; her nose in the air and her lips pursed. "Would you like us to serve?"

"No, 'tis just family here, Dolcie. We can pass the trays ourselves," Rycharde said with a smile. He waved her back to the kitchen.

Keena marveled at the comings and goings of his lucidity.

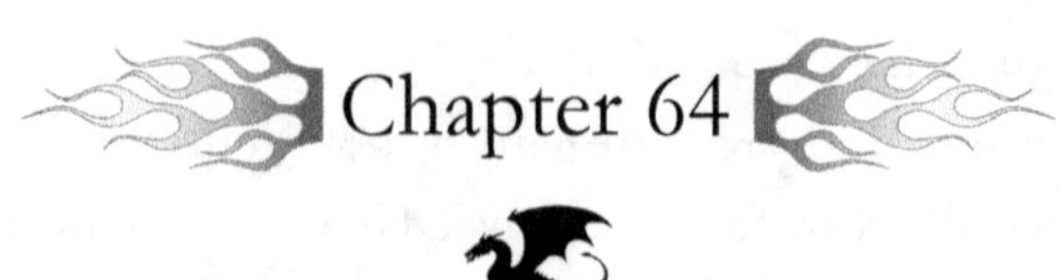

Chapter 64

Jydryn's stomach roared as the servants placed the food on the table alongside two metal pitchers. All but two maids left. They stood against the wall behind him.

Before anyone picked up a tray, Keena looked over Callum and Peyton to him. "Jydryn, will you bless our meal?"

He nodded and offered Peyton his hand. The girl took it and her brother's in the other. Callum reached for Keena and she took his hand while Rose, who sat in her lap, patted their hands and giggled. Keena turned her glance to her father and offered her hand. He looked at it for a moment, as if he didn't believe it was real, but he took it at last.

Jydryn hadn't expected the lord to offer his hand to his thane, but Herbert took it with a smile and offered his other to the fae.

Dusk glanced at Jydryn and then Keena. Jydryn was about to tell the fae he didn't have to link hands, but Dusk took the thane's hand and reached across the table to clasp Jydryn. A tiny ripple of magic tickled over Jydryn's skin.

When Jydryn ended his prayer, Keena, Peyton, and Callum said 'Amen' together as Rose tried to mimic their sound.

"Amen," muttered Herbert.

They released their hands, and passed the food around the table.

"It has been a long time since I heard a prayer," Rycharde said. "My mother followed the Way when I was young. There used to be a small chapel … somewhere."

"I think your father turned it into weapons storage." Herbert passed a plate of cheese to Rycharde.

"That's a shame," Jydryn said.

Keena selected a few slices from the tray and held it in front of Callum. "This is cheese." She pointed to four pieces she knew the boy had tried before. "You like these kinds, but you might like the other two as well."

He took one of each of the kinds he liked and Jydryn took the plate to hold for Peyton.

Rose snatched up one slice from Keena's plate and stuffed it in her mouth.

"Small bites or you'll choke and you won't like that," Keena warned as she took the next tray with meat pies the size of Jydryn's fist.

She glanced at the children. "These are big. Perhaps you two should share one."

"You can always have another if you are still hungry afterward." Jydryn placed a pie on his plate and another on Peyton's before he cut hers in half and offered a portion to Callum.

As Jydryn watched Keena attend to the children more than normal, tickles of her guilt and hints of shame crossed their bond.

Keena glanced up at Dolcie as the housekeeper strolled into the room again. Keena's words to the children were more for Dolcie. "Peyton and Callum, remember what you ate before we met? This is good food, prepared well, and good for you. It is not rotten or covered in mold."

The children wrinkled their noses when asparagus tops, pieces of Brussels sprout, and a few peas placed on their plate.

"I agree, not everything good for you is tasty," Lord Rycharde said to the children. "But I find if I eat the things I don't care for first, the rest isn't so bad." He stabbed a Brussels sprout on his fork, plugged his nose with his other hand, and stuffed it in his mouth.

The older children laughed, but Rose snatched up the remaining bit of the sprout Keena had cut up and shoved it in her mouth.

"She is too young for solid food. She should still be nursing." Dolcie glared down her nose.

Rose fisted her hands and spit the offensive leaves out as Keena's shoulders fell.

"She has only had goat's milk since she came to us," Jydryn tried to intervene. "She started eating gruel not long ago, mixed with a lot of milk, and mashed up fruit and vegetables."

The housekeeper's eyes widened as her brows rose to her hairline. "She is not yours?"

"Jydryn rescued her from a burning altar," Keena muttered as she tried to clean up the mess Rose had made.

"Her 'as sars on her wegs," Callum said.

"A despicable human practice." Dusk grunted.

"Agreed." Jydryn met his gaze with a nod.

"I will inform the cook." Dolcie turned and left.

"You have made a powerful enemy today, Layna," Rycharde's hushed voice drew everyone's attention.

Keena's head snapped up. She looked from her father to the door the housekeeper had disappeared through.

"Gallagher is a fool, but he is also king of the human realm. Make no mistake, Nash, he will come after us for defying him and marrying without his approval." Rycharde's mind slipped again.

"I seem to collect enemies wherever I go." Keena's voice was small as she glanced at the door again.

"You have also gathered a host of powerful allies as well, princess," Dusk said as he hoisted his cup in toast.

She managed a small smile as she pushed from the table. "I'm going to take Rose to her room."

"I can do that, my lady." One maid behind Jydryn stepped forward.

"Unfortunately, I need to change as well." As she stood, Jydryn noted a large wet stain over the lap of her dress.

"We need better nappies," Jydryn said with a sigh. It wasn't the first time either of them had to change after holding the toddler.

"You haven't even finished your meal, Nash. Let the maid take Layna and stay with me." Rycharde reached for her.

"My lord—" Keena said.

"Can I have a tart?" Peyton broke in on the conversation.

Keena looked at her with a raised brow.

"I ate my vegetables."

Keena tipped her head.

Peyton looked from her to the lord before she ducked her head and muttered, "Sorry."

As Keena turned back to give her regrets to her father, Peyton turned to Jydryn and whispered, "Can I have a tart now?"

"After you finish the vegetables you've hidden in your lap, young lady."

Her mouth opened wide.

Jydryn tapped his nose. "A dragon's sense of smell is powerful."

Peyton's lower lip pooched out and tears filled her eyes as she dropped the asparagus and bit of Brussels sprout on her plate again.

Jydryn let the girl pout as he looked up at his mate. *Do you want me to come with you?*

She shook her head and followed the maid from the room.

"She's had a long day fighting with her father. The king of the fae is not a kind man." Rycharde popped a bite of meat pie in his mouth.

Keena had had a long day, fighting with a human king, suffering the disapproval of a housekeeper, and the ramblings of a man who didn't always remember who she was. Jydryn would give her a few moments, assure the maids attended to the children, and then go to her.

Chapter 65

Keena entered the nursery ahead of the maid and continued to the two low, narrow beds at the far side of the room.

"The babe sleeps here." The maid pointed to a small basket on a stand near the door to her and Jydryn's chamber. Had Rose been in there last night? She'd been tired—was still tired—too tired it seemed.

Keena laid the baby on one bed and changed her. "Rose is quite an active child. She is already crawling and has pulled herself up to stand many times. If she were to attempt to do so in the basket, she'd topple out of it and get hurt."

The maid pursed her lips.

"I will inform Dolcie of my wishes to have Rose sleep with Peyton."

"Thank ya, m'lady," the maid said with a long sigh as she came to her side. "I can change her, if you like."

Rose kicked her legs and threw her hands over her head as if she'd understood and didn't want the maid to help.

Keena shook her head. "Thank you—"

"Ella, m'lady." The maid curtsied again.

"Thank you, Ella. I can manage. Then I'll sit with her a bit until she's asleep."

"As ya wish, m'lady."

Keena smiled as she pulled off Rose's soaked gown. "You are doing a fine job, Ella. I have not been apart from her this long before. I have missed her."

Rose giggled and pulled on Keena's hair as Keena blew raspberries on her little belly.

Ella settled into the large cushioned chair in the corner. "Thank you for saying such, m'lady." She paused. "I've only been 'ere a few weeks. Mistress Dolcie does not seem happy with my skill."

Keena turned to sit on the floor beside the bed with her back against the wall. The hum of the earth through the uncut stones soothed her. She stroked Rose's soft, loose curls and looked at Ella with a smile. "I have felt the same way. Perhaps the housekeeper is just not happy." She sounded more hopeful than she felt.

Ella snickered into her hands. "All the maids try to avoid her," she whispered.

Keena was already making plans to do the same. She let her gaze fall on Rose again.

Rose sucked on her fist as she fought to keep her eyes open.

"She's a delightful baby."

Keena's smile grew. "My sweet little angel."

With a jerk, Keena opened her eyes. Ella sat, working on some embroidery, and Rose was asleep. "How long—"

"Only a few minutes, m'lady."

Keena drew in a deep breath before she stood. The stain on her dress was dry, but still pungent. She crossed to her chamber with a yawn.

"I can take your gowns to the laundress with Miss Rose's things later if you leave them here." Ella pointed to a basket with a lid near her chair.

"Thank you, Ella." She suffered another noisy yawn.

The maid giggled. "If you don't mind me sayin' so, m'lady, you could use a nap as much as little Rose."

"I don't mind, and I don't disagree." She smirked and stepped into her chamber.

In a new simple kirtle with a belt, Keena took her soiled garments to the basket. Returning to her chamber, she sat on the side of the bed. Another yawn spoke of her deep need for sleep, but the thoughts rattling in her head only grew in volume the more she tried to quiet them.

She jerked the door to the hall open and strolled out of her chamber and through the castle. Before she knew where she intended to go, she stood on the battlements near the outer gate. The field of crushed grass where Gallagher's men had been earlier stretched in front of her. The trees she had summoned were gone. She already had one powerful enemy. To provoke another had been foolish. Yes, Wealdstone was Lord Rycharde's ancestral home—hers too—but when he reunited with Queen Nashala, they would most likely make their home in Shimmerbourne the capital of the fae kingdom.

Her deep sigh was almost a groan as she leaned her weight on her forearms as they rested on a crenel. If the fae were right, and she was this long-lost empress of all the land, then it appeared she and Jydryn would find their home overgrown by the forest in Crystalbrooke. Did they need Wealdstone any longer? Would it have been better to let Gallagher have it—*after* Nashala and Rycharde renewed their bond?

She leaned heavier against the wall as weariness nipped at every muscle. They could always offer it to him. But, somehow, Keena couldn't see the arrogant king allowing her to escape some punishment.

Now, with two powerful forces after her—one human, one fae—what was she to do with the children? Tears filled her eyes at the thought of being separated from Rose, and Peyton and Callum, even for a day. Her head dropped forward as the thought stole her breath and sent her heart into a frantic rhythm. How much more would Dolcie disprove of her if she took the children with her and then faced her enemies?

Jydryn's heat comforted her before he drew her back into his arms and held her. She tucked her head under his chin and let his strength fill her.

"You are a wonderful mother." His voice rumbled in her hair before he kissed the top of her head.

She whirled, planted her palms on his chest, and stared at him. "How can you say that? I didn't know Rose should still drink milk. The children almost died when Nightshade created a hole under the wagon, and—"

His lips covered her mouth, forcing her silent. He held her close again and kissed her forehead. "You are too hard on yourself, my love."

Keena rested her cheek against his warmth and fought to believe him.

Jydryn brushed up and down her back, soothing her like she had Rose. "There are a few things you must remember. Fifty-nine days ago, you were an emaciated woman full of fear that you'd caused the deaths of many and sickened even more. Forty-one days ago, I brought Rose to you. You gave her a name. Helped me tend her wounds. You kept her alive. Twenty-eight days ago, you came searching for me while men held me in magic chains. You carried Rose and dragged along a goat so she wouldn't go hungry. Twenty-four days ago, you found me, and before the day was over you learned you were fae royalty. Your parents had not abandoned you, but loved and cared for you. And you learned of your powerful enemy—who you have fought three times, losing none who fought with you, my love. You kept Rose safe against Cai and Willuma. Twenty-two days ago, you brought two starving children in off the streets. You have fed and clothed them and taught them how to be part of our family. We are all healthy, strong, and bathed in your love, Keena. That the children do not care for the sour Dolcie and want to be with you does not speak of your failure, but of their need to not stay with strangers and, instead, to be with their mother."

His hands gripped her shoulders and pushed her away only enough to see her face. "Fifty-nine days. Less than two months. The children want for nothing. You are an excellent mother. You are my perfect mate. There is no fault in you."

She searched his face.

"I find it disconcerting when you hide your thoughts so well from me, however." He leaned forward and kissed her forehead. "It seems you must tell me what still troubles you, my mate."

She bit at her lip.

"Please?"

"Why?" She swallowed, took a deep breath, and tried again. "Why did you want me to reveal the dragon? Shifters do not make themselves known to humans. You hadn't even told Rycharde and his men your real name."

Jydryn pulled her close again. "And you thought I did it because I doubted you?" His lips rested in her hair and his breath warmed her scalp. His love flooded into her spirit until it forced tears from her eyes. *I could never doubt you.*

 Chapter 66

Jydryn cradled her tighter. "Oh love, we have both been on a journey of growth and transformation."

She pulled from him, leaned her back against the outer wall, and looked up.

He'd have preferred her in his arms, but he sensed she needed to see his face. "When the gong sounded, summoning the dragon to collect another maiden, I saw it as any other rescue. But you weren't bound, washed, groomed, or dressed in a new gown like the others. The villagers risked getting close to me to assure you didn't escape. But you never tried." He shook his head as he grinned at the memory. "You ran toward me."

Keena's brows still pinched together as she studied him and listened.

"You climbed on my back—and cut your hands on my damaged spine spike. So, I brought you home—"

"Fifty-nine days ago."

His grin widened, and he drew in a deep breath of her fresh meadow scent. "Fifty-nine days ago my world tilted, and later it flipped upside down." His gaze returned to her hazel eyes flecked with blue and green. "It righted itself, but it is nothing like it was before."

Her head tipped.

He wasn't explaining this right. "You were so broken when you came to my home. Even then, before I knew of our bond, I imagined holding you until all the broken parts of you fused back together. They had deprived you of love. I wanted you to know God loves you. I wanted to be part of your mending and help you know the truth about how much God cares for you."

"And you?"

He chuckled and rubbed the back of his neck. "That came the day the Dragon Fire ignited between us." He brought his hand up, palm facing her.

Keena did the same, but she didn't press their hands together. Dragon Fire leapt from her hand to his, bringing the flames to life.

He drew in a deep breath. "I never dreamed of finding a life mate. It shook my world, and I understood at last why I had felt so possessive and protective of you. Knowing the bond between us, my goal became to protect you. I had to keep you safe. You were so small and frail— inside and out. That God saw fit to pair a dragon with a starved human made no sense to me."

Keena relaxed against the wall behind her.

He released a long breath and braced a hand on either side of her. "But when humans captured me, *you* came for *me*. You walked for days, argued with me, and fought to remove my chains. I have never been more terrified in my entire life. It was my job to keep you safe, and you endangered yourself and Rose to rescue me. You were so much stronger than I gave you credit for—so much more."

She brushed his cheek.

He leaned so their noses almost touched. "Then, I found you in the fae court. When I asked you to remove your shoes, it was only a test. I wasn't sure you were one of them." He smirked and wiggled his eyebrows. "Kind of hoped you weren't."

At last, she offered him a shy grin.

"If you were fae, I expected the dead natural surroundings to respond to you in some fashion. And they did. Seeing everything come back to life surprised me. But when I proclaimed your name and your birthright for all to hear …" His head shook at the memory. "… your magic is *powerful*. You aren't frail, or weak, or needing of my protection. You are a fae princess, and my goal altered to help you step into this new role. Like when I first shifted, and I had to become comfortable with who I am in both forms, you needed to become who you are as a fae."

"But …"

He stared at the beautiful half fae woman who was his mate. "But … we completed our bonding. We became one. No longer Keena a' Arlayna and Jydryn the Champion of Life, but life mates. I can't be who God designed me to be without you. I can't hide in my old fears of revealing my shifter nature, or remain in the shadows, if you are to be who God created you to be. We vowed before our Creator to face everything together." He pressed his forehead to hers. "Raising children, building a life for us, *and* sharing our battles."

A long breath slid out. Keena's arms slipped around him.

Still, something bubbled under the surface. Something she wouldn't say. Jydryn used a single finger to draw her chin up until he gazed into her eyes again. They danced in the late afternoon light. Her lips parted for just a moment and she tried to tuck her head against his chest again.

He cradled her face so she continued to look at him. "What? Why won't you speak the words and tell me what you need?" It cut him to know she kept things from him.

She tried to shake her head. "It's nothing."

"Can we decide that together?" His thumb brushed her lower lip.

"It's silly. Nothing important."

He kissed her cheek. "What do you want, my love?"

She bit her lip but the barrier she'd raised to keep him out of her thoughts slipped. He saw an image of her soaring through the clouds on his dragon, and she couldn't contain the excitement in that moment.

He laughed and then kissed her. "I would love to fly with you again."

Rose's shriek—though not as angry as earlier in the day—and the laughter of Peyton and Callum drifted up the wall to interrupt them.

Jydryn kissed her again. "They will call us to the evening meal soon —"

"Children. Come here! You can't run about the bailey in such a wild manner. There are people working," Dolcie scolded.

"And we need to rescue our children from that grumpy woman." He kissed her forehead as he drew her to the inner side of the battlement wall so they could look down into the bailey. "We will fly after sunset when they are in bed, my love."

# Chapter 67

Our children. Jydryn's words bubbled inside her along with his promise to take her flying later. "Do you really see them as our children?"

"Of course. Don't you?"

"I was afraid to."

In her attempt to get out of Dolcie's grasp, Rose flung herself backward, arching her back over the housekeeper's arm. She spotted them, righted herself, and reached for them, though Keena and Jydryn still stood high on the wall. She babbled as her hands opened and closed.

Her antics drew the attention of the other two children. Peyton's gaze followed Rose's reaching. "Can we come up too?"

"No. We do not allow children on the battlements." Dolcie scowled.

"We're on our way down," Jydryn said as he turned Keena toward the stairs.

"… to our children," she whispered as she snuggled against him.

"Aye, our children. They will grow with us, and we will care well for them. But in the eyes of the world, they are what you called them— wards. They can never inherit one of the seats held by our families. Those are for blood only. But in all other ways, they are our children."

Callum charged at Jydryn and slammed into his legs. Jydryn seized him around the waist and tossed him into the air.

"Oh, good heavens." Dolcie gasped as Keena pulled Rose from her arms.

"He is a strong dragon. The children are safe with him."

Dolcie pushed back her shoulders and glanced down her long, narrow nose. "Even so, it only serves to rile the children. They need to be calm and—"

"Why?" Keena stared at the housekeeper as Peyton moved behind her skirt. "They laid Rose on a pyre to take her life. Peyton and Callum's father abandoned them, and their mother died, leaving them to fend for themselves on the streets of a filthy city. Should we not now allow them to laugh, and run, and play with exuberance?"

Though it didn't seem possible, Dolcie's chin rose even higher. "How are they to learn their proper place if you leave them so unrestrained?"

"Because we shall teach them. There is a time to be stoic and serious, Dolcie. But there is also a time for fun." Keena reached for Peyton's hand, pulled her forward, and grinned at the girl. "I think the gardens would be a fabulous place to play."

Peyton's head bobbed with a vigorous nod.

"Absolutely not." Dolcie all but stomped her foot. "Do you know what kind of havoc these children will wreak on those delicate plants?"

Jydryn settled Callum on his hip and stepped beside Keena. "Are you suggesting, Dolcie, that the fae princess has not taught her children how to care for nature?"

"Don't pulled a flowder out of the grownd even if it are purdy," Callum said as he laid his head on Jydryn's shoulder.

"Look for branches on the ground first, afore ya break one off or cut down a tree. And be careful where ya step—" Peyton added.

Callum's fingers played in Jydryn's long hair. "Stays on a pass like the an-mals."

Jydryn drew Keena around the housekeeper, who still stood in their path, and turned them toward the inner gate. "Sounds like the children are ready to play in the garden."

They passed Ella, who had sucked her lips between her teeth to keep from laughing.

Keena sat Rose on a bit of grass, crossed the path, and sat on a bench next to Jydryn. He wrapped his arm around her and leaned them back against a tree. Callum and Peyton disappeared down the path with high-pitched squeals.

Ella curtsied. "There is a gate to the outside at the far end. I'll make sure they don't go through it."

"Thank you, Ella." Keena nestled into Jydryn and watched Rose scoot about and try to crawl to a small tree, though her long gown hampered her attempts. "Our children," she whispered again.

Jydryn kissed her hair. "Indeed."

Every time sleep weighed her lids, the two older children raced past them, and pulled her awake again.

Rose clung to a slender, white-barked tree and pulled herself upright. Before she found her balance, she whirled and landed hard on her bum and elbow.

Keena waited for the cry, but the tumble seemed to have startled the babe to silence, like she couldn't figure out how she'd ended up on the ground.

Keena felt like she was being watched.

On the balcony above us.

She glanced up over the dining room on the other side of the garden. Behind the branches of a tree, Dolcie glared with her arms crossed.

Rose righted herself and sat. Her lower lip quivered, and she drew in a stuttered breath.

Before she could burst into full-blown tears, Callum barreled down the path. "Da, Da, Pey gonna get me." He climbed Jydryn's legs, stood on his thighs, and continued to climb until one knee pinned some hair to the shifter's shoulder while the boy held on to the top of his head with both hands.

Doesn't that hurt?

Jydryn had the most ridiculous grin on his lips. *Yeah, but …*

"He called you, Da," she whispered.

Peyton came around the corner at a trot, breathing hard.

"Da, don't let 'er get me," Callum wiggled and Jydryn groaned.

Peyton frowned as she stood beside Keena, panting.

Keena brushed the girl's hair from her face. "What's the matter, my sweet?"

"I don't think he should call Jy Da," Peyton said at last.

Chapter 68

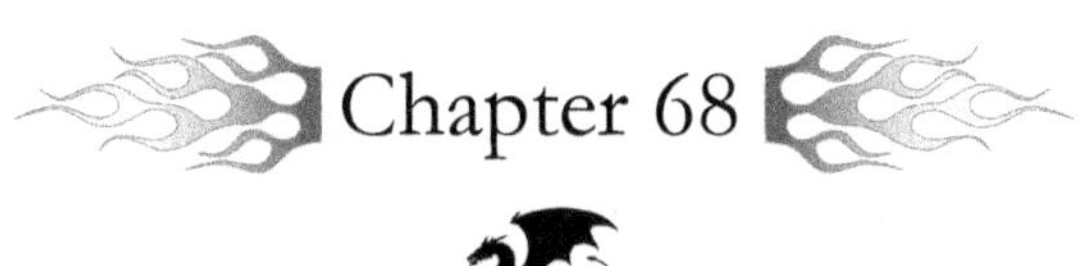

Jydryn swam in the exuberant emotions of being called 'Da' by little Callum. Peyton's word plummeted him back to earth. These were not his children, so why did it hurt that she didn't see him as one worthy of calling father?

"Oh?" Jydryn freed his hair from the boy and sat Callum on his thigh. "Why not?"

"Don't you think he loves you?" Keena asked.

Peyton stood out of reach and hugged herself tight. "Ya are both good to us. But … one day ya'll have kids of yar own. Then ya won't want us no more."

Keena stretched, caressed Peyton's hair and kissed her forehead. "We love you."

"But yar real kids will get yar love."

"Love doesn't work like that," Jydryn said. But how could he explain to such young children the nature of an emotion the best courtly poets couldn't explain?

"Ella?" Keena called. A moment later, the young maid came into view. "Can you fetch me five candles and a match?"

"Aye, m'lady." Ella stepped through the glass door of the dining room and disappeared.

Keena looked at both children. "When Ella gets back, I'm going to show you a little about how love works—but it will make you use your imagination. Do you think you can do that?"

Rose crawled across the path and grabbed Keena's skirt to pull herself up.

"What's maginasons?" Callum asked as he sat up straighter.

"It's pretend. Like when ya find a stick and act like it's a horse," Peyton explained.

Ella returned with the candles. Keena handed one to Jydryn, one to Callum, and another to Peyton. "Can you hold this one too, for Rose?" she asked.

Peyton took it in her other hand.

Keena placed the final one in her lap and opened the tin of matches as the maid stepped away.

"Now, we are going to pretend the candle you have is your heart." Both older children looked from her to the candle and back.

Keena drew out a match. "This is how love works. When Jydryn was growing up, his life was full of love. His father and his mother, grandmother and grandfather, and even his uncle the king, loved Jydryn." She struck the match and lit Jydryn's candle as he smiled at her. "But most of all, God loves Jydryn very much. The fire is like that love." She looked at each face before she continued. "When Jydryn met me, he gave me all the love he had in his heart." She picked up her candle and Jydryn lit it. "But see, even though he gave it all away, his love never went out."

Peyton scrunched up her face.

"Then, Jydryn saved Rose—" The baby giggled as she swayed in front of Keena's knees. "And we both gave all our love to her." Jydryn joined her in lighting the candle Peyton held for Rose. Admiration for his mate grew stronger as she continued the beautiful story of love.

"And then we met you." They lit Peyton's candle. "And you." They finished by lighting Callum's candle. He held it close and stared at the flame.

"That is the wonderful thing about love," Jydryn said, joining Keena in her explanation. "As much as you give it away, you always have more to give." He turned to Peyton. "As long as I live, I will *always* love you." Jydryn looked at Keena for a moment before turning back to the children. "Nothing will ever let me stop loving you."

"When we have more children, we will love them too, but your love will not grow smaller, and we will never take it away." Keena searched Peyton's face. "Do you understand?"

Peyton stared at the flame for a long time. Rose's candle drooped, forgotten in her other hand. Keena took it and blew it out along with her own. Jydryn blew out his, too.

"Mine." Callum jerked his candle away. "No blew out my wuv." His hand jerked the candle in wild loops, but Jydryn clamped his hand over the flame and snuffed it out before clothes or hair could catch fire.

"It was pretend love, remember?" Jydryn soothed the blubbering boy. "You still have all my love in here." He poked him in the chest over his heart and tickled him until Callum squealed with laughter.

When he looked back to Peyton, she'd blown her candle out too. She climbed up beside Keena and wrapped her arms around Keena's neck, as she sniffled. "I love you too, Mommy," she whispered.

"Forgive me, m'lord, m'lady." Behind Ella, beyond the window wall, servants bustled about the dining room. "The evening meal is almost ready." Her voice was soft.

Jydryn stood, settled Callum on his hip again, and offered his hand to Keena. "Come, let's get washed up so we are ready for dinner."

Each with a child on their hip and swinging Peyton between them every couple of steps, they made their way back into the castle.

"I'm afraid I left all the candles on the bench, Ella," Keena said.

The maid swiped at a tear. "I'm happy to collect them, m'lady." She paused before she stepped out of the way and met Keena's gaze. "Thank you, m'lady." Another tear escaped, and she hurried around them.

Keena glanced at Jydryn.

"You are a wonderful mother, my love—even the maid can see and appreciates it."

Dolcie stood near the door to the hall as they entered from the garden.

"We are all going to clean before the meal," Keena blurted.

The housekeeper stepped out of the way with a curt nod. "Well, at least you know to do that, but hurry. We are ready to serve now."

Keena ignored the comment as they entered the hall. "There is another thing about love," she told the children. "We can give it away without losing any of it, and it also stretches over very long distances."

Peyton jerked to a stop. "Are ya gonna leave us?"

Callum tightened his hold around Jydryn's neck.

Crouching in front of the young girl, Keena kissed her hand she still held. "Not right now, but sometime soon, we will need to be apart from you so you stay safe."

"You gonna fight tha ba' man," Callum said.

"Aye." Jydryn kissed his head. "We have to stop him, but we can't take you with us."

Keena nodded. "But we will make sure you are safe and with people we trust to take care of you. It is very important for you to listen to them and behave so we won't worry. Do you understand?"

"But you'll come back, won't ya?" Peyton leaned into Keena.

"Of course we will," Jydryn said.

Keena stood, and they started walking again. *Should you promise them we will return when we could die?*

Jydryn winked at her. *I'm trusting God to preserve us.*

Jydryn waited until they were almost to the nursery before he spoke. "Dolcie may never show her approval, but I think you are winning her over."

"If only all our enemies were so easy." Keena released a dry chuckle.

Jydryn let Peyton and Keena proceed him into the room, but stopped his mate long enough to kiss her temple.

He believed that, but he also worried. He was convinced Keena was to be the empress, but fulfilling her destiny seemed a far-off impossibility in the face of the power and strength of their enemies.

Perhaps tonight, when he took Keena flying, and they worshiped on the wing, God would show them the way.

Chapter 69

Keena floated on the memory of soaring through the sky at twilight and praising God on the back of her mighty dragon. The air still whistled in her ears while her hair had unwound and snapped in the wind.

Jydryn's arms tightened around her and pulled her from the dreamed memory into the new day. "It shouldn't be a surprise. God created you as my mate, but it fills my heart to find that you enjoy flying with me."

She snuggled into him and opened her eyes. Part of her still sensed the undulating movements of his great wings beating until she saw the firm walls of their bedchamber. "We could fly every night, or throughout the day, and I don't think it would ever get old."

He kissed her and slid out of bed. "When your parents re-establish their bond and we deal with the dark fae, I will enjoy taking you as much as you like."

She groaned as he dressed.

He paused with his shirt on his arms, but not over his head yet to glance at her. "Don't you want those things?"

"Of course. But at the moment, I would prefer you back here next to me. Can't the day wait a little longer?"

He drew the shirt on and stalked back to the bed. He leaned over and placed his hands on either side of her, making the mattress dip under his weight. His loving gaze covered her as he lowered and captured her lips. His cinder scent filled her again, and she closed her eyes as she wrapped her arms around his neck.

Far too soon, he pulled away and stood. "There will be time for us soon, my love." He tucked his shirt into the dark pants he wore. "This is our second morning here, and my concern grows for Echo. I pray your mother arrives today."

Keena sighed and threw off the covers as she sat on the edge of the bed. "Has there been any change in his condition?"

"Dusk sustains Echo, but he can't do so much longer."

"Can I help?" She pushed to her feet and went to her wardrobe.

"I asked him, but he believes we need you at your full strength in case Nightshade attacks."

"Then, we'll pray Lilly arrives today. I'll have the maids move our belongings to a chamber in a tower."

Jydryn drew her into his arms before she could get a belt around her simple blue kirtle. "Are you sure?"

"They have anchored the rough cut—and even the polished—stones of the castle into the bedrock of the rocky outcrop where the castle sets perched. I could sense the connection to the earth, even up on the battlements." She looped her arms around his neck again and savored another kiss. "Besides, I have you, and I'm only half fae. The queen—"

"Your mother."

She drew from him and finished dressing. "I know. There is still a distance between us. I pray it will be better once Nashala and Rycharde have renewed their bond."

"I'm praying for the same." He cradled her cheek and kissed her temple. "I'll check on Echo and see if there is anything new from the battlements."

"I'll help get the children up." She finished braiding her hair as she stepped through the doorway into the nursery.

"Honestly, Ella. What are you thinking?" Dolcie's sharp tone greeted her.

"But Mistress Rose is learning to crawl and even tries to pull herself up to walk," Ella said with her head down.

"You foolish girl. Children do not walk until they are over a year old. Rose is not even ten months by the look of her."

"Yet, even yesterday, she pulled herself up twice and stood for some time." Keena stepped beside Ella and faced the housekeeper. "What Ella did not tell you, for in her kindness she hoped to shield me from your ire, is I requested the maids to dress Rose in a shorter child's gown rather than the long christening gown she has worn since we arrived." Keena stepped to the bed where Peyton had been holding Rose and offered the baby her fingers. The sweet babe slid off and stood with a giggle. Rose picked up one foot and her knee kicked, but she didn't take a step. "Regardless of her age, Dolcie, this wee babe will walk long before she is a year old." Keena scooped Rose up and cradled her across her arms before Keena blew raspberries on Rose's belly and made her squeal.

"Oh." Dolcie snorted.

"You may leave, Dolcie. Ella is more than capable with the children."

The woman gasped as her hand pressed to her chest.

"You are the housekeeper of my father's estate. Not a nurse maid. As it is clear you do not care for my children, or for the manner in which I wish them to be tended, I will request Lord Rycharde return you to your normal duties of overseeing the maids of the house. I can see to the nurses who care for the children."

"Well … I …" The woman could not have stood more straight and rigid.

"That will be all, Dolcie. Ella and I can manage." She turned her attention back to Rose and made her shriek with laughter again.

At last, the door banged closed.

"Thank you, m'lady." Ella sighed.

"No, thank you for loving on my children and doing as I asked, even in the face of her wrath."

You need to come to the gate.

Keena turned to Peyton and handed her Rose. "You three listen to Ella. I'm needed elsewhere. Be good for me." The two older children nodded as Rose tried to reach for her again. Keena squeezed the maid's arm as she rushed past. "Watch them."

She dashed through the halls of the expansive castle, skirting servants and officials who startled at her reckless speed. At last, she burst into the ward and careened down the steps and out the inner gate, making guards and squires jump out of her way.

"Up here," Jydryn called as she approached the main gate. The portcullis was down and the drawbridge closed. Maybe the fae queen had not arrived yet.

Jydryn drew her between him and Dusk to glance over the wall. Six fae inched out of the woods. They spread wide apart and craned their necks to watch the sky. One rode in a round, open, two-wheeled carriage pulled by a deer with huge antlers. The woman inside seemed alert as she led them across the field where Gallagher's men had been yesterday. Her blue hair caught in the early morning light.

"Is she the queen?" Keena closed her eyes and tried to remember the confused woman from the fae court.

"Something is off," Dusk said.

"Where are Petal and Lilly?" Keena turned to the fae warrior beside her. "You don't think she can travel without them, like Rycharde couldn't without me." She turned back to the field. "I don't see Badger or Amethyst either."

"Or Doe." Dusk's bright blue hair brushed over his shoulder in a gentle breeze. "My mate." He turned and looked at her. "Doe should travel with the queen as well."

Keena stared down. "If they are not with this group, does it mean they captured our friends—or killed them? Or is this not the queen?"

Chapter 70

Jydryn watched the six fae as they inched toward the castle below him.

"Let us enter!" The blue-haired fae in the cart shouted.

Dusk leaned forward and braced his forearms on the wall. *Hmm.*

Jydryn's dragon rose to the surface. "It isn't the proper way for a fae queen to ask, is it?" Nothing about the woman reminded Jydryn of the queen he'd glimpsed in Shimmerbourne. "Is she your queen?"

Dusk shrugged. "I spend little time in court. Echo kept many of us away so we could work undetected."

"I'll see what I can learn." Jydryn already stood barefoot and now removed his shirt as several of Rycharde's men joined them on the battlements. He raced to the beam he'd propped up like a ramp yesterday.

"Why do they keep looking up?" Keena whispered.

The approaching fae caught the movement as Jydryn raced up the beam. As those walking stopped and crouched, the female leapt out of the cart.

"Wait!" Keena's shout echoed over the wall at the same moment a blast of dark fae magic exploded from a cannon where the carriage had been.

A scattered blast of fiery magic burned Jydryn's skin.

Two of Rycharde's soldiers stood on the opposite end of the beam to keep it on the battlement as Jydryn crouched on the other end in tattered pants after his partial shift to his dragon form. Blood ran from deep sores peppered all over his exposed skin.

"Are you—" Tears cut off Keena's words.

Jydryn turned and worked his way down the board to her. "I'll recover."

Shouts from below drew their attention. The fae were trying to reposition the weapon to fire above the gate where they stood. Keena gripped the stones and glared. In the next blink, the earth below the weapon opened, and it vanished inside, along with two of the attacking fae. Dirt covered them and grass grew, so it looked as though nothing had happened.

Keena stared at Dusk.

"Don't look at me. I don't have that kind of power from this distance, princess," Dusk said.

The remaining attacking fae raced for the tree line.

"If it was actual power, wouldn't I control it more?" Keena muttered.

"Lord Jydryn," Herbert raced toward them. He pointed to the back of the castle. "We have fortified the roofs of the two rear towers' with an extra layer of thick beams. You should be able to take your dragon form on either of them without fear of it collapsing."

Jydryn glanced at him with a raised brow.

The thane shrugged. "The last time Lord Rycharde came, he ordered it done to all the towers." Herbert pointed to the beam Jydryn had used as a ramp as proof.

"How could he know—half a year ago—we'd need strong enough towers to support a dragon?" Keena said.

"I don't know." Jydryn raced along the outer battlements until he came to the outer stairs leading up to the roof of one of the rear towers.

Keena followed close behind and climbed onto his back as soon has he shifted. They swung north of the castle to avoid going over where the dark fae stood to attack the castle, but flew west in their same direction.

Not far beyond the trees that had flanked Gallagher's army the previous day, bursts of light and dark fae magic lit the trees.

As they sailed over the battle in a narrow opening in the forest. Blue blasts answered black blasts from Nightshade and several dozen dark fae from a smaller group of light fae.

There was no order to either group of fighting fae. They spread out as nature fought against the dark fae. But anywhere a dark fae stood, the nearest vegetation was black and withered as they used the energy from the plants surrounding them to fuel the blasts of magic that erupted from their hands.

Jydryn remained high and out of sight while he assessed the situation.

We need to help them. Keena stood between his horns.

We have to form a plan to catch them off guard and to have the most impact, Jydryn countered.

A light fae group stood clustered together and took the brunt of the attack. Queen Nashala stood behind Lilly and Petal. They tried to shield her while at the same time tried to keep her from leaving.

Can you gather up the queen and several others and carry them back to the castle?

Aye. Jydryn dove to the battlefield. He released his fire at Nightshade and his warriors as he snatched up the queen in one paw and Lilly and Petal in the other.

Keena leapt from him, dropped to one knee, and stood. She blocked the black blasts. *Get them out of here.*

I'll not leave without you.

Get the queen to safety and then come back for me.

Several light fae climbed Jydryn's rear legs, and he leapt back into the air.

Keena shielded Jydryn as he flew away.

"Why won't you die?" Nightshade bellowed.

"Because God does not will it." Keena dug her toes into the soft turf. With one hand, she shielded herself. With the other, blue magic leapt from her palm to attack him. A handful of pine trees were still alive. They fought alongside by knocking her enemies off their feet for raining thousands of needles down on them. Amethyst, Badger, and five others flanked her to answer the attacks that came from every side.

While Keena focused her attack on Nightshade, a blast hit her in the side. Air fled her lungs, and she struggled to stay upright. Yellow hair waved in front of her as Badger leapt in front of her. The dark fae all turned their attacks against her while she swayed, dazed and defenseless.

A shaft from a broken tree branch surged through the air and impaled the female fae next to Amethyst.

A vine strangled a dark-haired fae behind Nightshade.

The dark fae forces closed in around them on all sides. No matter where Keena looked, there was dark fae. Nightshade laughed, which sent chills skittering down her spine.

Steadied and able to breathe—though it hurt—Keena shot a blast and a vine at Nightshade at the same time. The blast hit first. He staggered back a step; the vine wrapped around his legs, and dragged him down. Roots and vines scattered across the field sprouted from the ground and wound around the dark-fae leader.

Blasts of magic popped from his hands in a firestorm and incinerated all the vines and roots. He climbed to his feet again.

The earth opened under Nightshade, and he dropped. It encased him, leaving him poking out of the ground from the middle of his chest up. Every kind of plant tried to cover his head as he writhed and shouted.

As Keena fought to hold him and draw air into her aching body, the surrounding ground softened to thick mud and she sank past her ankles.

Before she could step out, the ground hardened and trapped her. Then, it turned frigid. Shards cut into her as she jerked to free herself.

Agony tore through her in growing waves as Nightshade pulled life from her body like the blackened vegetation.

Nightshade stilled and his smile grew as his glare narrowed.

Panting for breath, she swayed, but she didn't dare fall and give him more contact with the earth to draw her strength from her. Darkness tunneled her vision. Cut off from the life of the earth, she also lost her connection to Jydryn, who hadn't returned. As pain blinded her, Keena's faith faltered. Why had God abandoned her?

"You are an abomination no one could love." Nightshade's whisper came through the last moments of life in the blades of grass around her.

Badger blocked a blast aimed at her, but it hit an orange-haired, light fae on her other side. He dropped. Blood oozed from his head as he stared with unseeing eyes. He was free of the pain and the battle.

She neared her end, too. She'd never see her children again. Her heart fought to beat as she dragged in a wisp of air. With one last breath, a shriek tore up her throat and filled the air.

Chapter 71

Jydryn's claws brushed the tower roof to set the queen and the two female fae down when a mind-numbing pain laced through his body. The other fae leapt from his back as he pumped his wings and shot into the sky. His mate was dying. Her terror-filled scream propelled him back to her as he lost his connection to her.

Dead trees shattered under him as he crashed on top of Nightshade. He clawed and bit, but the dark fae had encased himself in a shield. Like a turtle hidden within his shell, Jydryn couldn't crush Nightshade. There had to be a way to stop him. Jydryn yanked the fae from the ground. A path of blackened, desolate grass snaked from where Nightshade had been stuck in the ground to Keena.

The dark fae tried to blast her in her weakened state but his own shield prevented him from firing and protecting himself against the dragon at the same time. Jydryn sprang into the air and carried him away. Nightshade laughed. "You are too late, dragon. I took all her strength and power. You can't save her or stop me now."

Jydryn continued to climb. The clearing where Keena fought for life vanished to a pin-point far below them. His dragon's large lungs full of air, and his heart full of rage, he continued straight up.

Jydryn held tight to the shield-covered Nightshade as the dark fae's attempts to free himself faltered. The wheezed breaths told Jydryn the fae captured little air. Blue light filled and strengthened the shield around Nightshade. The stolen magic recognized Keena's mate and seeped under Jydryn's scales and deep into his skin. Her love fueled the energy inside Jydryn.

Nightshade roared and tried to thrash as his protection grew thinner and weaker.

They touched the mist at the top of the sky and Jydryn prepared himself to enter the cold airless void of space. Pain exploded in his paw. It jerked open and Nightshade dropped. Jydryn spun and struck the near defenseless fae with the hard spikes of his tail. Nightshade's body crumpled and shot to the north as Jydryn tucked his wings and dove for his mate.

Keena lay still on her stomach as the five remaining light fae stood between her and a ring of dark fae.

Jydryn adjusted his flight at the last moment, sailed over her, opened his maw, and snatched up four black-hearted fae, crushing them in his jaws. Spitting out the bodies, he destroyed three more with an explosive blast of fire.

He ignored the last attackers and turned back to Keena. He scooped her limp body into his paw as Badger, Amethyst, and the remaining three light fae leapt into his other paw and clung to his back legs. His love held onto life by a breath.

His wings pumped in hard, fast strokes as he sped back to the castle. They landed on the other tower from where he'd left the queen. Jydryn released Keena, shifted, and knelt at her side. Leaves and vines appeared in the air and wrapped the lower portion of his body to form pants. Badger offered him a nod, which indicated that the leaves were his magic. Jydryn nodded back in thanks as Badger knelt opposite him on the other side of Keena, who lay almost lifeless. The other fae hurried to surround her.

Keena's skin was ashen. Long wrinkles fanned out from the corners of her eyes and mouth. Most of her hair was gray. The few breaths she drew were shallow and short. Her heartbeat thumped at such a slow rhythm, it hurt Jydryn to listen.

One fae put both his hands on one of Keena's ankles. Another did the same on her other leg. Badger took her right hand in both of his, and a pink-haired fae beside Jydryn took her left. Amethyst cradled Keena's face between her hands. Blue light filled each fae's hands. It seeped into Keena's body until she glowed.

"I took back some of her power from Nightshade," Jydryn said, not sure how to return it to her.

"Place your hand over her heart," Badger said.

When both his hands covered much of Keena's upper body, Badger and the other fae holding her hand each removed one hand from Keena and placed it on Jydryn's shoulder. Blue light pulled from him, up his back, down his arms, and filled his mate again.

Keena's back arched off the rough boards of the roof as she sucked in a large gasp of air. She relaxed, and the glow faded.

The fae dropped back to their heels with a deep sigh.

"She will live," Amethyst said through pants of air. "With your bond and time connected to the earth, she'll recover."

"Lay her on a stone floor or where her hand can touch the wall." Dusk appeared on the tower, crossed the roof, and pulled the orange-haired fae at Keena's feet into his arms. They held each other and kissed, oblivious to anyone else.

"I'm sure the queen can help—once she is restored—if the princess needs something more." Badger rocked back on his heels and stood.

"Where is the queen?" Amethyst asked as she stood too.

Jydryn caressed Keena's cheek. Much of her youthful appearance had returned, though her skin still held a gray pallor. At last, her eyes fluttered open. She blinked a few times before her eyes focused on him. He leaned forward, cradled her face, and kissed her.

She didn't return his affection and turned from him.

He shuddered.

Chapter 72

She was alive—and yet—part of her had died on the battlefield.

"Keena?"

Jydryn cradled her face and turned her to look at him.

But she couldn't. She'd failed, doubted, lost faith. Shame flooded her until she hoped she'd drown in it. She needed to get Jydryn away from her. But she was too weak to move. "Are the children all right?" Her voice rasped out of her parched throat.

"They're fine. Keena, will you look at me?"

"Where is the queen?" a female voice asked. They weren't alone. How many had borne witness to her failure?

"There," Dusk said.

Keena turned toward the voices, and Jydryn scooped her up in his arms. He carried her to the short wall that surrounded the flat roof of the tower. Dusk and four of the fae who had fought with her were there. Far below them in the ward, Lord Rycharde stopped as Queen Nashala exited the other tower and approached him with slow steps.

They stared at one another for the longest time, before he lurched forward. The queen leapt into his arms and he spun her around.

One of the fae watching with them sighed. "Everything will be all right now."

Their joy tore through Keena. She'd never experience such emotion with Jydryn again. She'd lost everything. Nothing would ever be right again. It would've been better if Nightshade had finished what he'd started. The vast emptiness of her soul consumed her.

Jydryn tightened his hold. "Dusk, do you know which chamber the maids moved our things to?"

"Inside this tower, one floor down. The chamber on the west side."

She waited until they descended the stairs away from the others to get out of Jydryn's hold. "Please," she whimpered. "I need to know if the children are all right."

Her husband tightened his hold and kicked open a door that stood ajar.

The maid inside yelped.

"Please send a meal up and leave it outside the door."

"Yes, m'lord." The maid scurried away.

Jydryn carried her to the bed, laid her on top of the covers, and remained so close he pinned her to the soft surface without hurting her.

Not that he could cause her pain now.

He cradled her face, and she closed her eyes. "Keena, my love. What is the matter?"

His spirit searched for hers; the sensation stuttered her breaths as she tried to shake her head in his powerful grasp.

"Keena, please." His voice cracked.

She couldn't tell him how she'd failed. Tears leaked under her lids and wet his hands.

His forehead rested against hers, and a long hot breath washed over her face. "Oh, love. Never. You did not fail me, our love, or God."

He'd seen her shame. Her tears increased until her entire body shook.

He laid beside her, brought her to him, and cradled her. "Remember what we told the children? Love doesn't work like that." He kissed the top of her head. "No doubt forged in a single moment of excruciating pain could ever make me turn away from you. You are my heart. And God will *never* stop loving you. His love is unconditional and mine mirrors it. There is nothing that can separate you from His love—neither death, nor life, nor angels, nor principalities, nor powers, nor things present, nor things to come nor height, nor depth, nor any other creature, shall be able to separate us from the love of God."

His continued faith in her only made her cry harder.

He tipped her chin up to stare into her eyes. "If you put Peyton or Callum on a pony and led them around, but they fell off and broke their arm—if they, at that moment, told you they hated you, would you stop loving them?"

She shook her head, unable to stop the tears.

"You never thought you hated God or me. For one moment, you doubted our goodness. Your faith that God would save you wavered—for a moment. Do you think I've never doubted? That my faith has never been shaken?" He stroked her back. "I was downright angry with God for bringing you and Rose into my life, only to let me get captured. I was ready to die and lose everything when you burst from the trees to free me from my chains." He kissed her again. "Even simple pain can override what we believe to be true. But what that foul fae did to you was nothing short of torture." He drew her chin up again and pressed a gentle kiss to her lips. "You did not fail. You have lost nothing. I am here. God has already told you He will never leave you nor forsake you."

She buried her face against his bare chest and let the grateful tears come and carry her into the depths of sleep.

Keena crawled out of the cavern of dark sleep. The memory of when she stopped believing in God's goodness accused her.

"There is therefore now no condemnation…"

She pried her eyes open, and they focused on her husband. He sat beside her on the bed and brushed her cheek. Keena lay on her side with her arm stretched out to touch the wall at the head of the bed. The connection to the earth strengthened her.

"Oh, love." He slid down to lie beside her and stared into her face. "You are so very hard on yourself. You've known God for even less time than you've known me. And though you are part fae, you are also mortal and—like all of us—not perfect. I know your love for me. I know your dedication and trust in our Heavenly Father. You've shown stronger trust and faith than I have in our time together. You cannot, for one moment when you lost sight of the truth, now condemn yourself."

It all made sense. It felt true. Why did she still feel hollow inside?

His thumb caressed her cheek. "Because our enemy wants us to focus on our flaws and not on our redemption. Not on who we are now. New creations who our fearsome enemy has no power over any longer."

To have someone so emersed in her thoughts, she didn't even have to say them, to hold no private feelings, made her uneasy.

He kissed her forehead. "You can have private thoughts again when we get that retched fae out of your head."

Keena tried to move. From her toenails to the hair atop her head, she hurt.

Jydryn slid off the bed and removed the covers. His warm hands cradled her right foot. As his thumbs drew deep circles along the sole, his fingers rubbed the top and her toes. He moved to her ankle next and up her calf to her thigh. He repeated it with her left leg and worked up her body until he sat beside her again and rubbed circles at her temples with his strong fingertips.

The pain eased as he worked her muscles with warm, firm hands full of love and the power of his dragon fed her through their connection. Sleep beckoned her again as a small tap sounded on the door.

The bed shifted, and Jydryn disappeared around the curved protrusion in the center of the room. Instead of being square like their former chamber in the castle, the tower room curved in a crescent around the central stairs winding down the middle of the tower.

The click of the latch and whispering seeped around the corner.

Jydryn leaned around the wall to glance at her. "The children are asking to see you. They have heard you were injured," he confessed. "You've slept for almost a day. Do you feel up to seeing them for a moment to assure them you are all right?"

She nodded.

He turned and vanished, only to return to her side and help her sit with pillows behind her.

Racing steps thumped outside, and the door banged open. "Mommy!"

Jydryn leapt off the bed, crouched, and caught Peyton and Callum around the waist with his powerful arms. He squeezed them as he stood and turned with the squirming children. "Your mother is still recovering. You will be gentle and not pounce on her like a cat on a rat."

Both children's heads bobbed in a repeated nod as Jydryn placed them on the floor again.

Peyton climbed onto the bed and curled against Keena's side.

Callum gripped the covers, pulled himself up, and crawled toward her. He sat on his knees beside her legs. "Did ya get the ba' man, momma?"

Keena stroked Peyton's face. "No, he got me."

Callum's small hand rested on her knee. "It's all righ'. Ya gonna be okay. Ya get 'im next time."

Jydryn squeezed the boy's shoulder. "From your mouth to God's ear."

Ella appeared beside the bed, carrying Rose. The baby leaned out of the maid's arms and reached for Keena.

Jydryn brought her to sit on the bed with the other children.

Jydryn brushed his hand over Keena's hair. *Their love—like mine, like God's—has not changed. It will only grow. Let it drown out the lies, my love.*

 Chapter 73

Jydryn gazed out the thick-paned glass, but because of the window's height in the narrow tower, he couldn't see any of the castle grounds below them. He'd kept the large window covered yesterday to allow Keena to sleep, but pulled back the heavy drapes earlier today. Keena had spent the last three days in bed. Between being fae, his dragon, and the earth giving her energy, her body was almost healed.

Her fractured mind still concerned him, however.

She again resembled the broken, fearful woman he'd met months ago. The wounds Nightshade had inflicted on her body would heal. The memory of the pain he'd caused would fade. But the horrid doubt the monster had created in not just her abilities, but in who she was, might never be silenced.

He sensed her wake and talked without turning around. "It's a beautiful day. Why don't we go outside? The children would love time in the garden and we can eat midday with your parents."

"The children can come in here and play."

They had been in several times. It was time to get Keena out again. He pushed a smile to his lips and turned. "No more playing in this damp, chilly tower. Come on." He threw off her covers and took both her hands.

She pulled from his grasp and curled on her side.

Jydryn scooped her up and cradled her in his arms. "This is not good for you, my love." He turned them toward the door. "Direct connection with the earth, outside in the warm sun with your family around you, is what you need. Perhaps we can get your parents to join us."

"Can I at least get dressed?" Her words had no life.

He looked at her, searching her thoughts, which she tried hard to hide from him.

She sighed. "I promise, I'll come. But I want to clean up and brush and braid my hair."

He placed her on her feet and pushed his fingers through her hair until he held the back of her head. He kissed her, and for the first time since the attack, she returned it. "I prefer it down like you first wore it. It lets the pink and blue of your fae nature show."

"What?" She pinched some strands between her fingers and pulled it forward to look at it.

He chuckled. "You didn't know you had areas of pink and blue in your hair?"

She pulled more of it over her shoulder. "No. Where?"

He drew her to a small table with a mirror attached to the back. After she sat on the stool, he turned her and showed her the different ribbons of color throughout the back. "It's faint, but there is fae coloring in your hair to be sure."

"But why two colors? And why hasn't anyone ever said anything?"

He kissed the top of her head. "Well, it was filthy when we met. Since then, you've woven it in a single braid, so it's harder to notice. As for two colors, you'll have to ask your mother."

Her reflection stilled.

With another kiss pressed to her head, he turned to the door. "I'm going to go tell the children, so you won't have much time to get ready unless you move now." He paused in the doorway and waited until she picked up the brush and drew it through her hair.

A few steps brought him to the chamber on the backside of the tower. He tapped on the door before he pushed it open.

"Da!" Callum jumped up from playing on the floor, charged, and slammed into his legs at full speed.

"I am taking your mother to the garden. Faces clean and shoes on, if you want to join us."

Callum raced back to the bedside table and reached for the large pitcher. He'd have dropped the whole thing on his head if Ella hadn't caught it in time. "El-la, 'urry. We go to da gar'en wiff momma."

Jydryn suppressed a chuckle and winked at Peyton as she scowled at her brother. "Slow down, little man. Your mother has to change her clothes. You will have enough time to clean and get your shoes on without making Ella crazy." Jydryn pulled Rose into his arms, freeing the maid to deal with the excited boy who splashed so much water getting his face clean, Ella insisted he change his soaked shirt.

With only one shoe on, Callum flew out the door and across to the other chamber.

"I hope Lady Keena has had time to dress," Ella muttered.

Jydryn nodded as he followed the boy with the girls.

Callum burst into the other chamber with a shout. "Ya and Da swing me. We go to da gar'en,"

Jydryn and Peyton stood in the doorway. Keena sat in a simple pink dress, weaving the last of a few small braids with the beads he'd bought her. She looked at the boy's reflection in the mirror. "All right, it's your turn to swing."

Callum jumped up and down and clapped his hands. "I swing."

Peyton inched forward and leaned against Keena and wrapped her arms around Keena's waist.

Keena hugged her. "Are you all right, love?"

Ella said she's been crying at night. She confessed she feared you were going to die like her other mother.

Keena turned and stared at him. She glanced down at the child and raised Peyton's chin to look at her. "I'm sorry I frightened you, Peyton.

I'm fine now." Keena smiled, though it didn't meet her eyes.

Keena stood and took Peyton's hand. They met Jydryn and the bouncing boy at the door. Callum reached up for both their hands.

"We have to wait until we get outside. The stairs are too skinny for all of us to walk side by side down them." The last words were still on Jydryn's tongue as the lad barreled down the stairs.

"It's a good thing there are only a few stairs to the bottom," Jydryn said, taking the lead.

Callum waited, hands in the air, as they stepped out of the tower. Rose sat on Jydryn's hip, and Peyton clung to Keena. They swung Callum between them as they walked from their tower in the outer wall to the castle. The boy's exuberant giggles filled the ward and bounced off the stone walls around them.

Jydryn glanced at his mate. Keena's shoulders relaxed. He sensed her spirit settle as a smile grew on her lips until it again reached her eyes.

It was there for a moment, then two, before it vanished.

Jydryn followed her gaze to see her father striding toward them with open arms. "Layna, my dear girl."

Chapter 74

Keena smiled at Jydryn who smirked back. Yes, he'd been right, she had needed to escape the tower and the nightmares plaguing her.

Callum's exuberant giggles worked a balm into her weary spirit, but Peyton's fear added to her burden. With Peyton clinging to one arm and Callum swinging from her other hand between them, Keena had nothing left to push against the renewed ache in her stomach. She stumbled. The dark fae still posed a threat. Jydryn had told her he doubted Nightshade was dead.

"Layna, my dear girl." Lord Rycharde strolled toward them with confidence. His back was straight and smile as wide as his open arms. He squeezed her shoulders and kissed each cheek.

When he drew back, he pulled her hands from the children's and held them tight. His eyes were clear and danced with contagious joy. Few wrinkles remained on his face and little gray in his hair. He looked closer to her in age.

"Thank you, my sweet girl. You found me and brought me home and made sure your mother arrived safe as well." His features darkened. "It near crushed me to know how you suffered." He closed his eyes and squeezed her hands again. "The thought of losing you a second time—" He drew in a stuttered breath, released it, and smiled as he looked at her. "But here you are. Oh, I love you so much, Layna. I regret everything—"

"It is all behind us now." Keena tightened her grip too and forced a smile.

Rycharde turned his attention to Jydryn and offered him a hand. The men gripped forearms. "Lord Jydryn, thank you."

"With pleasure, my lord."

"Call me, Ry. We are family."

"We goin' to the gar'den." Callum tried to take Keena and Jydryn's hands back.

"What a splendid idea." Rycharde braced his hands on his knees to look the boy in the eyes. "Have you found all the hiding places yet?"

Callum's eyes widened with a slow shake of his head.

Her father straightened and offered the boy his large hand. "I will show you all the places your mother found to hide from Dolcie when she was a wee girl."

As they turned, Queen Nashala stepped from the castle. "My love, there you are. You know I do not like you out of my sight." Her straight blue hair glistened and fluttered with her movement. Her long red gown made of a lightweight fabric and fitted bodice revealed the queen's youthful feminine figure while the skirt flowed around her like water.

She smiled at Callum before her gaze shifted toward the others. It dimmed when she met Jydryn's gaze and soured further when it met Keena's. The queen's lips pursed and her eyes narrowed. "Half breed. Mongrel."

The impact made Keena recoil from the muttered words.

"Nash!" Her father released Callum's hand and grabbed the queen by her upper arms and shook her. "Stop it."

When the queen's gaze shifted to Rycharde's again, her features softened, and she tried to wrap her arms around him. "There you are, Ry."

Rycharde gripped the queen's face between his hands and stared deep into her eyes. "Nix, fie, the hateful cur. Will we never be rid of him and the evil he has done to this family?" Rycharde pulled Queen Nashala to his chest and looked over his shoulder at Keena. "It's not her fault.

She loves you. Maybe even more than me. It's dark magic."

Keena's heart labored. "But I've seen her before."

Rycharde's loving gaze held hers. With clarity, she saw him as a caring father—her father. He sighed. "I think this spell only activated once we re-established our bond. If keeping us apart didn't work, then the despot had this as a backup. He'd make her hate any children she bore like he did."

An expansive shadow dampened the sun's warmth and drew Keena's eyes skyward. A deep red dragon meandered over the castle, turned, hovered above them, and released a long rumbling roar.

Peyton hugged Keena tighter, as Callum oohed.

Father released Nashala as they both stared up. "What is that about?"

"Shifters," Nashala grumbled.

Jydryn glanced at Keena. "I'm being summoned to the shifter high court."

"That's never happened before," Keena said after a quick search of his memories.

He set his jaw. "No, my uncle has never demanded my presence."

"Go." Rycharde nodded to him. "I'll meet with Lilly and Echo and see how we can undo *this* spell." He tipped his head toward the queen as she continued to follow the movements of the dragon overhead.

Callum stomped his foot and crossed his arms. Peyton tightened her grip around Keena's hand and arm. Rose seized Jydryn's neck.

"Should I go with you?" Keena asked.

"Aye." Jydryn gave a sharp nod and flashed her a smile. "When we are done with whatever my uncle wants, I'll introduce you to my father and show you my home."

Through the endless tears, Keena and Jydryn extricated themselves from the children. Father assured Callum he would still go to the garden, and Keena promised Peyton they would return with haste.

Keena and Jydryn stood on the tower roof. "Xurrod is still there." He pointed straight up toward the red dragon that she could no longer see.

Jydryn shifted, and she climbed on his back and they launched into the air. He turned west and passed over the castle's main gate, and the field where Gallagher's army had challenged them. They had restored the trampled grass after the next battle with the first wave of fae who came to kill the dragon. That attack, Keena realized now, was a delay to prevent them from joining the actual battle where Nightshade attacked the queen. She drew in a deep breath and closed her eyes. If the dark fae hunting her now knew that King Nix had poisoned the queen's heart against her own children before he died, would he still be trying to kill her and her family?

He wants the power. He longs to be king.

Xurrod came alongside them. His neck craned as he stared at Keena sitting on Jydryn's neck and grumbled.

What's the matter?

Jydryn surged forward. *He doesn't approve of you coming.*

Should you take me back?

No. You are my mate and we face all our challenges together. I left your side once. I'll never do it again.

Chapter 75

Jydryn approached Emberwick in the heart of the afternoon. The sprawling capital city of the shifters stretched out along the coastline of the Keyaral Kingdom. The waters of the Tilboro Sea sparkled beyond the city's fortifications.

As they'd flown for the last two hours, Jydryn tried to think of a reason his uncle had ordered him home. Perhaps they could stop to meet with Father before they saw the king.

Five royal guards in their dragon form launched from the various platforms used like guard towers in human's cities. They surrounded Jydryn and led him to the landing pad in the north part of the city, an area of the town that housed the military. Why did he feel like a criminal?

Forced to the ground under the weight of the air off their powerful wing strokes, he landed and waited only long enough for Keena to slide off before he shifted. All five of the guards landed and shifted as well.

Surrounded by naked men who made no move to cover themselves, Keena turned to Jydryn with red cheeks and handed him his clothes.

"Why have you brought us here?" Jydryn demanded as he dressed.

"The king instructed us to bring you to him under guard. That was before we knew you would dare to bring a *human* with you. The king's precautions were indeed justified." The captain's tone and words made no sense. They treated him like an enemy—not the king's nephew.

With the men now covered in loose, light leather pants that were easy to remove to shift, Jydryn took Keena's hand and turned her. Other than pants, as was the tradition of the military, they wore no shirt or shoes.

He glared at the captain and tried to assert his authority as a member of the royal family. "Take us to King Chozzrith that I might learn what has caused his concern."

As the group of fifteen warriors brandished unsheathed swords and surrounded them, Keena pressed closer to Jydryn. *Are we safe?*

They would not harm us until we have met with the king. I'm sure this is a misunderstanding. He glanced at her as they started through the streets toward the castle. *My uncle is honorable. Everything will be fine.*

Hoping to keep her calm, and himself, Jydryn pointed out places he knew from his childhood as they proceeded down the lanes wide enough for a dragon to walk.

She chuckled at the mischief he'd caused as a young fledgling and the tension dissipated as they passed through the inner gate into the castle ward.

The gleaming white stone of the shifter seat of power rose high above them as it reached into a clear, blue summer sky.

Carriages of all shapes and sizes lined the walls. Men in a myriad of colored surcoats representing the many shifter clans hustled between the buildings. The guards led them up the stone steps, each deep enough for a dragon to climb, to the towering doors. Royal guards pushed one side open as they approached and their military escort led them into the expansive chamber that could serve as a festive hall, for public gatherings, or—like it was now—an area for all the shifter clans to meet.

Keena tightened her grip and pressed against his side.

This was not good. It was one thing to be called before his uncle— not as family but as a subject—but to have their meeting take place before all the clans spoke of a grave matter.

His uncle sat on his throne on the long, raised dais beyond the chairs of the clans. An aisle sat open between Keena and him and his uncle in the tall rectangular room covered in polished marble. Rows of tables on either side of them faced the center. If he remembered the order of these events, the meat-eating shifters sat on one side and the plant-eaters on the other. But things may have changed since he'd last been in court during a clan meeting. He recognized a few faces of the angry men glaring at him.

His uncle's deep voice boomed in the cavernous room. "I summoned you, Jydryn Champion of Life, to answer to the charges that you have displayed your true nature before the humans on numerous occasions. Now, you dare bring one with you into our sacred hall?"

Keena stepped from his side with her head lowered. Her fears raised Jydryn's ire, but before he could respond to his king, Chozzrith leaned his head to a guard who now stood on the dais behind him and whispered in his ear.

King Chozzrith turned a narrowed stare toward Jydryn again. "Is it true this human despises our shifter ways so much she turned her back on my guards?"

This had to be some kind of joke. He knew his uncle as one who liked to make sport of him as a lad. He had to be doing so now. "Not so, uncle. Keena has seen perfection and didn't care to look on lesser males when I stood before her."

The clan leaders gasped. Some stood and shouted about his irreverence. Keena covered her face.

"Jydryn, I assure you, this is no laughing matter." Chozzrith's words were deep and slow .

Jydryn spied his father at the far left of the dais. Father shook his head to confirm the caution. Jydryn squared his shoulders and bowed. "Forgive me, King Chozzrith. I am dismayed about why you have ordered me to be brought here under such scrutiny. My words were foolhardy. Keena did not mean to offend. She has only ever seen one male undressed—me, her mate."

"What?" Chozzrith roared as he lurched to the edge of his throne.

The clan leaders rose from their seats with raised fists and shouts.

"Silence!" At King Chozzrith's boom, the windows rattled and Keena cringed. The hall quieted as he turned his attention back to Jydryn. "You chose the solitary life of an Activist, nephew. It is wrong to bring one simple human into your life and call her your mate."

"I do not call her such, Your Majesty. She is the mate the Almighty chose for me before the foundations of the world." Jydryn raised his left hand, palm up, for Keena to take and show them their Dragon Fire.

She didn't move, but brought the flames to life around her until he couldn't see her through it.

As the room erupted again, Jydryn brought the tongues of flame to life around him as well, though with less dramatic flare.

King Chozzrith leaned back in his chair, propped his chin on his fist, and stared.

 Chapter 76

Keena allowed the Dragon Fire flaring around her to dissipate as she quaked before the shifter king. A woman with flaming red hair—the only female with the handful of men on the dais—burst from her chair. She stomped to the red curtain covering the entire wall behind the king and vanished through it.

Keena dared a glance at her husband. *Who was that?*

Mirmash.

The shifter who hoped to be your mate?

He nodded.

"I would have hoped you would have done a better job of instructing your mate in our ways, nephew." King Chozzrith turned his hard stare on Keena. Her stomach clinched. "It is poor manners, young lady, to converse with your mate through your connection when you are in the company of others."

She dropped in a long low curtsy. "Forgive me, Your Majesty." There was a family resemblance between Jydryn and his uncle. The king's eyes, dark like her husband's, watched her with curiosity.

She did not think the way he sat on his throne appeared regal, though. He slouched, one leg bent and the other straight, and he leaned on his fist. He looked more bored than authoritative. King Chozzrith raised his nose in the air and drew in a deep breath. "You are more than human." His words accused her.

She swallowed hard. "Yes, Your Majesty."

"But you are not of the clans."

"No, Majesty."

Chozzrith placed both hands on the ends of the arms of his massive carved throne, elbows high in the air as if he would propel out of his seat at any moment. Instead, he slid to the edge of his chair. The entire room held its breath. "That can only leave one option."

Her voice squeaked. "Yes, Your Majesty."

His gaze flicked to Jydryn. "Your mate is a half human, half *fae*?" The last word ground out in a loud growl.

Keena rubbed at the gooseflesh on her arms.

"And she has mated with one of the clans," someone on her left shouted.

"The prophecy!" a voice answered from the right.

Keena lost track of the shouts as they piled on top of one another. She didn't know which voice belonged to which council member as the clammer turned into a discordant cacophony.

Then, a loud bellow rang over the den. "She comes to claim your throne, Majesty!"

Jydryn stepped to her side. "Let me speak to him," he whispered.

Chozzrith rose to his feet, fists on his hips. "Is this why you have come to my home without announcing your claim?" His voice thundered and shook her insides.

Keena slid forward two steps on quaking legs and dropped to her knees. She sat back on her heels with her hands resting open on her thighs, palms up. She bowed her head and begged the Lord for the right words to say.

In the quiet left behind when the room stilled at her odd behavior, she spoke. "The Lord God deal with me—be it ever so severe—if I should ever come to the hall of the great and good King Chozzrith to take anything the Lord has given him."

Her heart thumping in her ears was the only sound to remain in the immense room.

"My mate, Keena a' Arlayna, has made no claims regarding the prophecy, Your Majesty." Jydryn stood close enough for her to feel the comfort of his heat.

"My mother's people have thought as your people, King Chozzrith, that I am some long-waited-for empress of this realm, but God has not told me this. I fight for the fae against a dark faction among them. In our last battle, I almost died. I do not deem myself worthy to claim such a lofty seat." She sighed, took a deep breath, and raised her head until she met the king's gaze. "If—in the future—the good Lord should place this awesome burden upon my shoulders, I still would not come to take anything from you. I would only come in humility to seek your advice."

The king lowered back to his throne, but he sat forward with his forearms on his thighs. His head tipped and his eyes narrowed.

Without his objection, she continued. "You have built a city of wonder that welcomes all clans. I walked through your streets and saw laughter and joy among your people. This is something the entire kingdom should have. Your wisdom would be invaluable for *anyone* who claims the emperor's throne. To unite shifters, humans, and fae as one people as God intended, is a tremendous task, Your Majesty."

"You speak well, and you mention the God you follow. There are many among the humans and the fae worship nature itself. Which god do you claim, Keena a' Arlayna?"

She smiled. "There is but One, Your Majesty. The Lord Most High, Creator of the heavens and the earth."

He slid back in his seat, but his narrowed gaze never left hers. "I understand humans know little of my God."

She lifted her hand to her husband in gesture, but Jydryn used it to pull her to her feet. "Jydryn is an excellent teacher. On her deathbed, a prophetess even spoke a word over him. She told him to instruct the child he rescued, as Rose will be the next prophetess of the land."

Chozzrith's gaze snapped to Jydryn's as he sat straighter. "Which prophetess? What is her name?"

"Annabelle of Arrowfall, Your Majesty." Jydryn glanced at Keena. He appeared as confused as she was.

Chozzrith lounged back in his chair. "We will mourn her loss."

"You know of Annabelle, Majesty?" Jydryn asked.

"Aye, many of the clans have sought her out over the years. It was clear the Lord spoke to her."

Jydryn smiled and squeezed her hand. "Annabelle not only spoke a word from the Lord to me, Majesty, she also said one over Keena. One to remind her of God's faithfulness in the challenges she will face."

Chozzrith stood and stretched out his arms to encompass the entire room as he addressed all before him. "The afternoon is late. The hall needs to be prepared for the feast being readied for us. Please, take your leave for a couple of hours to think on what we have learned here, return to dine, and we will continue our discussion after the meal."

Though they grumbled, the clan leaders rose and filtered out.

"You." The king pointed at Keena. His hand rotated and his finger beckoned her forward. "Come with me. I wish to speak with you further."

Keena swallowed and rested her hand on her queasy belly as she stepped toward the front of the chamber toward the king.

 Chapter 77

Jydryn walked beside Keena as she followed the king off the dais and to the end of the hall. They wound through several corridors before they emerged outside the back of the castle, crossed a small grassy area where Jydryn had played as a fledgling, and exited through a gate onto the sandy dunes above the beach.

Chozzrith inhaled a deep breath of salty air. He stared at the waves as they lapped onto the sand.

"Your Majesty, can I inquire why you summoned me here if you knew nothing of Keena?"

His uncle turned to him with a small rise of one brow.

Jydryn smiled. "I go where my mate goes, Majesty."

A smirk played on his lips. "I think you are new to your bonding to be so unwilling to part with one another, nephew."

"Aye," Jydryn couldn't suppress his own smile as the tension between them evaporated.

Chozzrith strolled toward the waves. "As I said, I had heard rumors you had broken our laws and revealed yourself as a shifter among the humans many times." They reached the waves and turned to walk along the shore. "I understand now. Your mate prompted you to prepare the way for her to claim her place. It will come as less of a shock to the humans if they have some experience or knowledge of the other peoples who hid among them."

"I still make no such claim, Your Majesty," Keena whispered.

Chozzrith paused, turned, and look straight at her with a broad grinned. "Call me Choz, Keena. We are family, after all."

Keena's mouth gaped open for a moment. "Thank you."

Choz put his hands behind his back. "I suppose I should apologize for earlier. The allegations against my nephew were co-opting our meeting and the clans wouldn't let it rest. When I sent a messenger to fetch him so we might clear up the matter, Jydryn wasn't in his cave." Uncle Choz's brow rose as he looked at Jydryn. A moment passed before he laughed and his hand crashed down on Jydryn's shoulder. "That prompted more unrest, as you can imagine."

Jydryn nodded, and Choz turned his attention back to Keena. "You came as quite another shock, my dear. I almost feared the clans had been right." He inclined his head to her. "But you were a most welcome surprise." He winked.

"Thank you." Keena answered his grin with one of her own.

His uncle ambled down the beach again and Keena walked beside him as Jydryn followed. "As to you being our empress … The fae believe it to be true, as do my nephew and most of the clan leaders—by the sound of their shouts moments ago. I understand your reluctance to embrace the calling, but it does not make it any less true." Keena opened her mouth to respond, but Choz continued. "Have you ever walked along the shore, my dear?"

"No."

"As a fae, is it much different from a stroll through the forest?"

Keena remained quiet as the waves danced around her ankles. "It is. The natural energy our God allows me to access is more … chaotic here. The forest with its many plants has an order, or maybe it is more familiar. It's hard to explain. I've only known about my fae heritage and had access to my powers for a couple of months."

"You did not grow up in Shimmerbourne? Did your father raise you then?" The king remained silent and listened with interest as Keena told him of her life. He nodded when she concluded. "I see now why God chose you."

She stopped and stared at him.

Chozzrith chuckled. "You know suffering and what it means to be an outcast. He will use such pain to lead you to help others who are where you once were."

They turned back the way they had come, and Jydryn continued to follow in their wake. Chozzrith looped her arm around his and patted her hand. "Would you help me make a decision?"

"I wouldn't know how to advise a king, Maj—Choz."

"Talk this matter through with me, please." She nodded, and he continued. "There is a plot of land between two clans, and both request the right to cultivate it. I can't decide who to grant the request to."

"You know your people and their needs far better than I."

"Please, my dear." He patted her hand again.

Keena drew in a deep breath and allowed it to seep out. "Has either clan ever held claim to the land before?"

"No. It is a large patch between them which we cleared of a forest for its wood."

"Are either of the clans better at growing, or does either specialize in a high demand crop or something scarce among your people?"

Chozzrith's smile grew, and he glance back at Jydryn. "What have you been up to, Nephew, for the Lord to grant you such an intelligent and beautiful mate?"

Jydryn shrugged. "I don't know, Uncle, but I am forever grateful for the blessing."

"Indeed, you should be." He turned back to Keena. "No, both clans hold equal status as growers and producers of a variety of crops we all enjoy."

They had almost reached the path that led through the dune back to the castle when Keena stopped and looked out over the Tilboro Sea. The setting sun painted it in glorious orange and pink. At last, she crouched and pressed her fingers into the sand. "It might be an idea to divide the land into an even number of the same sized plots." The damp sand moved as though she drew in it, but her fingers never moved. An enclosed space divided by a grid pattern appeared in the sand. "You could assign the lots at random; each clan would get half the plots."

"Why not divide it down the middle?" Chozzrith tapped his chin as he looked at her illustration.

Keena stood and brushed the sand from her fingers. "What if one half has better access to water, or more sunlight, or shade, or ground with more rocks, which will require greater labor to prepare? This way, they can't accuse you of showing favor to one clan over the other."

He nodded, and they strolled away from the beach.

Keena skirted a large clump of sea grass. "If you wanted to further ensure their partnership on the land, you could require that each plot owner hire half of his workers from the other clan. Once they pay their tribute to you, the rest would be theirs to divide among their workers."

They stopped before entering the castle in the grass area. "You present me with an excellent plan to consider, Keena." He kissed the back of her hand. "Thank you for talking to me."

She curtsied. "It was my honor."

He turned to Jydryn. "The family apartments are available for your use. I'm sure you will both want to clean and change before the feast."

"I thought we might return to our children before it grew much darker," Keena said with a slight tremor in her voice.

"As the feast is in your honor, they might think it rude to leave before it even begins." He winked at her.

"My honor?"

Chozzrith opened the door. "Aye, my favorite nephew—the Activist, no less—has found his mate. I wish to celebrate." He disappeared inside.

"I guess we need to prepare for dinner." Jydryn offered Keena his arm, and they followed his uncle.

They climbed to the third floor and traversed the wide corridor to the south wing. It had been almost three decades since he'd been here. A guard inclined his head and opened the door to the expansive apartments his uncle let them use anytime his family stayed in the castle.

Mirmash rose from one of the velvet-covered divans as they entered the large seating area. "I thought you'd never get here. There is much to do and little time to accomplish the task." She looped her arm in Keena's and led her away as she spoke to Jydryn. "Your father is there." She pointed to one of the two doors leading off the main sitting area to the bedchamber his parents always used. "I'm sure you can find something appropriate to wear. I will see your mate is ready for her presentation." Before he or Keena could protest, the women disappeared behind the other door which led to the bedchamber he most often used.

Jydryn sighed. What was the red-headed dragon up to now? He recalled her as little more than a pest in his youth.

Putting the concern aside, he turned to the door and knocked.

Father beckoned for Jydryn to enter. "Come in," came a muffled voice from inside.

Jydryn pushed open the door as Father tucked a fine blue linen shirt into dark brown pants that ended below his knees. Hose covered the lower part of his legs and shiny shoes, with a small heel, waited near his feet.

Father turned, met Jydryn's gaze, paused, and smiled. He closed the distance between them in three quick strides, wrapped Jydryn in a powerful hug, and thumped him on the back. When they parted, Father held him by the shoulders and looked him up and down. "A mate," he said with a chuckle. "A human-fae mate, the future empress, and a child who will be a prophetess." He pounded Jydryn's shoulder. "You've done well, my boy. Very well indeed."

"I am blessed."

One more thump pounded his shoulder before his father returned to dressing. "That you are, son. I look forward to talking with your mate."

Jydryn turned toward the door. He hoped Keena would be up to the conversation. The sensations that leaked through their bond concerned him. What was Mirmash doing to her?

 Chapter 78

The red-haired dragon shifter bustled about as she pulled off Keena's garments and drew out a gown and several other items from the wardrobe and chest of drawers in the chamber of polished stone and massive windows. "You must make a good impression at the feast. After your surprise arrival, it will serve you well to assure the clans that you accept their ways. I don't know if you can overcome the claims of being the one to fulfill the prophecy, but we must do what we can to make you tolerable." Mirmash didn't give Keena a moment to speak as she whirled about the room. "Well, don't just stand there, dear. It would be an insult to arrive late. Clean the journey off and let's get you in a *proper* gown. You are the mate of the king's nephew, after all. Come, come, don't dally."

Keena moved to the washbasin and took the dampened cloth Mirmash plopped in her hand. She drew the icy water down her arm as Mirmash yanked the beads from Keena's hair and pulled a brush through the braids before she even attempted to unwind them. "I can—"

"There is so little time, Keena. Finish cleaning." Mirmash sniffed and crinkled her nose. "There must be something in here to hide the odor of your ancestry." Mirmash turned toward the dressing table where she'd picked up the brush and rummaged through the bottles. "Well, this will just have to do."

While Keena finished running the towel over her skin, Mirmash squirted a fine mist from a purple glass bottle. The most foul-smelling vapor dampened her skin. The scent of decaying plants—or maybe it was flesh—filled the room.

Keena pushed the bottle away before Mirmash could release anymore of the noxious scent on her.

Mirmash tossed her head with her chin high. "Suit yourself. But if you offend the king, it will be Jydryn who will pay."

Keena wanted to say they had walked along the beach for over an hour and his Majesty had made no comment, but she didn't. Instead, when the woman turned her back, Keena wiped as much of the horrid scent off as she could with the soapy rag still in her hand.

As Keena worked the braids out of her hair, Mirmash returned to her side. She carried an odd sheer skirt held in a wide circle by several stiff bands around its length. "Step into this."

"Should I put on braies—"

"No, shifters don't wear such undergarments. Come now. The time."

Keena obeyed, and Mirmash lifted the skirt over her hips and tied it tight around her waist.

"Arms up."

Again, Keena complied as the woman wrapped a stiff band of fabric around her ribs. Extending from her hips up to cup below her breasts and hoist them high. It contained the same stiff bands that lined the skirt and kept it in a wide ring around her. Only these strips went up and down. "Is this nec—"

"Corsets are the height of fashion, dear. I know they may be foreign to someone who runs about the forest in scant but leaves, however, you will dine with all the shifter nobility. For the sake of your mate, and to assure you bring no disgrace to the king who has been so considerate of you, you would be wise to follow my advice. Shifters are not ones to tolerate acts of dishonor. You could shame the king before his people." As she talked, Mirmash laced the corset up Keena's back and drew it tight. It forced Keena into a rigid stance and her bosom rose even higher.

Then Mirmash tightened it again, and again.

"My lady," Keena gasped, "It is hard to—"

"Yes, yes, I know. Fashion demands so much of us females to make our males look good before the people." She brought a heavy velvet gown the color of Jydryn scales toward Keena. "Arms up, dear." Mirmash laced the dress up and moved to stand in front of her. "Well, I had little to work with, but it will have to do."

"Keena, are you ready?" Jydryn called through the door.

Again, the dragon woman didn't allow her to answer. "You jest, male. A woman preparing for a feast is like sculpting a work of art. She will meet you downstairs."

As if Mirmash knew Jydryn's thoughts, she stopped Keena from responding. "You should not tell him the trials of preparing for the meal with his uncle, dear. Jydryn is a sensitive lad. He loves his uncle very much, and if he thinks you do not care for a little primping to honor the king, you will divide his loyalties." She patted Keena on the cheek. "Tell him all is well and you'll see him downstairs in a few moments. You don't want him worried. Perhaps the king will become cross with him again." Mirmash pushed her down on a stool and yanked on her hair to arrange it. The woman used a heated tool on her hair until tears filled Keena's lids and then put in clips and pins, which only made the tugging worse.

Mirmash made sense, but in her heart, Keena didn't trust the shifter. After her mother's rejection, Keena wanted King Chozzrith to like her. So, she bit her lip against the pain and did as she was told. Mirmash must know what the king expected better than Keena did as a first-time guest. Keena didn't want to fail again and bring shame to Jydryn's family.

Mirmash's thumb raked across Keena's cheeks and over her eyelids as the shifter smeared some thick goo on Keena's face. She stood back and looked. "Well, it is an improvement." Mirmash pulled Keena up to stand again.

Keena's chest ached as she fought to bring any air into her lungs.

"Only one more thing, and you'll be ready for a more proper presentation before the king's people."

Jydryn had wanted her to come. Wanted her to meet his father and uncle. He didn't ask her to change. Doubt tickled at the back of Keena's mind. Perhaps it was because of the haste with which the king had summoned Jydryn that he never thought to present her more formally?

Mirmash placed two odd looking shoes on the floor in front of her. The toes were far too narrow, and the heel rested on a long spike.

All other thought vanished. "I can't—"

"Go around the castle at a formal gathering with all the clan leaders with the bare feet of some peasant. Come, now." She reached for Keena's foot under the wide skirt and forced it into the horrid footwear.

Once she had the shoes on her feet, Keena swayed and her arms pinwheeled, trying to find some balance as her ankles bent.

"Gracious, look at the time. I've spent so much time with you, I fear I may now be late." Mirmash hurried out of the chamber door as she yelled over her shoulder. "Your mate will meet you at the bottom of the stairs, but there is no need to wait for the king to enter the hall and take your seat." The outer door clicked closed and Keena stood alone.

She wanted to take off the shoes and hurry to Jydryn's side, but she'd have to enter the hall in them, so she needed the practice. Using the furniture and walls to steady herself, she moved as fast as she dared out of the bedchamber, across the sitting area and toward the door.

Only by God's grace did she make it down the first flight of stairs without breaking her neck. Thinking she was getting the hang of it, she crossed the landing to the last flight, slipped, and landed hard on her rear. The stiff bands in the underskirt caused everything below her waist to fly up, leaving her uncovered and exposed. She forced the hateful garment down. No one was around. She crawled to the railing and pulled herself to her feet. Something had changed with the corset when she fell. She couldn't catch her breath. Her ankles rolled. Her head spun. *Jydryn.*

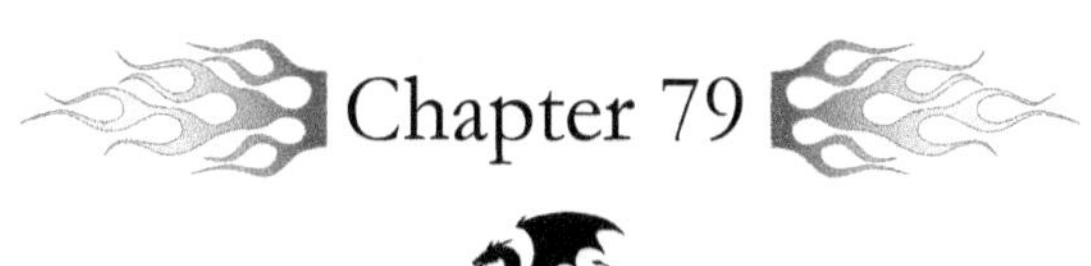

Chapter 79

Jydryn stood with his uncle and father outside the rear entrance to the hall. Mirmash floated down the stairs in a deep teal, flowing gown and flashed him a smile that made his stomach clench. She continued on to the women's entrance and vanished.

"I worry about that girl," his father said.

"Mmm." The king nodded his head. "Couldn't get it through her head …"

Jydryn stopped listening to their chatter. Odd sensations from Keena were getting stronger. Moments of pain washed over her, followed by fear, and then a resolute surge to press on. He remembered Mirmash's smile and shuddered.

Jydryn.

He turned and raced up the stairs at her weak plea.

She clung to the railing near the top of the first set of stairs in a hideous gray dress with an odd circular skirt. Her hair sat piled on her head in a dizzying mess, and heavy, garish makeup coated her face. Keena panted in rapid shallow breaths.

"What in all the kingdom are you wearing?" His uncle stepped up beside her.

Tears filled her eyes as she reached a quaking hand toward Jydryn. "I … can't …" She panted as her skin paled, and her lips turned blue under the thick layer of red.

"What can I do, darling?" Jydryn's aunt stepped up between him and the king. She took one look at Keena and pushed the men aside. Queen Sossi held onto Keena around her ribs. "Oh, good heavens! Jydryn get up behind her. Be quick, lad."

Jydryn climbed and stood behind Keena.

"Bring a claw forth, cut the ties on the dress, and then all the cords on the garment underneath."

Keena drew in a huge gasp of air as Sossi continued to hold her still. Breath after breath filled her lungs and her gasping at last slowed.

"My dear, where did you find this … *this*—" Sossi waved her hand in front of Keena from head to billowing skirt.

Keena glanced from her to the king. She bit her lip.

Jydryn sensed her reluctance to speak. A snarl rumbled through his chest as he looked over her shoulder at his aunt. "*Mirmash*—" the word growled over his tongue with a hot breath—"whisked her away when we entered the family chambers and insisted on *helping* her prepare."

Sossi crossed her arms. "Oh, that childish girl." She turned to the king. "Can you stall everyone for a few more moments? We can't let her join them like this."

"Aye." Chozzrith gave his mate a curt nod.

Jydryn's gaze blurred. "I will see to Mir—"

Chozzrith's hand covered Jydryn's chest. "Help your mate, lad. I will deal with that woman."

Sossi reached out her hand. "Come, Keena, dear. Let's make this right."

His mate didn't let go of the railing. "I can't …"

Sossi lifted Keena's skirt enough to peek at her feet. "Take those off. Take them off this minute." She looked up at Jydryn. "Your uncle is right; be a love and carry your mate to my chambers. Come on." Sossi picked up the hem of her dress and all but ran up the stairs. Though not considered elderly at one-hundred-eighty-seven, it still startled Jydryn how fast his aunt raced up the stairs.

"After you have delivered her, meet me in the antechamber." Chozzrith turned and stomped down the stairs.

Jydryn cradled his mate and carried her to his aunt's rooms. "Are you all right?"

Keena wrapped her arms around his neck as her tears wet his collar. "I thought I was doing the right thing to honor your traditions."

Jydryn entered his aunt's outer chamber as she raced through the room, calling to her maids. "Dorothy, Eden, and Biza, come, girls. We have work to do." He sat Keena on her feet outside the inner chamber and stormed down the stairs with no intention of joining his uncle. He'd pull Mirmash to the center of the banquet hall by her hair and give her a taste of her own medicine.

His father stood cross-armed in his path. "Not this way, son. Speak with Chozz as he asked."

Heat consumed Jydryn as his dragon threatened to burst forth. His hands fisted at his side as he leaned in to challenge his father for the first time. "Do you understand what she did to my mate?"

Father wasn't the least bit intimidated. In fact, he looked rather amused. "Which is why you need the king to deal with her and not you in a bond-crazed overreaction. Trust me, lad, we have all been there. Let him handle this so you don't cause an incident."

Jydryn narrowed his gaze and growled. His father shoved him through the door into the room where his uncle waited and kicked him in the behind for good measure.

Chozzrith paced with his arms clasped behind his back, though the tiny chamber provided little room for the king. It held two chairs used for Chozzrith and Sossi to wait while the servants prepared the rest of the hall. The large dragon shifter crossed it in three strides before he had to turn around. "Tell me everything you know about what happened between those two."

"Keena is my mate. I have a right—"

His uncle whirled and slammed his hand down on Jydryn's shoulder. "Mirmash attacked the empress while she was under my roof—my protection. As her king, I claim the right of punishment."

Jydryn stifled another growl and pulled memories from Keena. He told his uncle about her mother's rejection of her only hours ago, and the battle that had almost killed Keena. "Mirmash fed her lies. She told Keena *you* would lose respect before the clans if Keena didn't dress in that manner. Mirmash insisted Keena wear those monstrous heels when she knew Keena was fae. She didn't even allow her undergarments and when Keena fell, it left her exposed. God alone prevented her from being seen by anyone."

The room shuddered as Chozzrith punched a wall.

"Your Majesty?" A guard stuck his head in the room, eyes wide.

"Send Lady Mirmash to me at once."

"Aye, Majesty." The door clicked closed.

Jydryn's wrath brought his dragon near the surface again. Thoughts whirled of ways to deal with Mirmash. But a small part of him feared there might not be enough of her left after the king meted out his punishment. "I can deal with her. Your guests—"

"It will not take me long to throttle this woman," Chozzrith said.

Jydryn hoped to help.

Mirmash entered and dipped a curtsy; her smile bright. No shame or concern showed in her manner. "You wished to see me, Your Majesty?"

"By all that is holy, woman. What were you thinking to treat the Empress, Jydryn's mate, and my new niece, in such a horrid manner?"

Mirmash gasped as her hand pressed to her collar. "Your Majesty, I would never. I only hoped to help the poor woman. She was the one who—" Her words cut off as Chozzrith raised his arm to backhand her.

Jydryn had never seen his uncle so mad. In truth, he had never been so mad himself. "Are you too stupid to understand the link between mates? I've heard every word you said in the inner chamber, and experienced every pain you inflicted on *my mate*. Praise be to God above that He never paired me with you."

Mirmash cringed under Jydryn's shouts and the king's still raised arm.

Chozzrith fisted his hand but lowered it. "You are right, nephew. How could she comprehend a mated bond when she has refused to even greet any suitor in her addled hope you would come home and choose her?" Chozzrith towered over Mirmash. She had the good sense to back away and look down. "I realize you put her in clothes even my mother wouldn't have worn, hoping to bring her shame and, by extension, Jydryn and myself."

Mirmash opened her mouth but snapped it closed before she said anything.

"You put a fae in heels Queen Sossi wouldn't dare to walk in on the polished floors of the castle. You refused her undergarments to humiliate her when she fell." Chozzrith lowered his head and narrowed his gaze. "Had the Empress suffered an injury in my home, only your death would have reclaimed my honor."

Mirmash shuddered. "Your Majesty—"

"But she caused the poor woman injury, darling." Aunt Sossi's normal sweet tone grumbled as she stepped into the room behind Mirmash. "Keena's ribs show signs of bruising from the over-tightening of the corset. There is blood in her hair from where Mirmash yanked it out of Keena's scalp. And there are burns on her ear and cheek from the iron Mirmash used to curl it."

A growl rumbled in Jydryn's chest. His mate had suffered injuries only feet away, and he'd done nothing to protect her—again.

Keena stepped into the room next. Little space remained in the tiny chamber, but she slipped to Jydryn's side. She now wore a yellow silk gown that contoured to her pleasing form and floated around her like a flower petal in a gentle breeze. Her face was clean of the makeup, and her hair rested against her shoulders in several small braids adorned with beads. She touched one. "The queen cut apart one of her necklaces."

Jydryn wrapped his arm around her and drew her close. "I never should have left you with her." He brushed her hair with a tender kiss.

"This was not on you, nephew. The fault lies in only one." Chozzrith pointed a powerful finger at the quaking woman. "Mirmash the proud, the haughty, the arrogant, the *cruel*."

Tears soured Mirmash's voice. "Your Majesty …"

"Say nothing. There can be no excuse for treating anyone in this manner, let alone my honored guest and our Empress." He threw back his shoulders and crossed his arms.

Sossi scowled at Mirmash. "I have never been more ashamed of any dragon's behavior."

Chozzrith nodded. "This is your punishment, Mirmash. First, you will apologize to Lady Keena. Then you will take Jydryn's place and see to the protection of the innocent."

"You are banishing me? You can't. I'm a female—" she wailed.

Chozzrith seized her upper arm. "I can have you whipped first."

Sossi laid her hand on his arm. "Darling, we have guests we need to attend."

"Please, Your Majesty," Keena whispered.

Chozzrith released Mirmash. She staggered back a step. In the tight confines, his uncle almost struck Jydryn in the chest when his arm pointed to Keena. "Learn from her example, female. Even after all you did to her, she asks for mercy. This is the type of female I want in my court. For now, you will watch over the innocent in Jydryn's place. Until such a time as our Empress takes her throne and abolishes the practice of human sacrifice, you will protect the humans. If I hear of one child who has died in the flames or one maiden left to the elements because of your inaction, you will wish all I did was whip you." Chozzrith crossed his arms again and glared at Mirmash as she wept. "Perhaps some time alone will help you see the error of your ways."

They stood in silence as the woman sobbed.

"Your Empress is waiting for your apology, Mirmash," Chozzrith growled.

"I am sorry, Lady Keena."

Keena was quick to respond. "I forgive you."

Chozzrith stomped to the door. "You are a far better person than I, my lady." He reached for the door. "Nephew, I understand you wish to be with your mate at this moment, but Mirmash's antics already delayed us to the meal. I wish to present Lady Keena to the people. Jydryn, take only a few moments to tell Mirmash what she needs to know. She is to leave at once." He opened the door, stepped into the passageway behind the curtain, and extended both elbows to Sossi and Keena. "Come, ladies. Our guests have waited long enough."

Chapter 80

Keena looped her arm in King Chozzrith's and they walked between the curtains held open by guards onto the dais. Everyone in the full room quieted and stood. She wanted to be anyplace but here. She dared a glance back, but the curtain had closed again.

"He will be fine," Chozzrith whispered. The king kissed his mate, and she moved to the far end of the table where a few other women waited.

Keena tried to draw her hand from the king, but he closed his arm tighter, trapping her hand within the fold of his elbow. "Forgive our tardiness, my good people. A small matter of the realm drew our attention. But now we come before you to feast."

Subdued clapping answered him.

"We receive double honor this night, for not only does our long-awaited Empress, Keena a' Arlayna, dine with us. But we, the shifter clans of the Zarus Realm, are the first to honor our empress with a feast."

Smattered, lackluster clapping met the king's enthusiasm.

"Ynroth, would you bless our meal?" Chozzrith waved a white-robed man to the center of the room.

Ynroth raised his arms and tipped back his head, letting his ginger hair brush his collar. His wide sleeves slid down, revealing lean, muscled arms. "Lord God Almighty, provider of every good thing, we thank You for Lady Keena a' Arlayna, Empress of the three realms …"

The combination of her two names was a mouthful. She'd consider altering it if this empress thing ever came to pass. As Keena's mind wandered, she caught a bit of the thoughts railing in Jydryn.

She heard the words he spoke to Mirmash as if she stood in the room with them—*my only recourse against you now, woman, is whether I send you to my former cave/home, as the king instructed. Or feed you lies that will ensure your failure as you did my mate's.*

Keena spoke to her husband through their link. *Jydryn, God would have us show her mercy. You taught me vengeance belongs to Him. Please, love, tell her what she needs to know—the truth—and come join me. I'm frightened here in front of all these clans.*

Even now, Keena asks I show you mercy—

The priest's words caught her attention again. "… so we ask You, Father, to bless this meal and the work of our Empress as she unites our lands once again. Amen."

The crowd offered a dreary amen in response and sat, while Chozzrith led her forward to the seat at his right.

"Shouldn't I sit with the women, Majesty?"

He directed her into the chair and sat beside her. "Not this evening. You need to be at my side."

He took a tray laden with meats, speared several pieces with a long-tined fork and dropped them onto a plate in front of her. "Hand me Jydryn's plate, so he need not wait when he arrives."

She did as he asked and Chozzrith placed twice as much there.

As they brought tray after tray to the high table, the king continued to add to the growing mound before her. She put her hand up when he prepared a ladleful of some fruit in a thick sauce. "Majesty, please, I could not eat all I have now if given a week."

He chuckled, loud and deep. "I forgot for a moment you are not a dragon, my dear." He still moved the treat toward her plate. "Even so, you must try a little peach delight. We made it from the first peaches we've harvested this year." He dripped a little onto her plate.

Jydryn slid into the chair next to her and squeezed her hand.

"Now, you two." The king used his knife to point at Keena and Jydryn. "No discussing what happened with Mirmash while at the table. Let us forget the unpleasantness and enjoy the feast."

"As you wish, Uncle." Jydryn inclined his head and drew his eating knife from his belt. He cut a few pieces of meat before he handed the knife to Keena.

Chozzrith waved a servant forward from behind him and soon she had an ornate knife of her own.

"Thank you, Majesty." She returned his smile. "May I ask you a question?"

"Of course, my dear. You are family, and I have asked you to call me Chozz."

"Why are you so convinced I am the person who will reunite the peoples of Keyaral? I can't even unite the fae."

Chozzrith chewed for a moment as he stared out at the gathered clans. "While there is much to be said for your lineage—half-fae, half-human, mated to a shifter—it is not as unique as one might think. Over the last thousand years, some combination of this type has occurred a hundred times." Chozzrith glanced at her. "Some of what tipped the scales in your favor was the blessing you received from the prophetess in Arrowfall. But I saw something in your humility. When you knelt before me and swore you had not come to overthrow my rule, and you thought you could learn something from me, it intrigued me. The problem I posed to you as we walked along the beach was a bit of a test, I admit, to see if your actions matched your words. Your thoughtful questions and fair solution, which sought the best for both sides, convinced me. You are who you say you are, and you are also our empress."

"I wish I had your confidence." Keena nibbled on the many things on her plate. The king had been right. Peach delight was indeed special.

"There is one concern I have for you, my dear. I believe you sensed what Mirmash told you was a lie. You are too intelligent not to suspect. But you put those warnings aside out of fear. Fear we would not like you. Fear of bringing us dishonor. But in refusing to acknowledge the truth you sensed, you did us the greatest dishonor, for to appear as Mirmash dressed you would have been a scandal. You must trust yourself and what God is telling you."

"I will endeavor to do better, Majesty."

The king sat down his knife and covered her hand with his. "You cannot try, dear. If we are to be one people again, you must embrace who God made you to be. You must walk in the truth and the light so it can shine on the rest of us."

Jydryn covered her other hand. His huge smile greeted her. "Be strong and courageous. He will never leave you nor forsake you."

"Indeed." Chozzrith gave her hand a squeeze and then returned to his meal.

Keena continued to sample the shifter fare. Many things tasted familiar to the dishes Jydryn had prepared for her, but many were new. Her gaze swept over the clans gathered below. Many held her with a curious stare. Some smiled when their gazes met. She smiled back.

There was a group, however, who glared and bent their heads in conversation. A shiver of unease slithered up her spine. "Not all agree with your conclusions, Majesty."

He followed her gaze to the group stealing her appetite. "There are some who hate change, Keena. There are others who look to it as a chance to assert their power where they believe they were denied before." He turned his gaze to her. "Not everyone will welcome mixing of the clans of Keyaral again. While it is the way God intended us to live, some only see our differences and hate them."

Keena sighed. "How do I overcome such deep-seated beliefs?"

"Prayer. Lots of it." He smiled. "We will pray too."

Chapter 81

Jydryn pushed his empty plate away. He'd enjoyed the food, but the peaches were a little tart, and his mind swirled with the events from prior to the meal. He glanced at his mate. His uncle had heaped Keena's plate so high that even though she'd eaten, so much food remained that it didn't look like she'd touched her meal.

She sat rigid as she stared at the lion clan who glared at her.

Over the centuries since the dragons had taken the throne, the lions had risen in revolt against their king on several occasions. No doubt they were already scheming to use Keena's empress status and her close connection to the king to prove him biased and unworthy to rule. Jydryn could almost hear their accusation of the king being wrapped in her hair ribbons.

Chozzrith stood. "Clan leaders, I promised to return to our meeting. As the last hot chocolate of the season is served, why don't we address the petition of the elk and ram clans over the deforested area now known as Shortplains?"

Jydryn kept his gaze on his uncle as Keena glanced at him. She too turned her attention back to the king as he explained through their connection. *Hot chocolate is a special treat. I've never found it anywhere else in all my travels around the Keyaral Kingdom. Once we finish a cup, we can return to Wealdstone.*

Chozzrith outlined the parceling out of the land as Keena had suggested. While both the elk and ram clans had wanted all the land to themselves, they agreed it was a fair compromise.

If clan politics were the same as when he'd last been in court, Jydryn imagined both leaders were already concocting ways of buying or stealing the plots of the other clan to claim the whole Shortplains for their people.

His uncle must have been thinking the same thing. "Each plot will be held by the family who acquires it in the lottery for five decades. At which time, it can remain within that family, but if they pass it or another family purchases it, each plot must remain in the holdings of the original clan."

Jydryn sucked his lips between his teeth to suppress a smirk at the skill with which his uncle closed the loopholes the clans may use. It should keep the peace between the two clans for centuries to come—at least, concerning Shortplains.

They ratified the proposal with a spoken vote of all the clans, and the elk and ram leaders signed a written record.

Chozzrith thumped the table. "Good. I am pleased you found the Empress' solution sound."

"You discussed our affairs with that half-breed?" Kofa, the leader of the lions, burst from his seat with a shout, upsetting many of the goblets and mugs at his table. Others dining with him scrambled to sop up the mess before it flowed off the table into their laps. The dark-skinned shifter took little notice as his usual temper flared. The man was a hothead and an opportunist.

Keena sighed. *I wish King Chozzrith hadn't involved me.*

He has his reasons. Have you tried the drink? Jydryn responded.

My stomach is in too many knots. This empress business causes trouble wherever I go.

It will take time for all the peoples of the kingdom to get used to the idea again, but it is what God wants of us—to be united. He squeezed her hand. *Why not take a sip of hot chocolate before it gets too cold?*

Kofa thumped the table. "You presume too much, Chozzrith, to involve an outsider in our affairs."

Chozzrith leaned on rigid arms braced against the table. "That is Your Majesty, or King Chozzrith, Kofa. I'll not stand for your disrespect." He straightened and pointed first at the lion and then opened his hand to include everyone before him. "As all of you thought it a fair and equable plan when you believed it came from me, the issue is not with the resolution but with Empress Keena a' Arlayna."

"Even she doesn't claim such an elevated title," Kofa shouted back.

Grumblings grew around the room. Most sided with their rightful king and his decisions, but a growing number backed the lion.

"Yet." Chozzrith crossed his arms. "She does not claim it—*yet*. Our wise Empress thinks it best to eliminate this faction of the fae who threaten all the Keyaral Kingdom with their evil acts before elevating herself. But for those of us grounded in the Holy Word, we know our God wants His people—all of them, shifter, human, *and* fae—to be of one mind and one heart. We will achieve unity when He places Keena a' Arlayna on the ancestral throne of His anointed."

Keena pushed to her feet. Though she stood tall with her head up, her body trembled, causing her dress to flutter. "I welcome any who wish to assert their claim to the imperial throne to travel to Crystalbrooke and seek the group of sequestered fae, humans, and shifters living there who hope to learn the signs that will foretell of this new emperor. Or better yet, to prove any of you are the one the acolytes have been seeking."

Kofa ignored her as he again challenged the king. "What about the reason the clans demanded this meeting in the first place? Jydryn must answer for violating our laws. Do you refuse to punish your nephew?"

Jydryn remained in his chair as Keena sat again. He saw no merit in the lion's threat. "What law have I broken?"

A burly, bald man further back in the room stood. "You announced to the humans you are a shifter. You have exposed us."

Jydryn didn't recognize the man or what clan he was from. From his placement in the room, he might have been a rhino-shifter.

"There is no *law* against such a declaration," Chozzrith said. "We refrain from it out of safety, but Activists often reveal themselves in the course of their work."

"This was no rescue." Kofa raised his voice. "He told the human king who he was and shifted in front of him. Not to save some worthless human's life, but to show off in front of his mate!"

How did the lion shifter know of the events with King Gallagher and his men?

"Someone misinformed you, my lord." Keena thrust to her feet again. When she spoke, it was with powerful authority. "I was the only one to speak to King Gallagher as his army stood at my father's gate. I told the king and his men to leave or they would force me to use my abilities against them. A fae, who has sworn his loyalty to me, stood at my side ready to wield his magic, and my father's army marched at my back with their spears and swords. Lord Jydryn flew from the castle. No one saw him shift, and I introduced him as my husband to the humans, not my mate as I would other shifters. If any made the connection to the shifters, it would be because of their previous belief in them. But few humans believe in shifters and fae anymore. Both peoples have hidden themselves well."

The burly man from the back spoke again. "How do we even know she is a fae and can wield any of this so-called power?"

Chapter 82

Why couldn't Keena keep her mouth shut? It had been one thing when this angry group of shifters had attacked her, but when they'd falsely accused her mate, she'd been unable to remain silent.

"Show them, my dear," Chozzrith murmured beside her. "Reveal your power to my people so they will know you are the empress."

While Queen Sossi had insisted she not wear shoes of any kind, Keena still stood on cut and polished stones. She didn't have a direct connection to the earth below the castle's fortifications. It lay far beneath her. She could sense a hidden chamber below the floor further separating her from the ground that connected her to her power.

"I say she has no power at all. We know the fae are liars." The shout came from the dark-skinned man with his hair cut short so it hugged his scalp. He was first to challenge the king.

Keena reached out her power and called to a tree. Any fruit-bearing tree would serve.

A grumble rose in the room as the clans' challenges grew for her to do something.

The large bald man who had demanded she show her power banged his fist onto the table.

Screams from outside drew everyone's attention as the room fell silent. Guards at the doors shouted orders.

"Have them open the doors, Majesty," Keena whispered.

Chozzrith waved for the guards standing inside the doors to pull them open. The moment there was space between the two doors, a branch appeared and extended across the center of the room toward her.

As the branch stretched out, it thickened and produced smaller branches with long, slender, rumpled leaves. Shifters who sat on either side of the meandering and widening branch's path leaped to their feet and moved out of the way.

As it reached the dais, it grew up and across the table toward her. At the end of the branch near the base of a clump of leaves, a bud formed. It grew and opened into a pink blossom with long yellow spears topped with tuffs of dark pink in the center. Keena had time to acknowledge the blossom before it withered and a small fuzzy green ball replaced it. The ball grew and turned yellow and orange until it was the size of Chozzrith's fist.

Keena placed her cupped hands under the fuzzy fruit. "Thank you," she whispered to the tree. The fruit dropped into her hands, and the branch retreated out of the room.

"May I?" Chozzrith opened his hand.

Keena nodded and handed the fruit to him.

Chozzrith held up the fruit for all to see and cut a slice. Juice dripped into his hand. He popped the slice in his mouth. "Mmm. The sweetest peach of the season." He cut another slice and held it out over the table. "Would anyone else like to try?"

As the clan members settled back into their seats, a few came forward and took a slice from the king. They all testified it was, indeed, a sweet peach.

Weariness tugged at her. From her first outing since almost being killed, the confrontation with Nashala, Mirmash, the clans' resistance of her, and now drawing on her power with little connection to its source, she wanted to crawl into a dark corner and sleep for days. Before she could even sit, however, King Chozzrith spoke again.

"That was a powerful display of her earth magic. You all know the nearest peach trees lie at least three leagues from this door. Empress Keena a' Arlayna has the power to make us her subjects." He turned to her. "Show them, Empress."

"I don't think such a display in your fine hall is wise, Majesty."

"Trust me." He winked.

She turned back to look over the heads of those gathered. Energy hummed inside her. Vines grew over the doors, windows, and covered the curtains behind them. She lifted her right hand and a multicolored stream of light sprang from her hands to crawl along the ceiling over them. The floor rolled in waves under their feet.

Shifters leapt up with shouts and screams.

The walls shuddered as the vines covered every surface.

Keena squared her shoulders and drew in a deep breath. "I, Arlayna Bright Star of the fae, swear a royal oath on the name of my mother, Queen Nashala Ever Blossom, that I will never initiate an attack on King Chozzrith the Strong Minded, rightful ruler of the shifter clans or any *under* his authority. In this only will I resort to violence; in defense. Should any attack me, my family, or those under my authority, I and those loyal to me will defend ourselves." She picked up the knife Chozzrith had provided her, sliced the side of her palm, and let the small stream of blood run out on the vine now winding over the table. The wave of oath magic washed over the room. Keena waited one heartbeat, and then another, before she drew her power back.

The room stilled. Vines sank back between the cracks in the stone. Her rippling magic fell into her open hand and vanished. Keena lowered herself into her seat with quaking legs as she drew several breaths into her trembling body.

Jydryn took her hand, and his strength eased her weakness.

The room remained quiet as a tomb.

The first to speak at last was the king, and his voice filled with quiet awe. "You have born witness, my people, to a taste of the power of the

Almighty, which He has only ever gifted a few. If any of you should still doubt my claim that this is our Empress, it is to your folly. If not for Empress Keena a' Arlayna's restraint, we would all be dead. But for her to forever bind—not just herself, but those under her authority—to never attack the shifter clans is … well, it is … astonishing. I am grateful she had the wisdom to allow for the defense of herself, her family, and her people. I tell you the restraint of her unbridled power in the face of your hostility is only further testimony to her worthiness as our empress, and her honorable character as a child of the Most High." Chozzrith sat and turned to her with wide eyes. "With such power, I never want to hear of you bowing to the whims of another, Empress. I thought Mirmash was fortunate to escape your mate's wrath, but I now understand having survived you is the embodiment of the mercy and grace of the Father."

Keena forced a smile to her lips. "Thank you, Majesty."

"Uncle." Jydryn leaned closer. His warmth only added to her struggle to remain awake after such a display. "I bid your permission to leave and return Keena to Wealdstone."

"Our lady has had a rather long and trying day, nephew. Take her upstairs to the family chambers and help her heal through her connection to your dragon." Chozzrith rose to his feet. "The day is late. Tensions have been high. We are all tired. With rest and time alone to think, I hope we can return tomorrow with more level heads. Goodnight, clan leaders, your families, and all who have dined with us this night." He hoisted a cup in the air, downed the remaining contents, and *thunked* it down.

With a nod to the end of the table, Queen Sossi rose, came to him, and took his arm. Chozzrith waited for Jydryn to rise and help Keena up. Once more, she drew from her husband's strength to hold her upright. They followed the king and queen through the curtain into the darker hall behind it. Light from several torches in holders high on the wall lit their way to the stairs.

"Get some rest, you two. We will see you in the morning." Chozzrith ascended the stairs with Sossi.

Jydryn swooped Keena up in his arms. Secure in his hold, her eyes closed as he carried her back up to the chambers where she had met Mirmash. If he did not hurry, she'd be asleep before they arrived. Still, something in the dark-skinned shifter's gaze as she left the hall told her it was not the last she'd see of him or his threats.

Chapter 83

Jydryn woke from a deep sleep. Keena snuggled next to him. Whether awake or asleep, she exuded a peace he needed, and he let it soak into his raging spirit.

She'd fought him last night, not wanting to undress. The discoloration around her ribs had made him want to burst through the nearest window, fly to their old cave, and wall Mirmash inside it. But Keena hadn't allowed it, even after discovering her blackened and swollen ankle and a broken toe. He didn't know how she'd walked.

Knock, knock, knock. "Jy, lad. Chozz is here and needs to talk to you and Keena. Are you awake?" Father called.

Keena stirred next to him with a hum.

Knock, knock, knock. "Jy, 'tis important, my boy."

Jydryn rubbed Keena's arm. "The king needs to speak to us."

She mumbled and tried to snatch back the covers he stole.

"Coming," Jydryn called. He pulled on a pair of trousers and helped Keena sit up. She still wasn't awake and muttered words he couldn't understand.

He brushed her hair from her face and helped her into a robe. "Come on, my love. Something is going on." He pulled her to her feet, and she tipped forward to lean against him with her head on his chest. He chuckled. His mate was not in favor of early mornings. "Should I carry you?"

She shook her head but didn't move.

"Nephew? Empress? 'Tis a matter of some importance," Chozzrith called through the door now.

Keena pushed off him, her eyes only half open. "It had better be," she mumbled.

Jydryn laughed again as he wrapped his arm around her and led her out to the common area of the suite.

Keena tied the ribbon around the robe to close it as Chozzrith stopped his pacing and came toward them.

His uncle took her hands and drew her close to kiss her on both cheeks. "Forgive me for the early hour, my dear. Things have not gone well through the night."

Now more alert, she looked at him with wide eyes. "What's the matter?"

"Kofa has taken advantage of being within the walls of my home to exert his need for power and incited most of the cat tribes to rebellion." His uncle's gaze shifted to him. "They have the roof and internal launch pads secured. Do you remember?"

"Aye." As a child, Chozzrith had shown Jydryn the secret passageways within the walls that led from the family chambers, down through the castle, and out under the wall.

Turning back to Keena, Chozz offered her a sad smile. "I'd hoped for a more celebrated and dignified departure from Zarus, but this is for the best." He released her and took a set of clothes Father held. "These will be easier the way you're going."

Keena didn't move. "Will you be all right? We could stay and help."

Chozzrith squared his shoulders and Father matched him as both men crossed their arms. "Since when has a kitty ever threatened a dragon and it gone well for them?" Both men laughed. Chozzrith spoke alone. "We'll be fine, my dear, but I would feel better knowing you are out of harm's way. You are too valuable to our kingdom to get caught in our internal squabbles."

Keena still paused. "You're sure?"

"Aye. Now, off with you. I have a cat to tame."

She accepted the bundle of clothes as Father stepped forward with wide open arms. Keena accepted his powerful hug. "I have not had enough time with you, daughter." He pulled away and held her by her shoulders. "My brother monopolized all your time." He leaned in as though to share a secret, but didn't lower his voice. "Such a kingly thing to do to steal you away from me. He's been doing that kind of thing all our lives." Father winked.

Chozzrith's hand fell hard on Father's shoulder. "That is what big brothers do. And you make it so easy."

Keena giggled. "Thank you both."

"Time to go, nephew."

Jydryn took Keena's hand and pulled her back into the bedchamber they'd used. "Change quickly."

She glanced at the items in her hands for a moment and Jydryn had to smile. The tan pants and large, deep blue shirt were his from before he'd left Zarus. He must have left them in the castle the last time he'd visited.

They dressed in haste.

She took his hand but didn't move toward him as he faced the back corner of the room. "Where are we going?"

Jydryn turned a bit of decorative plaster on the wall a quarter turn to the right and pushed on the panel inside a border of white molding. A door opened in the wall, revealing a dark passageway behind. He smiled over his shoulder and pulled her inside. When he pushed the panel closed again, it clicked back into place and left them in utter darkness.

"Jydryn?" Her voice trembled as she reached out and grabbed hold of him with her other hand too.

We need to travel without a sound in the hidden passageways.

I can't see.

He brushed his hand along her arm to calm her. *Close your eyes.*

Why does it matter? I can't see either way.

He leaned in and touched their foreheads together. *You need to draw on my dragon and see through my eyes.* He waited as she followed her connection and strengthened it. *Now, open your eyes.*

Oh!

Better?

She nodded.

Okay. Follow me and stay close. He turned and led the way. The passage was so narrow between the two walls of large stones that he had to turn sideways to fit.

Keena jerked her hand away and failed to stifle a yelp. She danced about, staring at her feet when he turned. "Cockroach," she whispered in her distress.

He leaned in and kissed her cheek. *A bug might have scurried over your foot, but it could have just as likely been your pant hem.*

She continued to squirm as though thousands of the creatures crawled about her as she shuddered.

You could always threaten to have me squash them if they don't leave our path like you did the spiders in the shack in Cragholde. He tried not to laugh. She was a powerful fae—a creature of nature—who almost brought down the entire castle last night. Yet a tiny creature terrified her.

I know it's illogical, but I can't help it. I've always disliked bugs.

Jydryn chuckled. *I know. Come on.* He put his hands up in front of him to capture webs and stomped a little harder to send any scurrying beasts at their feet away. Still, she startled and jerked at any little thing that brushed against her. The faster they traveled through the tunnel, the sooner Keena would relax.

Chapter 84

Keena viewed the dusty stones through a golden haze. It was like making her way across a barn at night with a sliver of the moon coming through a high window. She could see enough to not run into a wall and find the stairs, but not much more.

Something brushed her toe, and she stumbled and danced. Her heart hammered in her ears, so she couldn't hear anything else. At the bottom of a second landing, a shadow stepped out from the right between her and Jydryn. She covered her mouth with both hands to silence her scream.

"Forgive me, my lady," the slender man, only a few inches taller than her, whispered.

"Fetmak?" Jydryn reached out and shook the man's hand. "How did you know about the tunnels?"

"Stumbled onto them one day when my father came for a council meeting."

Jydryn's words to Fetmak were terse. "What are you doing here?"

"Came to make sure you two get to where you are going." Fetmak waved for Jydryn to continue and lead the way, but something in the way he phrased his intentions didn't sit right with Keena.

He didn't say he was there to help them, or lead them to safety, but '…make sure you get to where you are going.' The shifter wanted to follow Jydryn. The tunnel came down from the family apartments, so no threat would have followed them. Did he want to know where they were going?

As she stepped into place behind Jydryn, with Fetmak behind her, her stomach tightened. *"You must trust yourself and what God is telling you."* Chozzrith's words filled her thoughts like a shout. She whirled.

Fetmak held a dagger raised above her.

The tunnel flooded with Dragon Fire, blinding her for a moment, since she was still connected to Jydryn's dragon vision. When her flames disappeared and she could see again, Fetmak stood encased in the inner stone wall. Only his eyes, nose, and the hand holding the dagger were visible.

Jydryn pushed her back a step. His heat covered her in sweat, as he hovered over Fetmak's face to keep his voice as quiet as possible. "Since when do wolves side with cats?"

Keena removed the stone from his lips but didn't release his entire face, so he had to force his words out from between his closed teeth. "Things in our realm will be superior for all shifter-kind when we are no longer controlled by an autocratic dragon."

Jydryn stared at the man. "What things will be better?"

"They promised any non-dragon freedom and status we've never had under your scaley claws."

"What more freedoms could you possibly want? There is no limit to the rank you can achieve in the shifter army. There is no business you cannot own. No position in the court you can't hold—other than king, and Kofa wants that for himself."

The wolf shifter searched Jydryn's face. His brows crinkled.

Jydryn leaned back and crossed his arms. "We trained side by side for two years before I left. You never had a problem with my uncle or your life. Not one you ever shared, anyway."

"Kofa promises it will be better," he muttered as his brows drew even tighter together.

"Someone has deceived you into betraying one you once called a friend and the king you swore fidelity to."

Keena covered Fetmak's lips again and touched a root growing between the stones. "Tell the king what has happened, and where to find this shifter." She turned back to Jydryn. *Do you think it's safe to continue?*

He didn't seem to know the way.

Keena glanced at Fetmak as she whispered. "Or he was just a coward who thought the bravest act of the rebellion would be to stab a woman in the back."

Jydryn took her hand. *Our only options from here are: to return the way we came, go out through the kitchens where he came in, or proceed the way we were heading.*

She closed her eyes and shared her prayer with her husband. *Lord, which way would You have us go?* She opened her eyes and lifted her hand. Just like when she searched for Jydryn, a ribbon of Dragon Fire left her finger and snaked down the tunnel in the direction they had been going.

Jydryn nodded, turned, and stalked forward.

She let the fire go out and rested her hand on Jydryn's bare back. Heat almost seared her hand, and she pulled away.

He reached back and took her hand in his. It was still warm but didn't burn. She followed him down into the earth and savored her renewed connection to it. Here, even she had to hunch over in the short narrow passageway. Keena stopped and brushed her fingers over many small roots poking out of the hard-packed earthen walls. She sent a message along it, searching for anyone else lurking in the dark. *We're alone,* she told her husband.

He nodded and continued to squeeze his body through ahead of her. *This was much easier when I was a child.*

Keena's feet slid along the cool earth and her connection to it completed the healing Jydryn had begun last night. Her heart calmed; her breaths were slow and deep.

Jydryn paused as they came to an iron door in a stone wall stretching out to their right and left, far into the darkness. He lined his heel even with the doorframe, stepped to his left, placed his other foot against the toes of the first, and stepped heel-to-toe five more steps. Next, he turned to the wall and counted down three blocks. Then he pushed on it.

Nothing happened. He tried the stone above, below, to the right and to the left.

You said you were smaller when you came here last. Maybe if I count off the steps? She moved the seven steps and ended an arms-length from him. She found the third stone down and pushed. It didn't move. She moved one stone to the right. It sunk into the wall under her touch.

Brilliant. He kissed her temple and reached into a hole carved in the exposed stone with the one above it depressed. Retrieving a key, he unlocked the door, returned the key, and pressed on the stone again. It slid back into place, unnoticeable in a wall of stones.

Once through the door, he had her walk ten steps to the right, retrieved another key from the bottom stone, locked the door, and returned this key too.

Keena had assumed once they passed through the wall, they'd be outside, but the earthen tunnel stretched on before them without end. She was glad for the trousers and shirt. Traversing the narrow passages in a skirt would have been impossible.

A boulder almost as tall as her loomed in their path. Jydryn placed his hand on it and glanced back over his shoulder. *I'll push this away, and then we'll be outside. The sun should be up, so it will hurt with my vision.*

She placed one hand on his arm and the other flat against the earthen wall. *Someone is walking around this opening.*

Suggestions?

Keena shook her head. *Anything I'm thinking about would make them suspect fae magic.*

Jydryn drew her close, and she snuggled against his warm body. He rubbed her arm as he prayed. *Lord, we need Your assistance to get out of here unseen by those who wish us harm.*

As they waited for a revelation to strike them, a tiny stream of light from around the rock vanished, and the sound of an animal sniffing came through the slender gap.

Keena held her breath and squeezed her eyes closed.

Chapter 85

Jydryn embraced Keena at the end of the dark tunnel, as someone with the scent of a wolf moved around their only escape.

"I smell something here," a rough voice said.

"Yeah, we're in the woods. I smell a lot of *something* too," a female called.

"*Human* something."

The woman's voice drew closer. "From what the alpha said, she's more fae."

"There's a crack here. I think I can move this rock."

Keena's magic hummed over Jydryn's skin as other rocks grew around the one that served as a stopper in the entrance and held it in place.

The scrapping of the two wolf shifters digging came through the stone in muffled waves. Some creature called with the growl of a bear and the baneful moan of an elk.

The female screamed. "By the alpha's fur, what was that?"

Aye, what creature makes such a sound? Jydryn glanced down at his mate, who rested against his chest with her eyes closed.

She looked up and grinned. *A moose.*

Jydryn had heard a man talk about them once while in a human village, but he'd never seen one. They live in the far northeastern territory of the human kingdom.

The female screamed again as the moose answered with another call.

"What is it?" the male wolf shifter said.

"It looks like a deformed monster elk."

Both wolves whimpered, and the ground vibrated.

Keena pulled from him and stood as best she could in the short tunnel. The extra stones receded back into the ground, leaving only the one stopping up the tunnel. "The moose wasn't happy about coming so far south, but I told him there would be wolves waiting for him." She flashed Jydryn a mischievous grin.

Jydryn moved to the stone. "Who's to say how many are looking for us? I'm going to move this, climb out, and I'll shift as you exit. Then we'll take to the air."

She nodded and stepped closer as he thrust the obstruction out of the way. Keena crawled up his leg before his wings unfurled.

He dropped the stone back over the opening and Keena caused dirt to cover it. Jydryn loved how in tune they were.

He flew to the west, away from the castle and out toward the sea. To remain unnoticed by those searching the skies for an escaping dragon, he flew so his belly brushed the coastal grasses and then the waves.

Keena settled in the middle of his long neck. The spot was her favorite. Her joy and excitement of flying filled him, and he fought a triumphant roar.

Once he could no longer look back and see the shore, he shot up into the sky, turned back in a southern trajectory to miss all Zarus lands, and soared through the clouds back eastward to Wealdstone Castle.

The sun had passed its zenith before they neared Wealdstone Castle.

Keena stretched. *A dip in a cool bath sounds delightful. I see why you prefer to fly at dusk.*

The heat feels good on my scales, but I think your fair skin is burning. There's a lake not far—

I want to see the children.

He did too. If a few hours of separation from the little ones, who were not his blood, frustrated him so much, he couldn't imagine how deep the bond would be when Keena bore him a child.

She tried to wrap her arms around him. *You'll love them all the same, you big-hearted lizard.*

A rumble traveled up his throat, but an exuberant squeal drowned it out as they flew over the inner ward of the castle.

Rose reached for him as Ella struggled to keep hold of her squirming form.

Callum shouted next. "Da!" He darted for the tower door that Jydryn flew to.

Oh, how that single word melted him. Keena was right; he couldn't love these three anymore if they were his blood.

Keena worked her way over his shoulder and down to his left fore-knee before she jumped the rest of the way to the tower roof. She handed him pants as soon as he shifted. It took a moment before he realized they were the ones she had been wearing.

While not appropriate for a human, his long shirt Keena still wore was no shorter than the skirts most of the common fae wore.

She sped down the stairs.

Jydryn followed in enough time to see her drop to her knees on the landing between their chamber and the children's. Her arms spread wide as Callum and Peyton charged up the stairs and crashed into her. She hugged and kissed them both. "Oh, how we missed you."

"Why did you have to go?" Peyton snuggled in close as she whined.

"We went to see Jydryn's uncle, the dragon king."

Callum looked at her wide-eyed. His little pink lips formed an O as his gaze rose to meet Jydryn's. "King of all da dagons?"

"Aye, indeed he is," Jydryn said.

Callum stepped from Keena's hold, but stopped and rested his hands on her arm. "What's a unle?"

"Uncle." She smiled at him. "The king and Jydryn's father are brothers."

Callum tipped his head as his features pinched.

Keena tried again. "When Peyton grows up and has children, they will call you Uncle Callum."

"Yuck." Peyton stuck out her tongue. "I'm never havin' no kids."

Callum stepped to Jydryn and stretched up his arms to be picked up.

Keena tipped Peyton across her thighs, where she still knelt on the floor and tickled the girl until she writhed in giggles. "Why not? Children are ever so much fun."

Peyton's fits of laughter made Jydryn hoist Callum up and pretend to bite his belly. "They are ever so tasty too," he shouted over Callum's squeals.

A sharp shriek stilled them for a moment as Rose spotted them. To avoid her falling, Ella sat her on the floor before they finished climbing the stairs.

Rose crawled with remarkable speed, used Keena's arm to pull herself up, and swatted and pushed Peyton to get the older girl off Keena's lap.

Keena captured her hand. "Be nice to your sister, Rose."

With one hand keeping her upright, and Keena holding the other, Rose resorted to using her foot to push Peyton off Keena's lap.

Jydryn had to return to tickling Callum to hide his laughter.

"What am I to do with you, child?" Keena held Rose around the waist and lifted her high enough to keep her out of reach of Peyton.

"Here you are, Empress," Lilly and Echo joined them on the landing. The fae woman still didn't have a glamor to cover her facial injuries.

Keena noticed it too. "Was Queen Nashala not able to break the binding on your magic?"

Lilly shimmered and stood before them as a beautiful fae. Then, her image wavered again, and she was the old woman who'd cared for Keena when she was little. But she returned to her true form. "This is who I am. I'm not ashamed of these scars. I earned them protecting you and your mother."

"She is who we've come to talk to you about, Empress," Echo said.

"Please, call me Keena."

"We could not break the king's spell on your mother, my lady," Lilly said. "It … we're afraid …"

"Dark magic forces the queen to hate me," Keena said with a long sigh.

 Chapter 86

Keena shuddered at the thought of fighting dark magic again. Her stomach soured to think her own grandfather had used it against both his daughter and his granddaughter. Who could hate so much they would resort to depriving another of love?

"Aye, dark magic is our fear." Lord Rycharde—Father. Keena had a father. A man who loved her as she'd always dreamed. He wasn't a stranger any longer, and she thought of him with the same affection she had for Chozzrith and Govam. They were all family. Father squeezed onto the landing along the wall near the chamber she shared with Jydryn. They did not design this space in the center of the tower for so many. "You, Layna, are the only one who can do anything."

Keena clung to Rose on one side, while Peyton snuggled in on the other. "She won't let me get close to her while under the spell."

"You're our only hope, Empress," Echo said.

Keena huffed. There never seemed to be a moment for rest. "We'll need someplace secluded where we can't cause a lot of damage."

"There is a walled-in alcove at the rear of the inner courtyard where we used to pen the bulls during mating to control the quality of the calves our holdings produced," Father said. "I'll have it cleaned and fresh hay laid."

Keena rocked back, and Jydryn helped her stand. Brows rose as the others glanced at her bare calves, but no one said anything. "Give me at least half an hour." It wasn't enough time but, with God's favor, she could return to the children in a short time and then retire early tonight. Would she ever feel fully rested again?

"I'll make sure your mother gets there." Rycharde smiled and kissed her cheek. "I know you can get through to her, my sweet."

Lilly and Echo bowed. "We'll prepare wards to keep the walls standing." They followed Father down the tower stairs.

Still holding the girls close, Keena turned her attention to their nurse. "I'd like to keep the children for a few more minutes, Ella."

The maid dipped a curtsy. "Of course, m'lady." She entered the nursery across from their chamber but left the door open.

Keena leaned against Jydryn with a weary groan. He kissed the top of her head. "Let's go play for a few minutes."

They entered their chamber and all five of them piled on the bed with wild giggles and squeals.

Keena stood out of sight just inside the high-walled pen. Echo and Lilly's magic vibrated against her skin. She'd prayed with Jydryn and now she prayed again as she waited. She filled her mind with the tender kiss of her father on her cheek. Chozz's acceptance and commission to follow God. Govam's hug, and Annabelle's prophetic words to be strong and courageous. Still, Nightshade's laughter as he drew life from her body made her muscles taut and her teeth rattle from a violent shudder.

"Rycharde, why do you want me to see this empty space?" Queen Nashala's voice bubbled with laughter and playfulness. Her mother stepped past Keena without seeing her. Nashala wore a long dress the color of cantaloupe. It shimmered in the late afternoon sun like a spider's web.

Keena closed her eyes and drew in a deep breath. Of course, spiders would come to mind in this moment.

"Rycharde, why are you being so—" Nashala turned. Her gaze landed on Keena. Her smile vanished and eyes narrowed. "You. You deplorable creature—"

Keena jerked forward, covered the queen's eyes with one hand, and her mouth with the other. Vines encircled the fae queen from her feet to the center of her chest. "Yes, Nix, I know well your opinion of me."

Nashala jerked and freed her mouth. "How dare you accuse me of being my father. I curse—"

Dragon Fire flashed over Keena's skin before she realized what was happening. The queen yelped and stilled and Keena jerked it back. "Your father hated you, and you hate me. What is the difference?"

"I …" Nashala tossed her head, but Keena kept her eyes covered. "I … I am not my father," she muttered again, sounding like the lost, vulnerable woman Keena had first met at the fae court.

"Well, you have chosen the darkness as much as he. You allow him to still control your life."

"He placed spells on me." She tried to raise her chin and her tone hardened.

Keena clamped down on her frustration and refused to allow it to taint her words. "He is long dead. You reunited with your husband and mate. Yet you let Nix's hatred infect you still. Your faithful servants can't draw it out because you won't allow it. You want to believe your father was right. In some misguided hope of still gaining his approval, you cling to this last bit of him and hate me."

"I want nothing from him. Father was cruel—"

"And you are not? Spitting venomous words at the child you once loved enough to sacrifice yourself for. How can you claim to love Rycharde when you hate his child? How can he continue to love you, knowing any future children you have together will fall under your wrath as you did under Nix?"

"I don't hate—"

Keena dropped her hand from Nashala's eyes. The queen blinked, and her gaze narrowed. "You horrid abomination."

Keena took a step back from the icy chill of her mother's continued rejection. Tears stung her eyes, but Jydryn's love filled her and reminded her of the children, of Rycharde, Chozzrith, Sossi, Govam, and especially God. She held the queen's gaze as the enraged woman continued to speak words of hate. "I love you, Mother."

Nashala jerked within the confines of the vine as though Keena had struck her.

"I will not answer your hate with my own. The cycle of my grandfather's hatred ends here. Today I choose to love you in the face of all your Nixian hatred."

"Stop accusing me of being my father!" Nashala screamed.

It surprised Keena that Nashala hadn't broken from the vine, called up nature to capture her in return, or tried again to speak a curse. Movement on the confining vines drew Keena's attention from her mother's face. A few tongues of Dragon Fire slid up and down the green tendrils.

Watching the dancing flames, Keena spoke. "You say you love humans, Mother. So perhaps it is the fae in me you hate."

"I don't hate my people."

"Then it is only me, and every child you may have with Father in the future. How does that make any sense? You are queen of the fae and one of the most powerful rulers in generations, according to your people. Yet, you allow Nix's curse to continue to steal your joy of family. It must be your choice to live with this hate."

"Humans. I like humans," Nashala mumbled.

"You married one. Bonded with him as your life mate." Keena sighed. Weariness encased her. With an exhale, she released her mother from the vines as she turned her back on her mother to exit the pen. It was a risk, but Keena wanted to be away from the woman and her hate. She strolled across the inner ward toward the castle and the gardens where her children waited.

Jydryn sat on the castle's wide front steps with the children around him.

She shook her head.

Rose pulled herself up and stood, holding onto Jydryn's shoulder with both hands. She babbled, and it made Keena smile.

Rose lifted her right foot and made to take a step but set it down in the same spot again. She repeated the action several times with no forward motion.

Nashala came abreast of Keena and hissed. "You—"

"I believe you could be free if you chose to, Mother. I have chosen to love these little cherubs with my entire heart, though they are not of my flesh. They fill my life with love and joy and … such contentment and purpose. Love is a choice." Keena tore her eyes from Rose and glanced at Nashala again.

The queen's face twisted. Her head tilted, and lips pursed together.

Rose giggled again and Keena looked back. She'd released Jydryn and stood on her own.

Keena slipped a little closer and lowered to her knees with her arms outstretched.

Rose swayed as Jydryn reached his arm around without touching her to protect her in case she fell.

Rose swayed more. She picked up her right foot again and pitched to the left.

Jydryn snatched her up before she hit the ground. He stretched her across his lap and nipped at her belly as she squealed in delight. "Good try, my sweet girl. You will walk soon enough."

Keena turned back to her mother. "Like Echo, Lilly, and Father, I can do nothing to change you. You will continue to be Nix's daughter for as long as *you* wish. Only you can change your heart now."

"Why you—" Nashala cut herself off and her eyes widened. "I sounded just like him," she muttered.

"Yes, you did. You don't even speak to a shifter with as much hatred as you do your own child." Keena looped her arm in Jydryn's and they strolled into the castle heading to the gardens.

"There is nothing you can do?" Jydryn asked.

"Pray, and hope she chooses love over hate."

"But you don't think she will."

"There is a part of her that wants to but something is holding her back, and I don't know if she can overcome whatever that is."

Jydryn kissed Keena's temple and Rose filled her hands with his beard and jerked him back to look at her. She turned her cheek to him as she pulled him closer. "Am I only allowed to kiss you?" He chuckled.

Rose babbled and tugged until Jydryn peppered her with kisses and her squeals reverberated against the walls.

Keena leaned into Jydryn more. Who would choose hate over love?

Chapter 87

Jydryn laughed as Callum roared and raced around between them as they crossed the inner courtyard. It was a new day, and they headed to the garden, Keena's favorite place to play with the children.

Laughter greeted them. Rycharde strolled toward them with Queen Nashala on his arm.

Rose squirmed on Jydryn's shoulders, tightened her grip on his hair, and whimpered.

Jydryn couldn't blame her. In the week since Keena had faced her mother, Nashala had changed little. Oh, she held her tongue now, but the hatred and disgust still flashed in her eyes when she looked at her daughter.

Callum roared again as he looped around their growing number.

"What is this now?" Rycharde left the queen's side and tried to snatch the racing boy.

"Ya can't catch me. I a dagon." Callum raced away with his arms outstretched at his side like he was flying.

"Oh, I see. So, I have two mighty dragons to protect my castle." Rycharde darted in Callum's path the next time the boy came near and made a big show of trying to grab him but missed. "Oh, Callum the Fast is too quick for me."

Callum giggled, but Peyton groaned. "He'll never stop running around now," she muttered.

Jydryn ruffled her hair.

Peyton pushed his hand away and smoothed her long brown hair again.

Rycharde crossed the distance and nodded to Jydryn. "Good morn, son."

Jydryn acknowledged him with a smile. The lord was a good man.

Rycharde's gaze shifted over Jydryn's head. "And good morn to you, my sweet angel."

Rose wiggled, jerking on Jydryn's hair, and kicked him as she babbled.

The lord then braced his hands on his knees to meet Peyton at her eye level. "Good morn, princess."

"Good morn, Grand-pére." She stepped forward and gave him a hug.

At last, Rycharde moved to his daughter. "Good morn, my sweet."

"Morning, Father." Keena stepped into his embrace and returned it. He kissed her cheek as he pulled away.

Nashala stood in stoic silence. Today, her gaze was not hard but pained. She watched the children, and a smile tugged at her lips. She inclined her head toward Jydryn without animosity in her gaze. When she dared glance at her daughter, she frowned, but it was not in anger or displeasure. Her brows wrinkled. She drew in a deep breath. "Good morn, Arlayna."

Keena turned and smiled. "Morning, Mother."

Rycharde whirled around and snatched Callum off the ground. Lying across Rycharde's forearms, the lad thrashed. "And a good morn to the mighty Callum the Fast, the quickest dragon in my lands."

Callum stilled. His eyes grew wide, and he gaped up into the sky. His finger pointed.

Jydryn looked at a dozen dragons circling overhead. The large bronze one in the center was Chozzrith. His father's deep pine green dragon was there, as was Aunt Sossi's dusty rose dragon. They passed over the castle again and back to the field outside the gate.

"That doesn't bode well." Rycharde glanced at Jydryn.

"Let's hope they come with good news of the end of the lion's revolt," Keena said with little hope in her voice.

Callum thrashed in Rycharde's hold until the lord put the boy down. "I go see the dagons." He raced for the inner gate.

"Callum," both Keena and Jydryn yelled at the same moment.

Rycharde turned toward the gate too and followed the boy. "With all the unrest, we keep the outer gate closed and the portcullis down. He won't get far."

Keena glanced at Jydryn as Peyton took her hand to be swung between them. "Maybe the children should return to their chamber with Ella?"

Jydryn shook his head. "Neither Father nor Uncle gave calls of warning. Whatever their reason for coming, I don't think there is an imminent threat."

"'Urry, Da!" Callum bounced as the gate opened, but the portcullis remained down. "I wanna see the dagons."

Jydryn smirked. "I'm sure they have shed their scales and now appear like you and me."

Callum continued to jump around. "I wanna see."

"Take my hand." Jydryn reached for the exuberant boy.

Callum snatched three of Jydryn's fingers and pulled. He ducked under the rising portcullis long before Jydryn could follow with Rose on his shoulders. They didn't make it to the end of the drawbridge before the excited lad let go and careened into the field where the human army had been several weeks ago. There, the group of dragons had finished dressing.

The boy stopped in front of Chozz, craned his head, and arched his back to gaze up to the dragon king's face. "Ya 'umongous!"

Chozz chuckled, took a wide stance, braced his hand on his bent knees, and leaned down to meet the boy. "Aye; a dragon king must be big and strong to protect his people."

"Ya the king?"

"I am, lad." Chozz thrust his hand to the boy. "I am King Chozzrith, and who might you be?"

Callum looked at the hand and glanced back at Jydryn, who nodded. "Greet him proper." The boy squared his shoulders and gripped the king above the wrist as warriors did.

Chozz laughed. "Well met, lad."

"Huh?" Callum stared up at the king.

Chozz straightened as the rest of them caught up with Callum. "Hello, Uncle." Jydryn clasped his uncle's arm. "Please, let me introduce you." Jydryn turned to the others. "King Chozzrith, the Strong Minded, Queen Sossi, the Merciful, My father, Govam, the Protective, please meet, Queen Nashala Ever Blossom, and her mate, Lord Rycharde of Wealdstone."

Chozz and his father offered a small bow to Nashala and clasped arms with Rycharde. Aunt Sossi offered a small curtsy to everyone.

"You've already met Callum." Jydryn said, gesturing to the boy who watched the adults with great interest. "This is his sister, Peyton." He had to pull the girl out from behind Keena's skirt. "And this is Rose."

At the mention of her name, the toddler tipped forward and reached for Chozz.

The dragon king was quick to snatch her up. As he held her, she stared into his eyes and held his face between her hands. Everyone stilled for a moment. Rose grinned and tipped forward to lay her head on his shoulder. Chozz cradled the girl close and looked at Jydryn and Keena.

"She's done that before. We're not sure why, but it seems to be a blessing or acceptance of some fashion," Keena said.

With Rose sitting on one arm, Chozz extended his other and beckoned Keena forward. He pulled her into a side hug and kissed her temple. "Hello, niece. It is good to see you."

Father and Aunt Sossi both hugged her too. Jydryn watched Nashala. A tear slid down her cheek.

Chozz introduced the remaining shifters with him, and then he cleared his throat. "I'm afraid this is not a social call, Empress. Might there be somewhere we can discuss the unrest that is spreading through the entire Keyaral Kingdom?"

"Of course, King Chozzrith." Rycharde waved the dragons to follow him back toward the drawbridge and gate.

With Rose still snuggled against him, Chozz patted the lord's shoulder. "We are family, my friend. Call me Chozz."

Rycharde smiled, but it faded as the children fussed about having to go up to their chamber with Ella. "You can take them to the enclosure at the back. Perhaps you can ask the tanner, Quinn, to fashion them a ball with some of his leftover leather."

The fae within the walls and Rycharde's captain and key fighting men were called to join them. They soon filed into the castle dining room. Jydryn rolled his shoulders to loosen tight muscles as everyone stood around the table but argued about where each should sit when a king, two queens, an empress, and the lord owner of the castle were all present.

Jydryn glanced at Keena. She pursed her lips.

Chapter 88

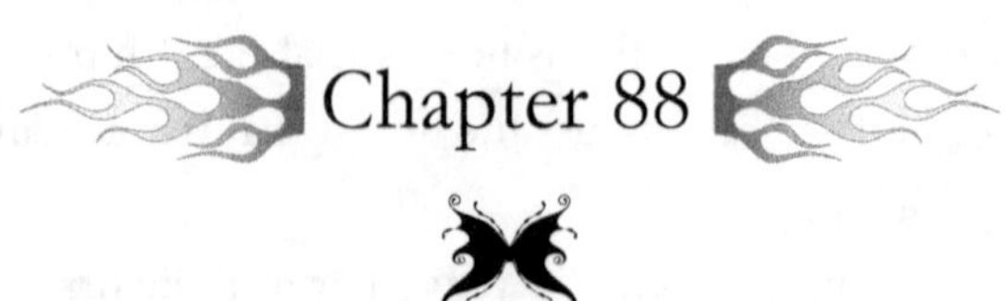

Oh, honestly … they wouldn't just take a seat and get down to the important business of forming plans in hope of saving the kingdom? Keena sighed. "King Chozzrith and Queen Sossi, gather your people at one end of the table. Queen Nashala, gather your people at the other. Father, take the middle of the table with your men."

"And where do you plan to sit, Empress?" King Chozzrith said.

"Are the fae at the head or foot of the table?" Nashala asked at the same moment.

Keena closed her eyes and pinched the bridge of her nose. With all her strength, she suppressed her urge to scream. "Who is to say if the head of the table is at the door nearest the kitchens, so they serve you first, or at the door nearest where everyone enters to greet all who arrive? Father can take one end and I the other. Then, the dragons on the side by the windows, and the fae opposite."

"Why do the dragons sit near the windows?" Nashala asked. "It is the fae who are already at a disadvantage by being inside, separated from nature."

Chozzrith crossed his arms. "And the dragons cannot shift without doing significant damage, so we are also at a weakness."

"I could have the table and chairs removed so everyone sits in a ring on the floor and rotate fae, human, shifter," Keena muttered.

Chozzrith considered her with a raised brow. "And why start with the fae?"

Keena threw up her hands. "Because you are a man of God and the last shall be first." She glared around the room. "There are enemies on every side. Our world, as we know it, will be saved or lost at this table. If you—the respective leaders of the three peoples of Keyaral—cannot even sit together without being offended by your place at the table, then we have already lost. For there is no hope that our land will ever be one again if we cannot."

Chozzrith's smile grew, and he gave her a sharp nod. "Now, that sounds like something an empress would say." His gaze rose to Queen Nashala as his arms dropped to his sides. "Your Majesty, choose your end of the table. We will take the other."

Mother sat nearest the door to the kitchen. Queen Sossi sat beside Chozzrith at the opposite end. The fae and the dragons took seats on either side of the table nearest to their leaders. Father sat on the window side at the midpoint of the long table and his men filled the remaining seats. That left the one opposite Rycharde for Keena.

She remained standing as most of the rest sat rigid, stone-faced, with their hands fisted in front of them. She glanced at the dragon king. "Please, King Chozzrith, will you tell us why you have come? What urgent news do you bring?" She sat as he rose.

"The lion shifters under Kofa are still in full revolt against my authority, but what is odd is the number of loyal followers that seem to have joined him from the other clans. When captured and questioned, they all say the same thing—verbatim. 'Things in our realm will be superior for all shifter-kind when …'"

Jydryn joined his uncle as the two men completed the words together. "'… we are no longer controlled by an autocratic dragon.'

Chozzrith nodded to Jydryn and continued alone. "Yet when pressed, they don't seem to know how things will be better."

"Fetmak said the same to us when he tried to kill Keena." Jydryn glanced at her.

"True." Keena nodded to Chozzrith. "He also said, 'They promise any non-dragon freedom and status we've never had under your scaley claws.' But he couldn't say what freedoms he didn't have or which he hoped to gain."

"There is also the issue of what had you summon me back to Zarus," Jydryn said.

Chozzrith nodded. "How did Kofa know what had happened here between Keena and the human king?"

"Are you suggesting the fae are behind this?" Nashala didn't stand. She leaned back in her chair and drummed the fingers of one hand on the table.

Keena popped to her feet. Tension crackled, ready to explode. "Yes. But not all—just one."

"Nightshade." Echo, Dusk, Lilly, and several other fae muttered.

"What is a Nightshade?" Sossi asked.

"Not a what—a who." Keena left the table and paced to one end of the room and turned to make her way to the other end. "Nightshade is a fae who served under my grandfather, King Nix. He uses forbidden dark magic."

"To what purpose?" Sossi asked.

"For power." Keena stopped and glanced around the room. "He wants to be king of the fae."

Chozzrith's brows pinched as his gaze narrowed. "But he is not of royal blood."

Sossi let out a small gasp as she stared wide-eyed at her mate.

Keena paused behind her chair again and met the gaze of those around the table. "He has fought me four times and not been able to defeat me—though he came very close to killing me last time. What I think he is doing now is gathering forces among the other tribes of Keyaral to join him." She glanced at her mother. "Not enough fae will turn their loyalties from their rightful queen to one outside the bloodline.

They understand the damage it will have on Shimmerbourne." Her gaze shifted to Chozzrith. "But the shifters would also not join forces with the fae of their own free will. The animosity among your peoples runs deep."

"You believe he has used this dark magic on my people?" Chozzrith said.

Jydryn glanced between his uncle and Keena. "Perhaps not all of them. I'm sure Kofa needed little persuasion to join forces against you."

"And you think, dear, that Nightshade has also influenced King Gallagher?" Rycharde's hand thumped a rhythm on the table. "To what purpose?"

Keena thought for a moment. "No, Gallagher chose to ally himself with Nightshade. You will never give up Wealdstone. As my father, I'd fight with you against him."

"And as her mate, I would aid you as well," Jydryn said.

"As Jydryn's father—" Govam spoke for the first time.

"And uncle—" Chozzrith interrupted.

"And aunt—" Sossi interjected with a smirk—"we will all join in fighting this human king."

"With such formidable forces lined against him, I think Gallagher sought a common enemy to align with him. Nightshade would have welcomed more soldiers on his side," Keena concluded.

Rycharde's concerned gaze caught hers and held it. "So, with the dark forces of the fae, desperate humans, and enspelled shifters, how would it be best for us to proceed?"

"We fight them, of course," Chozzrith thumped his fist on the table. "We have superior numbers of those who remain loyal."

They exchanged glances up and down the table, but no one spoke. It would never work. These three tribes couldn't trust one another at a peaceful table—the swords at their waists proved that. How would they ever fight shoulder to shoulder?

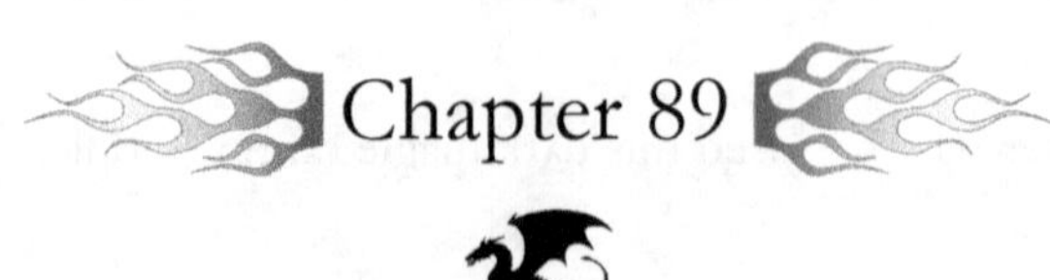

Chapter 89

Keena remained silent for so long that Jydryn squirmed in his seat. He could sense her whirling thoughts but not understand them.

She turned to the human soldier on her left, her father's captain, Wimund. "If our peoples were to go into battle together, and in this conflict, your brother, or father, son, or childhood friend fell at the hands of an enemy shifter or a fae, how would you feel? Though some are our enemies, some would fight beside you as comrades. Think on it and give an honest answer."

She turned to Echo and posed the same question, only changing who killed their loved one to humans or shifters. She finished by posing the question again to Chozz's captain with the culprits being humans and fae.

Her gaze swept over everyone at the table. Jydryn could feel her sadness before she even asked for a response. "Could any of you honestly say you would not hold a grudge against any of the other tribes if one of your family fell by their hands?"

Gazes dropped to the table as though they could read the most profound revelation in the wood's grain.

Keena pressed forward. "Can any of you assert, with all confidence, that you would welcome one from the other tribes to stand beside you in battle and believe they would protect you?"

A few had the guts to shake their heads as gazes crossed the tables.

"Father, how would you deploy your men to fight dragons, wolves, and lions?"

"Well, I … I might … well …" Rycharde glanced to Chozz at the far end of the table and shook his head.

Keena captured her father's attention again. "What about vines snaking out of the ground or trees swatting your men off their horses, the ground opening up, and spells being cast? How would you fight that?"

"I couldn't," Rycharde told her with a nod.

"We also can't fight nature and magic," Chozz said.

"And we have little defense against hordes of shifters in their animal forms," Nashala said.

Chozz smiled at Keena and leaned back in his chair. "So, what do you propose, Empress?"

Keena drew in a deep breath, as Jydryn sensed the plan solidify in her thoughts. "We divide the battle. No doubt they will try to fight as a unit to hamper our defense. Nightshade will count on us not wanting to kill our own kind while we mount fierce attacks against the others. He'll try to mix all his forces, but as we've just seen around this table, that will not work."

Keena's gaze swept to the fae. "As the tribes separate, can you provide wards that will keep each group apart? Then, we will focus on fighting our own." Keena sighed and stood a little straighter. "One day we may find a way to trust one another and fight side by side for the common good of all our peoples, but for now, it would seem best to fight parallel battles."

Mumbled agreement circled the room.

Keena glanced at Chozz. "Is there any word on where this battle is to take place?"

The king shook his head. "Not that I have been able to uncover, as yet."

"Let me see what I can learn." Echo stood and stepped out the glass door behind Rycharde into the garden.

Jydryn waited in silence with the others. He'd fought other dragons before, trained to fight with his uncle's army both in human and dragon form, but somehow this was different. He glanced at Keena again. She braced her forearms on the top of the back of her chair and her head hung low. She was praying. Something they should all be doing.

"According to the trees, many are moving toward The Soundless Flats." Everyone looked up as Echo came back into the room.

Keena tipped her head up to look at him. "Are they already there?"

"The humans are arriving and setting up tents. The shifters, who can't fly, and our dark brethren are on their way. We should gather everyone there by the end of the week."

"So soon," Aunt Sossi said on a breath.

Keena straightened and glanced at Rycharde and Jydryn. "How far are these Soundless Flats from our gates?"

The men exchanged glances. Rycharde spoke. "They lay north of the Tetling Ridge, at least four days on horseback."

"North but still on the east end. They lay several hours of flying away," Jydryn added.

"Is it a good place to engage them, or should we draw them to a location with better advantage for us?" Keena looked to each of the rulers at the table.

"The humans fought a tremendous battle there several decades ago. The blood and gore so tainted the ground, little grows there even now." Queen Nashala's voice stayed low.

"It is expansive enough for the dragons to fight with ease." Chozz inclined his head.

Keena straightened, and her arms drooped at her sides. "It would seem we have our time and location. Now, it is a matter of gathering our forces and meeting our enemy in battle."

Rycharde stood. "I would request we all share a meal together before each of us leaves to prepare. We can talk strategy and other matters. But our greater goal, as my daughter pointed out, is to become one in order to prevail in the war to come. What better way to do that than to break bread together?"

The others nodded their consent.

He called for Dolcie, and the door to the kitchen opened. A long stream of servants filed into the room, carrying trays of food and pitchers of ale and wine. As maids scurried to lay the table with them already seated, nervousness simmered under the surface, but they settled into an amenable time together.

Keena glanced at Jydryn as she moved to sit again. *I am not the person to lead us into battle. I know nothing of warfare and almost died the last time.*

We must trust God to go before us and preserve us. Jydryn took the tray passed to him. *We believe, Lord. Help our unbelief.*

Chapter 90

Keena stood on a rise surrounded by slender, white-barked trees. The setting sun warmed her back. The cries of her children as she and Jydryn had left still rang in her ears. She blinked back tears and closed her eyes. Dragon Fire covered her feet and kept her from a direct connection to the earth and, thus, shielded her from the dark faes' draining magic.

The tree in front of her exploded with a blast of magic, sending shards of wood in every direction. Only the shielding Mother erected around them saved her and those standing around them.

A flaming boulder from a human trebuchet arched through the air and smashed against the shield above them. Upon leaving Wealdstone, half of Chozz's guards had come here to the Soundless Flats to secure the high ground for her and mother's army, which left the low desolate flats for Nightshade's army.

Keena glanced back at Mother, huddled with the loyal fae who had arrived. Nightshade and his dark army hampered and delayed many light fae and even some shifters. Neither Mother nor the others took any note of the attacks. Exploding trees, the ground opening under them, and flaming arrows and boulders from the enemy had become common in the day and a half since they'd arrived.

Keena rubbed her arms as the attacks stopped. They were haphazard and infrequent, but kept them on edge. She allowed the Dragon Fire under one foot to seep into her skin and surveyed their surroundings.

Her and mother's army consisted of three separate camps. The fae held this rise on the north side of the flats. Jydryn, Govam, and Chozzrith held the rise to the west with the shifters who had managed to arrive. Father led what humans he could muster near the east end of the Tetling Ridge. While Keena remained connected to Jydryn, Mother and Father communicated through coded messages sent through the trees.

The enemy was almost all gathered in the flats, though she couldn't sense Nightshade.

Dark magic touched her and her Dragon Fire flamed to life, breaking her connection to the ground. Magic seemed unable to cross that barrier.

A few hours, Jydryn said. *Come sunrise, at the latest, we will engage the enemy.*

Keena wouldn't be able to sleep. She hadn't slept well since Chozzrith told them of their enemy's gathering army. After a life lived without love and family, now she had far too many she cared about, and no idea how to defeat this evil gathering against them.

"Empress?"

Keena sucked in air as she startled at Dusk's soft word.

"Forgive me, Empress. There is a group of humans who have arrived and seek a word with you."

She turned to the blue-haired fae. "Why do they wish to speak with me? Did you tell them Rycharde is to the east?"

Dusk shrugged in the calm manner that comforted her, though they stood in an ocean of tension. "They insist they must speak with you." He waved a hand toward the back of their camp. "I did not dare bring them within the shields—not after what happened to the shifters."

She nodded. One of Chozzrith's guards had consented to carry several shifters from the other clans to avoid the delays traveling over land were causing. One of them had turned traitor under the control of dark magic. He'd hurtled the others to their death and killed the dragon before he could land or shake free of the shifter. Since then, everyone was on guard for traitors among them.

Keena stepped to the shield and stared up at a mail-covered man with a bright yellow plume on his helmet. "You wished to speak to me?"

"Aye, my lady. We have returned to fight with you, as we agreed."

"Agreed?" It took Keena a moment to remember. "You must be Gallagher's men from the siege of Wealdstone a couple months ago." Had so little time passed?

"Aye, my lady."

She hadn't told the trees to call them. She'd forgotten all about these men. Keena stepped through the shield and moved to stand beside the hundreds of men who rode or marched in ranks behind the captain. Dusk followed and remained close.

She called a rock up from the earth to gain a little height so more could see her. "Forgive me, good sirs. First, I never should have asked you to turn against your rightful king by threatening your life. You gave the man your oath. It was not mine to break. Second, I did not call you to fight now by an act of will. The trees must have sensed my distress."

She took a moment to consider them. They could aid Father's small army, but they were not her men to command. "I release you from any obligation. You may return to your rightful king without fear or shame. I will not hold you to our agreement. You may join him or you may return home in peace."

The rock slipped back into the earth, and she turned to rejoin the fae in the waning light.

"All hale Empress Keena a' Arlayna!"

The combined shout of over two hundred men startled her. She side-stepped and collided with Dusk.

"We have made our choice, my lady. We fight with you," the captain said.

She glanced along the long rows of men as they placed their fists over their hearts. She lowered in a curtsy in her billowy battle trousers. "I am honored." She turned her attention to the captain again. "Please lead your men to the east, to where Lord Rycharde prepares the human warriors. Do whatever he directs, and may God protect you all in the coming battle."

"And may He guard you as well, my lady." In moments, the captain turned the men and marched through the darkness toward her father.

"We'll cover them in magic to protect them until they arrive," Dusk said as they moved back to the other fae.

Even the crickets were quiet tonight.

Another blast of magic hit their shield.

Keena rubbed her arms.

Pray with me, my love.

She moved away from the others and knelt in the darkness as Jydryn's thoughts filled her own with a plea to their God.

Lord, our God and King, Protector and Mighty to save. Look on the threats of our enemies. See how they plot against us? See the pain and death they cause? Go before us …

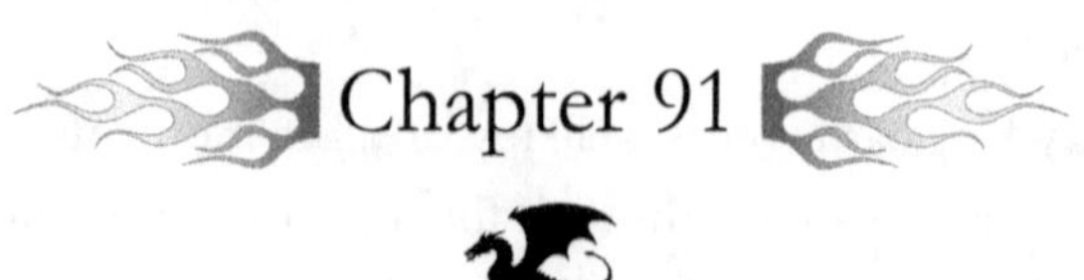

Chapter 91

Jydryn stood in his human skin, ready to spring into battle at any moment. The sun lit the eastern horizon, driving back the shadows of night and revealing a combined force of enemy shifters, fae, and humans who formed a ring around one green-haired fae.

The shifters with King Chozzrith, the fae with Queen Nashala and Keena, and the humans with Rycharde were a mighty war band of twice the number of those with Nightshade. Their armies formed an outer ring that faced those who followed the dark fae leader.

The air hummed with energy, both magical and emotional, until the hairs on Jydryn's arms stood up.

With the power only a dragon king possessed, Chozz shouted over the field. His voice shook the ground. "It is the Lord God who goes before you. He will be with you; He will not leave you or forsake you. Do not fear or be dismayed."

With a battle cry, the enemy sprang into action. They stepped forward in whatever direction they were facing and advanced on Keena's army. No one in the outer ring moved.

The humans with Nightshade drew their weapons. Dark fae filled their hands with balls of black magic. Kofa's shifters morphed into their animal skin.

Still, Keena's army stood motionless.

Jydryn's heart beat out a steady hard rhythm as he stood between his uncle and father. He could sense Keena. Fear still plagued her, but she did not jump or falter as the ranks of the enemy advanced.

Dark magic exploded in all directions and slammed into light fae shielding erected between the two armies.

The ground rolled and split beneath Keena's army's feet. Jydryn and all those who could fly shifted and sprang into the air, snatching non-flying shifters around them before they fell inside the growing caverns. Light fae shields extended under the human forces to save them, and the fae with Keena sealed the earth back up again.

Jydryn and the others landed but still did not advance.

"This battle is between the fae—Nightshade, and me, his queen. I challenge him to single combat," Nashala shouted, and the air stilled. "The shifters and humans have no interest in the affairs of Shimmerbourne. Come, Nightshade. Release the others and face me in honorable combat."

Balls of black magic flew and smashed into Nashala's shields in bright bursts of light. Kofa, and the lions with him, roared. Gallagher and his men thrust their weapons in the air with a confused shout.

Then, it happened; the moment they'd been waiting for. Someone in Nightshade's army broke formation. A human with Gallagher charged at an alligator shifter from Keena's army, who still stood in his human skin. A wolf with Kofa who'd stood next to the charging warrior leapt forward. He vaulted into the air with claws and teeth bared. Though the human and wolf stood with Nightshade, the shifter still defended one of his own against a human, his teeth found the opening between the helmet and armor and sunk deep. The weight of his attack took the man from his horse.

Keena had been right. Their people weren't ready to fight together. The enemy army dissolved into chaos as more of them fought each other than advanced against Keena's army.

One silent word between Jydryn and Keena, and their forces joined the battle, shifters with Jydryn dodged assaults by enemy humans and engaged only shifters siding with Nightshade. Light fae leapt over enemy shifters to confront dark fae. The Rycharde's men waited for Gallagher's forces to come to them.

Jydryn took to the air and raked the enemy wolves with fire to get their attention.

The battlefield filled with the cacophony of war; roars, shouts, clashing weapons, and explosions of magic. Jydryn pushed the din away as he dodged a metal net shot into the air from a ballista tucked near the tree line. Before it could open, he snatched it in his teeth, flew over the machine as they reloaded it, and melted the net, allowing drops of liquid metal to fall on the men and the machine. Flames leaped from the ballista. Sossi raced past him and followed his example with another machine as it launched a net into the air.

A blast of magic hit him in the chest, and Jydryn fell. Father caught him until he could get his bearings again. As a unit, they turned and moved back to drive the lions apart from the others. They were the genuine threat against Chozz. The dragon king's army had orders to focus their attention on Kofa and the lions with him.

Keena followed her mother. The light fae army stretched out beside and behind them. She had fought Nightshade and those with him four times, but it was nothing like this. The ring of sword against sword rattled above the clang of sword against shield. Lions and dragons shook the ground with their roars. Horses cried in pain and fear. Nature whirled around them in a chaotic tumult. Blue light fae magic answered blasts of black dark fae magic hurtled in every direction. The horrid stench of death made Keena taste bile.

Yet, she followed, safe behind her mother's strong magic shield. Keena struggled to draw nature into the battle where little nature remained.

Mother hit two fae which blasted them away from each other to open a path to Nightshade.

One of Gallagher's soldiers charged toward Keena atop a horse. She looked at the animal with his nostrils flared. "Stop." The horse stiffened his legs. His hooves raked across the ground. The rider hurtled through the air and landed hard at Keena's feet. She took his sword and filled her words with compulsion. "Go home."

The man blinked, rolled to his side, and stood. Without thought of the army he passed through, he walked from the battlefield without his mount.

A concentrated blast of magic hit the light fae shields. Blackened sparks burst through the cracks the dark power created.

Still, Keena followed her mother toward Nightshade—even as her fear grew.

Gallagher shouted, trying to gather his men around him.

The dragons swept between the shifters and the humans, dividing the groups further.

A group of fae around the outer edges erected walls of magic between the two tribes.

Another concentrated blast hit Mother's shield. Tiny black ribbons of dark magic leaked through the widening cracks. One struck Keena in the arm. Fiery pain laced through her body and ate at her strength. Dragon Fire covered her arm and broke the connection to the magic that attempted to drain her.

As Nightshade's fae army tightened their ranks to shield him, Keena's breaths grew quick and shallow.

The battles between the other tribes faded. Her connection with Jydryn dimmed. The dark fae raised their hands, preparing to fire again. The shield protecting Nashala and the light fae would fall with the next assault.

Keena stopped. The pounding of her heart the only sound that remained.

Pain exploded in her side. But it wasn't hers. Jydryn was falling from the sky. Keena didn't have the strength to scream. Govam, Jydryn's father, seized the base of his tail and pulled Jydryn up. A long agonizing moment later, her mate stretched his wings and took to the air once more.

"Empress!"

Fat ribbons of black magic squirmed through the crumbling barrier between the dark and light fae.

One hit the ground in front of Keena, sending clumps of dirt and debris in her face. Another sliced across her left shoulder.

A scream tore through the air.

Keena rubbed the tears and dirt from her eyes.

Dusk's blackened body lay beside her. Doe knelt over him, weeping.

A rage from the center of her being built until it consumed Keena and she locked her gaze on her enemy. "This ends today."

He smirked at her from behind the wall of dark fae.

# Chapter 92

Keena moved past her mother who fought off a combined attack of several dark fae. Keena saw nothing but Nightshade, heard nothing but Doe's cries. With rage fueling her every step, Keena fisted her hands and stalked toward her enemy.

As the light fae around her drove back the enemy, a path opened between her and her target.

He laughed.

Only the height of a man separated them.

"You know you can't kill me, little half-breed mongrel." Nightshade's hands filled with black, swirling magic. "You are alone. No one can save you now. This time, I will end you."

The magic surged from his hands but only covered half the distance between them before the flames of her advancing Dragon Fire stopped it. Her blue and pink flames overcame his dark magic with ease. Before Nightshade could do more than raise a shield around himself, her fire encased him.

"I am never alone."

He writhed as the Dragon Fire ate away at his shield.

"I am loved." Her flames tightened. "Love fills me. From my parents, my mate, his family, and our children. Yet there is a love more powerful than even that. The love of the One who created me for such a time as this." As her flames flashed and grew, Keena breathed with ease. Her heart maintained a steady rhythm. Peace filled her.

Fear laced his words. "You can't kill me."

"I won't. The choice is yours. It always has been."

Nightshade thrashed. The Dragon Fire broke through his shield, and he screamed as it touched his leg.

"Renounce your evil ways. Give up the dark magic. Let go of your hate. Stop your destructive pursuit for the crown that will never be yours."

"Never! I will never bow—" He screamed in pain again. "I'll never bow to a half-breed."

Keena widened her stance as she stared. Flames whirled around Nightshade, but a wave of peace filled her. "The choice is yours. Relent and step from the flames unharmed or perish. God's love rules and you need to bow to His will, not mine."

His shield dissolved and her Dragon Fire covered his body. His screams turned to howls. He glared at her until he turned to ash.

With Nightshade dead, her Dragon Fire extinguished.

The roar of the battle hit her ears. She stumbled backward. The stench-filled gore of the battlefield assaulted her.

Noticing their leader's demise, Nightshade's army fought in a chaotic frenzy.

Keena turned from the battle and raced to the rise on the outer edge. *Jydryn, I need you.* She directed him to a hill on the opposite side of the field from her and stretched her Dragon Fire toward him.

He shifted and reached his Fire toward hers. Their bright flames in every color covered the battlefield.

Sossi landed beside her, shifted, and stretched her fire toward Chozz's. As Keena called the leaves and flowers to clothe Sossi, the dragon rulers' orange and purple flames met. Others joined them from all the shifter clans encasing the battlefield in a rainbow until the flames of their loving bonds extended between each mated pair. The light fae walked through the flames untouched and clothed the shifters who followed them. Father and the soldiers with him rode beyond the flames, turned, and watched.

Soon, only Nightshade's army and her mother remained within the flames.

"As you can see," Keena shouted to those inside, "The Fire will not harm the pure in heart—those who choose love over hate. Give up your dark ways. Choose life, kindness, friendship, and love, and you too can walk away free. Cling to evil, and it will destroy you."

Keena nodded to those wielding the flames lined up beside her, and they stepped forward. Jydryn, Chozz and those on their side did the same. Step by step, the two groups walked toward one another, shrinking the bubble of Fire over those who remained.

Wolves darted from the flames; a few lions followed. Men rode their horses through. Mother glanced her way, closed her eyes, and drew in a deep breath. She moved to stand before Keena with only the flames between them.

"I love you, Mother," Keena whispered. "Please. Leave Nix's hatred and join me."

Mother stared and a shutter shook her body.

"Please. I don't want to lose you again." Keena stretched out her hands until her fingertips brushed the flames between them.

The Queen's eyes closed again. Her lips moved, but Keena couldn't hear what she said.

Keena held her breath. "Please," she whispered.

At last Mother opened her eyes as her shoulders relaxed. She smiled and passed through the flames. "And I love you, my precious girl." Mother turned, took Keena's hand, and called to her people still inside. "Turn your back on the dark magic and be free. I am ready to welcome you home."

A few of the fae answered her call and joined them outside the flames.

As the bubble grew tighter, it forced those wielding it to step over the bodies of the fallen. Tears streamed down Keena's cheeks and her flame faltered.

Be strong and courageous, Jydryn whispered in her mind.

A couple hundred remained in the middle. "This is madness. Repent and be free," Chozz called. "I will hold none guilty who step from the flames."

Riderless horses sprang from the bubble as the Fire bearers continued to tighten the ring around those who would not relent.

"The choice is yours. Is love not worth saving your life?" Keena closed her eyes and whispered. "Please, Lord, can't more be saved?"

A cheer rose from those outside the circle as a large group fled the flames.

Echo came to the edge and called several fae by name. "Bark, Willow, Chrysanthemum, we are elite warriors of Her Majesty's army. We have fought together. Please, won't you return to your places of honor?"

Men with Rycharde and shifters with Chozz did the same. More stepped from the flames and greeted those who had pleaded with them.

A fae who had fought with Nightshade locked his hard gaze with Keena, snarled, and hurtled himself against the wall of Fire. His screams died as the flames consumed him.

A few lions threw themselves against the flame near Chozz too, and met the same fate.

As the containing bubble of flames grew smaller, mated pairs had to step aside and extinguish their Fire. With less than one hundred inside, only Keena and Jydryn, Chozz and Sossi remained holding them.

Keena closed her eyes and let her tears flow. "It is not my wish that any of you should perish. Please."

Those inside raged.

Through her tears, Keena found Sossi's hand. They stepped forward until they could grasp the hands of their mates and those who had chosen death were nothing but ash.

Keena, consumed by her sobs, fell into Jydryn's arms.

"Now, Empress, take heart. Look at the number God saved." Chozz waved his hand out to the thousands standing around them. "Each made his own choice today. Their blood and fate are on their own head."

"Thank you," she muttered through her sniffles.

Nashala hurried toward her and pulled her into a tight embrace. "Arlayna, thank you."

"What would you have us do now, Empress?" Chozz asked as Nashala released her.

Father joined them as she scanned the littered battlefield. "We bury and mourn our dead. And we celebrate the lives that were spared." Her gaze shifted from Gallagher's bloody body, still impaled by a spear, to her father. "The humans will need to crown a new king." At last, she met the dragon king's gaze. "Then, on the summer solstice—the longest day of the year—I shall go to Crystalbrooke and see what the Lord says."

Chozz smiled and inclined his head. "As you wish, my dear."

As she accepted hugs and oaths of loyalty, Keena continued to look out over those who had fallen in the early part of the battle.

"You are alive." Jydryn wrapped his arms around her and hid her face against his bare chest. "God saved more than we lost. Take heart, for more mercy was showered on those who fought against you than in any battle in history. Which proves it was God at work here. Not you."

Keena pulled from his arms and lowered to her knees in the blood-drenched field. She raised her hands to heaven and called out in grateful praise. Jydryn, Chozz, Sossi, and the shifters were quick to join her. Soon, the once desolate battlefield turned to holy ground filled with worship of the one true God.

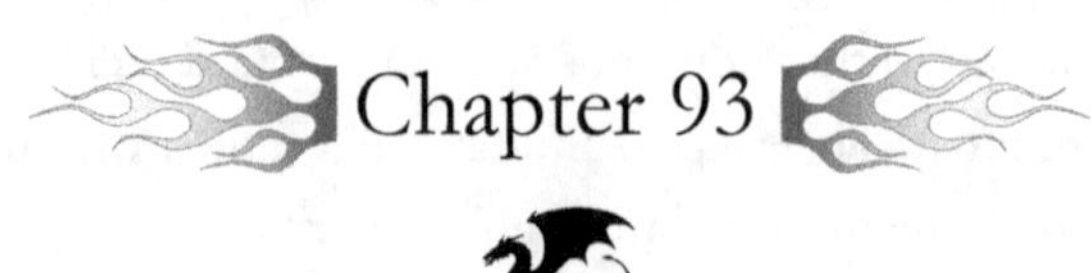

Chapter 93

Jydryn stood at the bottom of five wide crumbling steps and watched various individuals climb and face what little remained of a ruined palace overgrown by trees to the west and the tall mountain littered with waterfalls to the north in front of them. Each one behaved in the same fashion as the jaguar shifter there now.

The dark-skinned, muscled man raised his fists in the air and shouted. "I am Mazsar of the cat clan. I have come here to Crystalbrooke to take my place."

And as with all the others who had tried, nothing happened.

"Greetings, nephew."

Jydryn turned and found Chozz, Sossi, and Father approaching. Rose reached for the queen, and Jydryn lifted her off his shoulders.

"And where is my daughter?" Govam asked as he greeted Jydryn.

"She is in the hut of a fae acolyte praying. She has asked any other interested in the imperial throne to try to take their place." Jydryn turned back to the uneven stone platform at the top of the stairs that lay cloaked with tuffs of grass and weeds.

An orange-haired fae tried his luck this time with no better results.

Chozz chuckled at the human who staggered up next and shouted that he was their long awaited emperor. "I imagine her prayers are similar to our Lord's the night before His great sacrifice. 'Take this cup from me, but not my will but Yours, God.'"

Jydryn couldn't hear Keena's prayer, but he sensed her distress and the burden she feared she must carry.

"King, king." Callum jumped up and down in a vine enclosure behind them, alongside the path leading from the acolyte huts and the ruins.

Chozz strolled over and lifted the boy into his arms. "Callum, lad, how are you?"

"We getted to come with Mum and Da to the old broken castle."

"Mother didn't want to come," Peyton said as she sat in the grass beside Nashala.

Chozz inclined his head to the fae. "Greetings, Queen Nashala."

She beamed and waved at a stone seat she called up like the one she sat upon. "We are family, as you said. Call me Nash."

Jydryn let them play with the children as he turned and watched another try for the throne with loud shouts and waving arms.

Rycharde stood beside him. "All her life has led to this moment. I know she fears it, but she is the only one who can lead us."

Jydryn nodded. "We all know that, but she is afraid of the responsibility of so many."

"I think your God speaks of taking up *His* yoke to share the burden."

Jydryn smiled. "Aye. The Savior Himself said, 'For My yoke is easy, and My burden is light.' I think that is what she is wrestling with Him about now."

Rycharde patted his shoulder. "He and all of us will see this obligation does not crush her." He turned and strolled back to join the rest of the family.

Jydryn moved away from all those gathered about and knelt in prayer for his love.

As the sun reached its zenith, Jydryn stood beside Rycharde, Nash, Chozz, who held Callum, Sossi, who carried Rose, and Father at the base of the broken stairs. Peyton clung to Jydryn's back with her hands around his neck and her legs over his hips.

Without looking at them, or anyone else gathered to watch, Keena approached the steps. She drew in a deep breath and climbed. She dressed in a simple blue gown trimmed in pink, the color of her Dragon Fire. Instead of turning to the ruins or the mountain, she faced east and looked out across the large valley that had once held the mighty imperial city of Crystalbrooke.

She lowered to her knees, bowed her head, and rested her open palms upturned on her thighs. Keena released her breath.

Nothing moved.

No sound pierced the silence.

"I am your servant," Keena whispered.

The ground shook. Women yelped. Peyton tightened her grip as Jydryn and the others took a wider stance to keep their balance.

When Jydryn looked up again, Keena was prostrate on the pristine platform at the top of stairs of uncut stones that were like new.

"What's happenin'?" Callum asked.

A giraffe acolyte standing nearby spoke with awe-filled words. "God has chosen His empress and the very ground responds to her."

From where Keena lay, a path cleared to a flat area large enough for four dragons. It was back against the mountain and higher than the platform where she lay. The area smoothed and became covered in thick, short grass. Wood from the trees that had been there broke apart and formed two connected walls at each corner and at the center of each side. More wood created cupboards filled with all manner, styles, and sizes of clothes to form a third wall.

Chozz laughed. "It would seem she welcomes the shifters at court, but she expects us to be modest and step within the enclousers to dress in haste."

"I would expect nothing less from my mate," Jydryn agreed with a chuckle.

The ground rumbled again and wide, fat steps large enough for a dragon formed behind Keena. Seven human-sized stairs flanked the three enormous steps on either side. At the top, a circular platform of uncut stones formed. Four vines of a wisteria grew and laced together to form a trellis over the center.

A short, curved wall formed at the back with niches in it.

"Is Keena doing that?" Sossi asked.

The lean acolyte, so like his giraffe form, shook his head. "Not consciously. At the selection of each new Emperor or Empress, this place forms to their unique desires. Being a fae, everything created will be natural. The palace grounds will remain fluid and can continue to change for about a week before it will set. When Empress Keena a' Arlayna Bright Star passes on to glory, and her child takes the throne, the royal grounds will again meld to the new ruler's wishes."

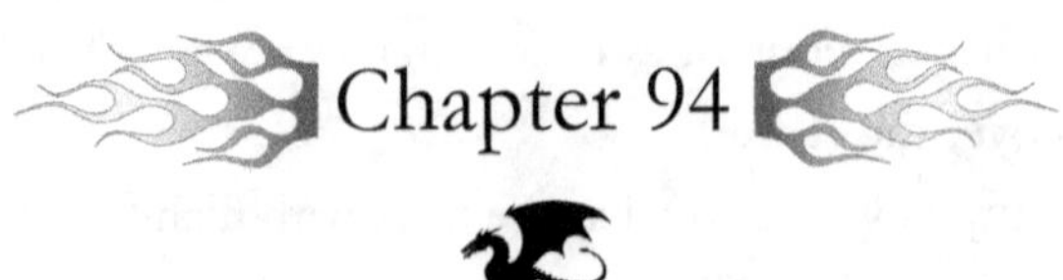

Chapter 94

Jydryn and those with him continued to watch the area change, while Keena remained prostrate on the stone platform. Small tables now filled each of the niches in the small wall behind the dining platform.

"What are those?" Chozz asked.

Jydryn's mind filled with what Keena was seeing. "Each is a table. We can pull as many as we need out to dine under the arboretum so we can meet together. Whether it is just her and me, or us and the children, or all of us, the tables link to accommodate all who will share the meal. Stone chairs will grow as needed too."

More stairs formed on either side of the table-storage wall. As the ground cleared, an enormous banyan tree came into view. The space between its many sprawling, rooted branches formed vast rooms.

One descending root grew from the nearest branch and stretched out toward Keena. It wrapped around her prone body and picked her sleeping form up. As the tree drew back, a living throne of white trumpet vines formed on another, higher platform. The tree sat her on the throne and her eyes remained closed.

Two sparrows fluttered over her head and placed a tall, jeweled, flower crown on her head.

The branches of the banyan tree shifted and reshaped to form a massive crescent-shaped building, which began on either side of the small throne platform behind her.

Jydryn could see each room as it formed and told the others. "Each tip holds the imperial guard's barracks with armories behind them. The next rooms are for the palace servants, males on one side and females on the other. Then, the kitchens fill the south end and the laundry on the north. There is only a small space at the entrance before the room opens into an immense hall for meeting and entertaining those of the kingdom."

The space was bright with light coming through the branches of the ceiling but filled with glass to keep out the weather.

Jydryn continued to explain what the building looked like inside, beyond what the others could see. "Hallways lead off from the back arch of the main hall. Some lead to administrative offices, a library, meeting rooms, living chambers for court officials, and guest rooms. At the rear of the arch are the living chambers for the family. Our chamber and the children's are at the center, along with chambers for Nash and Rycharde when they visit. Above these family chambers are ones for Chozz and Sossi, another for Govam, and yet another for the new human king, Luther. They all look out on a pristine lake behind the palace."

Balconies formed at various levels in the banyan tree's thick roots. "Guard towers," Jydryn explained.

The ground rumbled, and a vibration grew from the completed palace toward them. It passed underground beneath their feet and they turned as it continued southeast until a deep pool of water formed. This pool dropped into another and another. Algae covered the surfaces and a short wall surrounded each.

Jydryn laughed.

"What is that?" Rycharde asked.

Jydryn took a moment to explain the waste problem they had helped clean up in Cragholde. "There are small chambers within the palace where anyone can relieve themselves, bathing chambers, the scullery, and the laundry. These drain into the stone channels she just formed underground and carry the waste to those pools. She has filled each with different filtering plants to clean the water so that when it enters the stream at the bottom, it is free of all impurities."

"That's brilliant," Chozz said.

"We should have her make one for Emberwick," Sossi added.

They stood in awe as the valley wavered and changed like a shifter changing forms. Wide roads and smaller streets formed, areas opened for homes to be built, a village center ringed with empty booths and space for businesses arched around a monumental stone structure that grew out of the ground. It had windows that lined the sides and a tall spire at the top. A bell rang out over the empty village.

"A call to worship." Everyone whirled to see Keena standing on the step just above them.

She glowed with peace and light, not unlike how the Holy Scriptures described Moses after he'd met with the Lord. "Will you join me?"

"Of course." Chozz stepped aside to make room for her to pass.

She slid her hand in Jydryn's and everyone followed as they made their way to the cathedral in the center of the city empty of buildings and people.

Row upon row of six columns of polished wood pews filled the space between carved stone pillars supporting arches in the ceiling.

As they approached the simple altar, they found a gray-haired, bent man holding an open book. "Well done, good and faithful servant." He inclined his head to Keena.

She bowed and everyone found a place in the first few rows as the priest taught the Word, and they lifted their voices in praise.

Epilogue

Keena ambled through the streets of Crystalbrooke. The pounding of hammers greeted her at different times, reminding her of the city's continued growth. Almost every day, someone requested permission to build and open a business in the town center. Dozens of families arrived each week to build a home. Her only rule was there would be no tribal neighborhoods. There would be no shifter blocks or fae districts. Each family received the grant for their lot to build a home based on the next plot available in each quarter of the city. This meant fae lived next to shifters and humans. Within this valley, it worked. The larger Keyaral Kingdom beyond their ring of mountains had yet to embrace the ideas of unity between the tribes, but progress was being made.

"M'lady!" Victor, a young shifter, ran up to her. "Guess wh—" He shifted into a leopard, tearing holes in his clothes.

She squatted in front of him. "Oh, congratulation on gaining your fur, Victor. What handsome spots."

He returned to his human skin and remained on his hands and knees, panting for a moment.

"Don't worry; you'll have control of the transitions soon enough."

The lad sat back on his heels and stared down at his clothes. "Mother is going to be mad. I've already destroyed every pair of pants I have."

She smiled and wiggled her finger, beckoning him closer. He stood in front of her and she pinched his shirt between two fingers and his pants between two others. With a quick spell, the fabric knit back together. "It will be our secret," she whispered as she tapped the end of his nose.

Victor threw his arms around her neck in a quick hug. "Thank you, m'lady." He released her and ran off.

Keena stood and continued on her way. Jydryn crossed her path, coming from the soldiers' training grounds, where he helped with the instruction. One arm encircled her as his other hand cupped the bump of her belly. "How are you two doing today?"

She smiled and kissed him. "We get to celebrate the one-year anniversary of the re-founding of this town. It is a good day."

They continued arm-in-arm into the city center. Long garlands of flowers stretched between the buildings. Silk ribbons fluttered in the gentle summer breeze from the many posts. Everywhere she looked, decorations hung in windows and fluttered from roof tops.

"Momma, is the party starting?" Peyton darted up to them. Her hair was half out of her braid, her dress sat askew, and dirt smudged her face.

"Good gracious, what have you been doing?" Keena rubbed the dirt from her cheek.

"Playing."

"Can we eat treats now?" Callum plodded up to join them, his shirt dirty and torn.

Jydryn crossed his arms. "Laura is going to have a fit when she sees you've ruined another shirt, lad."

Callum glanced down with a shrug. "Don't know why, when Momma can magic it."

Like with Victor's clothes, Keena fixed and clean Callum's shirt. "We are never to be thoughtless of the work we cause others. Even if it's only saying a spell."

"Yes, Momma," Callum droned.

"Diddy up. Diddy up." Rose stood in front of Jydryn with her hands up.

He sat her on his hip. Her long curls looked like she'd been in a windstorm. Nothing short of magic could keep shoes on the child.

Ella and the maids who assisted her lumbered up and wiped their brows with their sleeves.

"Sorry," Keena said.

"They are wonderful children, m'lady," Ella said.

"Just rather fast." Jenny continued to gulp air.

Chozz, Sossi, and Govam entered the square from the far side and greeted them with a shout and a wave. Callum and Peyton raced to greet them and they exchanged hugs.

A face caught her attention, and Keena moved away from the others. "Mirmash?"

The red-haired dragon shifter lowered her gaze as her cheeks pinked. She dipped in a deep curtsy. "Greetings, Empress."

Jydryn was again at her side as Mirmash stood. She looped her arm in the man standing beside her, which turned him from the booth of scrolls he was examining.

"Father Aiden?" both Jydryn and Keena asked at the same time.

Mirmash's blush deepened. "We wanted to come and celebrate your coronation day. But more than that, I wanted to offer my profound apology for my behavior." Her gaze met Jydryn's. "You were right. I didn't understand."

Mirmash glanced at Aiden and back at them before she continued. "One year ago, as you were celebrating here, Greenburn sacrificed another baby in honor of the solstice. I rescued him and took him to Aiden in Arrowfall, as you had instructed." The couple glanced at one another again and flames of Dragon Fire fluttered over them.

Keena laughed. "God works in mysterious ways."

"Indeed, Empress," Aiden said. "It took some convincing on Mirmash's part before I accepted the reality of shifters and fated mates."

"I understand." Keena snickered. "I am so happy for you both."

"Thank you," they both said.

Keena glanced at the sky. "The celebration will begin with worship in about half an hour."

"Good, I have some time to examine the scroll this merchant has." Aiden turned back around.

Mirmash rolled her eyes with a smirk. "As if the man doesn't have enough scrolls filling our home."

Keena stepped forward and hugged the shifter. "I am thrilled for you, Mirmash."

"Thank you, Empress."

Keena and Jydryn wandered through the growing crowd. Many greeted them. She knew most of them by name, but more people came to make the city their home every day, so it was hard to keep up.

A couple on the steps of the church caught her eye next. Keena hurried to them. "Father." She hugged him. "Mother." Keena gave Nashala a sideways hug and stared down at her little brother in her mother's arms.

Keena had been in Shimmerbourne when Helio Pure Stream had entered the world last week. "I didn't expect you to come."

"We couldn't miss celebrating everything you've accomplished here," Father said with his chest puffed out.

"We have new friends who made the journey easier." Mother winked at Jydryn.

Keena glanced up as he joined them.

"There were already several dragons headed here. Shimmerbourne is not far out of their way," he explained.

"Beebee," Rose pointed at Helio.

"Yes, your Uncle Helio." Keena brushed his fuzzy head. The little hair he had was a shade deeper than hers. His skin was warmer too, more like Father's. It would be a few years before they knew whether he had strong magic and would inherit the fae throne after Mother, or if he was more human, and inherit Wealdstone from Father.

"He's too little to be a uncle, Momma." Callum stood on his tiptoes and peeked at the baby.

"Dragons and fae live long lives, son," Jydryn said.

"It blurs the generations a bit." Keena smirked as her hand caressed the skin over the child growing within her.

"Huh?" Callum stared with a curled lip.

The adults laughed as the church bell rang, calling everyone to worship as it had one year ago.

Keena drew in a deep breath and slid her hand into Jydryn's. They climbed the remaining steps and led the way into the church. So much had happened in the last year and a half. The day her town offered her in sacrifice but a dragon rescued her instead, had set her life on a course she could have never dreamed of. A life filled with an adoring husband, children, and reuniting with her parents, besides a terrible war. It had all culminated in God appointing her to reunite the kingdom one year ago and the rebuilding of Crystalbrooke.

"God is so good."

"All the time," Jydryn whispered in her ear as they took their seat in the front pew.

About the Author

Michelle Janene (Murray) the office manager/secretary/go-to-gal her her church by day
and writes Christian fantasy and historical fiction in all her free time.
She lives in Northern California with two crazy dogs and the characters of her imagination.

If you enjoyed *Dragon Fire* please review it on your favorite site.

Join Michelle's email list and get a free novelette at
MichelleJanene.com
You can also connect with Michelle:
Facebook: Michelle Janene-Author or Strong Tower Press
Twitter: @MichelleJaneneM
Instagram: michellejanene_author
Pinterest: www.pinterest.com/michellejanene
Goodreads: Michelle Janene
StrongTowerPress.com

Other Books

Check out these books also by Michelle

Mission: Mistaken Identity

The Changed Heart Series:
God's Rebel
Rebel's Son
Hidden Rebel

Seer of Windmere

Barbarian Hero

Guardians of Truth

Culling a Miracle

Lost Stones

Found in the Scars

The Last Good King

The King's Vengeance

Thrice a Bride